BLACK SWAN

A DEMON'S GUIDE TO THE AFTERLIFE
BOOK THREE

KEL CARPENTER

AURELIA JANE

RAGING HIPPO PUBLISHING

Black Swan

Kel Carpenter and Aurelia Jane

Published by Raging Hippo LLC

Copyright © 2021, Raging Hippo LLC

Proofread by Dominique Laura

Cover Art by Malice and Mayhem

Discreet PB ISBN: 978-1-957953-55-7

Discreet HB ISBN: 978-1-957953-66-3

 Created with Vellum

ABOUT THE AUTHORS

Kel Carpenter and Aurelia Jane are the hilarious team behind the international bestselling series, A Demon's Guide to the Afterlife.

They pride themselves in being absolute weirdos, spending hours on the phone coming up with detailed worlds, and laughing about crazy ideas for torturing characters. While they believe they each have the personality of a rabid badger, people still seem to like them okay.

They share a love of coffee, snarky t-shirts, and tacos, and they've made some adorable tiny people with their equally weird husbands. Best friends and work wives, Kel has the audacity to live in Maryland while Aurelia lives in Texas, but they try to see each other as much as possible.

patreon.com/kelcarpenterandaureliajane

To Uncle Chris
This world was too cruel for you.
If there's an afterlife, I hope you've found happiness in it.
-Kel

To my kids
You're my everything.
-AJ

The capacity for friendship is God's way of apologizing for our families.

Jay McInerney, *The Last of the Savages*

HADES

Good god, are you here again? You can't remember what happened, can you? I suppose you were expecting me this time around. Your memory is as bad as Fury's.

Okay, fine. I'll fill you in.

Where did we leave off?

Fury managed to get bit by her lover boys, and she was turned into some sort of majestic hybrid. Majestic might be a bit of a stretch. She still trips over her own feet. I guess you can majestically face-plant into the ground.

She started off in book two as a demon-shifter-vampire-fae. What does that mean? Well, her mates want to know too. The fun part about that is that no one knows. She finally spills the beans about who she was and what she was doing there on Earth. You know, the part where she's a demon that's come to rehabilitate them since they're prophesied to end the world? Yeah, that part. Ezra knew because he's the mind reader. Don't forget that tidbit. The other two were upset she'd kept that secret. Communication and honesty are important in relationships. But what would I know? I'm just a crow.

While our friend, Duke, searches for answers about what Fury is and why this mission has gone to absolute shit, Fury reaches out to someone that lives between worlds.

In the mirror realm.

You may know her as Bloody Mary.

She prefers to be called Jules.

Jules has access to all mirrors in the world. She's agreed to look for answers when Fury summons her.

In the meantime, Fury starts developing certain powers, and none of it makes any sense. Is our Fury graceful? Of course not. She starts haphazardly sifting in her sleep. She's bleeding from her nose and ears, fainting at random. And mysterious feathers are appearing. No, they weren't mine.

Why is this all important?

She's a hybrid. Weren't you listening?

Dorian teaches her how to sift, though she's absolutely shite at it. She was sifting objects to herself rather than sifting herself to locations. Although she was really good at slamming into things, much to my amusement.

They had their way of working that out and I am *not* sharing the details of that scene here. Go back and read it if you're thirsty.

What about all the bleeding? Fury has to be a special snowflake. She doesn't need blood like a vampire does. Nope. She needs to *give* blood. Ezra is good at being the recipient of that. You know, it works for them, but that bond isn't fully complete yet.

Fury fulfilled the mate bond with Roman and she accepted a mark from him. They have their thing going now.

As far as the mate bond goes, Dorian isn't willing to until she makes the choice to stay.

Now, in regard to shifting, that part is truly a work of art. See, Lyra—wait. I forgot to tell you about Lyra.

So Dorian's daughter is awake now, and let me tell you, that girl is a mess. She's under the influence of this angel, who at the time, we didn't know much about. Really. Who is this guy? What's his motive? Why's he such a dick?

Lyra's causing problems left and right, and she kills a good number of people. Shifters, mostly. Lyra grabs hold of Fury in a fight and sifts her to Avalon, where she Sparta kicks her off a cliff.

But not before the angel appears, wearing Fury's ex-husband's face. You know, the guy that killed her in her mortal life, beating her to death? Charmer.

Yours truly comes to the rescue, but she couldn't sift, and I couldn't really lift her.

So what happens?

She *shifts*.

Into a white raven.

And it was glorious.

Seriously, go back and read that chapter. It was fantastic, if I do say so myself.

Right, so back to story progress.

Lyra is being protected by an amulet given to her by the rogue angel, and no one can track her except Jules. Our girl in the mirror becomes a key player in this race to save the world.

Fury has an idea of how to cancel this amulet out. And she sends me back to the Afterlife to steal it. From Jake's office. (Jake is her Afterlife Resources caseworker, remember?) FFS.

Now we have a couple of things to figure out.

Number one, we need to neutralize Lyra. That's a big damn deal. But how do we do that?

Number two, why does this angel have this grand desire to kill Fury?

We all meet up at the end to figure out problem number one so that we can eventually solve problem number two.

And this whole time, the clock is ticking to the end of the world. No pressure.

Surprise! Duke shows up. *From the Afterlife*. And he brings some weird news.

The angel is none other than Azrael, the Archangel of Death.

Who also happened to be masquerading as Fury's husband while she was alive. Her real husband, John Adams, he never did those things to her. Poor dude was innocent.

Why, though?

What would cause Azrael to torment Fury in life, and then search for her in death?

She's an abomination.

A descendent of angels.

Dun dun dun.

What does that mean, you ask?

I'm not going to tell you, lazy ass. This is the part where you take over. I've done my part.

The setting where we left off?

Ezra's apartment.

Cast?

Duke: Dead dude from the Afterlife. Friend o' Fury's. Guardian of the portal to Earth.

Jules: Bloody Mary. Poltergeist. She lives in a mirror.

Tristan: Dorian's second. A fae. Pretty sure he and Rya banged for a while.

Rya: Witch that's almost as old as Dorian. Super power-ful. Maybe a little dramatic. She and Dorian put Lyra into stasis a thousand years ago.

Dorian: An old fae asshole.

Ezra: A kink-crazed bloodsucking vampire asshole.

Roman: A wolf-shifter-thing with a growling-problem asshole.

Rox: The wolf-shifter-thing's much more tolerable sister. Great hair.

Hades: The most glorious specimen of wit, wisdom, intelligence, and humility that the Afterlife has ever had to contend with.

All right. Read on, people.

Tick tock.

CHAPTER I

There were some things in life—and death, apparently —that were best delivered with a strong drink.

One of those being that my ex-husband—the same man that beat me for kicks, tortured me in my mortal life, and ultimately killed me—was an archangel.

Not just any archangel. The Angel of Death.

That gem was followed up with learning he was sent to kill me because somehow, in my human life, I was the descendent of an angel.

I wanted to call bullshit. Would have called it. But I couldn't. I knew for a fact that angels were anything but angelic. The images humankind had conjured were far from the truth, and that could be said of everything that happened when one died. I wasn't immune to being surprised either, as luck would have it. I'd spent a hundred years thinking I knew how things worked. Assuming I understood the inner workings of what people called Hell. But in the last month alone, I'd had everything about my life and my afterlife turned upside down.

I died, then became a demon. Demon magic wasn't

supposed to work with supe magic, yet now I was the only walking, talking, demon-shifter-fae-vampire—and evidently now angel-hybrid in existence. As far as we knew.

I was pretty sure none of that would fit on a business card.

One thing I'd come to realize was the more you think you know, the more you need to learn—and I don't know a damn thing about my life, or past life.

And my mates wouldn't even let it all sink in with a gin and tonic to numb the shock.

Fuckers.

I was seriously regretting that blow job I gave Fangs before this get-together.

A dark chuckle behind me broke the silence. Everyone in the room looked at Ezra like he was crazy, but I knew he wasn't responding to what Duke said.

"Only you would be thinking about how pissed you are at me for depriving you of liquor right now."

I pressed my lips together as Roxanne let out a sigh, clearly not amused.

I turned around to face Ezra, and he released me from his hold. "Just this once, I'm giving you a pass for intruding in on my thoughts and being so blatant about it, and only because I appreciate the distraction." I gave his dick a pointed look and lifted an eyebrow, making my meaning clear. *Next time you can take care of that with your hand.*

His lips twisted in feigned amusement.

In truth, my thoughts being listened to were the least of my concerns, but it gave me a moment to breathe. To process. Even if only for a moment, I appreciated it. Truly.

"You said Fury is a descendent of angels," Dorian said, apparently not needing the same amount of time as I did to recover. "What exactly does that mean?"

"The best place to start for that answer is at the beginning." Duke sighed. He gazed at me with a sad smile and squeezed my forearm. "Believe me now about taking a seat?"

I dipped my head in acknowledgement as Dorian sat, taking the only space on the couch available. He reached for my waist, pulling me down on his lap. I went easily, my back falling against his chest as he caged me in with one arm, letting the other fall to my thigh.

He wasn't the PDA sort. Out of all my mates, I'd have expected this from him the least. Under normal circumstances, I'd have questioned it. But right now, I had a feeling him touching me was as much for my comfort as it was for his security.

More so than Ezra or Roman, Dorian seemed to struggle with the idea of me leaving—by choice or otherwise. Hearing about a murderous sadist that wanted to kill me twice over? Probably a bit triggering, not that he'd show it through the cold mask he presented to the world.

"So about this beginning," Roman said, crossing his arms and looking at Duke.

"There's really no way to break into this easily. A thousand years ago, Azrael was caught breeding with humans," Duke started.

"When you say breeding . . ." I let my words trail off, not entirely ready to finish that sentence aloud.

"I don't know if it was consensual or not. Just as I don't know if he was doing it because he enjoyed it, or if he was breeding for a purpose. He'd created scores of half-angel children, generations upon generations. The Archangel Michael found out, and it was his duty to bring that knowledge to the other seven archangels. They unanimously ordered the immediate extinction of Azrael's entire lineage." Duke paused, taking a breath before continuing. "His punishment for putting Afterlife magic into the living world was that he had to carry out the execution of each and every one of his creations, all while Michael and the remaining seven watched."

My lips parted in shock, and I heard Rava and Caitlin gasp.

Oh my god.

I couldn't imagine . . . well I could, but only because he'd killed my baby before it was even born. Still, that was a thousand years—give or take—between the Azrael I met in my life and the Azrael that willingly created children. What was he like then? Did he laugh and enjoy it as he murdered them one by one?

Something told me he didn't.

"Is Fury," Dorian paused, and his hand tensed on my leg. What he was about to ask hit me, and with it came another wave of nausea. "Is she one of his descendants?"

Duke grimaced and shook his head. "Not that I know of. After the mass killing of his line, Azrael didn't father more children—at least as far as the person who wrote this was aware. If anything, the texts seem to suggest something in him changed. While children from the Afterlife were rare, they still happened on occasion. All the angels broke the rules. But there was a violent reversal in his viewpoint, and it was almost as if he declared himself the executioner. He tracked down every angel's hidden descendants and took them out. It was like he hated them and found joy in killing them."

"So having to murder his own line turned him into a sadist?" I asked, my voice terse and unforgiving. I might be able to see the gray in most things, but this was still the man that abused me. If he was sent to kill me, that's bad enough. But to spend years beating me? Deceiving me? To kill *our* baby while he stood over me and laughed? No. I wouldn't—I couldn't empathize with that.

"I'm not sure. I don't know who he was before, but he clearly was a sadist after."

"How did you find this out?" Ezra asked, eyes sharpening in a way that told me he already knew, and this rabbit hole was only getting deeper.

"I read through the journals of past archangels. Uriel, Gabriel, and Selaphiel. They all died within the last thousand years, and so did Michael—though he didn't have a journal in the Divine Libraries."

"That's . . . archangels don't just die. They've been around longer than living memory. They're eternal." I grit my teeth. "How does no one think this is odd?"

"Azrael's infractions weren't public knowledge; neither were the deaths of the archangels. It still isn't."

"But you read their journals in the Divine Libraries," I said in confusion. "How can that—" I met Duke's gaze and saw a slight twitch in his cheek. A shift in his eyes as his lips pressed together weakly. "Which library?" I asked quietly. "Which library did you read them in?"

He let out a long sigh before answering. "Bibliotheca Infernum."

"Only Upper Management has access to that library."

"Fury . . ." The slight pleading tone said it all.

I closed my eyes and turned my cheek. "You're Upper Management," I said. Part of me was hurt he hadn't said anything. The rest of me knew the facts: who was and wasn't part of the elite was a closely guarded secret. "I suppose it makes sense. They wouldn't leave just anyone in charge of the only portal to Earth. No. They'd need someone they could trust. That wouldn't be persuaded. It makes so much sense, but—" I broke off, because even as I pieced it together aloud, there was still one problem. "Upper Management gave me this mission. They assigned me because they thought I could fix things. They—you—did you know they were my mates when you sent me?"

"No," Duke said immediately. "I had no idea. If someone knew, that was kept from me, but to my knowledge, they had no idea. You wouldn't have been chosen. Them being your mates has complicated things. We never would have sent you if we'd realized." The arm around my waist tightened. I could sense Dorian's unhappiness over that declaration, and across the room, Roman let out a growl in response, equally as displeased.

They were irked someone would keep me from them knowingly . . . yeah, to say they weren't a fan was an understatement.

"And their previous mates? Did you know about the angels killing them when I brought that to you, and you told me that was a big accusation?"

"I didn't know. Not until after," he said, somewhat quieter. "I looked into it when you came to me. What you said, it made sense, but it also made me start to think something wasn't right. Too much was going wrong and was unaccounted for, and I realized someone in Upper Management was sweeping things under the rug. While angels are given cases that sometimes require euthanasia, it's rare. That it would happen to all three of you," he said, looking to each of my mates, "was no coincidence. So I dug deeper, and that's when I found out Azrael had been left in charge of this case for the last twelve hundred years. It was only recently that other individuals were brought in because the prophecy was getting closer."

I felt slightly better knowing he hadn't meant to betray

me, and that he didn't lie to my face when I asked the important questions. I pushed aside my hurt. I didn't have time to think about it. Not right now.

"So Azrael killed their mates and also fucked with Lyra in the process." The hand on my thigh pressed into my skin, holding tight enough at the sound of his daughter's name that the mark was sure to bruise. I put my hand atop his, squeezing it just as tight. "He killed me after spending years torturing me because he apparently hates descendants born of the Afterlife now." That was a lot to unwrap, and I still wasn't sure how to piece the information together. I took a deep breath, trying to figure out what else there was to consider. "What about the archangels? Four have died in a thousand years. How did it happen?"

"Michael and Azrael got into it some three hundred years ago and dueled. Azrael extinguished him. Not surprising that Azrael held a grudge. The other three are more complicated. They all chose to be extinguished."

My mouth dropped open.

"Wait. Three archangels chose to end their existence, and no one thought that was strange?"

Duke's brows scrunched together in disappointment. "Archangels are the top of Upper Management. Everything else comes down from them. When one dies, the only people that could look into that are other archangels."

"And magically, almost half of the nine died in the past thousand years. That's probably a good motivator to keep the others quiet. If Azrael were capable of somehow causing that, who's to say what he could do to them too."

Duke nodded. "Which is why I'm here. Something's got to be done about Azrael, but it's clear the others aren't going to step in. Upper Management is pretending that nothing is off. Meanwhile, the end of the world looms closer, and that prediction hasn't changed. You're going to need all the help you can get if we want to prevent this prophecy and stop Azrael from doing whatever he's planning."

I nodded absentmindedly. Was this it? The fate of the world was in the hands of my mates, my dead friend, and me—an abomination with a giant target on her back. This was my army to fight against a prophecy and the Archangel of Death. It was a tagline to a bad movie. It'd almost be funny if it weren't true. We had no choice but to succeed on both counts. If we managed to stop the world from imploding, but we didn't stop Azrael—he'd come for each and every one of us. No one was safe from him. A terrible thought slammed into me. "What about Henrietta? The girls?" I asked, jerking my head up to look at him.

Duke smiled, clearly having already thought of that. "They're hidden. No one on Earth or the Afterlife will find them," he assured me.

I lifted an eyebrow. No one in either place? That was a hefty claim. I wanted to know more, but I didn't expect him to reveal it in front of everyone. He'd tell me when he was ready.

"Good," I said. I hated to think they'd suffer in any way because of this.

"So now you know what I know. Hades has filled me in on where you are at with Lyra, but now is the time to fill me in on anything else."

"Exactly how much did Hades tell you?" I asked, looking over at the crow.

Duke gazed back and forth between us. "Judging by the looks you two are sharing, I have a feeling he didn't tell me everything."

I cleared my throat. "Well, I had an idea for how to—"

"I stole the starlight orb out of Jake's office," Hades interjected.

"Way to ease him into that knowledge, feathers," I snapped.

He shrugged his wings. "Time isn't exactly on our side here. Get to the point."

"Still. There was time to explain it."

"Tick tock," he said in response. I rolled my eyes.

Turning to Duke, I met his stare of shock. "You stole the starlight orb from the head of Afterlife Resources?"

I stood up, removing myself from Dorian's lap. "Yeah. That. I needed it. I have a theory on how it can cancel out the Afterlife magic that has a hold on Lyra. She's Dorian's daughter. I won't let Azrael hurt her anymore. So we're here to figure out a way to separate Lyra from him."

"All right," he said. "What's your plan?"

A small smile graced my lips. Duke was a true friend. He didn't question me. Shocked a little at the boldness of it, maybe, but he trusted me. If we were going to pull this off, I needed that trust more than anything.

"Jules?" I called toward the mirror. I didn't have a bloody Mary since it was all over the floor, but I'd make it up to her. I figured she would understand why I dropped it once she was up to speed on the details.

The mirror on the mantel warbled and shimmered. Jules' chestnut brown hair looked misty and far away before the image of her face came into view.

"You rang?"

CHAPTER 2

A few hushed whispers circled the room, which wasn't that much of a surprise. How many people had really seen a girl come to life in a mirror? I waved at her and started to speak, but Jules cut me off before I got a word in.

"It took you all long enough to finish talking. I've been waiting here forever. Had it not been for the really juicy information, I'd have taken a nap."

I stared into the hazel eyes of the young poltergeist. Well, young in appearance. She was anything but. "You heard everything?"

She flicked her long hair over her shoulder. "You mean the bit about Azrael being your ex, or the part where we only have five archangels left and we have no idea why?"

My expression flattened. "That about covers it."

"Then yeah, I heard. You invited me. You were late. I just kind of hung around until you were ready for me."

I huffed a laugh. "Okay, well, I'm ready for you. Let me introduce you to everyone."

I pointed around the room as I introduced her, purpose-fully skipping over Hades. I still didn't know what transpired between those two at one time, but I really wanted to find out. I would eventually. First, I had to worry about a rogue angel and a dangerous fae. "You've met Tristan and Dorian, and this is—"

"Hey Duke," she said. "Long time no see."

"Jules," he said and dipped his head.

"You two know each other?" I asked.

"Does that really surprise you?" she asked me.

"Uh, yeah. It really does. Why wouldn't it?" I said, looking between them.

Duke grinned and his eyes twinkled. "Upper Management always viewed Jules as an enemy and a threat. I never did. I have my own way of doing things. When I learned about her history with the Afterlife, I sought her out to hear her side of the story. We're friends."

"Mm hmm." My hummed response was filled with skepticism. There were an awful lot of secrets going on. But if they trusted me, I needed to trust them too. "Fine. But I want details later," I said.

Jules waved me off, but I saw the hint of a smile playing on her lips. "So what's the grand plan you wanted to share with everyone tonight?" She frowned when she looked down at the floor to see the shards of glass and her drink pooled on the tile.

I ran my fingers through my hair. "Well, it's not so much a grand plan as it is an idea. I figured we could hash out the finer details together," I started. "So, the orb we have, its magic source is from the Afterlife, and it's significantly stronger than what is protecting Lyra right now. That amulet she wears is made of supernatural magic. Ours should be able to break through the hold Azrael's amulet has on her. Once we do that, we have a small window of time to protect her and stop him from manipulating her."

I'd felt infinitely more confident before Duke's truth bomb was dropped. Beforehand, it was getting Lyra to safety, then deal with the angel, then work on the reason I was sent to Earth to begin with, though I figured parts two and three were intertwined a bit. Those were the bullet points of my plan. Finding out who the angel was complicated things.

But did it really? The more I focused on that question, the more I realized the answer was no. Not really. What it did do was complicate my emotions. Which was further complicated by my past and my trauma. But the mission was still the same. The base facts of the case were still the same. Someone was fucking with me and trying to make me fail. That wasn't new. The *who*. That was new. I knew deep down the *why* was only the beginning. All of those revelations should help guide me to finding a way to stop it all, right?

"I'm keeping an eye on her. If she moves, I'll know," Jules said, breaking my concentration.

Ezra waved his hand, bringing the attention his way. "How do we use this orb you have?"

I looked at Hades knowingly. "All we need is to be close to her. Really close. I need its power source to negate the one around her neck. Considering she really wants to hurt me, I think that'll be the easy part."

"She's the bait," Hades added, angling his head in my direction.

"Like hell you are—"

"I'm not asking your permission, Ezra." I looked at my mates, making sure each of them made eye contact with me. I wanted everyone in the room to understand. "I'm not asking for anyone's permission. Lyra desperately wants to hurt me. She blames me for what is happening to her again.

She threw me off a cliff. It's going to catch her off guard the moment she sees me, and that is the moment we strike. It's an opportunity we can't pass up."

Silence filled the room, but the tension was palpable. Roxanne fidgeted, pulling at a string on her shirt. Dorian pinched the bridge of his nose, and Ezra paced the room. Duke looked uncomfortable, but he was listening and learning. It was Roman that surprised me the most.

"She's right."

I jerked my head in his direction, raising an eyebrow in question.

He shrugged. "I don't like it. Not even a little bit. But it's a good plan. She won't expect to see you, and if that stuns her long enough for us to make our move, then so be it." His words weren't forced, but his voice sounded thick. He hated putting me in harm's way.

Ezra glared at him. "You can't be serious."

"I am. We all want the same things, right? So let's do what needs to be done to get there. She's our best shot at this."

A part of me warmed inside knowing that Roman was going against his wolf instinct. I needed him on my side.

My two other mates looked at each other and begrudgingly nodded.

"Good. It'll have to be timed and ready. We need to either lure her away—which I don't know how to do without dickhead tagging along—or we need to show up to her when Azrael isn't around. The former seems more likely," I said. "We run the risk of him showing up no matter which way we go."

"Then what?" Roman asked. He looked at Dorian and nodded respectfully before continuing, though I know he was hesitant to continue. "Her source of power isn't that necklace. You said it's only protecting her. She's incredibly strong and gifted in her own right, and she's—no offense—completely unhinged."

"Rya and I will be there to put her back into stasis," Dorian said, a hint of sadness leaking into his tone.

"Kelly has offered to help. It may take all three of us to put her back down," Rya added. "We don't know how much her powers have grown—"

"No," I said, stepping forward. "She's not going back into stasis."

A cacophony filled the room as everyone voiced their disagreement and questioned my reasoning—and sanity—all at once. I crossed my arms and breathed in deeply, waiting for it to die down.

Hades let out an obnoxiously loud squawk that left the shifters covering their sensitive ears. When the room quieted, he looked at me and whispered, "This had better be good."

I walked toward Dorian and looked up at him, craning my neck back in defiance. "You will not do it again."

"Fury, you don't know—"

"I don't know what? Don't know what she's capable of?" I asked, lifting my shirt to remind him of the wound she left on my abdomen. I pointed to Rava. "I don't know how she can manipulate people into hurting the ones they love? Or do you mean I don't know what her being in stasis has done to you for a thousand years?" I shook my head when he tried to speak again. "No, what we don't know is what stasis is doing to *her*. You don't know if you'll ever find a way to fix her broken mind. What I do know is that she'll never get better if she's put into a dream sleep. She's not at peace, Dorian. Convince me otherwise and I'll agree to letting you, Rya, and Kelly put her back into stasis, but it better be a compelling argument."

Dorian's shoulders tensed and he turned his neck, stretching as he considered his next move. "This isn't going to work."

I reached out, resting my hand on his arm gently. "It has to. Tell me how forced stasis is better than giving her death."

Dorian flinched at my words and shook his head. "I *will* find a way to—"

"When?" I asked. "*When* will you find a way to help her? It's been a millennium. You can't heal someone's emotional trauma while they're in a coma. Her mind has been shattered. He's played with her psyche. He broke her. Twisted and manipulated and hurt her. You can't fix that unless she's awake."

Trust me, I know. A hundred years later and it still haunts me, I said to myself.

"I need a moment with you," he said, signaling to Ezra as he was heading into his room. He grabbed my hand, sifting us there. One moment we were in the living room with an audience, the next we were in the bedroom, filled with privacy and soundproof walls.

"What the hell, Dorian?" I said, taking a step back.

"She has to go back into stasis, Fury," he said abruptly. "She can't die."

I stumbled backwards. "What? How . . . how do you know that?" I whispered, fear taking over my voice. "Did you try . . . to—" I couldn't finish. The mere thought that he'd possibly tried to kill her made me feel sick.

Dorian's brows creased deeply, and he shook his head. "Never. I would never." He sighed, his features softening into sadness yet again. "She tried to take her own life. Many times. Her pain was so great, the torture she was under was tremendous. She must've thought it was her only way. That's when she truly became what she is now. She couldn't break free in her mind, and whatever she was enduring caused her to crack."

"Dorian, I . . . I'm sorry." I sighed, now understanding another layer of Dorian's grief. I looked at the ground, thinking about Lyra on the roof. Worried that Roman would kill her. Seeing her in the ballroom, worried that Ezra would end up murdering Dorian's only child. "Why didn't you tell me earlier?"

"I'm telling you now," he said simply.

I wanted to argue. Remind him that keeping secrets did nothing for us. I wanted him to stop holding those things back. I wanted him to trust me. When all those thoughts came rushing through my head, a little voice reminded me this was him trusting me. This was him opening up and sharing a painful truth. As he said, he was telling me now, and that was what mattered.

I reached out, squeezing his arm, then wrapping myself around him in a hug. I didn't know what else to do or say. When I let him go, I looked up and met his gaze. "I'm sorry you both had to go through that." I turned my head, looking at the bedroom door. "I don't want to drag this out for you, but we have to tell them. They're in this fight too."

He nodded. "I know. I wanted to tell you first."

I pressed my lips together in a tight smile, whispering, "thank you," as he sifted us back into the living room.

I met the curious stares filling the room when we reappeared. Ezra's expression stayed flat, but I could see the twitch in his cheek as he read my thoughts, seeing the conversation that had taken place. He closed his eyes and breathed out for a moment. As respectfully as I could, I shared that Lyra couldn't be killed. The details of how it was known didn't matter. If Dorian wanted to share that later, he could. Rya's eyes told me she knew the missing information. After all, she was there a thousand years ago.

I turned in a circle, looking at everyone in the room. "I know you'll think I'm crazy here, but I refuse to accept stasis as the only way. We need another option. Anyone have anything? Something? A tiny spark of an idea?"

I was greeted with nothing but silence. Roxanne wouldn't meet my gaze. Tristan looked at the floor. Rava and Caitlin looked at each other. Everyone chose to focus on anything but me.

I groaned, running my fingers through my hair while I paced with heavy feet.

I stopped in front of the fireplace, turning my back on Jules to address everyone.

"We can't do this to her. It's no better than what Azrael is doing to her in the end. That's what he does. He takes away life, and if we capture her just to put her back in stasis, we are doing the exact same thing. She has the right to make choices and the right to live."

I thought of all the things John—Azrael, whatever his name was—had taken from me in life. I'd never known why. I still didn't. Not really. I couldn't save anyone he'd hurt before, but I had the chance to save Lyra. I felt the crushing weight of defeat starting to set in when no one made a suggestion.

"C'mon. We are a group of the most powerful supernaturals in existence, right?" I swung my hand around the room. "We have *four* beings from the Afterlife here, and we can't come up with one idea to subdue a single immortal fae?" I flung my arms up in the air. "Well that's just fucking great, you guys. Just great. If a group with this much power between them can't save one girl, then the world is just fucked," I said, my voice rising as my frustration climbed. "We're all—"

A loud sigh came from behind me before I felt a strong tug on the back of my shirt. My feet lifted off the ground. I was weightless, flying backwards, unsure what was happening.

A feeling like water rushed over my skin and I slammed onto the ground. My equilibrium was off balance, and I felt disoriented. My legs wobbled as I found purchase, trying to steady myself. The hold on my shirt lessened, and I looked to my side, watching as Jules released me.

"Will that work?" she asked.

My mouth fell open. "What in the actual . . ."

"Welcome to the mirror realm."

CHAPTER 3

I did a double take of my surroundings.

We were still in Ezra's living room. The mirror was still intact, but instead of being surrounded by my mates, friends, and everyone else that was working with us on the Lyra problem—it was empty.

I reached out, running my fingers over the couch to be sure it was real. "The mirror realm," I repeated. I thought only she could come here. I never expected to be standing on the other side of it with her. "So, what exactly is this place?"

I turned back to Jules, who now stood completely corporeal before me.

"My realm. Or, well, the realm I'm in charge of. No one can enter here without my help."

My lips parted and a sharp rap on the mirror to our left drew my attention. On the other side, Duke leaned forward, his knuckles tapping lightly on the glass. Mischief and amusement danced in his eyes. Behind him, Dorian, Roman, and Ezra had all jumped to their feet. While the former appeared concerned, the latter appeared puzzled, his lips drawn into a thin line and eyes flashing as he tried, and presumably failed, to find me. Roman's fists were clenched, nails sharpening to claws as he breathed heavily, demanding to know where I was.

"Might want to come back before these three lose it," Duke said into the mirror.

I shot a look at Jules. "He isn't weirded out like the rest of them. He knows I'm safe in here."

"Of course he does." She tilted her head to the side. "Where do you think his family is?" She winked at me.

Understanding of exactly what this place was only started to unravel as Jules extended her hand. "Just walk through," she said, touching my lower back and guiding me. "You'll be able to pass."

I took a tentative step and then reached for the glass. As my fingers loomed near, everyone on the other side froze, zeroing in on the movement. I tilted my head.

"They can see us?"

"Only when you're close to it. They couldn't when I pulled you through. Now they can. Like when you call me."

I lifted my eyebrows, taking a second look at Jules. I'd known she had the ability to pass through mirrors, but not how. The idea that she could bring others into her realm . . . it wasn't even a consideration.

My fingers passed through the other side and Ezra was there instantly, grabbing my hand and pulling me through. I phased from one side of the mirror to the other in a blink, landing against his hard chest. I took a couple quick breaths, pulling myself back to look at them. Each of my mates wore an eerily similar expression of fierce disapproval over what just happened.

"What the fuck was that?" Dorian was the first to speak.

Jules was the one to answer.

"That," she said in a singsong voice, "is the solution to your problem."

His eyebrows lifted slightly, dubious. "They couldn't hear us on the other side, could they?" I asked her.

"Nope," she said, popping the p. "They only see or hear us when we're within a foot of the glass, and that's only if I want them to see. Further than that and it's just their own reflection staring back."

"Care to tell me how you did that?" Ezra said, voice stiff. He gripped my upper arms like a lifeline, not easing up in the slightest. "I couldn't *hear* you. At all. There's nowhere on this planet that I can't—"

"That's because my realm isn't on this planet," Jules said. "It exists parallel to your world. It looks the same. Operates the same, mostly."

"Parallel?" Roman repeated. "Like a parallel universe?"

"I guess that's the best way to describe it. I was in Ezra's living room, only it was just me and Jules there. I could see you too," I told him. "On the other side of the mirror it's just like here, down to every detail." I turned, looking at her. "Is your world uninhabited?" I asked her.

"Not quite," Jules said as her lips twisted. "But close enough. Your girl will be safe there. Azrael won't be able to reach her, and she won't be able to reach anyone else."

"It won't work." Dorian sighed. I glanced over at him as he ran a hand over his jaw, his shoulders tense. "All Lyra has to do is sift. It would only confine her until she figured that out."

Shit. He was right.

Just when a seed of hope was starting to sprout, like we'd *finally* found one fucking solution to a problem, reality came to squash it.

Still, Jules was smiling, unbothered by his statement.

"She won't be able to sift," Jules said, shaking her head slightly. "Nor glamor. Or use any kind of fae magic at all. Supernatural magic doesn't work in my world. Only Afterlife magic."

I frowned, thinking of how easy it was for me to leave once I was there. "Okay, she can't sift, but couldn't she just walk out as soon as she comes across a mirror?"

Jules smiled, smug as ever. "The only reason you could leave is because I made it so. It's my realm." She wiggled her fingers at me. "Trust me. If I wanted you to stay, you wouldn't have been able to leave."

And just like that, my hope was restored. "She'd basically be a human in your world."

"Mhmm," Jules said. "Not even her fae strength will be of use, but she won't age here because it exists outside of time."

I frowned. "How is that possible? Even the Afterlife exists around time."

Duke cleared his throat, looking to Jules. "Mind if I cut in?"

She waved him on, unbothered. Hades fluffed his feathers, turning his head to look out of the window rather than engage in our conversation.

"The mirror realm is closer to a pocket dimension more than anything else. While nothing ages there, the surroundings shift to keep up with the current time on Earth . In that sense, it's like a smaller version of the Afterlife—except the only person that's ever been able to gain access to it is Jules. Humans enter the Afterlife upon death and no longer age, but the world still moves forward in time. It's the same in the mirror realm."

I sucked the air between my teeth, adrenaline coursing through me at the possibilities this presented.

Another Afterlife. Of sorts.

"Can people die in this realm of yours?" Dorian asked quietly. "If it suppresses her supernatural magic, and that's attached to her being immortal . . ."

His expression gave away little to nothing, apart from the solemn way he spoke. What if she became mortal there? She'd attempted to take her life before. Would she do it again? The giddy feeling that was surging through me cooled, knowing what was fueling his question.

"No," Jules said. "Not by your definition. People cease to exist on Earth, their physical body dying and their soul going to the Afterlife. In the Afterlife, souls carry on in a form of that previous body, but the soul can be extinguished. Neither can happen in my realm, but there is a form of dying, and there are consequences. They'd become incorporeal, like a poltergeist. Unable to regain form. If that happens, they can't leave my realm. Ever."

"Why?"

"They end up bonded to the realm, able to flip back and forth, but unable to leave. If Lyra were to somehow die here, she'd be stuck, and there's nothing I could do about it."

"But she'd live?" he questioned. "She'd be alive and conscious?"

"Yes," Jules said slowly, watching him with a sort of sadness I couldn't understand. "She would live. Forever. As long as Earth exists, so does the mirror realm."

He fell quiet for a moment. I patted Ezra's arm, silently urging him to let me go. Reluctantly the vampire loosened his grip but not before pressing a quick kiss to my temple. I turned from him, walking over to Dorian.

"This is our best shot," I said. "With me as bait, Lyra just has to get close enough so I can cancel out the necklace. We get her near a mirror and Jules can pull her through. She won't be able to live normally there, but she won't hurt anyone, and she won't be unconscious. I can work with her. I can't promise that she'll ever be the same as she was. The trauma she's endured . . . it's going to take time. And a lot of it. But I will do everything in my power to help her."

Dorian stared at me. There was something in his eyes, something intense and visceral and desperate. It was vulnerable, and yet strong. I didn't recognize it because I'd never seen that expression on his face. But something told me it was pivotal.

"One condition," he said. "We'll do this your way, but I want one thing at the end."

My chest squeezed. "What?"

"You stay. When this is over and done with, when Lyra is trapped and that fucker is extinguished, you do everything in your power to stay—even if the Afterlife wants you back, even if they try to take you away, *you choose to stay.*"

My mouth felt dry. My throat scratchy. Emotion clogged my windpipe, making it hard to breathe.

For weeks now I'd been avoiding this very question. Making no promises. No commitments. I'd danced the edge of what I'd do, constantly telling myself I'd cross the bridge when I came to it.

But that wasn't enough for him. Dorian wanted me to make a choice, whether or not I'd ever have to act on it. Whether the Afterlife came for me or not. Whether there was even a way back. He wanted me to choose them— choose him.

It was a monumental decision, not one I would have liked to make in front of so many people. Certainly not one without more thinking, then again, this wasn't the first time we'd talked about it. Maybe that was his way. He'd brought it up before to make me think, and now when the chips were down, he was asking me to lay out my cards. He was asking me for my answer.

I wanted his trust, their trust. I wanted their truths and their thoughts and their love, but I constantly held myself back. Giving the pieces that were safe, but not everything.

Dorian told me that things with him wouldn't be in half-measure. I wouldn't be able to dance on the line forever.

Here it was. The moment.

Either I committed to him and the life we had here, to staying, to fixing Lyra, to building something if we made it all through this . . . or I didn't.

For what? Retirement? To be a pawn forever? To be left alone for eternity, even though I had a feeling that wouldn't quite be the case given how much I was learning about Upper Management.

No. I may have wanted that once, but that's only because I couldn't even picture what I had now. I never imagined this future. As far as I knew, it wasn't within my grasp. It wasn't a possibility. That had changed.

I could fail. This could all be for nothing. But I was done being a piece on the board that others moved. I was done with accepting a half-future, and therefore letting Azrael win because I was too scared to care about someone.

I was done fighting fate.

"Okay," I said, my voice cracking. "I'll stay."

Dorian's expression didn't change, but there was an undercurrent of release. A tension that he'd been holding dissipated, and he wasn't the only one. Ezra's presence caressed my mind, and I felt his relief. Roman exhaled, and I knew without a doubt, the wolf inside him was sated. Their mate wasn't leaving them.

Without looking away, Dorian said, "Find Lyra and

Azrael. Keep tabs on them. If Fury is going to be bait for this, we need to set the stage."

"Did you have something in mind?" Roman asked.

"I do." Dorian cracked a half-smile , holding my gaze. "I think Fury's decision is cause for a celebration."

I scrunched my eyebrows together and tilted my head, working through his words to decipher the meaning. As realization hit me, I opened my mouth to speak, but Dorian beat me to it.

"Roxanne, are you up for planning an obnoxiously large party?"

She smirked, crossing her arms, and cocking her hip. "What'd you have in mind?"

CHAPTER 4
DORIAN

"A ball?" Fury asked. "That's what you've been working on all night?"

Roxanne shook her head. "A gala. It's different."

Fury sat next to me on the couch in my lounge, leaning forward over the coffee table and flipping through the pages of Roxanne's notes with a frown. "How so? It looks exactly the same."

"It just is, okay? This isn't a ball. You're not Cinderella. The focus is on you and to celebrate you. Not just to dance and show off a dress," she answered with a huff.

Fury looked up, a flat expression resting on her face. "Thanks for clearing that up."

Turning to me, she mouthed, "It's the same thing."

I shrugged. "Perhaps it is." I met Roxanne's annoyed glance and gave a small shake of my head. "However, that's not the point."

"Enlighten me."

I stood up and walked to a table that sat near the window. I picked up a folder and brought it back to Fury, handing it over. "Take a look inside."

I watched her carefully as she opened it, thumbing through the photographs. Pictures of a location. A historic building that had been transformed into a ballet studio years ago. Decorative wooden columns supported the balcony overlooking the center space. Ornate carvings on the banisters and railing showcased the character details that so many older structures boasted. The dark stained wood floors were a stark contrast to the bright light that reflected from the mirrors lining each wall. Her eyebrows raised slightly, and her lips parted as understanding inched across her face.

"It's wall-to-wall mirrors," she whispered, tracing her fingers over the pictures. "It's perfect."

I looked at Roxanne and gave her an approving look. She was quite pleased with herself, putting her hands on her hips and accepting her praise. She'd always been good at these things.

"Rox is working on the invitations already, and Roman and Ezra are pulling every resource into getting this ready," I said, fixing my cufflink while I spoke.

Fury looked up and twisted her lips. "Why all the pomp and circumstance? Can't it just be a party? Send an evite."

I suppressed the urge to laugh as Roxanne cocked an eyebrow at my mate. "I would be offended at the suggestion if we weren't setting a trap. An *evite*," she muttered. "In all seriousness, though, it has to be believable. We don't know who he has control over. You've had how many supes come after you that know your old name? That was all Azrael."

"Okay, fair point," Fury said.

Duke had been sitting in an armchair, silently listening to our exchange until he cleared his throat. "If Azrael hasn't yet figured out that Fury isn't dead, it won't be long before he does."

I pointed at him in agreement. "Duke is right. And I know my daughter. There's no guarantee she'll show up if we don't make it a spectacle. Something this large? She won't be able to ignore the opportunity to show off and destroy everything around you."

"Azrael couldn't resist sending his minions the opening night of the summit ," Fury admitted, nodding along as she talked herself through it out loud. "And Lyra downright enjoyed destroying that ballroom and turning it into a bar fight. She used the chandelier as a damn swing." Fury's face fell and she ran her hands through her hair, the sunlight filtering through the window and catching the deep red and making it almost shimmer. "She also managed to manipulate a surprising number of supernaturals, and some of them ended up dead. We're taking a lot of risks here. I wish there was a way it could be just us," she said.

I sighed. It was a topic that Roman, Ezra, and I had debated all night. We were putting the lives of hundreds on the line for this plan. None of us liked it. I had little in common with the vampire and the shifter, and Fury aside, one thing did remain. We were alphas, and we had a responsibility to our people. We had to protect them. Unfortunately, we were dealing with matters that were far beyond our control. As Fury had said, first we subdue my daughter, then we deal with Azrael and the prophecy. She'd come here with a mission, and that meant we had to put the lives of our people at risk in order to save them. If we failed, everyone died.

Roman and Ezra didn't carry the same weight I did in making any of the decisions we'd agreed upon. I also had a responsibility to Lyra. She was my child. I was there when she came into the world, and I was there every time she tried to take herself out of it. I'd seen the devastation she'd left and the lives and families she'd torn apart, and still I loved her. I'd watched the evolution of a monster, and it shattered me into pieces that would never again be whole. But I never stopped loving her, hoping that I could find a way to save her. The love for a child was truly unconditional.

The fact remained, to protect our mate and to protect our people, we'd have to put them at risk again. All of them.

I shook my head. "We know the risks, and so do those attending." I held my hand up as Fury began to ask another question. "There won't be children. A great number of guests are soldiers and enforcers, and the rest are going to be volunteers, so to speak."

"I'm working on vetting a list that Roxanne gave me," Ezra said, sifting into the room with James. He patted my assistant on the arm, thanking him before walking to the couch and sitting next to Fury. He reached for her hand, grazing his lips over her knuckles, and kissing the top. Then he winked at me.

I stared at the spot on her hand and regretted inviting him. I never was much for sharing.

"It's a solid plan, then," Fury said. "Keep the furniture and everything away from the walls. We'll need to get her close so Jules can grab her. That would be just my luck to get her close enough to it but then get blocked by some giant floral arrangement on a table."

"Of course," Roxanne said. "But if you find yourself in that situation, you can always slap her in the face with a bouquet of flowers. Pretty certain she wouldn't expect that. Might buy you some time," she added with a shrug.

Fury crumbled up a piece of paper and threw it at Rox's

head. She dodged to the side and smiled.

The circumstances were grim, but I was pleased they were able to smile in the face of it. It was more than I was able to do.

"Fury will carry the orb. Lyra will go for her, but on the off chance she wants to toy with others first, Fury is the only one that can sift it to someone else," I said.

My mate blew out a breath, no doubt wanting to practice that skill before putting it to a test. I had faith in her abilities. She was far more advanced than she gave herself credit for.

"We have a week until the date," Ezra said, leaning back on the couch. "We've got the guest list, Roman and the pack are handling the setup . They have the numbers to work fast."

"I've arranged a place for Duke to stay as needed," I added. "He'll be on the move but can reach us at any time."

"Hades and I have some digging to do." Duke smiled at her warmly, reassuring her that he was on board with everything. I could see that it mattered to her deeply, though I wasn't entirely sure why. They looked at each other, silently sharing some connection.

"Okay," Fury said after a moment. She rubbed her hands together and looked in my direction. "Where does that leave us?"

My lips curved up to one side. "You're staying with me."

～

FURY and I walked through the hallway after entering the castle on Avalon. Our footsteps echoed off the high ceilings, barely muted by the tapestries lining the walls.

She didn't argue when we told her she'd essentially be in hiding. It wouldn't have mattered if she had. I would always listen to my mate, but I had a feeling she wouldn't have liked our answers if she had chosen to disagree. We'd made the decision without her, and we were firm in it.

Ezra wanted Fury to himself just as much as I did, and Roman wanted more time with Fury to work out whatever issues they were having, but that wasn't my concern. The fact remained that Fury and I could sift, and they couldn't. She could communicate with Ezra from anywhere, but if Lyra showed up, I could sift Fury out of harm's way instantly. It was only temporary. She'd find us again, but it would give us a chance.

Ezra had certainly tried to remind me that Fury could sift herself to safety, but his point was moot. Fury could indeed sift, but she couldn't do it far, and she couldn't do it with a degree of certainty. We'd spent hours practicing her abilities. An entire night of edging her until she finally sifted out of her bindings. It was an unusual method. One that I didn't mind repeating if she were up for it.

Rounding a corner, we came to Fury's bedroom door. I turned the handle and opened it, gesturing for her to go in before me.

She stopped abruptly, pointing to a pale pink dress I had laid out for her. The bodice was a soft, pliable cotton with two thin straps over her shoulders. The skirt was a thick, billowing tulle that would sit at her mid-waist and drop to the floor. "What the hell is that?"

"Rox and I had Kelly make you a mockup dress for the gala," I answered, closing the door behind me. I put my hands in my pockets, dipping my head toward the garment. "She has your measurements on file. This is just a test run. You can change the color."

Her forehead wrinkled as she tipped her head to the side, considering it. "Why do I need a practice dress?"

I huffed a small laugh. "If Roxanne were here, you'd get an earful about it. You know that, don't you?"

"Oh, I learned that lesson already," she muttered with a smile. "But seriously. This isn't a real ball or gala or . . ." She waved her hand haphazardly when she couldn't think of another name.

"Try it on," I suggested. "Roxanne and Kelly ran through some details last night. They want you to be 'battle-ready'—that was the term used, I believe." I shrugged. "They designed it together, but if there needs to be tweaks made, we have more than enough time."

Instead she stared at the dress, looking back and forth between it and me. "I'm going to look like a ballerina." She grimaced and shook her head. "Is this Roxanne's theme, or whatever it is she calls it when she plans for a party?"

I tilted my head back and laughed. Fury did not seem amused. "It was her inspiration, yes, but stop complaining. It has a purpose."

"Ba-ller-in-a," she said slowly, enunciating each syllable. "What about me says delicate and graceful?"

"Literally nothing," I deadpanned, then snapped my fingers.

In an instant, Fury's jeans and T-shirt had been removed, replaced by the dress in question. She glared at me, putting her hands on her hips, preparing to yell at me. Her mouth opened, but nothing came out. I smirked as she looked down, realizing exactly what she was wearing.

She patted herself down, her hands grazing the curve of her body, under her breasts, over her hips, and down to her thighs. I wouldn't complain. I had every desire to do the same, but I kept my hands in my pockets and let her figure out what purpose that particular dress served.

She lifted the tulle skirt that pooled around her, sticking her foot out to see her Docs still on her feet. Her legs were covered in a skintight spandex, the same pale pink shade as the dress.

"It's a bodysuit," she mused, toying with the seam where the skirt met the waist. I smiled as she understood. "The skirt rips away, doesn't it?"

I nodded. "It does."

Fury turned, looking for her mirror. Standing in front of it, she twirled to look at the back. "Can I make some requests?" she asked, looking at me.

I took my hands from my pockets and strode forward. "Of course."

"Not spaghetti straps. They're going to break. Something thicker." I nodded, and she smiled. "Not so much tulle. Just a little less."

"Noted," I said. "Do you mind if I make a suggestion?" She raised her eyebrows in question and waited. "I would keep the same pink color on top, but I would suggest a black tulle. It'll be easier to hide your boots, unless of course you want me to change the color of them to match the pink."

"My boots?" she said, confusion filling her tone.

I hummed in response. "Roxanne said you'd feel more comfortable in your Docs, especially while fighting. The skirt is meant to hide every part of that."

"I'm good with black. It's dark and moody," she said, smoothing out the fabric. "Fits my personality quite well, don't you think?"

Standing behind her, I traced her bare shoulders while she watched in the mirror, waiting for an answer. I pressed my lips to her heated skin, looking up to see her eyes fluttering closed. "You are anything but delicate and graceful," I murmured between kisses. Her eyes shot open, her nose wrinkling, and I chuckled. I ran my fingers down the length of her arm, wrapping my hand around her waist and pressing her into me. "You are elegant and fierce."

"Nice recovery," she said, a hint of playfulness in her eyes.

"There's one more thing," I said, reaching into my pocket. "This is for you to wear."

I lifted my hands over her head and draped a necklace around her. A simple Celtic knot on a silver chain. It rested neatly on her chest, perfectly settled between the base of her throat and the top of her breasts.

"Knotwork has a long history with fae, dating further back than when humans think they discovered it," I said, scooping her hair aside and clasping it together. "Some knots are symbols for families or roles in society, some tell a story, and some have meaning beyond even that."

Her fingers reached up to touch it, tracing the lines of the metal. "It's beautiful," she said softly. "What does this one mean?"

I met her gaze in the mirror as something heated and feral coursed through my veins. She'd made the choice to stay, no matter what. To be with me. She wasn't going to leave.

"A knot has no beginning and no end. It's an interwoven continuous line, never breaking," I said, my voice thick. Grazing my fingers from the back of her neck, I wrapped my hand possessively around her throat, pressing my body to hers as my cock twitched. Her breath hitched and I waited in silence, feeling her heartbeat speed up beneath my palm. "This one means you belong to me."

CHAPTER 5

The intensity of Dorian's words sent chills over my body. The hum of his voice reverberated over my skin, and I shivered. The burning hunger in his eyes sent a shot of desire into my core and a throbbing ache to the place between my thighs.

"Say it," he whispered roughly.

I met his gaze, considering a challenge. Silence spanned between us, and I could hear the clock ticking softly. My heartbeat pounded in my ears. He waited.

In the past, I didn't want to belong to anyone. I was independent. A loner, graced with the free will to make that choice. Would I ever agree to belong to someone? No. Never again. But this? This was different, and I knew what it meant. It wasn't ownership. It wasn't patriarchal. It wasn't subservience.

It was mutual. Equal. It was unbreakable. It was my choice. *Our* choice.

If I belonged to him, he belonged to me.

I didn't break eye contact as I slid my hand over his arm, trailing my fingers up to his hand over my throat, placing it on top. I swallowed thickly, opening my lips as they peeled apart slowly after being pressed together for so long.

"I'm yours," I said hoarsely, my voice cracking.

A low growl in his chest rumbled against my back as the floor was pulled from beneath me, wind rushing around us and blowing my hair into my face.

I landed on my back, the soft bedding enveloping me as I crashed into it. I took in my surroundings, realizing I had no idea where we were. It wasn't the castle. We weren't in Avalon.

The room was brighter. Warmer. Modern.

I sat up, looking around the room. It was painted a soft gray. Wooden furniture with clean lines filled the space, and framed art decorated the wall. A chaise lounge sat near a dresser in the corner. Expansive floor-to-ceiling windows lined one side of the room, reminiscent of Ezra's high-rise without the balcony. Long, sheer white drapes hung on each side. The faint noise of a city made its way through the glass.

"London," Dorian said from the end of the bed, answering my unspoken question.

I started to ask more when he grabbed my ankles, pulling me to the very edge of the mattress.

"I bought it for us," he said, rubbing his hands slowly up the side of my legs, and pushing the tulle skirt up.

"No one knows about it." He bent down, kissing my calf, grazing his hand further. I exhaled a shaky breath, relishing the gentle touches for the time being, knowing that time with Dorian would always be a combination of rough play and soothing strokes. And I was all for it.

"No interruptions," he murmured against me, dragging his teeth over my skin.

I tensed, anticipating a nip or a bite that never came.

Not knowing what was coming next increased my need for him to touch me, and I reached for him, trying to guide his hands to the apex of my thighs.

Dorian smirked and shook his head. "Same limits as last time?" he asked.

I raised an eyebrow, unsure of what he was aiming to do. He'd already edged me for hours on end. I had no idea what he had in mind. "Yes," I said finally.

He tilted his head and narrowed his eyes, catching the tremor in my voice. "Are you sure?"

I smirked at him in return. "Don't mistake my anticipation as fear. I said yes. I won't ever agree to something if I'm not ready."

"I'll remember that." Dorian grinned, an incredibly sexy and almost cruel smile. He grabbed my wrists, pulling me off the bed as I slammed against his chest. One hand cupped my face, and the other traced to the base of my neck, taking a fistful of hair. His lips crashed into mine, and I opened my mouth to his, moaning against the heat of his tongue as he devoured me.

Dorian reached between us, and he tugged at the tulle skirt, the sounds of the rip-away fabric echoed in the room. He tossed it aside, pressing his hands up against the curves of my body, following over my hips, across my ribs, and up to my breasts. He ran his thumbs over the fabric, flicking my hardened nipples and sending a rush of electricity through me. My breath caught, and I smiled against his mouth.

Releasing me, he hooked his fingers under the small straps of the bodice. I reached for his shirt to unbutton it, but he grabbed my hands. Shaking his head, he said, "Not yet. This is about you."

I wanted to argue. I wanted his fucking clothes off. I

wanted to say if it was about me, then I wanted him to be as naked as I was about to be, but something about the husky tenor in his voice and his choice of words left a lump in my throat. For all the fire in me, all I managed was a measly "okay." Some demon I was.

He hummed in approval, taking the straps in his grasp once again, gently pulling them down my arms. The fabric slowly folded over the curve of my breasts, slowly curling over my waist. I pulled my arms away, moving to grab his hair and guide him down.

"Don't move," he ordered, placing kisses along my exposed skin as he dragged the bodice down. "If you move, I'm going to stop."

"You're a bastard," I muttered under my breath. His tongue ran a line down my skin, followed by a kiss, followed by tongue. I groaned, the throbbing ache between my thighs growing deeper.

Hooking his thumbs into the fabric of the leggings, he pulled it down my legs, just as slowly. Kissing and licking my skin as he went. Teasing. Never kissing or licking where I needed it the most.

I'd never once been undressed so slowly before. It was agonizing. I wanted nothing more than for him to touch me, or to at least touch myself. My fingers twitched at the thought, and I clenched my hands into fists at my sides.

The aching intensified. A flood of wetness coated my underwear.

Dorian was on his knees in front of me, the rest of my outfit around my ankles. He tapped my leg, and I lifted it out of the material, doing the same for the other side.

He took a step back, just staring at me as I stood there in nothing but dark green lace panties.

His eyes raked over my body, and I remained still,

holding my fists together. The bulge in his trousers throbbed, his need for more just as obvious as my own.

"Fucking beautiful," he said.

Striding forward, he grabbed my jaw and kissed me, reaching between us, grabbing the lace, and ripping hard. The delicate fabric tore instantly, leaving a mark on my skin. My breath caught, not expecting him to drop back down to his knees and grab my hips. He pressed his mouth to my center, licking and pulling my clit into his mouth to suck.

"Oh fuck," I gasped, and my legs buckled. I wasn't ready for it. I was, and I wasn't. I wanted it so bad, and he'd dragged out everything so damn slow that I wasn't prepared for it when it finally happened.

I almost toppled forward, grabbing his shoulders and his head—anything I could use to balance myself. He chuckled against my core, the vibrations sending delicious sensations through me, and I moaned.

Grabbing one leg, he hoisted it over his shoulder. My balance was well and truly gone. I was damn near curled over his head, threading my fingers through his hair for support. He gripped my hips hard, his hands pressing deeply into my skin. In a swift move, he stood up, my other leg swinging over his shoulder quickly before he slammed me into a wall, the artwork rattling next to me.

My back hit the flat surface, giving me a place to balance as he held my thighs apart, his face pressed between my legs as he devoured me.

Each suck of my clit sent shocks through my system, pushing me to the edge of an orgasm. My legs tightened and started to shake; he pressed the flat of his tongue against me, and I bucked, angling my hips and grinding against his face, chasing the release I so desperately needed.

He moaned his approval against me, and I shattered, screaming as I flooded into his mouth. My legs quaked around his head, and I held his hair tight as I rode the waves, my body shaking.

He nipped at the inside of my thigh, then looked up at me. He pulled back, sliding my legs over his shoulder, and catching my waist as he set me down on unsteady legs.

I let go of his hair and grabbed his shirt quickly, ripping it open. The buttons popped off, clinking on the ground when they landed.

Challenge flashed in his eyes, and he pulled away from me, walking to a chest of drawers. My mouth fell open in surprise that he'd just leave me standing there.

"Where are you going?" I asked, my voice just as unsteady as my balance. I pressed my flattened palms against the wall, holding myself upright. My breathing came in almost panting breaths. I wanted more, and I wanted it now.

"I told you not yet, didn't I?" he answered. Opening a drawer, I watched him shuffle some items before pulling out metal locking wrist cuffs. He turned his head slightly, side-eyeing me to gauge my response.

My heartbeat fluttered and my pussy clenched. That's where this was going. A small smile crept up my lips and I nodded. "You did."

Striding toward me, I couldn't help but watch the way his trousers hung low on his hips. With his shirt gone, I could see every ripple of his muscular chest. Every bulge in his arms. The sexy lines that curved down the side of his lower abs, leading toward what I wanted the most right now. He towered over me, hovering. I looked up, jutting my chin out. I held my wrists out, palms up, waiting for him to make his move. I trusted him. The anticipation and thrill made me wetter, and the unknown sent my thoughts spinning.

He leaned down, kissing my wrist before putting the cuff on, clicking to lock it in place. I closed my eyes, and tilted my head back when I exhaled, loving the sensation as he repeated it on the other side.

My body jerked forward slightly, and my eyes shot open. He'd grabbed the middle that connected the cuffs and pulled it, testing its strength. Holding it, he lifted my hands over my head and slammed it against the wall as I gasped. Pushing his body against mine, he ran his nose over my shoulder, kissing the crook of my neck, his mouth hovered over my ear, taking my earlobe between his teeth and pulling slightly.

"Are you okay?" he asked softly, his hot breath sending a shiver down my spine.

"Yes," I said softly, trying to maneuver and spread my legs so he'd touch me.

Keeping my arms above me, he reached between us and unfastened his pants, pushing them to the floor. I tried to look down. Tried to see what he was doing, but he kept my head up, using his own body to block my view. I could feel his cock twitch against my belly, hard and ready.

"Spread your legs," he ordered, giving me space to move and follow through.

He palmed his length, running the tip over my folds, stopping on my swollen clit, then moving to press against my entrance. I tried to angle my hips forward, tried to slide him inside me.

"Not yet," he said huskily, teasing me, sliding it over me

back and forth. "Tell me what you like, Fury. What turns you on?"

"You mean other than this?" I panted. He hummed in response against my neck. "Getting off. That turns me on."

"Wrong answer," he said, pulling his cock away from me.

I let out a loud groan, the lack of another release frustrating me.

"Tell me," he said slowly, enunciating each word. "What. Do. You. Like?" He shoved two fingers inside me hard, curling them and pressing into the pillowy G-spot.

I cried out, and instant electricity shot through me as my knees went weak. He pulled them out, depriving me of the oncoming orgasm.

"I like it when you lick me," I managed, wetting my lips with my tongue.

"Mmhmm," he responded, pushing his fingers inside my mouth so I could taste myself. "What else?"

It was hard to focus, and I cleared my throat, trying to buy time. "I like being shared. I like groups. I want to be the center of attention."

He rubbed beneath my thighs in slow, lazy circles. "What about that do you like?"

"I like . . ." I trailed off, my mind going blank in the heat of the moment. He bent down, taking a nipple in his mouth, whirling his tongue around the taut peak. Taking it between his teeth, he carefully pulled, not causing any pain, but definitely hitting some of that pleasure.

"You like?" he continued, my nipple still in his mouth. He pressed his fingers against my clit, rubbing until my legs shook. Then he took it away again. "Finish your sentence, Fury."

"I like being watched," I breathed out, my voice hoarse. "I like being on display."

"Interesting," he murmured against my chest. He stood up, turning his head slightly, a slow and intense smile curling his lips.

In a quick move, he put his shoulder into my belly, lifting me up and carrying me. I hung upside down, my hair creating a curtain around my face, not knowing where we were going. There was no one here. No one to watch us. He said no one knew about this place.

He palmed my ass while he walked, taking a handful, sliding his fingers down but never giving me the satisfaction.

"Close your eyes," he said, as he set me down.

The unknown elicited a flood of desire through me. I didn't know what was about to happen, but I knew Dorian wouldn't disappoint.

I kept my eyes closed while he held the middle bar connecting the cuffs, lifting it over my head again.

"Turn around, eyes shut," he said. As I did slowly, he held my shoulders, guiding me until he told me to stop. "One small step forward, then spread your legs again."

I stuttered a ragged breath as I stepped forward, then moved each foot to the side, doing as he had said. My heartbeat was pounding in my ears. Every part of me was shivering in anticipation of what he was going to do. There was a new chill in the air I couldn't place.

He licked my neck, and I tilted my head to the side, sighing. His hand grazed my belly, sliding over my skin, coming to rest as he cupped me between my thighs.

"Open," he said.

I did.

The pounding in my chest increased tenfold.

I inhaled sharply.

My pussy clenched and my clit pulsed and ached.

The floor-to-ceiling window was in front of me. The expansive glass overlooking a sprawling city. Buildings all around our own. Thousands of windows. Countless people. Bodies walking below, and those living or working in apartments across from us. Forty floors or more of nothing but people possibly looking at me right now, naked and entirely revealed, my cuffed arms held above my head . . .

"Like this?" he asked me.

"Yeah," I said thickly. "This is new . . ." I managed.

He chuckled darkly. "Good."

He nudged me forward carefully, and I faltered, the feeling of vertigo taking over.

"You're safe with me," he said softly, and I knew I was. His body pushed against my back, and I moved with him until my chest was pressed against the window. Dorian only put his weight onto me more, forcing me to turn my head and press my cheek into it.

I gasped as my skin flattened over the cold glass, my arms suspended and bound above me, unable to move. He gripped my hips, digging his fingers into my flesh, pulling my hips back so that my back was arched. Dorian angled himself behind me and took his length, rubbing the tip of his cock over me, coating himself in wetness. He slid in only an inch or two, then pulled out, repeating the shallowing actions several times over, but never once entering me completely. The teasing was so good it was almost unbearable.

"Fuck me now," I ground out. "Please fuck me now."

A dark chuckle escaped him, then he hooked his arm under my leg and lifted it, pressing it against the window too, leaving me to balance myself on one foot, my pussy perfectly exposed to anyone watching.

"Is this what you want?" he asked, positioning himself at my entrance.

"Yes," I mumbled, my face pressed against the glass.

"You like being watched? Then let them watch you," he said roughly.

He drove inside me, stretching me out, filling me more than I realized he would. I gasped and inhaled, my mouth forming an 'o'.

"Yes," I drawled out in a husky voice. This was what I wanted. What I needed.

Dorian moved slowly at first, dragging out the pleasure and the build-up as he found a steady pace. I tried to arch my back more, giving him better access as I felt the tingles of an orgasm start to spread with each thrust. I pushed myself against him, fucking him as he fucked me, meeting his movements as best I could in my limited position. He shoved in fully and stilled. My channel fluttered around him, begging for me.

"I love feeling you tighten around me," he said in a gravelly tone. Almost as if my body could speak, another spasm wrapped around his cock, and he hummed deeply in approval. He hovered by my ear, his breath heating my skin. "Keep your hands up."

I nodded, not trusting coherent words to come out while I practically panted with need.

He bit my shoulder, whispering against my skin. "Good."

I groaned when he let the cuff go but I kept my hands up, pressed against the glass. With one arm still hooked up my leg, he grabbed my hip to anchor us. I felt him twitch inside me and the anticipation made me clench around him again. He pulled out, then drove into me with a feral intensity I knew he'd been holding back. I exhaled in a loud cry, not expecting it, feeling the pain and pleasure all at once, but I didn't have time to recover before he did it again.

"Do you see them down there?" he grunted, sliding in and out of me. "Do you see them watching you?"

"Yes," I breathed out, my toes curling as I chased my release.

"When they look at you, when they see me fucking this pretty pussy, they know you're *mine*." His fingers and claws pricked my skin, digging in as he put emphasis on his last word.

"I'm yours," I moaned, another spasm wrapping around his cock.

"That's right," he rumbled and pounded into me at a fast rhythm, the sound of skin slapping skin echoing the room. Each time his body slammed into mine, the momentum pressed me into the cold window overlooking the city. Anyone looking would see me, my breasts against the glass, my legs spread apart and open as Dorian fucked me savagely from behind. They'd see each and every thrust, watching his cock slide in and out of me. They'd see my body move against the window, my face pushed against it, my cheek flattened and my mouth open as I panted in time with his movements.

With each pump inside me, with each thought of someone looking up to see us, with each time he slammed into me—his fingers marking my skin as he held on—the intensity of it all made the oncoming orgasm climb at an unprecedented rate. Tingling sensations ran down my legs and they started to shake. I could feel myself getting wetter, and my channel began to tighten uncontrollably.

Dorian felt it too as he started to fuck me deeper, dragging his cock over that spot inside me that made me damn near lose myself. I squeezed my eyes shut, a scream building in my throat as my body tensed.

"Come, Fury," he said, sliding his arm forward and reaching his hand over to pinch my clit. "Let them watch you come for me."

"Oh my god," I cried out, and an explosion hit me. White dots blocked my vision, my consciousness threatening to black out. I clenched tightly around him, pulling his cock in while a flood sprayed the window and dripped down my legs. My limbs shook, and the muscles contracted all at the same time. My fingertips went numb as I clawed at the glass, unable to do anything else with my hands.

Dorian grunted with a final savage thrust into me, leaning his weight into my back.

"I . . . I'm going to fall," I managed to say. I couldn't stand up anymore and I had only moments before my knees gave out.

He sifted us back onto the bed and I lazily mumbled my thanks, the post-orgasm exhaustion taking over.

"Not so fast," Dorian said, reaching up to unlock the cuffs.

I raised an eyebrow at him. He tossed them aside, then swiftly spread my legs apart, moving to settle between them. He ran his tongue over me, one long stroke from bottom to top, before he flicked at my swollen and overly sensitive clit, causing my hips to buck.

He grinned up at me. "I haven't licked you clean yet."

I opened my mouth to . . . what? Protest? I didn't know. But it didn't matter. He took my clit into his mouth and sucked. All that came out of me was a loud, completely undignified moan, and I shattered all over again.

CHAPTER 6

A dim morning light started to filter in the window, rudely awakening me. I grumbled into my pillow and rolled over, crunching myself in a ball and hiding my face.

"I'm afraid it's time to get up," Dorian said. He sounded like he was on the other side of the room.

I peeked out of the covers, cracking one eye open and looking at him. He sat in a comfortable-looking armchair, having what I assumed was a cup of Earl Grey tea. "Why are you up?"

After a night of what felt like endless sex, I didn't understand how he could even be awake so early.

"It's eleven in the morning," he answered, not looking up from whatever it was he was reading.

"Really?" I moved to sit up, somewhat shocked. It felt much earlier than that. I looked out the window and frowned. The sun was fighting with the gray skies, finding little moments to break through before being cast out again. "It's still dark out. Well, darkish."

"It's London," he said, as though that explained it. "It's this or rain."

"Lovely," I mumbled, scooting myself down to curl under the covers again.

"Up, Fury." Dorian's tone took on a sharper quality, and I shot back up, the sheets falling to pool around my waist.

"Why?" I asked, pointing outside. "It's perfect weather for sleeping in."

He leveled me with an unamused glare and raised an eyebrow. "For one, you don't need perfect weather for that. You'll sleep eighteen hours if I let you."

I sighed. "And two?"

He set down his tea, and stood up, walking across the room to stand next to me. He reached out, caressing my hair. I'd been giving him my most annoyed look possible, but one of confusion took its place when he pulled out a white feather, then he held it up. "And two," he repeated, "you have a molting problem that needs to be looked at."

I grabbed the feather from him, turning to search the bed. There were more than I cared to admit. "I don't know what you mean by 'looked at.' I'm not going to a veterinarian if that's what you're suggesting. Birds molt."

Didn't they? I wasn't entirely sure. But also, I wasn't a bird. Mostly.

An odd stirring in the back of my mind reminded me of my raven's presence. She scoffed at the suggestion that I wasn't a bird, very much insistent that she wasn't going anywhere.

He chuckled and shook his head. "No, I meant we need to look at how to prevent this from happening. You need to learn how to shift."

"Do you think learning to shift is going to stop—" I

looked at some of the feathers in the bed and pointed to them—"this?"

Tilting his head to the side, Dorian twisted his lips before answering. "Maybe. There's the possibility that this is just part of your shifter body now. You'll continue to molt at random, and it is what it is. The way you need to give blood as part of your vampire self. But there's also the consideration that your molting started, and continues, as a need to shift periodically until you understand that side of you. Much like your fainting spells before you give blood." He looked out of the window briefly, lost in thought, then returned his gaze to me. "You need to learn to shift, regardless. It's part of who you are now. Nothing bad will come of learning, but considering the way things have continued to go thus far, we can almost guarantee something will go terribly wrong if you don't."

That was an understatement. I had yet for anything to go right for me ever since I'd come back to Earth. I groaned in acceptance, throwing the sheets aside and pulling my legs over to the side of the bed. Reaching my arms up, I stretched, tightening my body and suddenly feeling every muscle that had clenched and unclenched over and over the night before.

"Fine. Let's get this over with."

"You really are charming in the morning, aren't you?"

I shrugged, getting up to walk to the bathroom. "I never claimed to be a morning person, but you're stuck with me now." I looked over my shoulder and winked at him as he blatantly stared at my naked body.

"Indeed," he said in a low rumble.

I laughed to myself as I shut the door and sat down on the toilet. I rested my elbows on my knees, letting the thoughts drift through my head.

How was I going to practice shifting? I didn't have the first clue where to start. It felt like it took forever when Rava had to help me learn to shift back. I wasn't sure I had the patience for it. If patience was considered a virtue, it definitely wasn't mine. I could feel my raven's irritability, but I didn't know what it meant. This was going to take some getting used to.

Was her emotion leaking into me?

No, I was never a morning person. Or an afternoon person. Mostly I wasn't a 'liked to be woken up' person. I didn't think she had anything to do with my mood at the moment.

I finished up and looked in the mirror, grabbing a brush from the drawer and combing my hair. It looked like it was on fire. Deep red, sticking out everywhere, and coated with sex sweat. I picked a small down feather off my shoulder, flicking it off my fingers as it got stuck. "Just-been-fucked hair and covered in feathers. Attractive," I said quietly to myself.

"You are," Dorian said from the other room.

Of course he could hear me. Supersonic bat hearing from the shifter and the fae, and nosy mind-probing from the vampire. I had certainly found myself with an interesting group of mates.

When I came out, Dorian was again in his chair, but this time he wasn't reading. His heated gaze traveled the length of my body before he took a deep breath. Then I was clothed.

It took me by surprise, and I looked down to see what he'd chosen for me. Shapely black leggings, an incredibly comfortable green sweater, and low-heel leather boots that came just below my knees.

"Not going back to Houston?" I asked, knowing full well

I would melt there if I were wearing anything short of a bikini.

He shook his head. "I spoke with Roman while you were sleeping."

"Well that was rude. What time is it there? Did you wake him up in the middle of the night?"

"He'll be fine," he said, waving it off. "Shifting needs to be a priority. You're much better at sifting now, and we know that'll improve as you continue to practice. Any other fae abilities you discover can be something we work on as well."

"What other powers could I have that would show up?"

"Elemental control. Persuasion. Glamour. Shielding. James is a hell of a baker," he said with a laugh. "I'm certain there's magic involved in his pumpkin streusel cake."

"Well, I am no baker. I don't even think magic could help me there." I thought through the others, thinking it would be cool if I had control of elements. With my luck I'd only be able to control something like fire. That'd be messy. I mentally shook my head, hoping that wasn't the case. Shielding, though . . . "Dorian? How do you shield someone?"

He raised a brow. "Do you think you have that?"

"I don't know. I knew about Lyra existing and somehow Ezra never saw that in my head. What do you think?"

He tilted his head, considering it. "It wouldn't surprise me if you could do it without knowing it. You're a natural, and sifting objects to yourself isn't an easy task. It's something we should explore." He tapped his head. "If you want to shield yourself, you're basically creating a mental barrier. Focus on it, building it around the thoughts you want to keep to yourself."

"Or in your case, around every thought," I pointed out.

"Yes. If that's what you want it to be." A small smile played on his lips. "In the meantime we have to get you started on shifting now that we know you're capable of it."

The memory of working through the frustration of sifting was burned into my mind. I thought of when he left me outside on the steps of the castle in Avalon, freezing my ass off. I wasn't keen on going through it again. If shifting was going to be anything close to that . . .

"Is it really necessary to work on that right now, like today?"

I felt my raven's anger as she crashed around.

Okay, okay. Message received.

Dorian looked at me in surprise, unaware of the exchange I'd had internally. "I thought you were a demon."

"I am," I said indignantly. "What's that supposed to mean?"

"I didn't expect you to be so averse to a challenge, much less whine about it." He smirked.

I narrowed my eyes at him. I knew what he was doing. And it was working.

"Touché, fairy." It was his turn to glare at me. "So when do we get this started? What's the plan here?"

He disappeared without answering, leaving me to stand alone in the middle of the room.

Well that was rude.

Fine. Leave me alone in the penthouse apartment. I was hungry anyway. I'd worked up quite the appetite.

I walked to the kitchen and opened a cabinet. A decanter of what I assumed to be fae wine was tucked next to other bottles of undefined substances. I grabbed it, taking a few swigs of the potent drink. I used the cuff of my sweater to wipe my lip marks off the crystal, wanting to avoid the shit I would no doubt get for not using a glass. Or just drinking in general. They'd laid into me for weeks now. It was getting old.

I turned to see a carafe of orange juice and a basket of bagels with some other assorted pastries I didn't recognize. Forgoing a glass once again, I sipped the juice and grimaced. Drinking that after fae wine was not a good combination. Grabbing the carafe, I picked up a bagel and stuck it in my mouth to hold, walking around the counter to sit somewhere comfortably and eat my breakfast.

As I entered the living room, Dorian and Roman popped in and I almost ran straight into them.

The juice sloshed, almost spilling, and the bagel fell right out of my mouth and landed on the floor with a thud.

"Really?" I asked them, annoyed with their choice of location.

"I didn't realize you would've left the bedroom. It's why I chose this room," Dorian said, looking at my discarded food on the rug with displeasure. "Also, I have plates, in case you were unable to locate them in the cabinet. The cabinets with clear glass doors."

Ignoring him, I turned to Roman. "Fancy meeting you here," I said, smiling obnoxiously and picking up my bagel.

Roman laughed, crossing his arms. "Nothing like orange juice and a lover's quarrel in the morning."

"He's got jokes," I muttered to no one as I sat on the couch and ate.

They took a seat across from me, uninvited I might add, and didn't even have the courtesy to wait for me to finish breakfast before they started talking.

"Dorian and I spoke this morning about your need to practice shifting," he said, leaning forward in the chair.

"I'm aware," I said around a mouthful. Swallowing a big chunk, I drank from the carafe. "I need to practice, yadda yadda yadda. I'm not disputing it. Let's go do the thing."

"We can't do it here," Roman said. "We'll need a safer location. It's going to be hard enough for you to learn this, but you need to be able to focus. When a shifter learns this part of their animal, it puts them in a vulnerable place. We can't do it at the compound, and this place is too—" Roman paused, looking for the right word—"unfamiliar. And clean."

I snorted. My mates most certainly lived two very different lives. I thought of Dorian's elegant castle. His estate in Houston and this penthouse. Clean lines, sterile, and organized. Then I thought of Roman's compound; earthy, rustic, and covered in dirt and nature.

I suppose I could see it. An animal learning to shift here wouldn't make much sense.

"Why not the compound?" I asked, wiping my hands on a napkin that Dorian had brought me.

"Lyra," he answered. "She knows about it and already came there once. Roman says you are vulnerable when you learn to shift. That's not a good position to put you in."

"We'll do it on Avalon," Roman finished.

I stopped fidgeting with the cloth and looked up. "Lyra is well aware of Avalon too. It's not only where she lived, but she kicked me off a cliff while we were there together. I fail to see how that's any safer." I looked at each of them. "Shouldn't we go somewhere else? Like the desert, or some remote island?" I liked the idea of an island, and I smiled to myself.

Dorian huffed a small laugh. He caught on to my train of thought about going to a beach. I hadn't done much resting in my Afterlife, and the beach wasn't a thing there. I wanted to go to one. A really pretty one that looked like it didn't belong on this earth, with shimmering black sand and sapphire blue water. I'd seen pictures. The contrast reminded me of, well—me.

"C'mon, Fury," Roman said. "We thought of that. We want you to be able to protect yourself further. We didn't plan on putting you in any danger while you practiced. Hades suggested—"

I snapped my head up. "Hades?" Shifting with him last time had been such a treat.

"You rang?" His familiar voice filled the room.

Where in this world or the next did he come from? How did he do that exactly? I wanted to ask. I wanted to know if I could do it too. It was a subject I would bring up once I mastered shifting.

Excitement rushed through me, but it wasn't my own. My raven heard the idea of mastering shifting, and she certainly seemed to like it.

"I guess I didn't expect to see you here," I said to him as he landed on the back of a couch.

He fluffed his feathers, reaching his foot up to scratch his neck. "Not sure why. I'm pretty crucial to the process, don't you think?"

I sighed. He was. Roman couldn't understand me in bird form. Neither could Ezra. If I needed help, I was screwed without him. Not that I would tell him that. Not in those words, anyway.

"I suppose you are," I conceded. Gesturing to my mate, I said, "Roman was saying you had made a suggestion?"

Roman held his hand out to the crow, letting him have the floor. So to speak.

"Mmm hmm. The cave," he said.

"The cave . . . the cave over the side of the cliff," I said flatly, trailing off.

"Yes, that cave. It's an excellent place for you to practice. Perfectly safe and away from humans." He watched me carefully, waiting for a response.

I hated that cave. And I hated how much he was right. No one knew that cave was there. It was pure dumb luck we'd found it to begin with, and it was only accessible depending on the tides and storm surges. I exhaled loudly. "Good idea, Hades. Point to you."

"I know it's a good idea," he said, his tone filled with snark. "That's why I said it."

"Well, aren't you pleasant this morning? Did you go play with a cat or something before coming here?" I asked, crossing my arms. Looked like we were having that kind of relationship today.

He fluffed himself up. "Considering you're also a bird— and not a very good one yet—I wouldn't joke about feline encounters."

I snorted. "I'm sensing there's a story there."

He glared at me in response but instead he chose to ignore me. Now I definitely wanted to know. Turning his head, he looked at Roman.

"Shall we?" he asked. "She's shifted once, but I have a feeling this isn't going to be like riding a bike."

CHAPTER 7

"I think we should toss her over the edge and see how that goes," Hades chimed in for the umpteenth time. I narrowed my eyes at the feather-brained asshole.

"You're here to be helpful, not"—I motioned to him—"*this.*"

He snorted in a very un-birdlike manner. "I *am* being helpful," he insisted. "We've been waiting for over an hour for you to shift and I'm freezing my feathers off down here. If you can't shift on your own, what better way to kickstart it than tossing you over the ledge?" I crossed my arms over my chest as he continued. "Better yet, we could Sparta kick you off the cliff again? Now that would make this worthwhile."

"Sparta what?"

He cocked his head, his little dark crow eyes staring at me.

"Sparta kick. You know, from the movie *300*? Where Gerard Butler was all like, 'This is Sparta!' And kicked a messenger into a hole, like how Lyra booted you."

I stared at him blankly, not at all amused. "I don't know

what you're talking about, so if you don't mind shutting your beak—"

"Oh come on! Really? You've seen every episode of *Grey's Anatomy* like fifty times, and you've never seen *300*? This is a travesty. Roman, we must fix this."

My mate scrubbed a hand down his face, amused and yet tired by the back-and-forth Hades and I had been volleying at each other since entering the cave.

"Not the time, Hades. As you pointed out, it's fucking cold down here and my balls are shriveled-up walnuts right now."

I choked on a laugh. My nipples were hard enough to cut glass and I wasn't even turned on. I understood the sentiment. None of us were crazy about the location.

"I'm sorry, shifting is just turning out to be as much of a pain in the ass as sifting was." And while Dorian's teaching method worked, something told me that wouldn't work here.

"Which is why wolf boy should toss you over the ledge and make you fall or fly—"

"Even if that would work—you still had to drag me to the edge of the cave last time. Forgive me for not being keen on the possibility of dying if you're not able to do it again, and instead I land on the rocks then drown in the damn ocean. I'm open to ideas that don't end in my death," I snapped at him, cocking an eyebrow.

Hades grumbled something about how I wouldn't drown if I flew—which I promptly ignored because it wasn't helpful.

Fucking bird. Why did he have to be the only one that could understand me in raven form? Ugh.

My inner raven also expressed annoyance over this. Not

happy with him, and not happy with me. The best I could tell, she didn't like that it seemed as though he was better than me because he could shift. Like that was my fault. Somehow.

"Does your raven want to shift?" Roman asked me suddenly.

"Yes," I answered without having to think. "She's annoyed I can't."

"Hm," Roman hummed. "Have you tried letting her take over?"

I stared at him like he was speaking gibberish. "Take over?"

"When my wolf wants to shift, it's because he wants to be front and center—in control of us. It's a give and take with our animals. While we have to hold the ultimate upper hand, being too firm can lead to them lashing out. I'm concerned that's what the molting is—that she needs you to let go so she can take the reins."

My raven's immediate liking to this explanation answered the question.

"That's what she wants," I said. "But I don't know how to. Is this like a feeling? Is there an actual switch of who's in charge here?"

"Right now, you're the one calling the shots. Try closing your eyes and letting yourself step back for a moment. See what she does."

I pursed my lips. This sounded like a lot of mumbo jumbo, truth be told, but what better option did I have?

Closing my eyes, I let out a sigh and mentally envisioned my raven. I wasn't entirely sure what she looked like, but I knew she was there, flapping her wings impatiently. Her thoughts and emotions rushed forward, as if attempting to barrel me out of the way. I recoiled at first, wanting to snap back—but a firm hand caressed my back, reminding me of what I'm supposed to be doing.

"That's right, cherub. Let her out. She might be a bit aggressive at first because she's impatient to shift. We can work on that with her later." My raven disagreed with that idea. She thought 'working on that' was a hard pass. Bossy bitch, she was. "For now, just let her come forward. You'll be relinquishing control of your body, but don't fight it. It'll make shifting much easier if you give her the chance to guide you through this. You have to build trust."

As he spoke, a rippling across my back made me wince. My raven continued to wiggle her way forward, filling up every inch and crevice of who I was. Fire burned along my spine. I opened my mouth to cry out, but it didn't come. My raven had stepped into control and gritted our teeth against the pain. She pushed our body to accommodate her, and I knew the moment my wings popped free, and my bones cracked. Blackness closed in, but she kept pushing, unrelenting in this assault.

Unable to stop her even if I wanted, I got carried along for the ride.

And when the blackness faded and my eyes opened, the world looked quite different.

It was disorienting. Bright. A world of color opened up that I didn't know about before. Last time I shifted I was in shock. I didn't pay attention. This was different. It was startling and beautiful all at once, to realize how many other colors existed that I normally couldn't see. Ones that didn't have a name and were impossible to describe—even if I could talk.

"Well look at that. She grew her feathers, after all."

My raven turned her head and narrowed her eyes on

Hades. She was not a fan of being insulted. Not when she knew what a majestic and rare creature she was.

I would have huffed a laugh if I could. *And Hades thought I was full of myself.*

He was in for a rude awakening when my raven charged at him.

Surprise flickered in his eyes before his wings snapped out and beat frantically, carrying him up.

"Not so bad now, are ya, you big heifer," Hades mocked.

My raven saw red, and her wings spread wide. In a mighty effort, half fueled by anger, the other half adrenaline, she took to the air after him.

"Oh shit," Hades squawked before ducking to evade us. Suddenly liking this dynamic a lot more, I egged my raven on, encouraging her to get him.

Roman doubled at the waist, letting out a booming laugh.

"You're going to regret talking shit now," he called out from the ground of the cave. Hades was more graceful, given he'd been at it longer—but my raven was a natural. She had this in the bag—and she preened under my praise.

Where he banked left, we followed, and when he skimmed the top of the cave, we closed in underneath him in an attempt to throw him off. When he did a wonky thing with his wings where he essentially rolled from the top of us to below us, my raven felt smug satisfaction.

All at once, she stopped flying and dropped onto him.

Hades let out a string of curses as we sank like a rock with us sitting on top of him, claws hooked into his sides. Hades went down, hitting the ground first, but my raven didn't let up. She continued to sit on him, lifting her head to gloat.

"Jesus Christ, you need to lay off the cheese fries—" he started.

She let out an indignant squawk at him and then shuffled forward. He tried to usurp us, but her larger size prevented him from making any real ground as she moved forward and then—

"YOU DID NOT JUST SHIT ON ME," Hades roared as she hopped off and pretended to inspect her wings. Inside I was dying. Roaring with laughter.

"You're beneath me, peasant," my raven responded. Her voice sounded similar, but intrinsically different to my own. She was haughty and aloof in a way I wasn't. To Roman, it would have simply been a croak of some sort coming from deep in my throat. Given the way Hades was muttering to himself with dark fury, I figured he understood her perfectly well.

"I thought Fury was bad," he grumbled. "I think I prefer her lazy ass over—"

My raven cut him off with a beat of her wings as she threateningly towered over him—nearly twice his size.

"You don't get to talk bad about her," she growled at him. I found myself very pleased with her for that, mentally nodding along. "Only I can."

Okay, not where I expected that to go. I figured I could live with it if she was down to give Hades shit. Literally.

My raven liked this change in power dynamic. She liked it quite a lot. Enough so that I was beginning to think maybe she should have been a peacock or cat because she really was a bit full of herself. My raven turned a critical eye inward over that thought and I shrugged. We are who we are, and she was a high and mighty bitch boss. Could be a lot worse.

"Wolf boy, I think we should put her in a bird cage until

she learns some manners," Hades chimed in, jumping back next to Roman when my Raven narrowed her eyes. "Maybe rig it up like a training collar and shock her every time she's bad."

Roman stroked his chin, a wicked smirk crossing his lips. "I'm not sure about the cage, but there are other possibilities in there." The rawness of his tone sent a shiver through me and my raven. I could honestly say I'd never considered that in my hundred and twenty-six years, but I was curious.

Hades flicked a glance between the two of us. "Oh—*oh*. You two are disgusting. Can't you at least save the freaky shit for Ezra's sex club?"

"Quiet, peasa—" My raven cut off in a croak.

Warmth ripped through me, burning like fire.

"I'm sorry, I couldn't hear that," Hades taunted in the background. "Cat got your tongue?"

We flipped sideways, curling inward as black edged into our vision. Without needing to be asked, she stepped back, letting me come forward in a panic.

The pain faded, but the blurred edges in my vision remained. I tried to lift my head but struggled to.

"Ezra," I rasped. "I need Ezra *now*."

CHAPTER 8

ROMAN

Feathers rippled over her human form, a wave that sprouted and then receded as fast as it came. Beneath her bare skin that unearthly light of true power went off.

I ran to her, knees buckling at the sight. Cupping her face, I tilted it back to see her elongated fangs.

Fuck.

She needed to give blood again.

"Hades get to Dorian; tell him we need Ezra."

"On it," the crow said, all previous anger and bantering between them was gone in an instant. I heard the woosh of his wings as he took to the skies, but my eyes were all on Fury.

"Stay with me, cherub," I commanded, my wolf's power reverberating through me, making the ground quiver.

"Running out of . . . time," she said through a tight breath. "Need to bite."

My eyes flashed to the mouth of the cave where Hades had disappeared only moments prior. I wavered with indecision, knowing she wanted Ezra for this but that we might not have another option.

Dorian appeared, sifting in on a cold gust as if the frigid air itself had carried him here.

"I can't reach the vampire," he said. "He's not responding."

In my arms, Fury whimpered. Around us the cave started to shake, causing stalactites to fall from the roof and smash into the stone flooring. That wild light beneath Fury's skin started to glow. Something told me that it wasn't simply the blood trying to get out.

"I can do it."

Dorian narrowed his eyes. "Are you sure?"

"She needs to give blood and we can't keep waiting for that asshole," I muttered.

"We don't know if her bite could harm you," Dorian said. "She is part vampire."

"I'll live." I wasn't thrilled about the idea of being poisoned, but it was the only reasonable way to alleviate her pain. "She's also part wolf and she bit him."

Dorian tilted his head forward, conceding the point.

In my arms Fury began to tremble. Red colored her cheeks, and I knew we had seconds at most. Without hesitation or fear, I brought my wrist to her mouth.

"Bite," I commanded, pressing my flesh into her fangs.

Worry shone in her eyes, but the feverish need that was taking over won the fight the second I nicked myself—the very top of her fang pushing in. She latched on with incredible strength, a moan of relief escaping from her. I shifted us, pulling her back to my chest so I could wrap both arms roughly around her while not jostling my wrist. The bite itself stung a little, but not much. More than anything, it aroused my wolf, who quite liked the idea of its female biting him back. While this wasn't meant to be a claiming mark, he took it that way—practically purring inside me.

"That's right, cherub. Get it all out," I whispered into her hair. The soft words were meant to encourage, though my wolf's tenor refused to leave my voice.

The shaking in the cavern stopped. The rattling of the floors diminished. Everything around us went silent once more. Judging by Dorian's expression as he cast a look around the cave, I wasn't the only one who noticed the strange occurrence.

"Either her power is growing, or the vampire side of her is still settling. That was worse than previous events," he said quietly.

"Her raven only just shifted on its own. She's still learning how to use her fae magic. I'd say it's probably some of both."

"She managed to shift?" Dorian asked. "That was certainly faster than her sifting."

"I believe she and her raven came to an understanding of sorts."

Mouth still pressed to my flesh but fangs retreating, Fury snorted.

She lifted her face, fangs slipping free. My skin healed instantly, leaving only a smear of red blood as evidence it ever happened.

"You could say that," she grunted, stretching her mouth in odd directions as her fangs slipped back in—still longer than a human, but not ferally so. "We have a common interest at heart."

"Pissing off Hades?" I guessed.

"Precisely," she hummed, wiping her lips with the back of her hand and giving the blood a foul look, as if it were somehow at fault for this. "That and she's hilarious, and full of herself." She chuckled, clearly speaking to her raven when she added, "Oh hush, we both know you are."

"Glad to see you've figured that out," Dorian said. "Did you realize that you were starting to bring down the cave when you needed to give blood?"

Her face paled a shade, which said something—because my mate was already pasty white. "I was?" she asked. "I hadn't realized. I've had such a firm grip on that ability for decades. I didn't think it would be an issue again."

"Does it feel unstable?" he asked. "Out of control?"

"No." She shook her head. "I feel the same as always."

Dorian hummed in contemplation. "Perhaps it's a one-time thing, then. Or simply a development related to you needing to give blood."

"Must be," she said, leaning back into my shoulder. "Thank you, by the way. For letting me bite you." Her nose wrinkled on the word 'bite'.

I leaned forward, letting one hand skate over her collar bone and down her arm. "If it makes you feel better, my wolf quite enjoyed it."

She squinted at me like she found that hard to believe. "Neither me nor my raven are a fan of blood. Unless it's someone else bleeding. We're okay with that."

Dorian chuckled, and I lifted my eyebrows in amusement. "Torture. You're okay with torture, but biting is gross?"

"Yup," she agreed. "That about sums up our opinion."

"I shouldn't be surprised," I said.

"You really shouldn't." She pointed to herself. "Demon, after all."

I shook my head, hoping she never changed. The first thirty-three years of my life were a bleak place without her.

A flap of wings made us all look up. Fury stilled, going cold as stone for a moment, then she visibly relaxed when she saw it was Hades. It occurred to me that she'd momentarily feared it was Azrael. It killed me that that bastard could instill a fear response. It ran so deep I wasn't sure she recognized it.

"Found Ezra," Hades puffed, landing on a rock beside us. "He was busy dealing with clan business and didn't hear Fury."

"I checked his apartment and the club," Dorian said stiffly.

"He was in the dungeon, apparently. Kendrick helped me track him," Hades said.

"I guess it's a good thing we know he isn't needed now when *our mate* needs to give blood," he said, clearly not happy with the vampire. I wasn't either, but not quite as pissed as Dorian seemed.

"Um, you can relay that to him. I'm not getting involved with mate politics," Hades said, ruffling his feathers.

Fury snorted. "It's fine. I'm fine. Shouldn't need it again for a few days, right? Now, back to this shifting thing . . ."

For the first time in weeks, her eyes glowed with something close to happiness as she shifted back into her raven form and chased Hades around the cave. I wanted to capture the moment. Freeze it in place and hold it close. I hadn't done that enough in my past, and I didn't want to make that same mistake again.

CHAPTER 9

I tightened the robe around my waist and sat on the edge of the bed, running a towel over my hair and squeezing out the excess water while I lost myself in thought.

Not bad for a day's work. I'd figured out how to shift, and I was pretty proud of myself for it. Wrapping my head around all the abilities was another story, but it would happen. In some ways it already had. I wasn't fighting it. It wasn't that I wasn't willing to accept it. It was still just a weird thing to understand when you really laid out all the details.

A lot had happened since I'd come to Earth , and I don't care who you were—supernatural, Bob-the-human, or a demon from the Afterlife—it was a lot to process.

Demon-vampire-raven-shifter-fae hybrid. And angel. Can't forget that.

In the Afterlife, I prided myself on being *The* Fury. I'd said I was one of a kind. I had no idea how true that would end up being.

Once we'd thought maybe Jules or someone else could

find a multi-hybrid that existed. It didn't matter anymore. I knew deep down, even if we ever did find one, there wouldn't ever be one like me. I was okay with that.

I finally felt like I was in control of my body again, and after my human life, I despised not being in control. Yes, there were aspects to learning it all that were still fuzzy. I wasn't entirely sure of the pattern for the blood-giving. When that came on, it came on strong. But I was trying to analyze it and look for the telltale signs. I felt confident that I could figure it out and cut it off at the pass.

I could sift, and I didn't feel like throwing up when I did. Definitely a plus. I still had work to do and needed a lot of practice. My aim, so to speak, wasn't that great yet. I couldn't go far distances, but I could get myself from point A to point B in a nearby area, and that came in handy. Rava and Dorian said it would get better with practice. She assured me it had been the same learning curve for her.

Now I could shift with ease. Not only did I like mastering that, because let's face it, I hated failure, but it also put my raven at ease. I still felt her presence, but it wasn't as jarring. It didn't feel like a bird in a gilded cage, rattling her prison bars and desperate to get out. She felt at ease, comforted, and . . . rested. She lurked in the shadows of my mind. There was a trust there now, as weird as it felt. Handing over control was not my strong suit, but it felt different with her. She was me, and there was no way that Rava or anyone else could have explained that to me. It was something I truly needed to feel to appreciate it.

It helped me understand Roman a little more than I did before. If the way she fought inside me when I'd struggled to hand her the reins was even a tiny fraction of what Roman felt with his wolf . . . I shuddered at the thought. He and his wolf sounded like they had to work out some issues of their own.

Roxanne had said he killed relentlessly after he lost Maya. He let too much of his wolf take over. He became feral. Otherworldly. He'd said he was determined never to become that monster again.

My raven had her own personality. Her own thoughts, and in the same sense, her own emotions. That meant Roman's wolf did too. A part of me wanted to know his animal. A part of me didn't know that it would be possible. My girl had her own voice. What did his sound like? But how could a bird and a wolf communicate? We hadn't figured that part out yet. I couldn't rely on Hades every time I needed to shift.

At the mention of Hades' name, my raven stirred, huffing in annoyance. I chuckled to myself, reminding her that he had saved me right before I shifted the first time. He wasn't all that bad. I rather liked his company sometimes. The bantering was fun. She questioned my logic, but I reminded her that we didn't have to tell him. She could torture him all she wanted, but when it came down to it, we all had the same agenda.

I felt her acquiesce, reluctantly, I might add.

I stood up from the bed, walking to the vanity and sitting down to brush my wet hair.

"Whatcha doin'?" Jules said, appearing in the mirror three feet from my face.

I inhaled in shock, and spit smacked right into my windpipe, sending me into a coughing fit from semi-choking. The force of my surprise as I pushed away from Jules was too much. I tipped myself back, teetering on the bench as I hacked up a lung. My feet went up in the air while I windmilled my arms, hoping to stop the inevitable. It was useless. I landed on my back with a thud.

A cackling came from the mirror above me as I sucked in air while my confused body tried not to die. Death from spit. Add that to what would end up actually killing me. I just laid there on the floor, my arms sprawled out, waiting for it to end.

"It really never does get old," she said through fits of tears.

I gasped, clearing my throat. "You're a twat," I said, my voice hoarse.

She only laughed harder. "For a demon, you sure scare easily. I expected better."

Lifting my head off the ground, I glared at her. "Dude, the devil himself would jump out of his skin if you appeared right in front of his face and he wasn't expecting you." I let my head down, resting on the floor again.

I craned my neck when I heard a knock at the door. "Come in," I said, coughing again.

Roxanne peeked in, then opened it wide to enter. "Am I interrupting something?" she asked, raising an eyebrow when she saw Jules. "You did it again, didn't you?"

Jules grinned and Rox shook her head, coming to my side and extending her hand in a gesture to help me up. I shot Jules another dirty look, then threw my hand to catch hers. She helped pull me up and handed me a glass of water.

Taking it, I sipped it until my raw throat felt better.

"I heard you coughing," Rox said, answering the silent question.

"Thanks," I said, before turning to side-eye the poltergeist. "I choked on spit."

Roxanne tried to hold in her snort, but she only just managed. She quickly shook it off and mumbled, "Sorry ."

"Laugh it up, you two. It's all fun and games until you piss off the demon."

"I'm trembling in my mirror realm," Jules teased, making the glass warble for effect.

I couldn't help but crack a smile. "Nice touch," I said as her mirror waved, then cleared my throat again. "I'd ask 'to what do I owe the pleasure,' but I feel like that would make me a liar. So instead, I'll ask, what do you want?"

She shrugged. "Nothing at the moment. Just saying hi. I've got eyes on Lyra, but nothing to note as of yet."

"What about Jo—" I stopped myself, knowing full well he never had been John. "Azrael. Where is he at?"

"Lying low. I haven't seen him." The disappointment in her tone was thick. "I'm sorry. I've been searching. But no news is good news, right?" Even she didn't sound convinced.

"Ha," I barked a laugh. "Not likely. He'll make himself known soon. He'll wait until we feel confident and comfortable. Then he'll show his face." It's what he did. I knew him. I wished so badly that I didn't.

A sense of grief washed over me quickly, and I pushed it aside, unwilling to let it grab ahold of me now.

"We'll be ready for him when he does," I finished. I pressed my lips together tightly.

I wanted nothing more in this afterlife than to make sure that bastard found a way to die. I didn't yet know how to actually kill the Archangel of Death, but it was now my mission to find out. Well, that and stopping the end of the world. Two missions.

Jules smiled big, showing her teeth. "You bet your ass we will."

Roxanne rubbed her hand over my back reassuringly and I looked at her with appreciation.

"You ready for tonight?" she asked me.

"Oooh, what's tonight?" Jules asked, her eyes brightening with excitement as she waited for an answer.

I turned to look at her. "It's a ritual with Roman and the pack. We're mates, so . . . we, um . . ." I tilted my head, turning to Roxanne in confusion. "What do we do here?"

"You're getting married, Fury," she answered, jutting her thumb over her shoulder and pointing to the door. "What did you think was going to happen? Rava is bringing your dress up any minute."

I felt the color drain from my face. "I . . . what?" I spluttered. My heartbeat raced and I could feel the pounding in my temples. *Married?*

Roxanne busted out laughing, doubling over, putting her hands on her knees. Jules snort-laughed, falling down in a hysterical fit and out of view in her mirror.

I glared at Roxanne, furrowing my brows. "You cackle like a swamp witch, you know that?" I got up while they had their fun, choosing to sit on the edge of the bed instead.

"You should've seen your face," she said, wiping the tears from her eyes.

"It wasn't that funny," I mumbled.

Jules reappeared, red-cheeked and catching her breath. "I assure you it was."

Rolling my eyes, I crossed my arms. "Care to tell me what really happens at this thing?" I huffed in annoyance. "For real this time."

Roxanne smiled, sitting on my vanity chair. "Oh, come on, Fury. It was funny and you know it. Don't tell me you wouldn't do something like that to me."

"She's more likely to strap you upside down on a St. Andrew's cross and leave you there," Jules said.

Roxanne nodded in agreement. "Probably. You should have seen it when she used a pool cue to deep-throat a douchebag shifter in my bar."

"What?" Jules exclaimed. "I miss all the fun."

I cracked a smile. "It was before I knew you."

"Will you promise to call me the next time it happens?" she asked, sounding hopeful.

I barked a laugh, thinking about how there would probably be a next time. "Why not."

Jules looked pleased as she smiled and watched Roxanne turn to the mirror, fluffing her gorgeous afro and playing with a curl.

"Rox?" I prompted. "The ritual."

"Right." She cleared her throat, turning back to face me. "It's the celebration of finding a mate. The whole pack is there, even the kids. It's really to honor the couple and to formally announce they're mated."

I nodded along as she spoke, not really picturing what it was. I only had one frame of reference, and that was the wake. "So . . . is there a bonfire and hot dogs again?"

Roxanne's smile was warm, and it reached her eyes. "I'm sure someone will start a bonfire somewhere, but it's more than that. To show the pack that Roman is worthy of you, he has to fight and prove himself."

"Fight? That seems pointless. It's Roman," I said. "He can't die. Why would anyone fight him?"

"That's the tradition."

"Okay, so who fights him, though?" I was trying to picture someone just raising their hand like an idiot and saying they'd fight Roman. The alpha. The immortal. No one would do that.

"For a hetero couple, the tradition is that someone from the female's family fights the male mate."

Not that any of it made much sense, but my heart sank. I didn't have family, and the evening was going to be really awkward in front of the whole pack when we all announced I didn't have someone.

"I don't have family," I said quietly. "So how do we . . . will the pack understand or make the exception?"

"I'm your family," Roxanne said. "I'm stepping in to fight for you."

What a weird turbulence of emotions. My heart swelled at the gesture and the notion that she considered me as her real family. The rush of worry swirled right through it, pushing it aside and taking hold. "You are going to fight your brother. You can't do that."

She threw her head back and laughed. "Oh yes I can. Just you wait."

She didn't seem worried in the slightest. She almost seemed amused by the idea of it, and that felt reassuring.

"How long do you fight for?" I asked.

"Well it used to be to the death," she said, using a hand to wave vaguely. "But that was a *very* long time ago when everyone was stupid. Now it's to first blood. Again, it's just following the traditions more than anything. It's more for show."

I sat there gaping for a moment, trying to process what she'd told me. It was Roman. This was his sister. Surely he'd pull his punches . . . right? He wouldn't draw blood on Roxanne. I scrubbed my hands down my face.

"You all need therapy," I said, exhaling loudly. "So you both fight. There's some blood. Then what?"

Roxanne pressed her lips together. "Then you fuck."

I stared silently, waiting for her to finish her sentence, but it seemed that was the end. "We fuck," I repeated.

She pressed her lips together in a smile, mumbling, "Mmm hmm."

"Are you going to elaborate?" I asked, holding my hands out in question.

"I don't think you need instructions," Jules piped up. "You're well-versed as it is."

I shot her a look that said, 'Shut up.'

"You're mates. So to prove to everyone that you have both been claimed, you do it in front of everyone," Rox said, watching me carefully. "I figured that wouldn't be a problem for you, all things considered."

A rush of heat coursed through my veins and shot straight to the place between my legs. Exhibitionism was certainly something I enjoyed. Damn, it was hot. In front of the entire pack . . . that would definitely be more eyes on me than ever before. The sex clubs in the Afterlife were a busy place, but you picked rooms. Areas. Not everyone was in one location. Even then, I'd stopped going long ago. Got weird when you saw someone that irritated you so much you wanted to drive a stake through their forehead for entertainment. Everything after that was smaller groups where someone lived.

Roman's entire pack was huge. I wasn't sure what to expect, but I had a feeling I would enjoy it.

I finally met Roxanne's curious stare, twisting my lips into a side smile, doing what I could to hide the excitement. "Yeah, no. I'm good."

"I know you are." She put her hands on her thighs, pushing herself up from the chair. "Finish getting ready. I'll come get you at sundown."

"You aren't staying?" I asked. It was unlike Roxanne to

leave when it came down to me getting dressed or prepped for something. She enjoyed that sort of thing.

Walking toward the door, she stopped right before it and looked over her shoulder. A feral grin showed an elongated canine. A faint glow flashed in her eyes before she winked at me. "I have a fight to prepare for."

CHAPTER 10

Feet pounded the earth. A steady call. A battle drum.

The sound of over a hundred shifters, eagerly awaiting the upcoming ritual.

I heard them about a mile out. Their whoops and hollers in an otherwise quiet forest was akin to a bulldozer rolling through. Pebbles skittered across the ground the closer we got, jumping in rhythm with the deep boom of the earth as it shook beneath their feet.

It wasn't until we were right on top of them that I could really see it.

An arena for this ritual had literally been carved away into the land. Fifty yards in diameter, the massive circle plunged straight down, rows of makeshift seats acting as the stairs that led to the very bottom. Almost thirty feet below ground, where the dirt was thin and bedrock thick, was the center of where the fight would take place—followed by a truly indecent amount of sex that had my pulse hammering if Roxanne was to be believed.

I hoped she was.

"How long has this been here?" I asked as we

approached the edge. It was mostly full, with a few scattered spots left open, apart from one section at the very bottom where I spotted a head of light purple hair. Rava.

"A hundred years or so," Rox said, waving at a few friendly faces that I was starting to recognize but still couldn't remember names. I smiled back in what I hoped looked like approachable politeness, but probably better resembled a grimace. "The mating ritual dates wayyyy back before Houston was picked as an official epicenter. Before shifters even came to America. Most of the larger packs have their own ieró zevgároma that's hidden by enchantments or what not. Kelly did ours, so unless you've been here, you'll never be able to find it."

"Clever," I murmured as we made our way around the side. "What was that word you called it again?"

"Ieró zevgároma," she repeated. "It means—"

"Sacred fucking? Coupling?" My eyebrows drew together.

Roxanne squinted at me. "You speak Greek?"

I tilted my head from side to side. "Somewhat. I'm rusty."

"Sacred mating," she said, correcting my translation. "You know, because shifters."

I snorted. "Why am I not surprised the ancient Greeks came up with this? Totally speaks to their quasi-orgy-fetish style."

She chuckled right as a kid around eight years old yelled, "AUNTIE ROXY," at the top of her lungs. I lifted both eyebrows.

"Um. Do you have another sibling I need to know about because Roman didn't mention he had any kids?" Not that it mattered if this was a child he'd had with another shifter, but this sure as shit wouldn't have been the time to tell me.

"No." She shook her head while smiling at the little girl. "She's Caitlin and Rava's daughter."

"Move, people!" the girl yelled. Some shifters scooted to the side to try to make space, but not everyone was listening . . . until wisps of hot pink magic shot from her fingers. It snaked straight up the seats to where we stood, shoving everyone to one side to clear a path for us.

My mouth dropped open.

"Pria!" Rava sighed, shaking her head. She shot a look of apology to the now bristling shifters, who immediately relaxed when they realized what had happened.

Beside me, Rox tried to hide her smirk behind a cough. "Pria is a hybrid. Like you and Rava. Half shifter, half witch."

"No shit," I said, watching as Rava scolded her daughter quietly. The girl didn't seem to be paying much attention as she watched Roxanne start down the seats toward her. Mirth shone in her dark brown eyes as she ignored Rava and bolted up the last few stairs to meet Roxanne. I followed down at a slower pace, nodding awkwardly to the shifters I made eye contact with on the way.

"I missed you sooooo much," the little girl said, throwing her arms tight around Rox's waist.

"I've missed you too, kiddo." She hugged her back just as tightly, putting her cheek to the top of Pria's poofy black curls. "How's school going? Magic lessons look like they're progressing."

Pria let her go to rock back and forth excitedly on the tips of her toes. "They're good. Ms. Jenn says I'm the best in the class. Which made Ashley maaaad. Her mom says I shouldn't be there because I'm not a full witch."

"Well, that's not nice," Rox said with a frown. "Did you tell Ms. Jenn this?"

Pria nodded. "She told me to be the bigger person and ignore it."

Roxanne hummed, sharing a look with Rava over the girl's head. Neither looked pleased with that answer.

"Pria, come down here so Roxanne and Fury can take a seat," Rava said now that the initial excitement passed.

A guilty smirk crossed the young girl's face before she turned on her heel and skipped down the seats till she reached the bottom. Rava crouched down in front of her, blocking her view as we followed behind. She spoke quietly; calm yet assertive as she scolded her daughter.

"We've talked about this, baby. You can't just use magic on people without their permission. You wouldn't like it if they used magic on you, would you?"

As I reached the bottom, I caught a flash of water welling in the little girl's eyes while she stared at her light-up sketchers. "No . . . but Mom , they weren't listening."

"First of all, you didn't give them a chance to. You yelled for them to move and then you made them. Second, not everyone is going to do what you want, when you want it. That doesn't give you permission to use magic on them."

Pria's bottom lip wobbled, but she sucked it in with her two front teeth, biting down to stop the tremble. Beside Rava, Caitlin sighed. "Leave it be for tonight. She's excited, and she misses the pack. We can cut her a little slack."

At her other mom's words, the girl perked up, all traces of guilt vanishing. Rava groaned. "Do you have to do that in front of her?"

"It's just for one night," Caitlin insisted, winking at Pria.

"It sets a bad precedent when she needs to learn about respecting boundaries," Rava replied, a little tersely. She let out a breath she must have been holding and slid back into the seat beside her mate. Pria sat next to her, followed by me and Roxanne. Below ground level, the thundering of shifter feet pounding the earth reverberated through my body, pulling me in. If not for the advanced fae-shifter-vamp-hybrid hearing, I wouldn't have been able to hear a damn thing.

"So Pria," I said quietly, trying to find a way to word my question. Rox must have sensed my confusion because she filled in the gaps.

"Was sent away after the first attacks on you, for fear the attacker might focus on people surrounding you—and their loved ones," she said without missing a beat. My lips parted.

"That was over a month ago."

"And Pria's been gone all that time. Caitlin and Rava enrolled her in a private school for witches so she could work on her magic." A trace of guilt flashed through me. I knew it wasn't my fault. Not truly. I didn't ask for my ex to be an archangel that was hellbent on killing me—again—because of my supposed angel blood I knew nothing about. I certainly didn't ask to put them or anyone else in danger, but still, being just a kid and taken away from everything you know, the guilt was there. "It was going to have to happen at some point," Rox added softly. "They'd just been putting it off despite Pria's growing magical outbursts. Don't beat yourself up too much. Sending her killed two birds with one stone."

I picked at a fraying edge of my jean shorts, ignoring the worming feeling beneath the surface. "This mating ritual must be a pretty big deal if they brought her back for it."

"You could say that." Roxanne nodded. "It's not every day the entire North American pack gets a second alpha."

My eyebrows rose as I stared at her dubiously. "They do know I'm not a wolf, right?"

Roxanne snorted. "Not all of them do, but it doesn't matter. You're Roman's mate and he's chosen to publicly stake that claim. Shifters respect that—if they know what's good for them."

It was my turn to snort at her. "Right. So Pria and the other kids are here to—"

"Watch the fight," the little girl chimed in. "Obviously."

I nodded once. Clearly, there was shit I needed to learn.

"I'll be taking Pria home after I beat Roman," Roxanne said under her breath. "Obviously," she added with a wink at Pria, who was swinging her legs while we waited for things to get underway. "I love you, but I have no desire to see what's going to happen after."

Given it was her brother and me, no other explanation was needed.

"You seem awfully confident about this," Caitlin said, speaking a little louder to be heard over the shifters around us.

Roxanne smirked. "Roman may be *the* alpha, but I taught him everything he knows."

All at once, the shifters quieted. Shouts turned to whispers as a hush fell over the crowd, and on the other side of the ieró zevgároma, Roman stood like a wolf god. His black locs were pulled back, showing the warpaint that dotted his cheekbones and outlined his jaw. Shirtless and glistening beneath the moonlight, the white paint travelled across his proud shoulders, down the hard edges of his chest, sweeping a story across every inch of his beautiful brown skin.

Suddenly I saw the appeal of this whole thing.

You know, apart from the very public and gratuitous sex that I was also totally down for.

"You can pick your jaw up off the floor whenever,"

Roxanne snickered.

I elbowed her in the side, which caused her to let out a demented cackle. "And to think, you told him 'hard pass' when he declared you his mate in my bar."

I did. Repeatedly.

If past Fury knew what present Fury did, she might not have run.

It had worked out so far, so I couldn't say I truly had any regrets about how things had run its course.

"You know what they say. Treat 'em mean, keep 'em keen."

From a distance, Roman heard what I'd said, and he lifted an eyebrow.

I had a feeling he was going to ask me about that later. Or better yet, take it out on me here. Tonight. My skin flushed at the prospect.

"Thanks for that. Getting him all worked up before his ass kicking," Roxanne whispered.

"That's a bad word," Pria said, semi-scolding Roxanne.

Caitlin snorted, which led to Rava throwing her another glare.

"She's an adult. She can say what she wants," Rava said under her breath. "Now quiet, unless you want Mama to take you back home and put you to bed."

Pria's mouth snapped shut with an audible clank of teeth that had even Rava grinning as Roman descended into the arena. Silence ensued for a suspended beat.

Then he spoke.

"My family, my pack, my people—" His voice carried loud and clear, yet low and intimate at the same time. "I stand before you to lay claim to my mate in the rite of ieró zevgároma."

With his final word, the pack let out a collective howl

that not even the wind could compete with.

"Who here stands for Fury, to test my worth as a mate? Who here fights for her, to first blood?"

"I do."

Beside me, Roxanne stood, moonlight casting her face in partial shadows.

Across the space, Roman answered, "Very well. At first howl, we duel."

Roxanne stepped forward into the circle. She reached for the hem of her T-shirt , whipping it off to reveal a sleek black sports bra and spandex shorts underneath.

A certain swagger entered her step as she strode forward, stopping only feet from him. While he towered over her smaller form, the confidence she wielded was undeniable, and I was curious to see how this played out.

From the stands, a lone howl cried out, and others joined in.

Roxanne and Roman went from utterly still to a flurry of motion as he tried to grab her and she ducked, sending a knee to the kidney while she was at it.

Something brushed against my side. I glanced over at Pria who had scooted closer but was watching them with nothing short of awe.

"Who do you think is gonna win?" she asked me while Roxanne executed a perfect rolling maneuver to avoid his outstretched claws. She popped back up and turned to face him, but Roman had done some sort of movie-worthy flip over her head, landing behind her.

She must have sensed it, and swung a roundhouse kick in a full one hundred and eighty degrees.

"No idea," I said honestly as Roman caught her foot. He twisted it and she spun with the movement, landing on her back. Roman grinned down, thinking this was the end.

"I think Rox will," the little girl said, very assured. I didn't want to pull my eyes away, but the calm, collected way she said it made me want to read her expression.

"What makes you say that?"

Roman dived, going to strike against her forearm. I really thought it was over until Roxanne's legs shifted in a fraction of a second. They went from the human limbs of a woman to the ginormous, fur-covered legs of her wolf. The strangest and most extraordinary part was that they were the only thing that did. The rest of her remained in human form as she kicked him off with incredible strength.

Roman went flying straight up into the air.

In a flash, Roxanne shifted her legs back and rolled out of the way as he came falling back down. She was on her feet before he hit the ground.

Pria grinned smugly. "Because girls rule and boys drool."

I snorted. Her answer was so . . . eight. Roxanne was definitely gaining the upper hand, but it had nothing to do with gender and everything to do with her speed and strength.

Roman hit the bedrock hard and took a face full of dirt.

Rox flashed a victorious smile, sauntering forward to land first blood. Roman may have been down, but he wasn't out for the count.

He rotated his hips, kicking her legs out from under her, while getting his hands beneath his form and using his still moving leg to gain enough momentum to get his other leg up and under him to stand.

I half expected him to dive on her when she went down, but he seemed to have learned from the last time he tried and instead backed off, taking a breather to reconfigure his strategy.

Rox landed on her butt in a plume of dust but grinned up at him, clearly enjoying the duel despite the seriousness the ritual started with.

"You call this worthy?" she said, egging him on. His eyes flashed blue, his wolf surfacing at her insult.

"Watch it, sister," he said in a deep gravelly voice that I'd grown to associate as his more feral half.

"Watch yourself," she replied with a wink.

Roxanne charged him, shifting mid-stride without faltering for a second. Roman barely had time to follow her lead in their dance of claws and teeth. He shifted quickly, albeit not nearly as fast, in an attempt to stop her from plowing him over.

I wasn't sure how it would go when they met head on, but it seemed Roxanne had a plan. As she approached—he lunged for her, and she shifted back. She dropped into a slide that would have made any Major League Baseball team proud. She slipped straight between his legs, vanishing underneath him before he knew what was up. In the second that passed for him to realize, she popped back up behind him and leapt onto his giant furry back, gripping the scruff of his neck harshly.

Roman rolled, trying to unseat her, but Roxanne wasn't giving up so easily. She took the weight of his entire wolf form as her back hit the ground. Other than a wince, she didn't let it show that the action caused her any pain, instead persisting with the hold on him. Roman shifted to his human form, lifting up from the waist before slamming back down in an attempt to crush her—or at the very least, jostle his sister loose.

And to think I had assumed they would pull their punches.

Rox wrapped her arms around his neck in a headlock,

then twisted her body, flipping them before he could do it. With his hands and knees flat on the ground, Roxanne sat on his back, choking the life out of him—so to speak.

I was just beginning to wonder how far they'd take the ritual when Roman lifted a hand from her arm and, in the moonlight, a dark red liquid smeared over his fingers.

"First blood," he coughed.

Roxanne released him instantly and took a step back.

"Is it?" She smirked, a red line running down her forearm but healing quickly.

Roman stood up and followed her line of sight to the matching red mark on his bicep that was healing and had left behind a swipe of blood where it had been.

Roman glowered, not pleased she may have kept going if she had been the first to draw blood. Roxanne smiled, shrugging a bit, and the crowd let out a laugh.

"We both drew blood, but who was first remains unknown. Roman, I declare you worthy of the sister to my soul. However, it is not my choice to make."

All eyes fell on me, and Pria elbowed me in the ribs, stage whispering, "It's your turn."

Caitlin and Rava chuckled at their daughter's antics, shaking their heads.

"Fury," Roxanne said, summoning me forward. "Beneath the night sky and before this pack, do you find him a worthy mate to bind yourself to, from now until the earth takes you both?"

My heart hammered, the silence around us screaming for me to answer.

"I do."

Roxanne smiled at me. "Then come forth and let the sacred mating begin."

CHAPTER II

I approached Roman slowly.

Roxanne patted my shoulder on the way back to grab Pria, who was excitedly chatting about their sleepover and how she was going to show off her rock collection and the stuffed animals she'd acquired. Other kids and their caretakers made their way up the seats. A few teenagers grumbled about how they wanted to stick around and were promptly told to come back when they were paying their own bills. I snorted, especially since I didn't currently pay my own. Then again, I didn't really live in any one place. I bounced between my mates and their homes.

Through it all, Roman and I stood toe to toe, staring at one another with something far deeper and more profound than lust. We shared each other's amusement in listening to the younger generations. We shared our impatience and delicious tension as we waited for what came next. We also shared a quiet sort of intimacy, just being near each other and not simply content—but happy.

I valued that more than I could ever find the words to say.

As the last of the kids left, Caitlin walked forward, carrying a clay pot with some sort of black substance. I cast a curious glance as Rava stepped up beside her.

"We will now paint you in the symbols of our pack to represent our acceptance," Caitlin said quietly. Around us, a subdued pulse of feet meeting earth began again, but unlike before, it didn't resemble a battle drum. Instead, an almost soothing sort of rhythm that seemed to aid the interpretation of them accepting me.

When I hadn't moved, Rava stepped in front of me and slowly reached for my shirt.

"May I?" she whispered. I wasn't sure if it was part of the ritual, but I appreciated it all the same.

I gave her a small nod and lifted my arms for her to begin undressing me.

With each piece of clothing that came off, my heart beat faster. A heat creeped over my skin.

There was a different sort of vulnerability in allowing them to undress me like this, for all to see. It wasn't driven by the same kind of heat that made me an exhibitionist, but instead was incredibly revealing.

Intimate.

Sacred.

When Rava pressed her fingertips to my cheek bones, I began to understand the ritual in a way I hadn't before. The paint was cool but not cold, and it thankfully dried quickly.

We stood in the center, not speaking as she painted my face and neck. Her fingers dipped in the bowl and then swiped across my shoulders in steady strokes. Down my arms and around the curve of my breasts.

Roman's eyes glowed an icy blue the entire way. His wolf was very much at the forefront and ready to claim its mate.

About halfway down my body, heat started to settle in under his watchful gaze. There was something erotic about being watched by him while Rava painted my naked form.

When she dropped to her knees to start on my thighs, her fingers brushed across a sensitive patch of flesh, and I shivered. A low rumble escaped his chest, the alpha starting to grow impatient.

My body flamed hotter. I was glad for the moonlight and shadows in concealing the flushed shade my skin was no doubt turning.

Rava's fingers moved quickly, painting the rest of my legs and feet. When she was done, she stepped back with Caitlin to observe me. They both bowed their heads in respect, and the crowd behind them followed.

When I turned to Roman and saw that he was on his knees, doing the same, I wanted to combust. A cool wind whipped through the circle, lifting the sweaty strands of hair from the back of my neck.

No one told me what I was supposed to do now.

There were no instructions.

So I followed my heart.

Running my fingertips down the sides of Roman's face, I cupped his jaw and tilted it back. The eyes of his wolf met mine and the primal hunger I saw there—it shattered us both.

He stood up, pulling me into him, our lips meeting in a clash of teeth and tongues. I fisted his dreads, and a growl rippled through the clearing.

"Mine," Roman declared. His voice was mottled. Deeper. Rough.

He grabbed my ass with both hands and hoisted me up.

"My mate," he continued when he broke away to kiss

down my neck. I tilted my head back, wrapping my legs around his waist.

"My equal," he purred, tilting my body in such a way his already hard cock touched my entrance. After minutes of standing in front of him, unable to touch, to tease, I was more than ready.

"My queen," he whispered reverently. Teeth pricked my skin on the opposite shoulder that he'd claimed before. I tipped my head to the moon, mouth falling open in pleasure as he bit me. A moan worked its way up my throat, turning to a gasp as he thrust into me.

My pussy spasmed, locking tight around his cock. Roman groaned into my shoulder, his fingers turning to claws that pricked my ass as he started working me over his length.

I dropped my hands from his hair to his shoulders, raking my own nails down his back. Roman released the flesh of my shoulder with a pop, throwing his head back to let out a howl. The wolves around us followed suit.

I opened my eyes to stare at them as they watched me, their eyes filled with lust. Several of them were touching themselves. Others undressing. Then there were the couples like Caitlin and Rava, who looked like they were most of the way to finishing the deal themselves.

Their ravenous stares urged me on, and I bucked against him. My hips bounced in rhythm against his, the smack of flesh meeting flesh and panting moans the only sounds now.

I couldn't remember a time in my life that I'd ever felt so alive.

I never wanted it to end.

That was the thought that filled me when my body tipped over the precipice. My cunt contracted. Blackness exploded behind my eyes as a visceral shudder ran through me.

Roman dropped to his knees, tipping me backwards. My head touched the ground, followed by my shoulders. He kept pumping into me, holding my ass and hips off the ground to guide them to his engorged cock as he fed it to me.

I gasped, looking down at where our bodies joined. The black paint on my body smearing and mixing with the white paint on his. It was the most erotic sight I'd ever seen. I loved it.

"So tight," he said through gritted teeth. "So perfect."

I was approaching another peak when he pulled out, then set me down. He maneuvered my legs around him, turning me over so that my face was pressed into the ground and my hips pulled up, ass in the air.

"I love this ass," he muttered, before biting it. My back arched and I let out a hiss as pleasure shot through me, putting me on the very edge.

"Need you," I groaned, rocking my hips back.

He released me from his bite and gripped me tight. I didn't even feel him at the entrance until he was shoving inside me, and I tightened around him.

My mouth fell open as I let out an anguished cry. My body wound up, then snapped. My legs turning to jelly. The second climax wasn't as strong, instead leaving me wanting more. Needing more to truly finish the job.

"Open your eyes, cherub," Roman commanded. "Look at them."

And look I did.

In the time between my first orgasm and my second, the seats around us had turned into an all-out orgy. Men and women fucked. Sometimes two men and a woman, one taking her from the front and the other behind. Then there were the groups where one man fucked another, and the one being fucked ate a woman out. No one was truly alone in the public act taking place, where we all embraced our desires together. I never felt more like I'd truly found my people.

"Roman," I breathed.

"What do you need?" he asked, his voice thick with restraint.

"You. Your cock." I groaned in frustration, reaching for that pinnacle again but failing to grab on. "I need to come."

Roman pulled out. I wanted to cry from the emptiness when my blood was pounding, yearning for a release only he could give me.

"What are you—" I started to protest, but my words were cut off when I felt him brush the inside of my thighs, his mouth covering me and latching onto my clit. He grabbed my hips, pulling me back so that I was sitting on him, spreading my pussy wide open for his taking.

I rocked into him, letting out another moan as his tongue swirled around my sensitive nub, then sucked.

"Yes," I breathed, finally gaining ground.

He blew on my clit, and I broke.

A mix between a guttural moan and scream escaped me. My body locked tight in the sweetest ecstasy. The best and worst sort of pleasure, where it felt so good it hurt.

My back arched so far back it threatened to snap as I clamped tight. He rubbed his tongue over me through the entire orgasm, drawing every last drop of pleasure from me until my body turned soft and pliable, too at ease to fight anymore.

With one last lick, Roman lifted my hips and pulled out from under me. I fell back, my butt hitting the heels of my feet when he let go. There I stayed, kneeling and half-dazed, when Roman stepped around in front of me. His cock was hard and heavy as it swung between his legs.

He gripped its base, lifting it to position the tip a few inches from my lips. I opened wide, taking his head. My tongue swirled around it, tasting my release and his precum.

"I'm close," Roman panted as he ran his fingers through my hair. I relaxed, taking him deeper. The rough pad of my tongue running along the underside of his length as I rocked into him and pulled back, going a little further each time.

My lips curled around my teeth to keep from hurting him. I pressed them tight to his skin, sucking hard. The way he twitched and pulsed told me how much he loved it.

"I want to show my pack who you belong to," he groaned. I hummed my approval around his member, bucking my head up and down.

Roman pushed in and out twice more before holding the sides of my head with both hands, twining his fingers through my hair, gripping tight. I parted my lips, widening my jaw so he could fuck my face.

I stilled while he thrusted in a fervent rhythm, his cock hitting the back of my throat repeatedly while I grasped his muscular thighs, keeping balance. A loud grunt sounded, then he shuddered as he erupted in my mouth. His salty release coated my tongue, mixing with saliva as it dripped down my chin, splashing against my chest, and running down the slope of my breasts.

Roman cupped my cheek, rubbing his juices into my skin, slightly possessive yet still sweet. "I love you," I said, the words slipping out of me.

Roman got on his knees with me and kissed me softly.

"I'd destroy the world for you—and I don't even think I'd care anymore. That's how much I need you."

We kissed again, falling into the haze of lust and love that consumed the circle. But in the back of my mind, where I couldn't ignore it, I thought about what he'd said.

While I hoped it would never come to that, I believed him.

The part that scared me the most was that I was starting to believe that too.

I needed him. Them.

And I'd destroy anything that stood in the way. Even the Afterlife itself.

CHAPTER 12

Jules leaned forward on her elbows, cradling her face in her hand while she watched me get dressed.

Kelly had put the final touches on my 'battle-ready' gala gown. We'd replaced the spaghetti straps with a thicker piece that clasped behind my neck. I twisted around, making sure it felt right and my boobs stayed in place. The black tulle of the skirt had been lessened as I requested, but it was still more than enough to cover my legs. Beneath it all, black leggings connected to my pale rose-colored halter , the rip-away function of the skirt cleverly hidden by a thick black ribbon tied around my waist.

The shade of pink was muted and not something I would have likely chosen, but Rox liked it and my hair more than made up for it. I put on my Doc Martens and double-knotted the laces for good measure. Standing in front of the full-length mirror, the boots were lost under the long skirt. Kelly had measured that tulle perfectly, and it touched the ground without dragging, but also without showing any part of my feet. I looked like I was floating.

"That's pretty," Jules said. "You look like a ballerina

princess." Looking down at where she knew my boots were, she added, "Well, almost. Like a ballerina princess assassin."

I snorted. "I'd much prefer the latter. The whole pink tutu thing is not really my style," I said, trailing off. After a long pause, I added, "But it does serve a purpose. And it fits with the theme of that room. Gotta make it look real, after all."

"What's that mean?" Jules asked, pointing at my neck.

My fingers grazed over the intricate lines of the Celtic knot necklace. "It's, um, it's what Dorian gave me as his mate. It claims me as his and claims him as mine."

Jules waggled her eyebrows. "Fancy. So he gives you a necklace, Roman fucks you like a savage in front of everyone . . . what does Ezra do in this brother-husbands scenario?"

I busted out laughing. "Brother-husbands what?"

"You know that show, right? *Sister Wives*?"

"I've heard of it, but it's not really my kind of show. How have you seen it? Do you have TV in the mirror realm?" I asked, now genuinely curious as to what went down on her side of the world.

"I watch shows through mirrors in people's houses," she said and shrugged. "Anyway, it's like that for you, except the opposite. I don't know what that's called, or if it's even got a word for it. But you're the girl, and you've got three husbands."

"I do not have three husbands. I had one once, and that was enough," I said firmly. I wasn't so sure why the thought of calling them my husbands would cause such an adverse reaction. They weren't Azrael. They were my mates. I felt it. I knew it with every fiber of my being. This was real, and it was forever. Why it happened, I didn't know. I no longer cared about the why. It just . . . was. And I was happy for it.

Being called mate and allowing them to claim me while I claimed them didn't bother me. Why then did the word husband?

"Fine, *mates,* then. But it doesn't have the same ring to it," she said, frowning. "You still didn't answer the question, though. What does Ezra give you?"

"You know . . . I don't entirely know. Ezra is different. He's . . ." I paused, trying to find the right way to explain what I had with my vampire mate.

Ezra was the easiest in some ways. While his mind-probing was infuriating at times, he was also the one that could probably understand me more than anyone else. There was a comfort factor in that. He'd been trying so hard not to invade my space, giving me peace of mind and not showing up or listening without permission. Or, as he said it, not reacting to it and allowing me to feel like my thoughts were private.

He was also more detached as a mate. I'd started to think on it as I accepted the mate bond with them all. Dorian and Roman were adamant about claiming. Dorian didn't like to share, but he acknowledged the bonds and wouldn't come between them. Roman wasn't that dissimilar, but I had a feeling he was maybe willing to share a little more than Dorian would. My cheeks warmed at the thought, reminding me of the ritual. Ezra was firm that he would never come between me and my other mates. He knew what pain it caused when you couldn't be with them. He certainly seemed like he would be fine sharing. He had no problem letting Kendrick watch us before. I assumed we'd easily take things further one day.

But the fact remained, he'd not only lost his mate, but

he'd been burned so badly by her when she rejected him. It didn't make her loss any less, but I could see how it would be hard to fully open up to me. I figured he wore a mask when he was charming and flirtatious, in some ways getting close to me but still keeping me at arm's length. Before I had made my decision to stay, there was one thing I knew for certain. Of all three mates, he was the only one willing to accept me going back. Dorian refused to get close, and Roman would have followed me into the Afterlife if he had to.

I traced the outline of the scar on my shoulder where Roman bit me when he claimed me the night of the bonfire.

Who knew? Maybe I was wrong. Maybe I was over-thinking things. I certainly had plenty of time in my after-life to do just that. Now it would seem I continued to do it in my post-afterlife-life.

"Yo, Fury," Jules said, pulling me from my thoughts. I refocused my eyes, looking up from where I was staring off in the distance.

"Yeah. Sorry, I was just thinking," I mumbled.

"You sort of disappeared there. You were saying that Ezra is different?" she prompted.

"Mmm hmm," I answered, reorganizing my thoughts, and sitting on a cushioned stool. "He's just more laidback about the whole mate thing, I think. He believes in it without question, and he takes it seriously, but he was rejected once before. That probably takes a lot of time to get over."

She gestured toward me as she said, "Well, take a look in the mirror, no pun intended. It's been over a hundred years and you're still not over what your ex did to you."

I stared at her, wide-eyed. "Wow. Tactful."

She shrugged again. "Look, I don't people much anymore, okay? I call it how I see it."

Straightening my posture, I tossed my hair over my shoulder. "I don't think you can compare the two, but you're not wrong. There is, however, a massive difference between being rejected by a mate and being beaten repeatedly and then murdered."

"How do you know? You've never been rejected, and he's never been beaten and murdered."

I let out a frustrated sigh. "What is your point?"

"Not sure anymore. Maybe I don't have one. Who knows where thoughts come from?"

I groaned loudly, but before I could tell her off, she turned her head as though she were listening to something. Turning back to me, she said, "I'll be back. Lyra is on the move. I need to watch."

"Wait, how do you kn—" I stopped my sentence when she disappeared fully, knowing I wouldn't get my answer.

How did she know that, though? Was it possible she could be in multiple places at once? She had to have some system set up. I wondered if she would take me back in there when this was all done. I wanted to see more, and not when she was yanking me from the middle of Ezra's apartment and into her world, freaking everyone out.

I sat alone in my room at Dorian's Houston estate. Somewhere down the hall, Roxanne and each of my mates were getting ready.

I grabbed a lock of my hair, twirling it around my finger while I waited and mentally prepared myself for how the evening would go.

If Lyra was on the move, our plan had worked. She was coming to the gala. She'd been dormant for over a week, not causing trouble or showing up anywhere. Jules had seen Azrael with Lyra once, but nothing more. She couldn't hear them, but she'd said it looked like a quarrel. Azrael ended it the way he always did; striking her down, standing over her, and commanding her compliance. Then he disappeared, leaving Lyra on the floor. Jules hadn't seen him since.

A knock on the door pulled me away, and I said, "Come in."

Ezra entered, his charming half-smile lighting up the room. His tuxedo jacket was on, but he'd opted out of a bowtie, instead allowing the inky black tendrils of his tattoos to peek out of the open collar.

"You look beautiful," he said, coming toward me and kissing me gently on the cheek. I held the side of his arm as he leaned in, lingering for a moment longer than I expected. "You smell delicious too."

"Thanks. Roxanne got me a perfume," I said by way of explanation. "I'm not entirely sure it was for tonight or for use in general. I'm guessing the latter because she said she could smell sex on me, and she thought it was gross."

The look on Ezra's face shifted briefly before he caught it and corrected it. If he didn't think I saw it, he was dead wrong. He reached into his jacket, pulling out a flask. After unscrewing the top, he took a swig, then another. He traced his fingers over his lips, wiping off the excess before extending it to me.

Thank the stars he was giving me a drink without being a prick about it. I took the offering, downing several gulps before returning it.

"I wanted to say thank you," I started, trying to steer us into a good conversation.

"For?" he asked, raising an eyebrow.

"Giving me space," I said, tapping my temple with one

finger. "I know it's not easy to just stop listening and probing, but I know you're trying. Even if I know you're listening in, you've been quiet about it. I appreciate it."

"It's what you wanted." Reaching his hand out, he grazed his thumb and forefinger down my cheek, stopping on my chin and leaning in for a peck on the lips, leaving behind a tiny tingle. Pulling away and stepping back, he said, "I always want to give you what you want."

I smiled, looking him up and down in a suggestive way. I hadn't been able to spend much time with him, and I missed it. "I want to see more of you."

He looked at me in surprise, then turned to look at the door. "What'd you have in mind?" he asked, giving me his full attention as he sauntered toward me like a predator tracking prey.

I walked backward, raising an eyebrow coyly. My back hit the wall, and Ezra ascended on me. Wrapping my arms around his neck and throwing one leg around him, I pulled him toward me in a deep kiss as I opened my mouth to him. Tracing my tongue over his, I inhaled deeply, drinking him in. His hands gripped my upper waist before he moved them up my body, pressing into me and following my curves. We released, and I gasped for air, feeling the familiar ache between my thighs when he moved his hips against mine, his hard length pushing against me.

"Hurry," I said in a husky tone, need taking over me. "I don't know what time we are leaving."

I reached between us, rubbing his cock with the flat of my palm, and started to unbuckle him. He let out a throaty growl, licking, kissing, and nipping down my neck, moving to my shoulder. As I turned my head to give him better access, I felt him freeze, and he inhaled sharply.

"What?" I said, my breathing somewhat heavy.

Ezra stared at the mark left by Roman.

"The shifter claimed you," he said quietly.

I looked at him in confusion. "Uh, yeah? I told you about this, and it's not like you can't see that shit in my head." I dropped my leg from his waist, taking my hands away from his trousers. Talk about a mood ruined.

"I didn't think I'd be able to see it. The bite should heal."

I looked at him incredulously. "I . . . the mating bite doesn't fade or heal. The mark stays there, even on me, apparently."

Ezra stepped back, eyeing between the necklace and the bite. He rubbed the bridge of his nose while the silence spanned between us.

I reached up, feeling the scar tissue under the pads of my fingers. Ezra's reaction felt awful. For a brief moment, I felt like I needed to cover my mark. Like I had done something wrong . . .

That moment quickly passed. Fuck that. We all knew what this was.

I took my hand off it, walking forward and pushing past him.

"Fury, wait," he begged, reaching out to grab my wrist. I yanked away.

"No, don't lay your bullshit on me, Ezra. It's not cool," I said, reeling on him. My hands were flapping wildly as I yelled, pointing at him and waving them about. "You can't make me feel bad for this. You were there when I said I would stay. I made a choice. My choice was my mates. All three of you. You said you would never come between us. They would never come between you and me. Honestly, I can't even process this right now. Out of the three, I expected jealousy least of all from you."

He held his hands up in surrender. "I know, I know." His

entire demeanor had softened, and the appearance of jealousy melted away.

"What is this, Ezra? Tell me what's going on." I crossed my arms, jutting out my hip.

He put his hands back in his pocket and met my annoyed glare. "It's been a weird week, that's all."

I could feel the heat of my glower. It would melt an iceberg. "No. That's not enough."

He sighed. "I've spent the past week tracking Azrael, trying to keep you safe. Interrogating vampires across the southern borders. Roman has shifters out doing the same, but the only one I can rely on is Kendrick. Too many vampires were infiltrated last time. I just can't trust them."

I softened slightly. "What does that have to do with Roman claiming me?"

He frowned. "It's not jealousy. It's . . . longing for something I haven't had in a long time."

I held my hand out toward the wall where we had just been. "Um, you were about to have me over there, fangs. Not sure what you're longing for."

He huffed a laugh, looking at the floor. "Not exactly."

"Then what?" I asked, feeling the frustration starting to creep in again.

"I haven't claimed you, but they have," he answered.

Oh . . .

The tension and anger left me. "I . . . I'm not rejecting you, Ezra. We just haven't . . . you've not been around much. It just sort of happened with Dorian. The ritual with Roman was planned, but . . ." I trailed off, not knowing what else to say. I met his reluctant smile with one of my own. "What happens when vampires claim?"

"We tattoo each other," he said.

I raised my eyebrows in surprise. "Really? As in we are

the ones that put the ink on each other?" I wondered what that would look like. That took artistry and skill.

Ezra opened his mouth to answer, then shut it quickly. He creased his eyebrows together in concentration and it looked like he was focusing on something behind me. Looking back at me, he rushed through his words quickly. "I have to go. Kendrick has something." He walked toward me, placing a hand behind my head, and kissed me on the forehead. "We'll talk more. I promise. I'll make this up to you," he said before going to the door.

I stood in the middle of the room confused as hell, wondering what had just happened. I'd managed to make Ezra feel rejected. I'd told him to give me space. To get out of my head. I couldn't feel bad for wanting privacy. I had a right to that. But still, that combined with the other two claiming me first probably felt like a giant slap to his ego.

I scrubbed my hands down my face and stormed over to the bed. I grabbed a pillow, took a deep breath, then screamed into it.

"Um . . . are you okay?" Jules asked tentatively.

I jerked my head up and saw her concerned look. "Yeah, I'm fine."

She deadpanned. "Did you really just say you are *fine?*"

I sighed. "Did you hear or see any of that with Ezra just now?"

She shook her head. "Afraid not. What'd I miss?"

"My first encounter with juggling the emotions and commitments to three brother-husbands, as you put it," I muttered, tossing the pillow back onto the bed.

"Oh, well, I don't actually know anything about marital bliss." She grinned awkwardly and looked away. "Anything you want to talk about?"

I laughed. I had made a friend with a girl in a mirror.

She was significantly older than me, and younger all the same, but it didn't matter. Even if it made her uncomfortable, she was willing to listen to me vent if I needed to. Knowing that I had that with her felt good. At the moment, it was all I needed.

I waved my hand, dismissing the weirdness that had just taken place. "Nah, don't worry about it. I'll talk to him more later. I think I figured out what's wrong. Now we just have to make it better."

A subtle pop sounded in the room, and I turned to see Dorian as he walked toward me.

I smiled at him, feeling content that this encounter would at least not feel emotionally overwhelming. A warmness spread through my body, making me wonder if the temperature in the room had risen.

"You look stunning," he said, eyeing the necklace that he'd given me.

"Thanks," I started to say, but my tongue felt thick, and the word came out warbly.

Fuck. Not again.

I reached out, trying to grab something to hold me up as my vision began to swim, but I missed the edge of whatever furniture was next to me.

"Fury," Dorian shouted, catching me in an instant and bringing me gently to the floor.

So much for not being overwhelmed.

My fangs grew, pressing into my lips, and I groaned. The need to bite was increasing, and the buildup inside was creating a pressure in my head. "Need . . ." I slurred. It was all I could get out.

"Ezra just left," Jules said. I turned to see her mirror shaking just before she disappeared.

Dorian looked at the door, then back at me. He looked

like he was vibrating. My vision distorted further, making it appear like the room was rattling.

I felt my consciousness fading as the room started to spin violently. I pawed at Dorian's arm, mumbling his name.

I had seconds to spare before blood would start pouring from my ears and eyes, and he knew it.

"Need . . . you," I managed.

Dorian looked up at the ceiling and around the room, muttering curses. He pulled his jacket off and readjusted our bodies, laying me between his legs, cradling my head and back with his right arm. With his mouth, he ripped the sleeve of his shirt, exposing the thick muscles of his left forearm. He pressed it against my mouth, my fangs piercing the skin as blood came rushing out.

Instant relief flooded my body as I poured into Dorian. He grunted through it, resting his head on top of mine as I reverse-fed. His fingers stroked my skin while whispering reassuring words I couldn't even make out.

When everything had been expelled, I let go, grimacing at the metallic taste leftover in my mouth. The puncture wounds started to close and heal.

"Sorry," I mumbled hoarsely. "I didn't—"

"There's nothing to be sorry for," he said, snapping his fingers to make a glass of water appear. I took it gratefully, gulping and swishing it in my mouth.

"Thank you for catching me and letting me . . . you know." What? Thank you for letting me bite you and inject you with an overflow of blood? Didn't feel right, so I left it at that. I looked at the tattered material on his arm and groaned. "You ruined your shirt. Did I ruin my dress?"

Dorian scrunched his eyebrows as he held me, staring

at me with concern. "Did you just ask if you ruined your dress?"

"Oh, shut up." I smacked his arm, moving to sit myself up. "You know what I mean."

He chuckled. "I don't know. Seems like a situation where you'd be using a secret code to call for help, when you're worried about ruining your dress." He smiled at me while I rolled my eyes. "And you're welcome."

I squeezed my eyes shut, inhaling deeply. "That one came on fast. It felt faster than it did in the cave with Roman."

He pressed his lips together. "Mmm. You almost collapsed the cavern that day." He looked up, and I followed his gaze to see a crack in the ceiling. My mouth fell open. "Looks like that's part of the deal now."

I felt horrible. There were too many people in this house. Something could have gone terribly wrong. "I have to get this under control."

Dorian stroked my hair. "We're going about it all wrong. We need to tackle it from another direction."

I turned to look at him in question. "Meaning?"

"Maybe give blood before these symptoms come on. Perhaps it would lessen the severity of your reactions and cause less"—he gestured above us—"whatever that is."

I nodded along and sat up, my body starting to feel like my own again. "You may be onto something there."

I was willing to give anything a try. I was with my mates almost all the time, and I had given blood to each of them. They were fine. I was fine. We'd be able to figure it out.

I wanted to ask what could go wrong, but I honestly didn't want the universe to answer me anymore when I asked stupid questions.

CHAPTER 13

The ballet studio turned ballroom was even more beautiful in real life than it was in the pictures. The renovated building in the historical district was classic and restored on the outside. Inside, the wooden details in the columns, window trim, and archways showcased those characteristics missing in modern architecture.

The balance bars that lined the walls around the entire room were draped in sheer white and pink fabric. There were thirty large round tables covered in elegant black tablecloths, each one carefully moved away from the mirrored walls, leaving more than enough space for us to get Lyra near one when she showed up.

The centerpieces were grand vases filled with floral arrangements in different hues of pink and red. Sprigs of tiny white flowers filled the gaps between the roses and greenery. Each one sat on a mirrored plate, giving us one more opportunity to get her near Jules.

We weren't willing to unnecessarily risk anyone for this operation. Instead of hiring musicians, Roxanne opted for music playing softly through speakers. A bar had been set up at the end of the room, but I'd been informed it was all for show. No one was drinking on this particular evening. Each shifter, fae, and vampire invited tonight was here for battle. We even had a couple of witches on hand.

Roxanne had outdone herself. I had no idea how she was able to coordinate all of it, but she'd managed to make it stunning. I almost believed it was a real celebration to publicly acknowledge my acceptance of taking three mates. Almost.

Rox came to my side, handing me a red drink with a cherry. A 'drink.' I smiled and took a sip of the brightly colored liquid. I winced at the sweetness and coughed through the carbonation. "What is this?" I asked hoarsely.

"A Shirley Temple. It's a kids' drink. Grenadine and Sprite." She smiled brightly. "I thought you'd like to feel like you were having a drink at the party."

I frowned, setting it down on a table. "I appreciate the thought, but it's just a bit too sugary." And not enough alcohol-y.

She reached out, handing me another drink. A purplish red color filled the rock glass, a wedge of lime pushed into the rim. I grimaced, but she said, "Not sweet. It's cranberry and lime."

I took it tentatively, sipped it, and nodded. It wasn't bad. Whisky was better, but I would take it.

"It's your mocktail."

"My what?"

She pointed to the glass in my hand. "A mocktail. A mock cocktail. I serve them to pregnant customers, and some that just want to play pool or cards but don't like drinking."

"I'll keep that in mind." I pressed my lips together and held it up in a sign of 'cheers'. Mock cheers for the mocktail.

I didn't plan on making this a habit. I liked drinking, and I sure as shit wasn't pregnant.

It was boring expecting someone to arrive when they didn't know they were even invited. I knew Lyra would show up, but the wait was mind-numbing. Everywhere I turned I saw mirrors. I knew Jules was watching, I just didn't know where she was. I patted my dress, feeling the orb in my hidden pocket. All around us, couples and groups were mingling. Holding mocktails in their hands while they had their fake conversations.

I saw Elena talking to Rya and Kendrick. Her high ponytail was traded out for intricate braids. She wore a rich black off-the-shoulder dress, but I knew full well she could sift into her armor at the drop of a hat. Kendrick and Rya appeared to pay attention, but I knew they were watching every move in their periphery.

I looked up to see Dorian on the balcony overhead, watching the entire room. His posture was relaxed but commanding. I knew he was tense, but somehow he didn't show it. I scanned to find Roman and Ezra as they spoke to each other quietly, strategically placed near the center of the room. I made eye contact with Ezra, and he smiled, winking at me. I hoped that was his way of telling me things were okay with us.

Caitlin and Rava were on opposite sides of the room, bringing Kelly around to chat with fae and vampires I didn't know. It was an odd thing. I was told the summit was the only time all three factions were on equal ground. The only time they conversed and socialized together. From what I was seeing, it looked natural. Like it could easily happen more often. The three groups were getting along fine. They all had a common purpose. I knew this was a façade, but they seemed at ease with each other. Their interactions didn't look forced or uncomfortable. It made me think it could happen more often if they didn't try to stay segregated. Nothing good had ever come from it. I wondered if I could talk to my mates about it. Would that be overstepping boundaries? Getting involved in their duties as alphas?

Turning back to Roxanne, I asked, "Hey, do you think Roman would mind if I talked to him about the pack and working together with the vampires?"

She raised an eyebrow, giving me her attention. "Working how?"

I shrugged my shoulders. "It just looks like everyone here gets along better than I thought they would. Common goal and all. But maybe it's more than that. Maybe we can work together as factions and not need to have this need for a summit every decade."

Roxanne pursed her lips as she thought about it. "I imagine more would get done if everyone wasn't always in a pissing contest. Besides, we all hate the summit. Talk to Roman. He's a good listener. You're his mate. It's not out of line."

I nodded along. "I'm just thinking it would have been easier to spread out resources, especially now. Like with the southern borders. It just makes more sense to work together."

A crease developed between Roxanne's eyebrows, and she waited a moment before speaking. "The southern borders? What are you talking about?"

I stared blankly. "Ezra interrogating vampires at the southern borders? He said Roman had shifters out doing the same thing."

Roxanne gave a slight headshake. "We don't have any

shifters at the southern borders. We aren't interrogating anyone, vampires or shifters."

I blinked several times, processing her words. "Maybe I misunderstood what Ezra had said. My bad." I bit my, lip feeling like I'd missed a part of our conversation earlier. "My point still stands about working together, though," I muttered. I excused myself suddenly, leaving Roxanne by the table with furrowed brows and twisted lips on her expression.

I walked toward Roman and Ezra, trying to give a small smile even though something ate at me inside. Why had he lied to me? I didn't miss part of that conversation. I wasn't crazy.

As I approached, Roman's attention went to Roxanne. I turned my head slightly, seeing in my periphery that she was waving him over. Her confused look was gone, now masked by a beautiful beaming smile, playing her part in the evening's charade.

Roman nodded, then bent down to kiss me before he left. I turned to Ezra, feigning happiness and pretended to start a general conversation like the rest of the supernaturals in the room.

"Hey angel," he said, giving me a half-smile .

I jutted my chin towards him in a casual gesture, acknowledging his greeting but hating that he'd called me that. "No kitten?" I asked, tilting my head to the side.

"Is this really the place for it?" he asked, looking around.

"I didn't know there was a place for it," I countered. "I just don't like being called 'angel'. Never have." I lifted my drink to my lips, sipping the cranberry juice. Ezra looked at it like I was drinking mud. "When you left earlier, I wasn't sure if we were okay. I know this isn't really the place to hash out the details, but we need to talk more, and I want you to know I want to talk about all of it. I never meant to make you feel that way, but I'm not sorry I asked for space."

Ezra looked at his shoes briefly, then nodded when he looked up. "We're good, I promise." He reached into his breast pocket, pulling out the flask from earlier. I glanced at Dorian on the balcony, and he rolled his eyes, shaking his head when he looked away. Ezra unscrewed the top, taking a swig and then offering it to me.

I cocked an eyebrow as I accepted it, tilting it back and taking a mouthful of real bourbon, no mock about it. I swallowed, letting out a heavy breath.

You're a fucking liar.

I waited.

Nothing.

Ezra waited patiently until I handed him back his flask and he tucked it away.

"Good. I'm glad we're okay," I lied in return, since that seemed to be what we were doing now. I reached down to smooth out the skirt on my dress for absolutely no reason. "I want to do that tattoo you were telling me about."

"Hmm?" Ezra mused. "When?"

"You tell me. Do vampires plan the claiming thing like the shifters do? Is it a public event, private? Does someone like Kendrick do the tattoo?"

Ezra and I scanned around the room, continuing to look for anything out of place. My eyes landed back on him, and I stared.

"We do it whenever we want, however we want," he answered, grazing his fingers down my arm from shoulder to elbow.

"I like the idea of that," I said quietly. "Will you show me what it looks like?"

"Of course. Anything for you," he said, taking my hand and leading me over to the fake-bar. I held my drink glass up to the bartender, asking for another as Ezra asked her for a pen.

She handed him one, and she handed me another drink. While he grabbed a cocktail napkin and started to draw, I waited, squeezing the lime into the cranberry juice and swirling it around with my finger.

I moved my eyes around the room, checking the location of my other two mates and their seconds. Everyone had shifted their places somewhat, finding a new person to talk to. Everyone looked casual and laid back. Everyone except Roxanne. Her gaze was pinned on me, watching my every move. Roman stood facing her, his back to me, but I saw him in the mirror. He watched me carefully.

"Here, kitten," Ezra said, sliding the napkin toward me. I took it from him, cocking my head to the side as I looked at the specifics of the tattoo. The symbol he'd drawn wasn't Chinese. They were runes connected to each other inside a circle. It was hard to tell where one began and one ended. "You look disappointed." There was a tone in his voice I hadn't heard before.

I shook my head. "I'm not," I said truthfully. "I thought it would be something in Chinese, to be honest. What does this mean? The only rune I can make out is 'eternity'."

He scooped his hand around my waist, pulling me closer to him. Setting the drink down on the bar, I slid into his embrace.

"It's a vampire thing, not a cultural thing," he said vaguely.

I moved the symbols through my mind, focusing on the curves and the details. It had to mean something. I felt like I'd seen it before. Runes were complicated. So many cultures had them. If there was a vampire language, I certainly wouldn't know about it.

I was willing to let it go, setting it aside in my mind. He was not okay yet, and he was pushing me away as a result. Fine. We'd deal with each other when Lyra was shoved into a mirror and I could think straight.

Ezra started to dance to the music, pressing me against him and taking me along for the movement. I tried to sway gracefully, keeping in time with him. My mind was tripped up, still trying to decode the symbols in my head, arguing with myself that I couldn't figure it out if they were in fact some sort of ancient vampire language. But I focused. They were attached to each other. Where did they break?

Ezra released me, turning me into a slow spin, holding my hand gently. I fixed my face into a demure smile as I separated from his body, falling back into a deep concentration when I came back to his chest, resting my hand on his shoulder. He hummed softly in my ear, sucked my earlobe, then whispered, "You'll be mine in life and death."

I stumbled over my feet in our dance. The runes. Where they broke apart . . . it meant life and death. I'd seen them before. I'd thought it was a hallucination back then. I'd been hit so many times, my vision was blurred. My eyes were swollen, nearly shut, filled with what felt like endless tears. I was balled up on the floor, covering my head with my arms as he'd yanked me up. I'd sworn I'd seen his hands glow with strange markings as he reached back to slap me again. It was when I knew my consciousness was waning. It was the only explanation at the time . . .

Bile rose in my throat, and I shoved it down, catching my breath. In an instant, I regained my steps. Then I put all my weight and strength into an uppercut into Ezra's jaw as

I screamed bloody murder, shaking the room and cracking mirrors right down the middle.

My fist made contact with his face, shattering bone and sending him flying into the air. He crashed to the ground, breaking floorboards on his impact.

The room stilled, unsure of what to do. Dorian, Roman, and Roxanne were at my side in an instant, all three of them holding me back before I charged Ezra.

"What the hell are you doing?" Dorian said. I could feel an inkling of his persuasion crawling over my skin. He was trying. And failing.

My eyes flashed with anger and hatred as I looked at Ezra when he stood up, his jaw healing quickly. He rubbed it with his hands, opening and closing his mouth. "Where the fuck is Ezra, you piece of shit?"

"Fury?" Roxanne asked in panic. "What's going on?"

My chest was heaving as I tried to catch my breath, never taking my eyes off his body. "It's him," I choked out. "Azrael."

Azrael looked at me with Ezra's green eyes, but the fire and rage that filled them didn't belong to my mate. A feral grin widened on his face, and he started to clap slowly.

"Miss me, angel?"

CHAPTER 14

A chill of disgust reverberated through my entire body, rattling my bones, making my stomach roil. My shoulders shuddered, trying to shake it off. I wanted to get the slimy feeling away from my skin.

"Where is he?" I said through clenched teeth. He laughed at me in response. Roman threw his arm over my abdomen protectively, pulling me into him while a low growl sounded. Dorian's ire vibrated, moving the air around me.

Racing thoughts took over, clouding out reason. Ezra. My Ezra. I knew something was wrong. The distance. The silence in my head. He didn't look at me the same way. It was too much. He felt off. It was jealousy. It was Azrael's possession. It was never Ezra's. The sick feeling resurfaced, sending a flood of adrenaline and anger as it coursed through my veins.

I needed the ones I loved to get out. I didn't know how he trapped Ezra, but my mates were in danger of the same fate. If he could get one, he could get them all.

I didn't know if Ezra was safe. I wasn't even sure how long he'd been gone.

"Tell me where, or so help me—"

His laugh echoed in the room, cutting through the silence. No one moved. No one attacked. Dorian held his hand out to the fae, ordering them to stay still. Rya and Kelly stood with them, prepared to take direction from their friend. Roman's shifters remained alert, their hands fidgeting, their fingers twitching, aching to shift. The vampires froze in their confusion, looking to the other alphas for direction now that their own was absent.

"You'll what?" Azrael mocked. "Kill me? Go ahead. See what happens."

The torrent of emotions swirled inside me. Anger that he was standing in front of me. Frustration for what I was, why I existed, and why he even cared. Bitterness at the path my previous life had taken. A searing and intense rage that *he* existed at all—that he had been in my life just to torment and kill me. And an overwhelming fear that he had taken Ezra from me when I'd only just found him.

I hated him. I wanted him to die a thousand deaths, and I wanted to be the one to hand it to him. Could I? Surely my powers could end this motherfucker. Just blow him up. I couldn't have access to all this magic, just to have it end up being all for naught. What a sick joke that would be.

"What did you do with Ezra?"

He shook his head slightly, a crooked, vile smile on his face. "No, no, angel. You won't find him, and I have no intention of telling you where he is. What purpose would that serve?"

A tiny rush of hope surfaced. Present tense. He hadn't found a way to destroy Ezra. If someone could take my mates from this world, I didn't doubt it would be him that was capable.

I had been scanning the room all night, waiting for Lyra to show up. Hoping to see her crazy ass at any moment. Shove her in, then get us all out. Find a way to safety. I wasn't sure if safety existed or if it was just something we convinced ourselves we could find, but that was the only plan we'd had.

Yet here we were. Azrael wasn't supposed to be here. He wasn't supposed to be Ezra. My mate wasn't supposed to be gone. It was a show the entire time, and he'd been in on it. Everyone here was in danger. Every single fae, shifter, witch, and vampire in the room was in danger of becoming extinguished into nothingness. Lured here with bait. Bait I fed them. I wanted to choke.

"What, then? What do you want?" My words were strained. All the powers I had within were dying to get out. Explode. Level this damned building if it would end him. Roxanne reached down, squeezing my hand. From the corner of my eye, I saw her. My friend. My sister. Giving me support . . . and the reminder to keep my cool.

"What I've always wanted." He reached into his pocket, taking out the flask. He looked down as he opened it, then brought his eyes up to meet mine. His tongue slid over the metal opening, licking slowly. The lewd gesture sent another wave of nausea through me. Then he hummed. "Tastes just like you."

"You're going to make me vomit."

His eyes narrowed briefly, a flash of his temper shining through. "Now, angel. That's no way to talk to your husband."

Dorian's and Roman's growl shook the walls. I was

tempted to stop suppressing the need to throw up, just to make a point.

I turned my head slightly, never taking my eyes off the imposter in the room. "Get them out," I said quietly. "Now."

I could feel Roman's desire to protest as he tensed against me, but Dorian understood, though I felt his hesitance. For a moment he considered, then he met Elena's ice-cold glare, nodding his head once.

Fae had been strategically placed in the room. Always near vampires and shifters. Their safety net. Their escape route. We didn't want to lose lives. We just wanted to get Lyra into Jules' realm. Every fae was ready to sift the other supernaturals to a different location Out of this room. To a healer, if needed. Now? Now that plan was sift everyone out permanently. Don't return. Just go—anywhere but here. Take everyone with you, even the witches. There was no time for magic or spells.

In what felt like the blink of an eye, fae reached to the supernaturals nearest them, grabbing hold and disappearing from the room in droves.

Then it was just us.

A showdown with the Angel of Death.

"Why?" I shouted, feeling the hot sting of tears ready to come out. I pulled them back in, steeling my spine and swallowing the desire to cry. I would not give him anymore of my tears. Never again. "Why now? Why all this?" I shouted. "What is the fucking point? Why didn't you just kill me when you had the chance? You did it once. Why not just do it again and get it over with?"

He looked back at me, still wearing my mate's face. Still looking like Ezra, but the evil in his eyes and in his voice were one hundred percent Azrael.

"I could have, yes. I was going to. You shouldn't be here,

angel. You shouldn't exist," he said, drinking from the flask and then tucking it away. He inspected his nails, drawing out the time between his answers. "But that first day you'd arrived back on Earth, I couldn't. You smelled too sweet. It would have been such a waste."

My jaw fell. He had been near me. He'd been following me for . . . how long? Was he there in the Afterlife, watching me and waiting? A fuzzy memory surfaced, reminding me of my initial arrival. "It was you. Outside the apartment . . . with the doors . . ."

He dipped his chin, the sneer on his face never dissipating.

"So, what? I smelled like a dessert, and you just changed your mind?"

"You were always my favorite, you know that? I wanted to watch you again. I loved the way you writhed and screamed."

"Kinda screwed that one up when you tried to have me killed by a shifter, huh?" I waved my hands around wildly, mocking his absolute failure in trying to torture and kill me all over again. "Azrael, the all-knowing. Didn't know that trick wouldn't work, did you?"

"It was certainly unexpected," he admitted. "That made it a whole new game. I like it. You're different now." He chuckled. "You think you're stronger, and you put up a hell of a fight, but you're still Sunny and I know how to break you."

My heartbeat pounded in my head when he said my dead name, but the only thing I did was roll my eyes. "Then why haven't you, hmm? Oh, maybe it's because you can't."

His expression darkened. "Give it time, angel. We've only just begun."

"There is no *we*," I scoffed. "There never was."

"You were mine once. You will be again." He closed his eyes, breathing in deeply. He opened them as he exhaled, pinning me with a glare. "I couldn't let these *animals* have you. No," he said, slowly shaking his head. "Nor could I have you fawning over them. *That* was unacceptable."

"They're my mates," I said through clenched teeth. "You can't have me."

He cocked his head, raising an eyebrow. "I almost did," he paused, looking at his watch, "about an hour ago, right?" My stomach sank as he winked at me.

"I'm going to kill him," Roman said, his voice low and rumbling. He moved forward, and I planted my feet, keeping his body behind me. Placing my hand over his arm that had been holding me protectively, I reminded him to stay back.

"I wanted Ezra," I snapped, looking him up and down in disgust. "Not whatever *you* are." The mere idea of it sent a shudder of revulsion through me. "But there you were, knowing you'd never be good enough, so you had to pretend to be a better man instead. You're so weak and cowardice that you couldn't show your own face. All it knows is rejection."

A rumble of thunder rent the air, a warning of an oncoming storm both inside and out. Had the weather been any different, I'd have assumed it was Azrael's wrath that sent the heavens into disarray. Maybe it was.

"Careful, angel," he warned, the furious tenor in his voice starting to shake. "This won't go the way you expect it to."

"Oh, go fuck yourself, John. Azrael. Not-Ezra. Whoever you are."

"I take it you don't care what happens to your dear vampire, do you?"

My insides twisted. He was lying. He had to by lying. I *needed* him to be lying.

Dorian put his hand on my shoulder, doing what he could to reassure me. He tapped my shoulder with his thumb, where Azrael couldn't see. Over my ex's shoulder was Jules, safe in her mirror realm, completely unable to help. She raised her hands and shrugged her shoulders, the panic and worry on her face unmasked. She disappeared just as quickly. A solid moment to let me know she was here. Moral support, but nothing more.

We didn't have Lyra. We couldn't beat Azrael. My mate was gone.

It was at that moment I realized what he was doing.

"You set me up," I said quietly. "How long? How long have you been Ezra?"

He smirked, but the darkness and anger that had been taking him over as I insulted him didn't dissipate. I hated seeing Ezra's beauty marred by the evil that encompassed Azrael. "I wonder if you already know the answer to that," he said, evading my question.

I shook my head, taking my hand off Roman's and beginning to move his arm. He held tight, refusing to let go. "You were going to keep me. That whole charade in my room tonight. The jealousy. Calling it 'longing'. Making me feel sorry for you. All the shitball qualities that have always been your piss-poor calling card. You were going to weasel your way into my life and pull me away from them because it amuses you to watch me suffer inside and out." I let out a humorless laugh. "You're nothing like Ezra. Never could be. He's my mate. You're just . . . death. To everything and everyone you touch."

A crease deepened between his brows, and this time, the rumbling came from him. I hated him. I didn't see Ezra anymore. Ezra would never look at me like that. He'd never enjoy my pain. He didn't look at me as though my existence was vile. The hate inside me was burning. I felt it crackling in my veins, begging for release.

"Oh, you're angry? You're gonna growl at me now? I'm not fucking scared of you. Sunny is dead. You killed her. Now it's me, baby," I shouted, throwing my arms out. "And you. can't. have. me. But I will end you, motherfucker."

"I told you, Sunny. You're mine, in life *and* in death." His arms shook as he held back, his temper rising, ready to strike me like he'd always done.

I met his glare with one of my own. "Then fucking kill me, asshole. Death is the only way you're getting me."

The words flew out of my mouth before I could think them through.

In that moment, two things happened, only one of which made complete sense.

Azrael retaliated, losing his hold as I openly defied his authority and challenged him. His palms glowed, his face straining with rage. He thrust his hand toward me while I stood with arrogance, not regretting the words I'd said.

Expected.

As I stared at his palm branded with the rune of death, I have to admit, I was taken by surprise.

His blast hit me in the chest, a crackling sound like lightning burning metal echoed in the room. My skin was searing, my veins burning, feeling like my blood was boiling. The air in my lungs expelled as I was knocked back by the force of his power . . .

And it fucking killed me.

Again.

Unexpected.

CHAPTER 15

I crash landed.

My head bounced forward then smacked into the hard ground, eliciting a crack. I groaned, rolling onto my side in the fetal position, waiting for the ringing to stop.

"What the hell are you doing here?" A familiar squawk broke through the static. I cracked one eye open, streams of light illuminating a flurry of dust particles around me. Through them, Hades sat on the edge of a familiar desk with papers strewn all over it.

"Hades?"

"Fury?" he quipped back, tilting his head.

I jumped up, turning in a full circle while patting myself down. It was my body. It was real. "Holy shit—mother-fucker—we're in the Afterlife." That realization turned from excitement to dread as I repeated, "We're in the Afterlife. Fuck." I dropped my head in my hand, pinching the bridge of my nose.

"Yes. We've established that, but not the how—" Hades started, using a slow voice to speak to me like he would a small child.

"Because Lyra never showed up—" No, no, no. I stopped, feeling for the orb in my pocket. I came up empty. It was gone. I looked down at the ground, checking to see if it came falling out.

"And?" he prompted.

"And then my asshole ex, who has been posing as Ezra, killed me. Again."

I may have taunted him into doing it, but that was irrelevant.

"Ah shit," Hades groaned.

"Shit is right, because the other two now think I'm dead and—"

"That's not the actual problem," Hades interrupted. "Or at least not the immediate one."

"What are you talking about?" I demanded. "Of course it's the problem. Have you met my mates? Jesus Christ. They think I'm dead-dead." Even I thought I was dead-dead.

Instead of answering, Hades landed on my shoulder and said, "Stay quiet and don't move please."

My eyebrows drew together. This bird must be smoking crack to think I was just going to let this go. Before I could say anything, my body disappeared, along with Hades. We were still in the office. I still felt him there, nails digging into my skin through the straps of my dress.

No sooner did we disappear did Azrael storm into the office. I froze to my spot, fight or flight trying to kick in. He'd dropped the face of Ezra, instead taking the form of my ex-husband—albeit even colder and more beautiful than my true husband was. His high cheek bones were sharp enough to cut glass and his skin was so pale it looked like bone. He scanned the room, blue eyes cold and distant.

I tensed when he looked straight at me . . . then kept searching.

He couldn't see me. Because of Hades.

Slowly he stopped, a cruel smile gracing his lips.

"You're mine now, angel. In life and death."

My heart froze, assuming we were visible again. But he disappeared in a blink, taking the chill his very presence exuded with him. I was slow to uncoil, not truly trusting that he was gone.

Another minute or so passed before Hades exhaled in a woosh. Our forms appeared again, and he sagged on my shoulder.

"What was that?" I asked, my voice quiet, deadly. It wasn't the outrageous cursing and yelling he was used to. No, this was a quieter kind of Fury. And far more dangerous. It was the Fury I'd become right after my death. The demon that underwent over a hundred years of anger management because the rage I'd held in was too much.

Hades must have sensed it because he didn't dance around the question.

"Jules isn't the only one with her own realm. A handful of beings from the Afterlife have the powers to unlock other pockets in reality. Azrael is one of them."

My lips pressed together. "I don't see how that has anything to do with what just happened, or how you knew he'd come for me."

"Azrael is the Angel of Death. The *literal* personification of death itself. When someone die-dies—like for good—they go to his realm."

My mouth popped open.

The air rushed from my lungs but wouldn't go back in.

I gasped, crushing my hands into fists to control the emotions rolling through me.

Because if he was death's true master . . .

"He looked for me here so he could finish the job," I said quietly.

Hades sighed. "But because he didn't find you, he's probably going to search his realm and see if you're already there. Judging by the creepy smile on his face, he thinks that's the case."

I turned toward the desk, putting my hands flat on the surface to lean forward.

"You've known that this entire time." The squeezing in my chest wouldn't let up. "As soon as we found out it was him, you knew he was trying to kill me—to trap me for *eternity*." My voice choked on the last word. I'd yet to truly understand time in that way, but I was beginning to. With it, all I wanted was to have that future with my mates.

I never knew the other outcome wasn't simply death, but a fate worse than that. While I was in a state of shock, a part of me said I shouldn't be surprised. Nothing about the Afterlife was what it seemed. But *this* . . . this was more than I could have ever imagined.

"Can you blame me, Fury?" he said, hopping off my shoulder to land on the desk. "I know what he did to you. I knew his end goal was to do it again—and that you'd truly rather die than face that. Except death wouldn't even give you peace. How could I tell you that if we lost this, if he got you, that's what you had waiting for you on the other side?"

"You should have told me," I snapped. "I had a right to know."

"Why?" he demanded. "So you'd be petrified with fear? So that you'd turn back into that shell of a girl you were when you came here? Why in the Afterlife should I have told you that if you lost, that your worst nightmare would come to pass?" I closed my eyes, looking away. "Telling you doesn't change it. All it does is let fear steal away the life you're currently getting to live with your mates, and if the only life you get is the here and now, I wasn't going to take that from you."

The tightness in my chest eased as I sucked in a breath and slowly released it. We'd shared some moments before. When the bantering was over and the emotions were real, he was something I'd never expected.

"Thank you," I said after a long moment. "For keeping him from finding me . . . and that."

"I do what I can," he said, dipping his beak down. "But you said he was posing as Ezra. Is he . . .?"

I shook my head. "He told me I wouldn't find him, but he didn't say he'd found a way to kill him, so there's that," I said quietly.

Hades exhaled. "Okay, first things first. We need to get you out of here."

I nodded, leaning back to stand. "Great plan, but I don't know how to use the portal, and Duke isn't here." I ran my hands through my hair. "I don't even know where to go. It's not like going back is safe. Nowhere is safe right—" I gasped, stopping mid-ramble. Something brushed my mind. A familiar presence I hadn't felt in days.

Water gathered in my eyes and my lips parted, making Hades cock his head as he looked at me in confusion.

"What is it?" he asked.

I couldn't speak, too overwhelmed for words, when a voice whispered through my head.

Fury?

CHAPTER 16

DORIAN

I watched in slow motion as Azrael lifted his palm in retaliation, a glowing mark illuminating the magic that was ready to come forth as he rose to Fury's challenge.

I couldn't stop it.

It happened so fast I didn't even have time to sift.

It hit Fury squarely in the chest, its force sending her and Roman flying backwards. Roxanne and I had been standing next to them, all providing a level of protection. In the end, it meant nothing.

The force of the unexpected blast sent me flying to the side. The same for Roxanne as she landed with a thud on the ground, the floorboards rippling under our powerful frames.

For the first time in my very long life, I heard a ringing in my ears and the air felt heavy. It was a magic I had never come in contact with before.

A maniacal laughter echoed in the background, though it sounded further away than I knew it to be. The only words I could make out were, "You're mine now."

I heard Roxanne coughing, and I rolled over to the side, pushing myself up.

Across the room, Roman's arms were locked tightly around our mate where they landed, never having let go, keeping her protected as I knew he would. He groaned, but she didn't move or make a sound.

I looked for Azrael, but he was gone. For one foolish moment, just one, I felt relief. Clarity slammed into me, the voice in my head asking why he would leave. A part of me knew the answer.

Roxanne and I stumbled to them, regaining our composure as our bodies quickly healed from the injuries of being thrown.

As Roman turned to lay Fury on her side, the hoarse scream that came from him made my blood run cold and I stopped dead in my tracks. "Fury! No," he shouted, repeating her name over and over.

Roxanne rushed over, dropping to her knees beside her brother as Fury's body turned to ash, disintegrating before our eyes.

Roman grasped at what was left, as though he could hold on to her. But his hands came up empty, and he pounded into the ground, roaring, his body going into a shift as the electricity in the room sparked and flickered.

I stood there, looking at the empty space where my mate had been. My love. The one who had given me purpose again. She'd given me something I had lost so long ago. *Hope*. Hope for our future, and she'd further extended that prospect for my daughter's future. We were in it together. A family.

The loss was all-consuming. Grief tried to swallow me, reminding me I would never have another chance with either of them.

Everything I had ever loved had been ripped away from me. By the same. fucking. person. Hatred for that angel began to burn at the very core of who I was, devouring what little soul I had left.

The denial in me screamed for her to reappear. To come back to me. To us.

The air stayed silent.

A single tear streamed down my cheek while Roman howled, losing himself quickly.

She was dead. For real this time.

Azrael had killed her.

The anger inside me pulsed through my veins, but I was silent.

"No," a harsh whisper sounded in the room.

I snapped my head to the mirror, seeing Jules with her hands over her mouth, shaking her head softly.

A new flood of rage washed over me, and I stormed toward her.

"Where the fuck is he?" I hadn't even raised my voice and the entire building shook in my wake. In all my life, in all my loss, my power had remained under my control. Whatever restraint I had managed in my past was gone. The magic inside me swirled brighter, undulating as my emotions soared.

Her eyes widened, tears sitting on the brim. "I don't know. I can't see him. I don't know if he's even on Earth. I don't know what he did with Lyra, or where she is," she choked out. "They're just gone. I don't know."

"Then what do you know?" I shouted.

She threw her hands out, the glass between us warbling and moving like waves. "I don't know, okay! This wasn't the plan." She sniffed as she cried. "This wasn't supposed to happen."

"You were supposed to—"

"I was supposed to what, Dorian? Come out and fight the Angel of Death with you? I'm a poltergeist. I was supposed to grab Lyra and keep her safe with me here. I was doing that for Fury. My friend. I was doing that for you too. I was doing it so I could help save everyone, but you can't blame me for this!" The tenor of her voice started to make the mirrors shake.

I held my hands out in a gesture to show her I was giving in. "I'm sorry," I breathed. "It's not . . . it's not your fault . . ." I sighed and pressed my hand onto the mirror, giving what comfort I could to the dead girl on the other side. "It's not your fault," I said.

"She isn't dead," Roxanne whispered, but the sound of her voice carried all around the room. She was still kneeling beside Fury's ashes, holding a hand over them as though she wanted to touch them. "She's not dead."

Roman angrily pawed at the ground, communicating with her in a way neither Jules nor I could hear. She shook her head at him. "Turn back." He growled at her in response, baring his teeth, and she stared him down, repeating herself to him. "I just want to talk to my brother."

Roman took his time considering, and for all I knew, they shared more conversation. He shifted back, his chest heaving as tears marred his face. His icy blue eyes flashed as though streaks of lightning were hidden within them.

I walked toward them. "What do you mean?" I asked, coming to stand beside her.

She looked up at me, her silent tears dripping onto her chest. "She couldn't die before. She shouldn't be able to die now. It's Fury. I don't think the end of the world would have killed her." She let out a tiny huff. A humorless laugh.

"She's ash, Roxanne," I argued, pointing to the ground. "When she died before, *that* didn't happen."

She pressed her lips together firmly, humming her disagreement before speaking. "That was different. Before she had all this power. Think about it."

"Think about what, Roxanne? We turned her into a supernatural to save her life," I countered, shaking my head. "You heard what she said about death for our kind. They don't have anywhere to go. They just stop . . ." I couldn't finish it. I couldn't say it. Not out loud. Then it was real. I wasn't ready to speak those words. To admit what I knew to be true.

She shook her head vigorously, never taking her eyes off the place where Fury disappeared. "You're wrong. She was only part supernatural. Nothing about her was what we thought. When you all changed her, that should have been the end, but it saved her instead. Maybe he just killed the supernatural in her. Maybe her demon part is still there, and it's enough. She has angel in her too, and none of us knew that. She can't have survived this long to have those parts of her be worth nothing."

I didn't know who she was trying to convince.

"What are you saying?" Roman asked through clenched teeth. His nostrils flared as he exhaled forcefully between breaths.

Roxanne turned her head, facing her brother. "I'm saying give it time. Before either of you try to level the building." She looked up, and we followed her gaze. Cracks lined the walls, and a slow rumble in the room finally eased when she pointed it out. "And before you both try to destroy everyone and everything on this planet, give her time. Trust her. She'll come back to us."

Roman dropped to his knees next to his sister, defeated, staring at a pile of ash and waiting like an absolute fool.

I would do no such thing.

She was dead. Taken from me.

I didn't care what I had to do, or where I had to go. I was going to end Azrael myself.

He may have been the Angel of Death, but Duke had said angels could die. I was going to find out how and kill him.

I was immortal. He couldn't do shit to me. And if he could? What the fuck else did I have to lose?

I strode to the mirror and looked straight at Jules. Meeting her wide hazel eyes as she stared back at me in surprise, I took a risk, knowing it could lead to the end of all things, and I didn't even have it in me to care.

"I want you to take me to the Afterlife."

CHAPTER 17

"E zra?" I whispered, scared to speak for fear that it was all in my head. That I'd cracked under the immense pressure that was weighing me down. The guilt that I'd failed my mate so horribly—

You haven't failed me, kitten.

Relief slammed into me, immediately followed by worry. While I was certain it was him, he didn't sound like himself. There was a heaviness in his mental voice. As if speaking to me was exhausting him.

"He's here," I breathed. "In the Afterlife."

Hades let out a low coo that I thought was his crow version of a whistle. "No wonder Azrael was confident you wouldn't find him."

"Ezra, I need you to tell me where you are. What you see."

White, he answered immediately. *White walls. White furniture. White everything. The minds around me are being tortured. I feel their pain, so I've pulled back. I can't . . . I can't hold on much longer.*

"He's in Hell," I whispered softly.

Azrael had placed him literally in the only real version of Hell that existed. The cookie-cutter houses on the bottom levels that housed billions of souls—each one living their punishment. It seemed he'd picked one that hadn't been assigned yet. The white on white on white was the Afterlife version of the base model. Before a soul was assigned to a demon and house, they simply existed as empty spaces waiting to be filled.

"The houses?" Hades clarified. I nodded.

"He put him in an empty one. Unassigned."

"Well, that's helpful," Hades said, shaking his head. "That only narrows it down to a few hundred million."

"I know," I sighed, rubbing the skin on my forehead as I tried to think. "We don't have time to search them all on foot."

"I sincerely doubt he officially logged it in the database," Hades said. "Even if we could break into the demon guild HQ without being noticed, the chance of us finding it before someone—namely Azrael himself—finds you, is slim to none."

I agreed, but that wasn't going to stop me. "I'm not leaving him here."

"I wasn't suggesting you do, but we need a plan and sticking around here isn't one."

Fair point. I inclined my head. "Got anything else in your bag of tricks, like you did back there?" I asked, somewhat hopeful.

Hades cocked his head at me. "I'm a crow. What the fuck do you think I can do?"

"Well, I don't know," I huffed. "You can pop up places and go between the realms, I'm guessing. You made me invisible. How am I supposed to know what you can or cannot do since you're apparently more than a messenger pigeon?"

Hades groaned. "I can cross dimensions. Veils. Slip between the realms. Like what poltergeists can do. It makes me good at watching and sending messages back and forth, but I'm not a homing device. I can't just find someone out of all the places that exist simply because I want to find them. If I could have, I would have found you instantly when you were stupid and got yourself captured by rogue supes."

I sighed, knowing he was right. Not about me being stupid, but the getting captured part.

"Fine, so you're basically useless here—"

"Hey," he squawked in protest. "Now hold up a minute there. Last I checked you're the one with all the badass powers."

"Because bleeding profusely then passing out is so helpful," I deadpanned, lifting an eyebrow. "Or maybe you mean my demon strength that is also useless here. As is blowing shit up. Or letting my raven take over. Or sift—"

Sifting.

That was it. My answer.

It seemed so obvious, were it not for my rudimentary skills.

"Sounds like we have a potential solution. Let's try it," Hades urged, jumping up and flapping his wings to push him high enough he could land on my shoulder.

"Wait," I hesitated. "I've never sifted very far. Let alone from Duke's office into one of the lower circles of the Afterlife. What if I don't make it?"

I wasn't sure what happened when someone failed to sift because of distance, but the idea of falling out of the sky or popping up in a random location didn't seem good.

"I don't think we have another option, unfortunately," Hades said. "Even if we could find a spare Apple Watch lying around, you still don't know where he's at. If you sift, you can focus on him to bring us to his location—or bring him to us."

I gnawed on my bottom lip, mulling over the options. "Ezra's in bad shape. If I fail to sift him to us, that's worse."

Hades dipped his head in acknowledgement. "As long as you don't land us in Upper Management, we *should* be okay." He tilted his head, thinking on it. "Probably."

So helpful, he was.

I closed my eyes and focused on my mate.

I'm coming for you, I thought, hoping he heard me despite the lack of response.

The ball of anxiety in my chest squeezed tight as all the scenarios of what could be happening to him right now ran through my head. Knowing what Azrael was capable of, it was all too easy to let the fear take over.

"Breathe, Fury," Hades said, pulling me back from the edge of a spiral I couldn't afford to go down.

I swallowed past the lump in my throat, nodding once. "What if Azrael's there? With him?"

"We hope you're not tapped out sifting and can grab him and go before the shithead tries to extinguish you."

Extinguish. Dead-dead. Or so I'd thought.

"If he succeeded . . ."

"Don't go there," Hades said quietly. "Cross that bridge when we come to it."

I took a deep breath and nodded. "All right, let's do this." Closing my eyes, I pictured Ezra. Focusing on the bond between us. I felt a tug, followed by the whoosh of my feet leaving the ground, but I didn't let myself get distracted in my destination for even a second.

Ezra. Ezra. Ezra.

His name became a chant, a calling as I pushed through the exertion that weighed me down, until I found him.

I could not fail. I refused. Success was the only option.

My feet slammed into the ground, sending me to my knees. I gasped, filling my lungs with air, and slowly releasing it. My fingers uncoiled, the dampness in my palms turned cool against the faint breeze.

I opened my eyes.

We'd landed on the porch of door number 19348.

I squinted, trying to recall why I recognized that number. It seemed familiar somehow . . .

"We're here," I said softly, slowly standing.

"You're sure?"

"Positive," I answered. "This was our house number when we were married."

Should have guessed that sick fuck would have found a way to make this even more unsettling.

Hades cursed as I reached for the doorknob—hoping, praying that Ezra would be alone.

The door turned easily. The wood panel swung without a single creak.

My breath left my chest as I laid eyes on my mate, but the relief didn't last for even a second.

Red.

It painted the walls.

Spilled across the carpet.

Stained the furniture.

And lying in the middle of it, on his back, breathing harshly—was Ezra.

"Jesus Christ," Hades uttered. I took a single step into the space. My heart shattered into a million pieces at the sheer carnage Azrael had committed. I'd tortured people in my time, but this . . . it was something else.

I ran to him, falling to my knees.

"Ezra," I whispered, brushing my hands over his face.

His eyelids fluttered.

Then he reached up, grabbing my hand. He squeezed it softly, as if in reassurance.

I knew you'd come.

I ran my hands over his face. His chest. I was looking for injuries initially. Until I noticed something that made my blood turn to ice.

His tattoos were gone.

Every single one of them.

I knew it was him with every fiber of my being. The voice in my head the only true way to tell. But if they were gone, that meant . . .

I slowly lifted my head, taking in the living room once more.

It wasn't simply blood that covered the walls. Beneath the smudged reddish-brown stains that were dry and peeling—was *skin*.

Ezra's skin. His tattoos mounted like trophies.

Bile rose in my throat, and I had to look away, swallowing it back down.

That son of a bitch.

"We need to go, Fury," Hades reminded me, staying on my shoulder as a mostly silent witness to what happened here, but he remained an unwavering voice of reason.

"I know," I said. "Can you take us through the birdie-back door or whatever veil it was you passed between earlier?" I asked.

"I'm afraid I can't. Hiding you was one thing. I can't take you and Ezra through veils to get to Earth. That's strictly a me-thing," he said. I could hear the apologetic tone in his voice.

I blew out a breath. Sifting it was, then. If I sifted us here, I could sift out.

Looking at Ezra once more, I mentally asked, *can you move?*

His answer was short and acted as a spear to penetrate the ice filling me.

Barely.

The part of me that was his mate shut down. I had to. The horrors I'd found here were too great to process. I just needed to function in this moment. So I rose, methodical and calculated.

I lifted my wrist to my face and bit down hard, grimacing at the pain. I snapped my neck to the side, tearing my fangs across my flesh to open the vein further.

Ezra's lips parted, scenting the blood.

You need your strength, he murmured.

"You need it more," I insisted, refusing to yield. Kneeling back down, I shoved my bloody wrist between his lips. At first Ezra did little more than lick at the wound. But slowly, some semblance of strength filled him. He reached up, grasping my wrist tenderly but still firm, as he sank his fangs in.

I watched as color filled his face. Still pale, but no longer deathly white.

A moment passed where he drank deeply before releasing my wrist and thrusting it away with great restraint. I tried to shove it back at him, but he refused, his lips clamping shut as he swallowed hard. A muscle in his cheek twitched, as if he were struggling to deny himself.

"No, no more," he rasped, voice hoarse.

"Yes, more," I argued. "You're not well—"

"And I won't be until we leave," he replied, then switched to mentally communicating. *It's going to take a lot of blood to deal with the extreme deficit I'm in. More than you can give right now. I can't sift. You're the one that needs to be strong for both of us right now.*

I pressed my lips together in a hard line, knowing he might be right but not liking it.

"Look at me," I insisted.

"Fury." The way he said my name was firm and harsh.

"You need to be strong enough to at least open your eyes. If I'm not strong enough to sift us out of here, it's going to hurt. A lot."

He sighed. *Don't ask this of me, kitten.*

"No," I said, voice flat. "I need to see—"

His eyelids lifted, and I stopped speaking.

Thinking.

Processing.

Where beautiful green eyes should have been . . .

There was nothing.

Pits of flesh. Hollow, empty holes.

I couldn't contain the bile this time. It rose, and I hardly moved fast enough, turning to the side as I vomited.

He'd been blinded.

It's not what you think, he said in my mind, sad and consoling.

"He took your eyes," I said once the saliva stopped dripping from my mouth. I wiped it off with my arm. "He fucking butchered you."

"He didn't take them," Ezra rasped. "I did."

Shock ran through me, followed by confusion. "Why would you do such a thing?"

"Azrael took your face when he . . ." Ezra let his voice drop off, not needing to explain further.

Azrael had taken my form to torture him, just as he'd taken Ezra's to fool me.

I couldn't bear to see that. I knew it wasn't you, but I wouldn't let him play with me like that. If he was going to take me apart piece by piece, he was going to do it without me looking at him wearing your face.

I shuddered. Just when I thought he couldn't get any worse—anymore fucked up—he'd found a way.

I reached down, placing his arm around my shoulder as I slid mine under his back. Then I twisted, putting my other arm under his knees. It was probably uncomfortable, and certainly looked awkward, but if he couldn't stand yet, I'd carry him.

I guess demon strength came in handy, after all.

I went from kneeling to standing, pulling him up with me.

Resolution settled in. The fight or flight I'd been struggling with fell away.

I was going to make that motherfucker pay.

Come hell, come death, I was going to end him.

But first, I was going to save my mate.

I walked out of the house of horrors and onto the porch. Lamplights filled the quiet street, warm and inviting. It was meant to be that way. You'd never know what happened here behind these doors. You'd never guess the pain inflicted on the inside.

It was exactly the same way on Earth.

I shook my head, ignoring the light, because the path I was taking led only to one place.

Darkness. Death. Destruction.

And for the first time, I would welcome it.

As I secured my grip on Ezra, preparing to attempt to sift out of the Afterlife and back to Earth—a force rocked the very foundation I stood.

I looked down, then up.

This explosion wasn't like something you would see on Earth. It wasn't like a building with a gas leak, and it wasn't as though dynamite went off. The night lit up in flashes like a bomb had been dropped, but that was clearly impossible. There was no impact prior. Buildings weren't on fire. It may have been Hell, essentially, but it looked nothing like the images of fire and brimstone.

Bolts of lightning shot out from another detonation, breaking apart and splintering across the sky. The entire display was the embodiment of rage.

I would know.

"What in the absolute . . .?" Hades said under his breath, flying up for a better view. "That looks just like your handiwork."

Not taking my eyes off the blasts, I asked a question even though I feared the answer. "Can Azrael . . .?"

"This isn't him. It can't be."

I breathed a sigh of relief. I was not ready to face that tool right now. Ezra was my main concern. I felt the heat of his body against mine as I held him, and it gave me a small measure of comfort.

"If you weren't standing with me, I'd think this was you," he murmured. "No one has this power, Fury. No one except . . . but he's—"

I snapped my attention back to him. "What?"

Hades looked at me gently, his bird eyes somehow softening. "No one except Michael. It's where your powers originated from. Make things go boom, yeah? That's not a demon thing. That was an angel thing. Specifically, Michael's."

"I'm descended from Michael?" I asked, breathing heavily. "Why didn't you say something? How did you know?"

"I told you, I know a lot of things, and some things are better left unsaid."

I looked back to the explosions. "Yeah? Then why say something now?"

"Because he's dead, and we know this isn't him. I don't know what this is," he said. "But I think that's our cue to exit the Afterlife," I said.

From above us, somewhere in the higher levels of the Afterlife—someone was using my power. And it sure as shit wasn't me.

I briefly debated whether I should leave and let Upper Management deal with whatever was going on here.

That was until the wind carried a voice over the entirety of the realm.

A voice I'd know anywhere.

"Where is Azrael?" Dorian commanded. "Where is the angel who murdered my mate?"

CHAPTER 18

ow did he even get here? I groaned internally and squinted my eyes, seeing the fires in the distance, trying to judge exactly where it was coming from. "That's headquarters, isn't it?"

"Ugh." Hades waited a moment before continuing, sounding exasperated. "You want to go get him?"

"Yup."

"Of course you do," he muttered. He swooped down to land on my shoulder.

"You're joking right now, right? Dorian is in the Afterlife and now shit is blowing up. It's like this realm is revolting."

"Probably because he shouldn't be here," he grumbled. "Supernatural and Afterlife magic don't mix well. Present company excluded, of course."

"All the more reason we need to get him out," I said slowly.

"I know, I know," he said with a sigh. "If it's not one mate falling apart, it's the other. Go on. Sift us there."

"You can't take us?"

He shook his head. "Like I said before, I can hide you,

but I can't walk you through the veils. Not even here. You sifted us here. Just take us to HQ. No pressure. At least you aren't falling to your death though, right? That's an improvement."

"I would have just ended up here apparently," I said quietly, finding an inner focus so I could sift us there.

"Not necessarily. You may have only ended up here because of Azrael. Angel of Death and all that. There was no magic involved in those rocks and they could've just crushed you and you really would have been dead-dead," he said, tilting his head as he mused. "But dead-dead means—"

"Not the time, feathers," I said, and he snapped out of his contemplation. "I've got this. Even if you could take us, I can't rely on you or anyone else. I've got my own magic."

"Is this one of those 'put on your big girl panties' pep talks?" he asked.

"No." Maybe. "Let's go before Dorian fulfills the prophecy on his own." Which I really hoped wasn't possible.

He sighed through his beak, shaking his head. "Okay, I'm coming with you. You need all the practice you can get," he said, fluffing up his feathers like he was psyching himself up for the ride. "Onward, steed."

I side-eyed him, then turned my head and focused. Holding tight to Ezra, I imagined a hallway at headquarters. It had terrible geometric tile and reminded me of the carpet in *The Shining*. I turned my mind to it, pinpointing the details. The doors on either side. Their silver knobs. The obnoxious lighting. The color of the wood frames. (This place needed a makeover. We really did work in Hell, didn't we?)

SIFT, I told myself.

A sudden rush of wind brushed my skin while the ground I stood on felt as though it had been pulled out from under me.

Then I smacked my forehead straight into the doorframe, a loud resounding crack echoing the hallway. Hades had jumped off my shoulder in time, and my face politely blocked Ezra from hitting the wall.

I grunted at the impact, crossing my eyes at the sudden pain. It dissipated quickly, but the whispers of a headache were still there.

"Think about that wall a lot?" Hades asked.

"Clearly."

"Try thinking of the middle of the room next time," he offered, landing on me, shrugging a wing.

"Really? Right now?" I said, raising my voice.

"I'm being helpful," he said, flapping his wings to take flight.

"Be helpful and find where—" The entire building shook, cutting me off as I stumbled. I lost my footing, and my shoulder hit the wall while I held Ezra close to me. Hades fought the current in the air, trying to find space to fly.

Cracks appeared on the ceiling, traveling across like they were chasing some unknown creature. Thick pieces of what appeared to be concrete in nature crumbled, dropping chunks of it at random.

When I looked up, tiny pieces of lightning traveled the walls like electricity covering metal.

"Hades," I said, my voice trailing off. He landed back on my shoulder, and I turned to look at him. "You see that, right?"

He stared above us, and I followed his gaze, watching

the crackles moving along the wall, rumbling as if they had a life of their own.

The room rumbled slowly, no lightning, just a deep resonance beneath the surface. Above us. In the walls. It was *everywhere*. We looked up again, watching the vibrations.

It was at that moment I felt a tingle across my skin. It sent a chill up my spine. I didn't know what it was either, but I sure as shit didn't want to stick around to find out.

I hoisted Ezra's sagging weight to give him more support, and he mumbled what I assumed was his thanks.

Shouts of frantic citizens of the Afterlife reached my ears as they ran away from the blasts. They were beyond confused. Nothing like this had ever happened. Our realm couldn't be attacked, and they knew this. Everyone knew it. On occasion, demons would lose their tempers, and yes, weird things happened. A building or two would get knocked over. Limbs were lost—and then they reappeared. Sometimes another demon was lit on fire. But it's not like any of them could die. It was the *Afterlife*.

I'd blown a few things up in my earlier years. I was *The Fury*. I'd made a name for myself.

I turned to my crow, pinning him with a stern look. The unnerved expression on his face was not at all comforting. Dorian's presence might have been driving this explosive bus, but I was worried that it would somehow attract Azrael's attention. Judging by the look on his face, I feared he shared the same concerns. "We need to find him," I said. "Now."

"Well, the screams are coming from that direction." Hades took off down the hallway, flying quickly.

I needed a better way to carry Ezra if I planned on running.

For someone that couldn't die and was able to continuously heal, he was in a lot of pain. I mumbled my apology to him in advance, knowing what I was going to do wasn't going to feel good. I set him down, but bent over, putting my shoulder into his belly, and lifted him over my back. Holding an arm and a leg, I got his weight situated on me and he moaned.

I took off after Hades, following him around corners and making turns I didn't know were there. He'd said he couldn't take me through his veil, but I no longer knew where we were, and it sure felt like he'd crossed some invisible lines at some point.

Another explosion.

More screams.

Another rumbling earthquake-like wave shook the floors and I almost toppled over. Holding my hand out to the wall, I felt the tremors rocking the ground beneath us as another surge of power pushed through. The energy it held throbbed against my fingertips, welcoming itself into my skin, edging around my very core, nestling itself like it was home. I gasped, pulling my hand back in shock. "Well that was weird," I whispered, taking a step back.

Hades rounded in the air, coming back and hovering above me as he dodged bits and pieces of falling ceiling. "What are you doing?"

I looked at him, wide-eyed. "This is my power," I whispered. "I'm doing this."

"It's not, you aren't, stop talking, keep moving," he said, speeding through his choice of words.

I snapped at him. "It is. I mean, I'm not blowing things up, but this is my magic. I can't explain it. It's like it's reaching out to me. Calling me."

"Well then tell it to lead you to Dorian," he said. "Follow it."

I stared at him in surprise. He was on to something. I put my hand back on the wall and my power spoke to me, the vibrations traveling through my limbs. I looked to a hallway on our left. "That way."

He curved his body, rounding a corner when I felt a new burst of power—my power—readying itself like a current in the air.

Hades was in the path of the next shockwave.

Without giving it much thought, I dropped Ezra to the ground. The grunt as he landed made me grimace, but there was no time to dwell on it. I shouted for Hades to turn around as I rushed toward him, screaming for him to get out of the way. Like slow motion, I could see the streaks of lightning, the explosions ripping through space and time.

I ran towards it, letting it envelop me, pulling the magic back inside my body. Instead of reaching around my frame, it came straight to me as I blocked the damage from reaching Hades. My ears were ringing as I took the impact, my body absorbing the power it knew so well. Hades' claws sunk into my skin and dug into my back as he tried to pull me away with a strength I didn't know he had.

He cried out for my safety as I sank to the ground, shaking my head, trying to stop the tinnitus.

"What the hell were you thinking?" he shouted, landing on my lap.

"Saving your life," I said hoarsely. "You're welcome."

Before he could answer, Dorian's voice boomed in the corridors, the sound bouncing off the walls and carrying through. It was filled with anguish and a rage so deep it hurt my very soul, shattering the edges of my heart. Demanding to find out what happened. Demanding to know where I was.

I stumbled to a standing position when I heard him, my

mind going into overdrive with the impossibilities that had become possible over the last few hours.

"Dorian!" I yelled.

My mate stormed around the corner, the room shaking as he did. When he saw me, he came to an abrupt stop. "Fury?" he asked, completely disbelieving.

His amber eyes were on fire. His tuxedo jacket was gone, his shirt ripped and shredded, hanging off his body in random tatters. Lightning crackled beneath his skin, traveling across his body like a stormy sky.

My mouth fell open.

I'd thought that somehow his presence in the Afterlife had shifted my magic. I was an abomination, and nothing about me made sense. My grief, Ezra's pain, Dorian's presence—I thought I'd inadvertently caused the explosions. It was my power. When I touched it, the source of it was enraged, but it still felt like home.

But none of this was my doing. It was Dorian's. My power had transferred to my mate.

I threw myself at him, wrapping my arms around his neck. He stood still for a moment before he returned the embrace, threatening to crush me. He buried his face in my hair, breathing me in, taking my scent to know it was truly me. If he questioned it and there really was an imposter-me running around, I don't think she'd be wearing a pink halter dress with a black tutu.

All the questions rushed out of me as I pushed him away, holding his arms. "How are you in the Afterlife? You can't . . . did you die? You can't die. You can't be here. How are you here? What are you doing here?"

"I . . . we thought you died. Azrael killed you. Your body turned to ash in the ballroom . . ." he said, struggling to get the words out. "I didn't know you'd be here. I thought it was real this time . . ."

If my body had turned to ash, I was pretty sure that orb went right with it.

"How the hell are you here?" Hades interjected, not at all caring for anyone's emotions at the moment.

Dorian snapped his head toward him, the room suddenly starting to shake again. "How about you tell me where the fuck you were when Azrael was killing her?"

I slammed my palm into my mate's chest, pulling on the power and telling him to calm down. "I'm not dead. Hades was here, working on his own part. Azrael wasn't supposed to be there."

My crow narrowed his eyes. "Unanswered question, fae. How did you get here?"

Ezra moaned from the ground, trying to push himself up and failing.

I cursed under my breath, rushing over to him. I stroked his hair, apologizing in a soothing voice. I glanced up and down his body. He wasn't healing. Worry shot through me.

Could he die?

Over the course of his life, attempts had been made on his life and none had succeeded. But had they tried this? Assassins on Earth went for the quick kill. That didn't work. In this case, the Angel of Death was no assassin. He was a sociopathic serial killer, and he enjoyed every minute of the pain and suffering he'd put Ezra through. I shuddered thinking about all the innocents he'd gone after in the past.

I turned to Dorian. "Azrael's had him here. He's been tortured, and he's seriously depleted in blood. I need to get him back." I started to lift him, getting him situated so we could sift when another familiar voice broke through the silence.

"I thought you got that temper of yours under control," Jake said. "But here you are, taking out the entirety of HQ."

Looking up, I saw him leaning against a wall, arms crossed, and his ankle crossed over his other. He looked like he did any other day. Khakis. Collared shirt. Bored expression, but just a twinkle of amusement in his eyes. Hades landed on his shoulder.

"I never thought I would say this," I said, sighing in relief, "but I am so happy to see you right now."

"I can't say the same. You're blowing up my building, Fury," he said, eyeing the cracks in the walls.

I shook my head. "It's not me, and I can explain, sort of. I only know the 'whats' and not the 'hows' at the moment."

Jake's gaze turned from me to Dorian, and his expression changed. His eyes narrowed in confusion, and he looked at Hades. "How did he get here?"

The crow shook his head. "He hasn't answered that yet."

Jake furrowed his brows, returning to my mate. He waved his hand in a circular motion. "Waiting for an answer. But add to it *what* you're doing here, if you don't mind."

The hallway began to vibrate in Dorian's anger.

I rolled my eyes. Now was not the time for a pissing contest. Dorian didn't know how to control these powers yet, and they were far more devastating than he understood. And what did Jake do? He *laughed*.

"I came here for some fucking answers," Dorian said. He balled his fists at his sides, but I wasn't sure if he was controlling the roiling anger or trying to contain it.

"Well. Ask your fucking questions," Jake retorted.

I smacked my palm to my forehead, scrubbing my hand down my face.

"Dorian, you can't burst into the Afterlife blowing shit up, acting like Karen the Horrible and demanding to see the manager of the Afterlife," I said, completely exasperated. Pointing to my co-worker, I added, "This is Jake. From AR. He's my case worker. Now isn't the time for this."

"Oh, I beg to differ. Now's as good a time as any," Jake said, uncrossing his arms and pushing himself off the wall. "Your mate here has figured out a way to get into the Afterlife—a feat that shouldn't be possible, might I add. He's come here to ask questions. To whom? Upper Management ? Is that what you wanted, Dorian? You wanted to meet with them and find out what? Ask away."

From where I sat kneeled beside Ezra, I glanced at Dorian's arms, seeing lightning crackle across his skin.

"Dorian," I said quietly, slowly standing. "I need you to focus on me."

Without warning, Dorian sent out an explosion of power aimed directly at them.

My heart stopped.

The blast cut through Jake and Hades, shattering the nearby walls, sending their bodies into a million pieces of ash and flame.

It was my unique gift he was carrying, but he had no idea how to control it.

It was my unbelievable curse to bear, and he only saw it as a weapon.

I'd learned early how to wield the power. I had to. The destruction was immeasurable.

The quakes and the explosions? Those could be fixed. That was easy.

The core of my power? The boom? It could *extinguish*.

It had before.

Twice on accident, and once on purpose. All three were terrible mistakes in the end.

I screamed, unable to pull the power back before Dorian had done his damage. I watched as my power killed my friends. It felt as raw as though I'd done it myself. I reeled on him, hitting him in the chest with a force I didn't expect. He flew back, not prepared to take a hit from me.

"Why did you do that?" I cried.

Dorian shook his head. "I didn't know it would . . ."

Emotion clogged my throat, threatening to start pouring out of my eyes.

I was lost, in more ways than one. I had one mate that had just killed Jake and Hades. My other mate was in desperate need of blood and a healer. I was part angel. Azrael wanted to kill me and keep me as a bloody trophy. I was in the Afterlife, and all I wanted to do was go home. *Home.* That word repeated in my head, making the longing worse. At least the end of the world wasn't an issue when I had two of my mates with me in literal Hell. It was the only thing I had going for me. I wanted to scream. I ran my hands through my hair, trying to process what I could possibly do next.

"I really wish you hadn't done that," Jake said, breaking the silence.

I spun around in shock, finding Jake standing in the same place he'd been in, massaging the bridge of his nose. Hades' body shuddered, feathers flying about. "You're a dick, Dorian," he muttered, stretching a leg out and snapping his beak. "Ugh, I hate it when that happens."

I almost choked on tears, but confusion and curiosity overrode every other emotion I was feeling.

"Wait . . . how did you . . ." I was unable to find the

words as I tried to piece it all together while I stared at Jake. He met my gaze, letting me trail off before he spoke.

"Your powers can do a great many things, but it would take more than that to kill the devil."

My mouth fell open once again.

"The *what*?" Dorian and I said in unison.

CHAPTER 19

I stared at Jake dumbfounded. There was no possible way he was anything more than another body behind a desk in Afterlife Resources. Not *Jake* . . . he was so . . . so . . . normal. I'd known him for over a hundred years. He was boring. And plain.

"Expecting someone else?" he asked, rubbing his temples as though a headache was coming on.

"I mean, technically, yeah." It was all I could manage. I looked at my feet, massaging my head in the same way. This didn't make any sense.

Dorian leaned into me as he whispered, "You said there were no such things as gods and devils."

I snapped my head up. "If you're Satan, is there a god too?"

He cringed. "Don't call me that." Turning to the side, he faced a door in the hallway that had not been there before. "Come into my office. I think we have a lot to talk about."

He twisted the knob, walking through with Hades perched on his shoulder, not saying another word. Dorian and I didn't move. I crouched down, feeling Ezra's skin. It was clammy and paler than it should have been. Dorian kneeled, scooping my other mate in his arms. "He'll be okay," he assured me. "I've got him."

In that moment, Dorian did more for me than he could have imagined. I was still angry at him for attempting to kill Hades and Jake. He had no idea what my powers could really do, and he made some terrible decisions in his anger. I would've expected Roman to lose his shit this way, but not him. When he picked up Ezra, the vampire he shared me with, it showed a strength and caring in him I didn't know was there. He didn't want to see me hurt, and that meant he didn't want to see my other mates hurt.

He'd said I was the only thing they had in common. It was true in a sense, but it was also more than that. A by-product of caring about me meant caring for each other too. We may never live together under one roof, but I had a feeling when all this was over, we'd still spend more time together than any of us realized. If the world didn't blow up, that is.

"Are you coming or not?" Hades called from the room they'd entered.

We followed them in, and the first thing I saw was Francine, Jake's secretary. I raised my eyebrows in surprise.

"Hi, Fury. He's already in there," she said, casually nodding to his office door without looking up from her crossword puzzle.

I narrowed my eyes. I knew it. Acting like she didn't know which Fury I was all these years just to agitate me. "Thanks, twat." I tossed the insult at her and stomped right into Jake's office.

It looked exactly the same as it always did.

"How can you tell me you're the freaking devil, then keep this shithole as your office?" I asked, crossing my arms and sitting down in a chair in front of him. Dorian held Ezra, standing up against the wall.

I'll get you home as soon as I can. I promise.

Ezra caressed my mind weakly. *I know.*

I shot Hades a look. "You've been keeping secrets."

"They aren't my secrets to tell, Fury. I know you understand that," he countered.

"What about you, then? What secrets are yours to tell? Are you someone special? Are you God? Are you really some hellhound dressed up in a feather costume?" A heat started to crawl up my chest, reaching my face and turning my cheeks red. My temper was on edge, and I didn't know what I was more angry about. There were too many things to choose from.

"There is no god," Jake cut in. "At least not the way you think."

"What is that supposed to mean?" I asked, throwing my arms out. "Everything I thought I knew has been a lie, so I don't know what to think right now. Up until five minutes ago, I didn't think there was a devil." My voice was rising, and the room began shaking.

I'd had these powers under control for years, but I was at my wit's end. There was entirely too much on the line right now, and I was done with the secrets.

"I think you and Hades have some explaining to do," Dorian said with authority. My fingers were pressing into the chair, and it started to splinter and crack under the weight of my hands. "Just tell her what she needs to know."

"This coming from you, who kept Lyra a secret, is that right?" Hades shot back, tilting his head. There was some obvious resentment that my mate had aimed a blast at him. I didn't blame him for it. I just couldn't find it in me to care.

"And look how that turned out," Dorian snapped in

return. "I'll admit to my mistakes, crow. You should do the same."

I wasn't here for a standoff. "I don't care who admits to what mistakes. Just start talking. Here's what I know so far. I'm part angel. Azrael wants to own me in his hellhole pocket realm of madness. You're the devil. There is no god, at least not how I think. Tell me what that means. Let's start there."

Count to ten. No stabbing.

It didn't matter. What would I even stab?

Probably Francine.

Breathe and count to ten.

Jake cleared his throat before speaking. "The concept of a god and a devilish entity crosses over into multiple religions. Some have several on each side. The good and the bad, the dark and the light. It's all just made-up stories."

"I know this part. Where does that involve you?" I asked, impatience leaking into my voice.

He pointed his thumbs at himself. "I'm all of that."

I sat quietly, trying to process what he'd said. "You're all religions? Or you're all the entities?"

Jake shrugged his shoulders. "Tomayto, tomahto. It's all the same. Yes to both."

I inhaled, ready to respond, but the words failed me. I just blew out air, losing the ability to speak intelligently. After several suspended moments where they stared at me in the silence of the room, all I managed to say was, "But . . . you're Satan. Lucifer. How can you be God?"

"Because that's how it is," he answered simply. "I didn't make the rules—well, that's not true. I did make the rules. I didn't make up all the stories that humans passed down." He pointed to the table, wanting to emphasize his next statement. "I don't go by all those other names, so don't call me them."

"He goes through phases. Changes his name over the years," Hades supplied, rolling his eyes.

"If that's the case, why did you call yourself the devil? You say there's no god, but that there is. The story I knew was that Lucifer was an angel, and he pissed off God and fell from Heaven , but when I got here, I learned none of it is true."

Hades snickered, then quickly apologized when Jake shot him a look. "That is indeed another made-up story. By someone who thought he was being funny."

"I don't follow," I said, looking between them.

Hades avoided eye contact with Jake, who stared at him pointedly. He coughed quietly, then said, "Uh, that was me." I waited for him to go further, and when he didn't, I raised my eyebrows, motioning with my hands for him to get on with it. "I started that rumor. It was a joke. I didn't think it was going to get passed along at the rate it did, but it got away from me. You know how things go. It's a game of telephone, then it gets bigger and bigger and bigger until some guy writes a book and makes a religion out of it."

"You . . . started a rumor . . . that included a god—and a heaven—and then said Jake rebelled and was cast out?" I asked incredulously, piecing it together in order. "Because you thought it was funny? And it started an entire religion?"

Hades nodded his little bird head. "Yep, that about sums it up."

I blinked rapidly, not sure what to say, so I just looked at Jake and waited for him to speak.

"You asked why I called myself the devil. I said that because that's what makes sense to you. It's how you can comprehend who and what I am. How else would I explain it? This is part of why no one knows. It's a mind-numbingly frustrating conversation. In the end, I'm neither the dark nor the light, yet both at the same time. I'm everything. I just *am*."

"Well that clears that up," I said, not even trying to hide the sarcasm in my voice. I couldn't believe they kept this from everyone in the Afterlife. I couldn't even understand the point of it all.

Dorian cleared his throat, gaining the room's attention. "What about Upper Management?"

That was something I wanted to know as well, but Jake didn't immediately answer. Hades kept unusually quiet, which didn't exactly send warm fuzzy feelings through me.

"I'm what matters. It's like I said, I make the rules," he said, evading the question.

Every emotion came flooding through me as I listened to him. The circumstances of my life, and my death. Of how I came to be in general. What my mates had been put through. What my friends were beginning to suffer as a result of me being in their lives. The way Ezra looked when I found him sent another pang of anger through me. It was like the mercury rising on the thermometer, and it wasn't going to ever stop. It'd just burst through the top, shattering the glass.

"Well, you suck at it," I said, not considering any of my words before they came falling out. I was pissed. Jake looked surprised at my response, "If you're in charge, and you make the rules, then why was Azrael out there fucking humans, making babies? Why was Michael out there doing the same? How did Azrael start killing off other angels? That shouldn't even be possible. And more importantly, why didn't you stop it? You're all-knowing, right? You made the rules." My tone turned mocking while I waved my hands around erratically. "Azrael killed me in my real life, and you let him. Then he found his way back to me on Earth and is at it again, trying to end my afterlife and stick me in a place I didn't know existed but that I would apparently end up in for eternity. So if you are in charge, you are doing a piss-poor job at it, *Jake*."

He took my tongue-lashing, sitting silently as I let it all out. He pursed his lips and took a deep breath. "Are you finished unloading now?" I shrugged. "Right, well, I'll move on as though you are."

"Don't count on it," Hades muttered under his breath. I narrowed my eyes at him, giving him a dirty look.

"I needed a break. A vacation, if you will," Jake started.

"Wait," I said, interrupting even as he gave me an annoyed stare. "A vacation from . . . being Lucifer?"

He sighed deeply. "I. am. not . Lucifer. Stop calling me that. Satan, Lucifer, Beelzebub, Shaytan, Maara, Mephistopheles, Thanatos, Mors—these aren't my names. I'm vibing with Jake. You don't like your *other* name, right? So, I call you Fury, you call me—"

"Jake," I said through clenched teeth.

"Very good. And yes, a vacation from my role. I've been at it for a long time, you know. It's tiresome. It gets lonely. I'm as old as time. Look at your man here," he said, inclining his head toward Dorian. "He's been around fifteen hundred years, and time is crushing him slowly. That's a blip in my existence."

When I turned to see Dorian, his eyes were cold, but I knew he was trying to cover his pain. Jake was right. I knew he was.

Returning to him, I motioned for him to carry on. "Fine. You needed a break. So what?"

"I left Azrael in charge."

"You *what*?" Well, that fire and rage that had started to cool just crawled right back up my face. "Why would you do that? What's the matter with you?"

Jake held his hand out, palm facing toward me, then dropped fingers down until only his index finger was left. "Look, in my defense, he wasn't always like this."

"*In your defense?*" I repeated, my voice rising an octave. "You don't get to defend yourself for that. How long have you been on 'vacation'?"

"Eh, who's to say what time really is." If daggers could have come out of my eyes and stabbed him in the face, they would have. "I've been enjoying my work here in Afterlife Resources. It was a nice change of scenery. I jumped around, doing a little bit of work here, a little bit of work there. I found this role, and it's been surprisingly enjoyable."

An anger-filled sadness washed over me. Maybe all of this was fine. Maybe this was how he ran things, and this entire conversation was a total waste of time. "Do you care what's happening right now—what has been happening—or is this not something that matters to you?"

He softened for a moment, looking like the Jake I had known for a long time. The Jake that was my friend, who'd guided me through some rough patches in my afterlife. I really needed him to care. I wasn't sure I could take the heartbreak if he'd admitted that everything that had happened was of little concern to him.

"Very much," he answered. "That's why I've been doing what I can to help you through this."

While his answer was a relief and I released a breath I'd been holding while I waited, I couldn't help but scoff now. "You call this help?"

"Yes," he answered, clasping his hands together and setting them on the desk.

I ran my fingers through my hair, pulling on the strands. "Am I a pawn in some fucked-up game of Afterlife chess? Because that's what it feels like."

Hades flapped his wings in response. "Of course not. You were meant to stop the prophecy. Every bit of this is real." He hopped off his perch, waddling on the desk to come closer to me. "When I learned there was more to this than the basics of what your assignment had entailed, I came and told him everything. Your targets being your mates, Azrael waking Lyra, them coming for you. All of it."

"Did you know it was Azrael that sent that shifter to kill me?" I asked him point blank.

"Keeping that secret from you doesn't serve a purpose. I'll always tell you what you need to know," he answered. "That shifter knowing how to extinguish you was a tip-off that it was bigger than we realized, but no, I didn't expect him, and I didn't expect you to live through it, or their bites," he said, angling his head toward Dorian and Ezra. "There was a moment where I was certain we'd lost you."

I looked to Jake. "Why was that? How did I survive? Is that the angel in me?"

He shook his head. "It's because they're your true mates. Each one of them. It's happened a handful of times in history where someone from the Afterlife finds a mate on Earth, though three at once was a new development."

"Duke never found that in his research," I pointed out.

"Of course not. Why would he? I kept that out of the Divine Libraries for a reason. I don't need the dead taking assignments just to search the human population for a living mate. It could be catastrophic."

"The angels certainly did their share of damage without that knowledge written down," I tossed at him.

He cocked an eyebrow. "That they did."

I sighed, feeling some of my energy die out. "Why, Jake? Why were they allowed to do all this? Why didn't you stop him?"

"At first I didn't know what was happening. I was busy doing this," he said, gesturing to his office.

"Okay, but you know about it now. So? You say you're helping me, but why haven't you just made him stop? Ended him or extinguished him or *something*. Anything. You're . . . well, *you*."

He pressed his lips together, not disagreeing with me. "That's a complicated answer with a lot of layers to it. When I left Azrael to run things, I didn't look back. I'm not a micromanager. I trusted him. He wasn't what he is now. He was capable of running the show behind the curtain. Apparently he wasn't capable of handling what time does to us. I didn't know that Uriel was gone. Michael. None of them—"

Hades scoffed loudly, shifting his body, and fluffing his feathers up. I narrowed my eyes at him. "What was that for?"

He looked at Jake before answering. "I never liked Azrael."

"You didn't like him because you thought I favored him," Jake retorted, crossing his arms.

Hades bounced around to face him. "I don't care who you favored. I never liked him because he was a cunt, and I told you he was a bad choice. You just don't want to admit I was right." He squinted his little eyes at him, muttering, "Like I always am."

I was intrigued. Not that Hades thought he was right.

He frequently was, and clearly he knew it because he never shut up about it. I didn't want to stroke his ego and tell him that even I agreed with him most of the time, but I hoped his emotions were running high and he'd tell me what I wanted to know.

"Why didn't you like him? Why was he a bad choice?"

"Because he *wanted* to be favored. He *wanted* to be in control of everything. Those that are good leaders don't want the power they are imbued with, like this asshole." He jerked his wing out in Jake's direction. "Despite some truly terrible decisions, he's good at his role. He doesn't relish in the control he has. Azrael is the Angel of Death, and he *loves* it. How anyone can be surprised that he went down a rabbit hole of fucking crazy is beyond me."

"You didn't want the job when I said I wanted a break," Jake said by way of explanation, but Hades just gave him a deadpanned look. It was quite the accomplishment for a crow.

"Of course I didn't."

"That's what a second is *for*."

"No it's not," Hades groaned. "By your side as a second, not in your place."

"Wait, what? You're a crow," I said, looking at him, then to Jake. "He's a crow." They both stared at me, as if they momentarily had forgotten that Dorian was here holding Ezra, and I was sitting in front of them. "What am I missing?"

"Nothing," they said in unison.

"Oh, that's believable," I said flatly.

"I don't care about who favors who, or why. What are you planning on doing about it?" Dorian asked, and the room rumbled with his frustration.

Jake tilted his head to the side, considering Dorian. "Fascinating."

I turned and exchanged a look with my mate. "What is?" I asked.

"He has your powers, but I'm not entirely sure how," he muttered. "You've done something to transfer it to him." He looked back to me in question.

I scrunched my eyebrows. "I don't know. I have aspects of their powers after they saved me. Maybe when they bit me—" I stopped, thinking about a newer development. I closed my eyes. "I bit them."

"You bit them?" he repeated.

"My vampire parts are sort of backwards. I don't need to take in blood, I have to give it. Ezra wasn't exactly available each time, so I've bitten all of them now. If I survived because they're my mates, I guess that works both ways." Which meant it wasn't just Dorian . . . fuck my afterlife.

He pursed his lips. "That would explain it." He looked Dorian up and down. "You need to work on your temper and managing those powers before you cause more damage than you're capable of cleaning up."

Dorian's mood darkened further. "Considering the cleanup you're involved in right now, I'm not sure you should be giving advice," he said coldly. "You left Azrael in charge, and he's wreaked havoc right under your nose for centuries. More. I don't know. Duke said he chased down every angel's descendants and was able to kill each one of them, including Fury, but she's evaded being extinguished. Now he's—"

I'd been pressing the palms of my hands into eyes as he was speaking, trying to massage the tension out from the overwhelming onslaught of discovery, but his last statement made me snap my head up, setting my train of thought aside. "You knew who I was."

The day I'd arrived came flooding back to me. I was a scared kid, just having found out I was dead. That I'd been murdered. Learning there was no god or religion as I had believed when I was brought up. Jake was there, gently leading me through it. Understanding. Soothing. He had a file about my life, and he knew everything in it.

"Of course I knew, but no one else would have. I was the only one who could know. Angels have a signature. I created them. I sensed it in you when you showed up in my office." Jake put his elbows on the desk, crossing his fingers and resting his chin on top.

My chest constricted, feeling the pain of that day all over again. I swallowed a lump in my throat. "Why? Azrael killed countless of Michael's offspring. Duke said I was an abomination. That's why I was being hunted by him. If you knew what I was, why did you let me in? Why didn't you extinguish me?"

He considered my questions, but the way he looked at me told me he already knew the answers. "Because I wanted to let you in. I liked you. I make the rules, remember? You interested me. I could see parts of Michael in you that I admired. His power flowed through your veins, but your heart was different."

"Ha," I laughed, but there was no humor in it. "By different, do you mean broken? Because that's what my life was. Broken. My parents despised my existence, my baby sister was taken from me, I married a guy I barely knew thinking I had a small chance at maybe being happy—or at least content—until Azrael wore his face and made sure the baby I carried never had a chance. Then he killed me, but not before he beat me senseless for years."

Hades looked away from me at that moment, and I could sense his discomfort. Jake dropped his hands, lowering his voice. "Your time on Earth was short-lived no matter what. You would have died in childbirth."

"I . . . what? How do you know?" The implications of what he said sent a spike of anxiety through me. Did he know the future? Was that written out? Was free will not a thing? Were we all about to die, anyway? That might have been easier to hear.

"Your mother, your real mother, died in childbirth. All women carrying an angel's descendent do. Humans aren't meant to contain that power. Men continue passing down the line, and females give birth to the offspring," he said. "They'd go on for years, trying to grow their line. It's why I forbid the coupling between the realms. It's suffering to humans, but it doesn't stop it from happening. Your suffering would have been greater. You are already part angel, and you were carrying an Archangel's child."

My jaw fell. My stomach roiled, threatening to let whatever I had left come out on the floor.

My eyes filled with tears. The loss and the grief I'd felt tore through me as fresh as the day it had happened. I'd held on to the memory of hope I'd had when I'd missed my first period. Then my second. When I realized I had a life inside me. To the dreams I'd had of being a mother. Of being with my child and loving it the way I loved my baby sister. Those memories were all made up, but they'd gotten me through so many days. Honoring my lost child and honoring the future we would have had together. My heart was ripped out now knowing it never would have come to pass. I would have died, and he would have killed my baby right afterwards. Learning it was kindness to have had a miscarriage instead of having a child shattered my heart beyond measure.

Ezra's breath stuttered as he felt my pain. It was too loud, and I knew I couldn't keep it from him.

I'm so sorry, my love.

Please don't listen to this . . . it's too much . . .

I'm not leaving you alone in this. I'm always here. He mentally caressed my face as though he were wiping a tear.

I knew the energy it took him to do that, and I could sense his exhaustion and pain as well. *I am going to fix you.*

I'm fine. Get the answers you need.

I turned back, directing my attention to Hades. "You knew," I said through my tears.

He shook his head. "I didn't. I pieced it together." He looked down at his feet. "Jake confirmed it."

I felt a small measure of comfort that Hades hadn't kept that from me. He had his reasoning for not telling me about Azrael's realm, and that I could accept. But this . . . Another thought crept into my mind.

"Azrael didn't stop me from having his baby. He stopped me from dying. To keep me longer. To just *keep me.* He killed me by accident." I met Jake's gaze, seeing the fire in his eyes. "He was going to hold on to me for as long as he could, torturing me until he extinguished me, then take me to . . ."

"Yes. But instead, you died and came to me. I don't think he expected me to allow you to stay. He'd lost you, and he wasn't getting you back. Until I sent you to Earth. Once he learned where you were, he had a chance again. And now we find ourselves here," he said, a dangerous undercurrent in his tone making its way to the surface.

An intercom buzzed and Francine's voice came through.

"Boss? Risk Management is blowing up the phone, but I told them you weren't to be disturbed."

"Send them through."

Hades and I met each other's gaze, then I looked back to Dorian. We hadn't captured Lyra, but I had two of my mates with me. "We should be okay for now," I said. "If Dorian and Ezra are here with me, they can't cause the end of the world without Roman. We don't even know how they'd do it yet, but I figured it had something to do with . . . me . . ." I trailed off, feeling a tendril of something reaching out, begging to make the connection.

I rested my head in my hands as the call came in on speakerphone. I looked up at Jake in question, but all he did was raise a single shoulder. "It's your assignment. You should hear what they have to say."

Static connected the line and a hollow voice greeted us.

"Speak," Jake commanded. That was it. No formalities, just authority.

"The prophecy has altered at an alarming rate," the voice said. "The supernatural trio are now joined by . . . others."

Jake leaned forward, toward the speaker. "What *others*?"

An uncomfortable silence spanned, freezing the moment in time. I could hear Hades' feathers ruffle. Ezra's shallow breathing. Dorian's quiet stewing.

Finally, the voice spoke again. "The Dukes are present."

Jake slowly closed his eyes, exhaling loudly through his nose. "What else has been seen?"

"It is the same ending, but the suffering and devastation leading up to it are significantly more," the voice answered.

"It would be with those twats in the picture," Hades said, gently banging his head into the desk on repeat.

Who? Ezra asked me.

I don't know, but it looks bad. His unease passed into me, furthering my own suppressed anxiety.

"Background?" Jake asked, running a hand through his hair.

"Night. The moon is a waning crescent. No location."

Jake hung up but didn't speak. Hades had the top of his head resting on the desk, as though he had stopped mid-banging.

"Who are the Dukes? What does that mean?"

"My asshole brothers," Hades muttered.

"My asshole children," Jake said, leaning back in his chair and rubbing his eyes.

"YOUR *WHAT*?" There was no holding back any longer. I was shouting at the 'boss' and I didn't care. I slammed my fist on the desk, sending a crack down the middle. "You both better explain this to me right now. RIGHT. NOW. What do you mean your brothers? What do you mean 'your children'—oh my god . . ." My eyes widened as I reached another conclusion. I did a double take between them, then I looked Hades up and down. "You're his son . . . you're a duke of hell . . ."

"I'm *The* Duke," he corrected, inclining his head as though he was bowing.

"But you're a crow." I had to sound stupid, stating the obvious. Who wouldn't be confused in this case?

"Yes, thank you for that astute observation." Hades flew over to a shelf, grabbing a book, and flying back to the desk where he dropped it. It landed with a thud, its dusty pages sending a plume of particles up in the air. "I wasn't always a crow. It's a form I take."

"Change back, then," I demanded while he flipped through pages.

"I can't. Punished. Bad choices and breaking rules and all that," he mumbled.

"Um, explain."

"We're off topic," he said, finding his page and turning the book to me and pointing his clawed foot at it. "Read."

I opened my mouth then shut it. We were so coming back around to this. He wasn't getting off that easy. Duke of the freaking Afterlife. Son of th—Jake. My head was going to explode from too much information.

I scanned the old text, trying to see what he wanted me to find that was so important. When I found it, I froze. I muttered to myself while reading, and then I heard Ezra's breathing change. Dorian felt the change, asking me what was wrong.

The bloodshed . . . the death and destruction they'd caused. It made Lyra look like the warm-up act. "The Dukes are . . . they're the Four Horsemen . . ."

Jake stifled a small laugh and shook his head. "They are definitely *not*."

Hades scoffed. "Oh, don't call them that. First of all, there's three of them—"

"Dude, you're their brother. Aren't you the fourth?"

"No." There was nothing more to it. Firm. Concise. To the point.

"He's technically the first," Jake supplied. At least now I knew where he was in the lineup. "And he never got on board with their little games."

Hades fluffed his feathers. "They are *not* the Four Horsemen. It's a stupid name they gave themselves like a shitty boyband and it stuck around with humans."

I snorted. "Well they can't be that smart. They can't

even count." Something twinkled in Hades' eyes. Oh, we had so much to discuss now. "Are they like what humans think the Four—er, are they like what we think they are on Earth?"

Hades shrugged. "Depends on the lore you're reading."

That wasn't comforting. All the lore and legend was bad.

"Where are they?" Dorian asked, shifting his weight carefully while he held Ezra.

Jake placed his elbows on the table, rubbing the sides of his head with his eyes closed. "In Lethe. Azrael's realm."

"You extinguished them?" I asked in awe.

He opened his eyes, and I could see wisdom there I hadn't ever seen before. Old and ageless at the same time. The depths of knowledge, of happiness, and pain. It swirled in a black galaxy, flashing at me just once. If you could describe how time looks, that was Jake's eyes at that moment. Then it was gone. "They're imprisoned there. I had to," he said simply. His eyes traveled to the book in front of me. "You see what they were. The floods. The plagues. The decimation of entire civilizations. You see what they became. I can't allow that. I won't."

I nodded, not pushing the conversation. There was no reason to. He didn't need to explain it further. I completely understood.

A spark of hope made its way to the surface. "Wait, if they're in Lethe, they can't come out. Nothing comes back from that. The prophecy is wrong." When neither Jake nor Hades agreed and they sat there in silence, the ember faded. A pit grew in my stomach. "They can't come out, right?"

Hades closed his eyes, and Jake answered. "Azrael has the power."

"For the love of—*why* would you give him all this

power? Why would you put these dangerous asshole kids of yours under his domain? That's a lot of freaking eggs in one basket, Jake."

"In my defense—"

"Enough with your defense! I don't want to hear about it. Azrael wasn't that bad, blah blah blah. Well he bloody is now!" I sucked in a breath, realizing I let all that out in one fell swoop. "Why would he let them out? Why can't these stupid risk witches even see Azrael doing this?" The answer slammed into me. All this time, they couldn't see me either. I jerked my head up, glaring at Jake. "They can't see angels, can they?"

He shook his head.

"Well that was a bit of an oversight, don't you think?"

"In hindsight, yes. You know what they say. Twenty-twenty."

"I can't believe you right now."

Fury . . .

Ezra's weak plea reached me, and I didn't need him to say more to know what was wrong. He was fading, and fast. What little I had given him had already pushed through his system, fueling what it could, but it was nowhere near enough.

"I'm going to go out on a limb here and guess you can't just stop your rogue boyband trio of death by snapping your fingers?" No answer. Great. "Are you planning on coming to Earth and stopping them?"

"I can't."

"What do you mean you can't?" I asked incredulously. "You made the rules. Don't you get to do what you want?"

"I mean I can't leave the Afterlife. Its very existence relies on my presence," he said, reaching into a drawer and pulling out a box and pushing it across the table. "But I can give you whatever you need to help you."

I blew out a breath. "These are the layers you were talking about, aren't they? This is why you haven't stopped Azrael. Lethe, the power he was given . . . and you're essentially imprisoned in your own realm." He inclined his head, confirming it all. This was so messed up. I threw my head back and groaned loudly. "How much time do we have until the waning crescent moon?" I asked.

Jake looked at his Apple Watch . "We have one day."

I grabbed the mystery box and stood up, walking to Dorian, then rested my hand on Ezra's cheek. "One day until Azrael unleashes your hellspawn on Earth and tries to take me back to his castle on nightmare island . . . no pressure."

"Tick tock," Hades and I said together quietly.

It'd be funny if it weren't true this time.

CHAPTER 20

We stepped out of Jake's and before the door could close, Hades swooped in from the back, landing on my shoulder once more.

"You should visit us more, Hades," Francine called out, giggling like a lovestruck fool.

"I'll see what I can do," Hades replied, with a little wink.

If not for the weight of everything I'd learned, I might have made a gagging noise at the flirting going on between them. As it was, exhaustion was hitting me hard, and it wasn't even the physical kind. It was mental, where my mind felt tired, my emotions felt raw and exposed.

I turned to Dorian. "I don't suppose you sifted here?"

"Uh, no. I had Jules give me a one-way ticket through the mirror realm."

"Unbelievable," Hades muttered.

I lifted an eyebrow at my mate. He and I were going to talk about all of this later. After Ezra was recovering and Roman knew I was safe.

"All right, in that case, let's hope my powers are strong

enough to handle sifting us back." I wrapped my arms around his waist from behind, trusting he had a strong enough hold on Ezra. His muscles tensed under my touch.

"I'm not sure that's the best idea. You've never gone that far—"

I didn't let him finish.

For so long, I'd been *The* Fury, one of the biggest badasses in the Afterlife. Then I became their mate and took on new powers I struggled to control.

The truth of it was, I was just as strong as before. If not more. It was my own fear holding me back. Fear of the unknown. Fear of Azrael. Fear of getting close to them.

But after today, fear had no place in my life.

I couldn't overcome it when it was solely for my benefit. Not when it was just my life on the line. After seeing Ezra . . . I would overcome it for him.

And it started now.

If I could extinguish souls and blow up the Afterlife, I could sift us back to Earth.

I would.

Because success was my only option. I wouldn't accept failure. Not anymore.

Pressure crushed me as the sifting process began. It started in my head, then worked its way down, pushing me into Dorian so tight that if he weren't immortal, I'd worry there would be a Fury-shaped dent in his back forever.

My jaw compressed, teeth gritting in pain as the invisible weight that smothered me reached its peak.

I focused on Roman; on going to wherever my third mate was located. I knew without a doubt he needed to see me and know I was okay.

My feet slammed into the ground, pressure releasing at

once. If not for Dorian's indomitable form holding me up, I would have collapsed to the ground in relief.

Hades croaked. "Remind me to never hitch a ride with you aga—" His statement was punctuated with gagging as he vomited onto the grass beside us. The longer trip must have hit him harder.

"Sifting can be a real bitch to get used to," I said, easing away from Dorian to look around.

"Your fae magic is stronger than I thought," Dorian said, casting me a wary look.

"What can I say? When the things holding you back are stripped away, we're capable of more than we think." I gave him a knowing look. We still needed to talk about teaching him how to control my power, but now wasn't the time.

"Fury?" Roxanne asked, disbelief in her voice. I turned to her and smiled almost sheepishly, if not for the sadness weighing me down.

"Hey, Rox."

"How—what happened—wait, is that Ezra?" Her questions spilled out one after another. In answer, I walked up to her and wrapped my arms tight around her shoulders.

"I can't answer everything right now, but yes. I died and showed up in the Afterlife. Turns out that still happens. Ezra was there, and we rescued him—"

"We?" she questioned, pulling back to look between Dorian and me.

"We meaning me and Hades in this case, but yes. Ezra's in bad shape and I need to take care of him. Dorian can fill you in, but first, I wanted to see Roman so he knows I'm not dead."

"About that," Roxanne sighed.

In the distant trees, an anguished howl warped the wind—followed by an explosion.

I turned to Dorian, sharing a look.

That explained why they were in the middle of nowhere. Roxanne took him to a secluded area to keep him from killing anyone accidentally.

"Rya and Kelly are out there doing damage control," she added. "He's destroying a lot right now. He's not quite . . . himself."

Yeah, about that, I thought.

"Can you help him without making things worse?" I asked Dorian.

He narrowed his eyes, seeming offended. I sighed and added, "It's not an insult. I'm being realistic. You don't have a handle on my power either. Do you think you can calm him down without accidentally using it? You two together could do a lot of damage."

Understanding flashed. He heard what I wasn't saying.

That the two of them may not end the world, but who was to say how much of it they could hurt with my power combined. As it was, Roman had to be trying to restrain it because this entire forest would be levelled if he wasn't.

Dorian nodded. "I can do this. Leave Hades here with me, though. In case he thinks I'm Azrael in disguise. He can't exactly impersonate a bird."

Hades puffed his chest in indignation. "I'm *far more* than a bird."

"We know," I said testily. "And we'll be talking about that when I can catch my breath for two fucking seconds."

He deflated, a guilty look crossing his beady eyes.

"I'm taking Ezra to your estate in Houston. Bring Roman and Roxanne there once he's not liable to blow it up —actually, take them to the compound and get Caitlin, Rava, and Pria. I want them kept close too. Azrael can impersonate anyone. We're safest in numbers right now."

I looked to Roxanne to make sure she understood the plan. Her chin dipped. "Thank you for thinking of them too."

One corner of my mouth dragged up. "Of course. We can't bring everyone, but I'll try to protect who I can."

She ran off, shifting into a wolf as she tore through the forest. I heard Roman's howling cut off . She'd shared with him that I was here, stopping him from causing more damage.

Dorian silently passed Ezra to me, then pressed his lips to my temple.

"Stay safe. Stay vigilant."

I lifted my chin. "I need you to do the same. Roman's in a vulnerable place right now. Don't let whatever he says get to you."

"For once, I understand completely where the wolf is. I was there myself. He'll be safe. I'll pull him out of it."

"Thank you."

I stepped back and focused on Dorian's mansion. Specifically, my room in it.

After crossing literal dimensions, this sift was nothing. The slight pressure didn't even register until after it was done. We landed in front of my bed, and I hitched at the waist to lay Ezra down.

"How are you hanging in there?" I asked quietly, retreating to the bathroom to grab several washcloths and running them under warm water.

I'll live, he answered, a hint of amusement in his mental voice despite his state.

"Is that meant to be a joke because you can't die?" I asked, unable to hide the follow-up thought, *that we know of. If anyone could have found a way, it would've been Azrael.*

Poor timing? Weariness leaked through his smartass

comments despite the humor I knew he was trying to use to put me at ease.

"The worst."

I returned to his side and started to wash away the blood and grime that covered his skin. I had to bite the inside of my cheek, seeing his tattoos stripped away from him. Over a hundred and seventy years gone, just like that.

Tattoos can be reinked. He caressed my mind. *When all of this is over, I want to put mine on you.*

My hand froze where I'd been washing over his hips.

"That's real?" I asked, hesitant to show him what Azrael had done, but unable to stop it from playing through my mind. His jaw tensed.

It's real. We ink our mates ourselves with a design of our choosing. I've had mine picked out for you since that night in the pool.

The first night I gave into him. It seemed so long ago now.

"Will you show me?" I murmured, continuing to clean him.

When it's on you. Tradition is we don't show until after. You're trusting me to mark your body as I see fit because I'm your mate.

I pursed my lips in amusement, washing the rest of his waist before starting to peel his pants away. "That seems a little miso—"

The ring of dried blood around his cock made it hard for me to stay casual. I'd tortured enough people to know what that meant.

Ezra lifted his hand to mine and squeezed.

Don't blame yourself.

"I . . . I don't know how I can't. I feel like I should have known sooner."

There was no way for you to know. He's been doing this for thousands of years.

Perhaps. But Ezra was my mate. I should have realized . . . I certainly should've picked up on it before I nearly fucked him.

The thought stopped me cold. Self-loathing filled the space in my chest.

Kitten, we've been through a lot. We'll be through even more before this is over. I don't blame you for what happened. I'm not angry with you. If anything, I feel so incredibly lucky that you were able to find me. That destiny or fate or whatever it is that put us together gave me you. We're going to have to work through all of this later, but right now, more than anything, I just need you.

The raw need in his mental voice cooled the fire and put a cap on the self-loathing. I stuffed it away for another time and finished cleaning his body of the ordeal he'd been through. When a pile of dirty wash clothes sat next to the bed, I laid down next to him and pulled him toward me, placing his face at the crook in my neck.

"I'm here for you. Always."

Ezra groaned, his fangs testing the firmness of my skin. The bite was quick. The pain brief. While I wasn't into biting them, the heat that filled me as he took my blood had me squirming beneath him. I tried to keep still, knowing he was too weak for that.

So warm. He moaned, one hand curling around my waist and sliding up my ribs.

So sweet. He cupped my breast, rolling my nipple between his thumb and forefinger through the fabric of my dress.

My breathing grew shallow, and my chest heaved as desire coiled around me.

He drank deeper, pulling harder. His movements became stronger. Surer.

Ezra rolled onto his back, pulling me on top of him. My legs fell to either side of his hips, straddling his waist. He pulled back, releasing my neck with a pop. His hands drifted up, to the center of my neckline. He grabbed either side and pulled, ripping the fabric down the middle and baring me to him.

I gasped as he leaned up, wrapping his arms around my waist once more as he took my breast in his mouth. I groaned when he bit me again, feeling wetness between my legs as I shifted downward.

"You're not strong enough for this yet," I gasped, pushing through my own lust to be the partner he needed.

Ezra lowered his hands to my ass, grabbing a fistful of each cheek. His nails dug into my flesh as he pulled me down, running my center over his bare cock that was very much aroused at our friction.

"Do I feel strong enough to you?" he purred, pulling off my breast and licking the puncture holes until they shut. He lapped at my nipple, teasing it between his teeth.

"Hard enough?" he prompted, thrusting up against me. My lips parted in sweet agony.

"You haven't healed," I ground out, struggling to continue finding cohesive words to form an argument.

"Look at me," he commanded. I obeyed without question and found myself staring into his emerald green eyes .

I cupped his face between my hands.

Tears pooled as emotion overwhelmed me. My chest swelled with this feeling of completeness.

"I'm immortal, or as close to it as anyone can get. It's going to take a lot more to put me down."

I ran my thumbs over his cheek bones.

"You were in really bad shape."

"I was." He nodded. "But my mate's blood will heal me faster than anything else could." I didn't know that, but I was glad for it. "And thankfully, because she's exceptionally powerful, it worked quickly and I didn't have to drain her too much."

"I'd let you," I said, unable to stop myself. "It's not like it would kill me."

"I know." He pressed a soft kiss to my lips. "I'd rather avoid that if it's all the same to you."

The corners of my mouth drew upwards.

"Try not to get captured again and I won't need to," I said. He grinned up at me, that devilish gleam entering his eyes that told me he planned to fuck the sass out of me.

"Who's a mind reader now?" he asked, licking his lips. His fingers ripped into my underwear, completely shredding them.

He lined me up with the head of his cock, rocking my hips back and forth to smear my wetness over the tip. "Fucking tease," I groaned.

He dropped me on his length, filling me in one swift movement.

My head tipped back in ecstasy.

"What was that, kitten?" he growled, lifting me to bring me back down.

"Don't stop."

"As you wish." He thrust up into me over and over again, licking and sucking on my nipples while he did. My hands fisted his hair.

"Ah," I gasped when he hit a sweet spot. "Fuck, I love you."

Ezra turned, pinning me to the bed so he could fuck me harder. "My mate," he purred against my chest. "Such a romantic."

A chuckle escaped me before he took my mouth with his, devouring me whole. I moaned into him, and he worked me harder, taking my body with a fervor that one could only describe as need.

I pushed back against him, meeting his hips, thrust for thrust.

It wasn't enough. I needed more.

My hands curled into claws, raking up his back, but careful not to break skin. It was an effort to be so restrained and not cause him further pain.

Ezra broke away, giving me a hard glare.

"You're holding out on me."

I pressed my lips together. There was no point denying it.

He lunged forward, grabbing my bottom lip between his teeth, and biting down. Copper smeared my mouth as he sucked it clean. I groaned.

"If I have to make you come unhinged, I will," he growled.

His cock slammed into me hard enough the headboard hit the wall.

He reared back, pulling out except for the tip before entering me again. This time the drywall cracked.

My back arched, legs straining as I reached for my release. Ezra delivered on his threat, fucking me harder than anyone ever had. His hands grabbed mine, holding them above my head while he pounded into me, breaking the wall a little more with each thrust. I squeezed his hands back, giving him my mind, body, and soul.

His next movement made the bed rails snap.

We fell down, and the headboard tipped forward. He released my hand and caught it in one swift movement, not slowing for a second.

My pussy clenched, that peak steadily approaching. My lips parted as a groan left me. My legs went taut as every muscle in my body tightened.

"That's right, kitten. Milk my cock."

His dirty words made me see stars. I blacked out and came back to his cock twitching inside of me. His eyes were closed in something like rapture.

When the aftershocks faded and his shallow thrusts stopped, we both laid there. He tilted the headboard back, resting it against the wall so it wouldn't fall on us.

"For the record, I love you more than anything or anyone, but I'm romantic enough not to say it while fucking you."

I laughed as he pulled out. His come slipped down my thighs, but Ezra didn't seem to care as he pulled me into him, dragging one of my legs on top of his.

We stayed like that for a long time. Silent but content. Enjoying each other on a level more intimate than sex itself. Words didn't need to be said to convey everything between us. The love. The fear. The insecurities. The anxieties. The hope. But above all, the desire to protect each other from what was to come.

It was that thought that kept me from sleep, even after Ezra drifted off. His body relaxed as soft snores told me he was finally resting in the way he needed.

I slowly pulled away, careful not to jostle him. My feet were near silent as I padded into the bathroom and grabbed a robe, tying it around my waist.

As I exited the bedroom, I left the door cracked. The need to keep an eye on him after everything that had happened was all too real. The hallways were dark and the mansion was silent as I made my way into the kitchen and poured myself a glass of fae wine.

Then I took a seat and waited.

CHAPTER 21

S ilence screamed.

The ticking of the clock was like a hammer to my anxiety, chipping away at what little self-control I had.

With every passing second, the night turned darker. The living room grew colder. Emptier. I waited in the silence with my wine and drank to numb the feelings.

To numb the fear because it had no place here.

To numb the regret because I couldn't change it.

To numb the guilt because it wasn't going anywhere.

Not when I could see that house of horrors painted red every time my eyes closed. I could see the strips of skin decorating the walls. I could see his hollow eye sockets, all because he would have rather suffered losing his eyes than be mentally fucked over by Azrael wearing my face as he tortured him.

I could see it all, but I didn't want to, because all the feelings—the hollow ache in my chest that felt like a gaping black hole—they wouldn't go away.

So I drank.

And I drank.

And when the glass ran out, I turned to the bottle. Then another. Another.

I didn't know how much I drank. How fast. How much time had passed.

All I knew was the spinning in my head and the ticking of the clock that had turned into a mantra of sorts.

The end of the world was coming, and I had one fucking day to find a solution.

Azrael was an angel that couldn't die.

He controlled a realm where extinguished souls went—and apparently—the Dukes of Hell were trapped.

The Dukes that would end the world.

Subsequently sending us all to the Afterlife or Lethe.

All except my mates, right? Because unless Azrael knew of a way to kill them, they couldn't die.

But me? Something told me I could. That even if I couldn't die here, I could be extinguished and trapped in his realm forever.

Alone. Isolated. Tortured for eternity.

I shook my head, fighting the emotions trying to surge.

It wasn't enough. Me. My powers. Jake gave me this mission, and I wasn't enough.

The bottle of wine in my hand exploded. Glass cut my palm. Dark burgundy liquid mixed with blood, running down my forearm. I stared at it, unable to truly feel the pain I knew should be there.

A childlike giggle made me pause.

I tilted my chin, eyes narrowing in the direction it came from. The hallway shifted the harder I tried to concentrate.

I frowned, taking a step toward it. A strange light-headedness hit me. Or maybe it was heavy-headedness . All I knew was I felt weighed down, my feet dragging like lead bricks whenever I tried to lift them.

Somewhere beneath the haze that wrapped around me, I sensed my raven. Unlike me, she was very much not numb and fighting. For what? I didn't know, but I wasn't all that interested in finding out.

"Sunny," a lilting voice said, making me freeze. "Darling Sunny. Beautiful. Broken." I felt the air shift behind me before a soft fingertip was running over my shoulder.

"Blameless," Lyra breathed, the scent of lilac and pine filling my nostrils. I turned, or at least tried to. But my balance was off. All I succeeded in doing was stumbling into the counter.

"Azrael send you to fuck with me?" I groaned, liking the way the cool granite felt against my forehead. I lifted it, attempting to face the fae once more.

"Azrael," she repeated, his name sounding lovely and yet haunting in her voice. "The angel. My angel." I sensed it then. The burning fire in her eyes. The way she watched me with not just childlike cruelty, but something *personal.*

"Find Sunny. Play with Sunny. But don't kill. Never kill." Her lips pressed together, pursed tight in anger and hatred. "Sunny's too precious for Lyra to kill. She belongs to the angel. She's *divine.*"

I shook my head, wanting to deny it even though it didn't matter. Lyra wasn't listening to me. She came here with a purpose, and for once, I didn't think it was Azrael's.

"Did he send you?"

Lyra's eyes glowed brighter for a moment. "Yes."

Then she lunged. I barely had time to dodge, if you could even call it that. I fell to the side, landing on shards of glass. A low moan slipped between my lips as the world continued spinning.

"Lyra is worthless. Useless. A mistake." She spat the

words with disgust. "The angel doesn't want Lyra anymore. Only Sunny. Always Sunny."

I squinted, seeing the amulet she'd previously worn was no longer hanging around her neck. I was starting to get a real clear picture of how we ended up here and it didn't look good. "He's using you, Lyra. He doesn't care about you, and he never did."

For a moment, her eyes turned sad. The rage dimming in the light of sanity.

"I know," she whispered. "But he's all I have."

Oh Lyra...

Some part of her knew and understood what this was. It was the same part that was buried deep beneath the trauma she'd endured. "That's why I can't take you to him. The angel wants Sunny for his queen. His prisoner." Her words broke through the numbness, filling me with dread. I twisted, trying to pull myself up and her foot came down on my back, pinning me to the ground. "Don't you see? I have to kill you to save us *both*."

Well that was a charming notion. A part of me wondered if that tiny voice inside her was breaking through and influencing her. If she recognized the prison he'd put her in—that he would put me in—and she thought death was better. She couldn't die, after all, but as far as she knew, I could.

In her own fucked-up way, she might have been attempting to save me.

Or I was seeing something that wasn't there and she actually just wanted me out of the picture. Either way, it looked like Azrael learned I wasn't in the Afterlife or Lethe, and he wasn't pleased.

I just needed a mirror. I knew there was one in the room. It was framed in an ornate gold design, hanging on the wall. Where was it? I tried to picture it in my head. I had to get to it.

My body hurled through space before landing on something hard. A crack sounded before whatever it was collapsed downward. My body slid sideways, letting me get a quick look at the coffee table that had broken my fall. I rolled away and cursed, seeing I'd missed my location by more than half.

Not great. I just wanted to get to the other side of the obnoxiously large room. Why was the room so damn big? Stupid design.

I tried to haul myself up, as much as I was struggling to figure out which way that was.

A soft hand clamped around the back of my neck and Lyra hoisted me off the ground.

"Drop her," Dorian growled, appearing out of thin air. On one arm was Rox. On the other, Roman. Beside them, Rava sifted in holding Pria and Caitlin, with Hades on her shoulder.

Lyra bared her teeth at him in a snarl. "No."

"You can't kill me," I gasped. "I can't die."

"So sure of yourself," she said, lifting an object for me to see.

My heart spasmed in my chest. I stopped breathing.

She had a deathstick. I'm sure it had some official name, but I never knew it. I called it what it was.

The rod was made of stardust and the essence of death. It was said the archangels' combined power created them. The only tangible weapon that could extinguish a soul— that we knew of.

I had my doubts about their origin now and I knew that at least I had an ability that could do the same, but for Lyra to be wielding one . . .

She really could end me, sending me straight to Lethe.

No one came back from that. Unless you were Jake or Hades.

"I smell your fear. You understand," she said. I swallowed hard.

"How did you get that?" I whispered.

"I stole it from my master. He'll be angry, but with you gone, things will be better. They have to be." Her hand moved. The deadly end of the rod looming near me. It glowed with darkness, blacker than obsidian, emanating shadows.

"Goodbye, Sunny."

Her eerie words hit me in a way that little else could.

Then a wine bottle went flying. I saw it, almost as if time slowed down. The bottle appeared in my periphery, wielded by an unknown assailant. It slammed into the side of her head, cracking into a thousand tiny pieces upon impact. Her face caved, contorting in pain.

Lyra's grip on me slipped as she crumbled, releasing me as I dropped to the ground—right alongside the stick that lay on the floor.

Making a snap decision, I grabbed it just as someone grabbed me.

I twisted; weapon poised to end someone—before his mind brushed against mine.

Just me.

My body sagged.

Ezra grabbed me and backed up just as Dorian came forward.

"We don't want to hurt you, Lyra," he said, voice calm and controlled—even if his eyes were begging and pleading for her to understand. I knew it had to kill him to be doing this.

Lyra slowly lifted her head, sparkling glass shards embedded in her cheek, healing as the moments ticked by. The image made her into a strangely beautiful and terrifying piece of art.

"*You*." Her tone was thick with disdain, haunted and plagued by centuries of hatred. "You're the reason he came to begin with. You're the reason Mathair is gone. Then you forced me to sleep . . ." Her eyes turned hazy, a faraway memory surfacing. "But there was no peace. Only nightmares."

The blue of her irises turned frigid.

Outside, the wind blew. Her skin began to glow a faint illumination akin to moonlight. The shards of glass stuck in her face created prisms that danced on the walls.

"You tortured me for a thousand years," she said, sounding strangely aware and not nearly as insane. "My angel may have broken me, but he also saved me."

Windows shattered.

Glass blew through like a hailstorm, wicked edges cutting anything in their path. They ripped through the drywall as if it were nothing. Pieces of fiberglass and insulation lifted in the air, creating a hazardous void that was going to consume everyone in this room.

My mates would have survived.

I probably would as well.

But Roxanne? Caitlin? Rava? Pria?

"I can't live this way," she said to me, completely at ease in the chaos she'd created. "He *wants* you, but I *need* him. Only one of us will survive tonight. Then he'll see."

I panicked, sifting to Lyra before she killed the ones I loved with the debris in the twisting tempest she'd created. Their bodies, supernatural or not, wouldn't provide protection from her destruction.

I forced power through me, slamming into her and sending her across the room. She smashed into that damned decorative mirror, her head leaving a star crack on its center before she landed on the floor. The glass shattered, raining fragments and slivers out of its gilded frame and onto the ground, the delayed sound ringing in my ears. But I'd overcompensated in my efforts, shooting that same blast outward and into everyone else.

Caitlin, Rava, and Roxanne went crashing into the hallway, rendering them unconscious. My mates went in different directions, breaking through walls. Even Dorian didn't see it coming.

Fuck.

I shook my head, trying to clear the fuzziness that was clouding my vision, squeezing my eyes shut so I could force away the haze, and focus.

When I opened them, Lyra was up, but her sights had shifted targets.

Hot pink magic hit her again, swirling around her body.

Across the room, Pria stood behind a piece of toppled furniture, laser-focused with a crease between her brows. Her powers wafted from her small fingers, sparking in bright bursts with her efforts. It shot out again, hitting Lyra in the chest. Its damage was minimal, but the follow-up Pria sent singed across Lyra's bloody cheek, leaving a singular line in its wake. Her face jerked in the opposite direction, and she turned back slowly.

"That was a mistake," she said, narrowing her eyes.

My stomach roiled, and a tight knot developed in my throat.

Lyra's eyes flashed, but Pria didn't move. I was going to be sick.

"Pria," I choked out, telling my body to sift to her. "Go," I shouted, hoping she would run away.

Concentrating hard, I sifted through space, and landed by a toppled bookshelf. I tumbled over it, slamming my shoulder into the splintered wood. I snapped my head up, trying to get my bearings.

Everything happened as though I was watching it from another dimension, peeking through a fuzzy veil. I had no control. My mind said to do something, but my body was frozen, impaired, and unable to follow any sort of proper direction.

Caitlin screamed, coming to and scrambling to crawl out of the mess and reach her daughter.

She wasn't going to make it.

My body flickered, trying to sift again, but nothing happened.

Lyra sifted, landing in front of Pria, claws extended and poised to swipe at her with a kill shot her tiny supernatural body couldn't survive.

I raged at myself to sift. I did, but not where I needed to be, landing on the other side of the room, opposite of where I had been. It changed my view of what was about to happen, and that was it. A scream built in my chest. Pria was about to die.

In a fraction of a second, a blur went by, and Pria was no longer in Lyra's path, her strike missing and going through thin air.

Ezra rolled out of the way, keeping the young girl tucked against his body. He came to a stop, and Lyra set her eyes on sifting to them.

"Dorian, catch," he shouted, then forcefully threw Pria away from him, knowing he was now the target. Pria shrieked, her body flying across the room, but Dorian sifted, grabbing her in mid-air, disappearing with her as quickly as he had appeared.

Lyra roared in anger, aiming for Ezra as she landed in front of him. He was crouched down, a hand behind his back, ready for her attack, but the look on his face wasn't grim. He smirked, a fang peeking through and touching his bottom lip.

I looked around the rubble, trying to find that stupid stick. I had nothing else to help me, so I ran. It was all I could do. My feet were as heavy as lead, and I had no speed. Just like Caitlin, I was never going to make it.

Ezra winked at Lyra, then pulled his arm from behind his back and thrusted the deathstick toward her chest.

My heart stopped. My emotions conflicted.

My mate would be safe. My mate's daughter wouldn't be.

Lyra gasped, stumbling back, clearly not expecting it.

Roman came from behind her, sliding a large shard of mirrored glass on the floor.

I watched as it swirled around, catching the light, twisting around in circles on its path, coming to a stop just behind Lyra as Jules' hand reached out, grabbing Lyra's ankle.

In a flash, she was gone.

With the exception of my heart pounding in my ears, silence filled the room. Roman was kneeling, resting on one knee with his forearm laid across it. He was staring at the spot where Lyra had just stood, unsure if it was over.

Ezra stood up, tossing the deathstick to the side and wiping his hands off.

Roxanne was pulling Rava out of a pile of debris, grasping her hands to help her.

Dorian was handing Pria over to her mothers.

Me?

I stood there. I did nothing. I said nothing. I helped with . . . nothing.

This was my plan, and I almost threw everything away.

I almost lost.

Pria almost died.

Lyra had said Azrael called her useless when he threw her away.

Not tonight. She'd been anything but.

I scanned the destruction of the room.

Caitlin and Rava held Pria's face, checking her body, crying and hugging her, then repeating it all over again.

Useless.

No, that title was reserved for me.

What had I done . . .

CHAPTER 22

DORIAN

I stepped into the mirror realm behind her. A perfect replica of my Houston mansion surrounded us, including the damage she'd done. In the center of the room stood my daughter.

Barefoot, dressed in one of the light, airy dresses she'd always preferred. Her white hair fell around her face in messy locks. Her blue eyes were vacant. Empty.

"I can't sift," she said. "I can't feel the wind. The cold." Her hands curled into fists. The action had previously filled me with dread. It meant she was planning something and preparing to strike. I'm not sure if she knew it. If the motions were intentional, or if I'd simply seen it too many times to know my daughter's tells.

"Your magic won't work here," I said quietly. "You won't be able to hurt anyone, and they won't be able to hurt you."

Her eyes lifted. Accusing. Damning.

I may have come off as a heartless bastard to most that knew me, but when it came to my daughter, I felt all too much. It suffocated me.

"You hurt me."

Her words did what they were intended, cutting worse than any blade.

I lowered my head and nodded. "I know," I answered gruffly. "I never meant to. I didn't know that nightmares plagued you the entire time you slept. I thought . . . it doesn't matter. I know I hurt you. I accept my fault in that choice. But I can't let you hurt anyone else either."

Lyra tilted her head, and I longed to know what was going through her mind. While her body gave away signs of emotion, her thoughts were a mystery to me. Just as they had been to Ezra.

For the first time, I wished the fae didn't have a predisposition to protect against mental attacks and psychic abilities. Lyra had never been taught. She was only a girl when her mother died and Azrael shattered her mind, but she was more powerful than any of us. Even me.

It didn't matter that she'd had no training. Her sheer strength allowed her to force her way into sifting, persuasion, and eventually—the wind itself. Elemental abilities were rare among the fae, even when I was born. It was a sign of truly remarkable power that came from our ancestors before us.

While I'd been able to manipulate the wind in limited ways with great practice, my daughter made what I could do seem like a parlor trick. Where the air might listen to me, it bowed to her.

I knew when she was born that she was gifted with my powers, and I suspected greater, but not even I knew how powerful she truly was. Since learning of the Afterlife and becoming privy to so many of its little secrets, I wondered if she were some sort of new god, brought into existence by supernatural magic but still beyond what this world understood. Maybe if we won this fight and Fury was able to help her, I'd find out.

"I won't go back to sleep," she said eventually, breaking the silence.

"I won't put you back to sleep." Stepping sideways, glass crunched under my feet. It littered every inch of the living room. "You can't use your abilities here, which means you're safe and so is everyone else."

She still hadn't moved, though I sensed her restlessness by the way her fingers twitched. "I'm a prisoner all the same. You won't lock me in my mind, but you'll make me powerless. Weak. A body in a cage—"

"No." I shook my head firmly. "You may see it that way, but I want to help you. Fix—"

"Me?" she said, her tone arrogant. Haughty. Above me. "What makes you think that you can fix me? That you can make the voices stop? Piece together my memories? Unravel the threads of the angel's influence?" She looked at me and waited.

"You're right," I admitted. It earned me a callous yet girlish laugh. "I can't, but that doesn't mean that it can't be done." Her jaw rotated as her teeth ground together. "Fury thinks she can help you."

"She and I are cut from the same cloth," Lyra said. "She is just as broken, even if her pieces broke differently."

I swallowed hard. She wasn't wrong. For someone with such a thin grasp on reality, she saw beyond the obvious, past the surface emotions, to the heart of people. She always had, ever since she was a little girl. It used to be unsettling, but also sweet. She wanted to help them. Fix them. That changed when Morvain died, and Azrael tortured her.

"She is," I said eventually. "Which means she knows better than anyone how to help you."

I stalled. Not sure what to say. This was my daughter. My one and only child. I loved her more than life itself, but in trying to help her I'd made things so much worse. No apology could fix that, and I wasn't sure if I'd even mean it. That was a harder truth. She was slaughtering people by the hundreds. The thousands. I couldn't let that continue. But if making her sleep had been a torture to itself, I'd have to live with that.

I didn't have a better way when I was forced to put her under. That doesn't mean there wasn't one, but I simply didn't know it. While maybe I could learn to live with that, she might not. The pain she'd endured could be too great for her to ever understand the choices I had to make.

But I'd live with that too.

Left without words to say, I turned to leave and go find Jules. She had to be somewhere around here, just far enough for privacy but still able to pop in when needed.

"I hope you're right."

She spoke softly. So quiet I might have mistaken it if not for the silence that weighed us down.

I pressed my lips together and took one last look at my daughter, knowing if we failed and Azrael could not be defeated it might be the last time. The only comfort I had, was that she was here, and he couldn't hurt her again.

"I do too."

CHAPTER 23

I sat with my elbows on my knees, cradling my head in my hands.

I replayed that moment in my head, over and over and over.

Pria.

Lyra was moments away from killing her. Ending her existence.

I saw the fear in Pria's defiant eyes, but she stood her ground. There was so much fire and bravery in her little body. So much more confidence than any of us could have had at that age. She had so much potential. That was almost cut short, and no matter how hard I tried to picture it differently, I never made it there in time to save her. Each time it ended with her death. An outcome that was solely my fault.

This wasn't about guilt. This was about truth. I couldn't have prevented Lyra from showing up. That wasn't my fault. It was my fault that I wasn't in my right mind. It was my fault that I couldn't function. Had Ezra not been there, Rava and Caitlin wouldn't be tucking their daughter into bed right now.

A dull ache filled my head, throbbing in time with my heartbeat. My hybrid metabolism burned through the alcohol in my system, leaving only the echo of its presence. I could feel it leaving my veins as I began to sober up.

My eyes burned as they welled with tears. I couldn't believe that it almost happened.

"Fury." Roxanne's voice broke through my thoughts, causing me to snap my head up and look at her. My vision was clear. Nothing was rocking or fuzzy. I could hear every vibration in the room with clarity, including the sound of disappointment.

Maybe it wasn't theirs. Just my own.

I wouldn't blame them, though.

"Hmm?" I responded to her, watching as my mates all came to gather around me. We'd left the room of destruction when Dorian left, finding another place to sit and wait.

"He's back," she said gently. "And we all need to talk to you."

Understanding washed over me, and I cleared my throat before speaking. "Intervention?"

Ezra pressed his lips together, acknowledging my guess. Roman nodded his head slowly, and Dorian remained still. I knew he had so much on his mind, but I could see the answer in his eyes.

"Right. There's really no need—" I began.

"Fury, you have to listen to us first," Roman said, keeping his voice even. "Please. You owe us that."

Listen, kitten. I know what's in your mind, but they don't. Let them share their concerns before you tell them. Every single one of us has a right and a need to say these things out loud. Don't deny them that.

I inclined my head to him—to all of them, really.

Mentally, I had that quiet support from Ezra, reminding me that everyone in the room was in it together. *Thank you,* I told him.

Hades flew to the couch where I sat, coming to sit beside me. At first, I wasn't sure if he was there to berate me or be a friend, but I was pretty sure I had an idea which one it was when he remained silent.

"I'm listening."

And I did.

I listened for an hour as Roman expressed concern for my long-term mental health. For how I would continue to make decisions that could affect the lives of others. I cringed as Roxanne said she'd carefully tiptoed around giving me drinks, trying not to feed the habit, but respecting me enough to give me control of my own life. That was no more. She wasn't going to look the other way when she knew I was sneaking bottles that I hid in drawers in my rooms. I listened as Dorian reminded me that he'd been there once, hundreds of years ago. It had changed nothing, and only made him feel worse. My past was my past. Liquor wouldn't change it. I felt another pang of disappointment as Ezra told me he didn't want to check every space we were in, emptying it of alcohol and treating me like I was going to raid the liquor cabinet.

Then I listened to how it affected them.

How they worried about what state I would be in from one minute to the next.

How they questioned if they could trust me around members of each faction, especially the younger ones.

How they hated watching me self-destruct.

When they'd finally said their pieces, I let it all sink in.

With the exception of Ezra, they were expecting pushback.

"So this is rock bottom?" I said, trying to break the ice. "I thought I'd been there before. Turns out I was wrong."

"You probably were there once. It just looked different," Hades said, dragging a claw on the sofa slowly. When he saw the questioning look on my face, he added, "It was rock bottom for where your life was at the time. Life, Afterlife, new life—whatever this is now, it's different. Your rock bottom has a different view. Your circumstances changed, but it's still the bottom. Still dark."

I nodded, whispering, "I suppose you're right."

Roman shuffled in his seat, shifting my attention to him as he spoke. "We've had our chance to say our piece. It's your turn."

I gave him a small smile. The concern in his voice ran deep. It was the alpha wanting to protect those he loved, wanting to fix whatever he could. He couldn't fix me, and he knew it.

"Okay," I said.

"What does that mean? 'Okay'?" Dorian asked, getting agreements from Roman and Roxanne.

Ezra smiled to himself, allowing me to speak on my own behalf. He gave a subtle wink, reassuring me as I continued.

"It means I'm done. You aren't going to hear any arguments from me. This was it tonight. My rock bottom. I blamed myself for what happened to Ezra and what he went through. None of you know the extent of it, but it doesn't matter if you did. I chose to try and numb it. The blame, the guilt, the self-loathing. When Pria . . ." I took a deep breath, shaking my head. "Her death would have been my fault, and not because I'm placing some bullshit blame on myself. My choices slowed me down."

"It's more than tonight, Fury," Roman said, leaning

forward and clasping his hands together. "Your past . . . this is what you are doing to cope."

"Oh, I know." I ran my hands through my hair, keeping my fingers tangled in the strands at the base of my neck and I stilled. "Tonight was just the final straw. It was seeing her life in my hands, and seeing that I would have failed her, failed all of you, because I was plastered."

"You drink because of him," Dorian said, though he was careful as he spoke to me, worried I would react. "You always have, yes?"

I huffed a humorless laugh. "Pretty much." I let go of my hair, dropping my hands to my lap, and shrugged a shoulder. "It numbed the pain in my mortal life. I carried it into the Afterlife, though it didn't have the same effect there. Believe me, I tried."

Flashes of my past entered my mind. Strikes to my face. Kicks to my crumpled form. My body flying into furniture and door frames. Ezra winced, watching my memories as the uninvited thoughts played out in my head.

"It wasn't your fault," Ezra said. He tapped his head when my mates gave him a questioning look, sending his thoughts to Roman, with Dorian catching on.

"I know," I whispered. "I don't think I did know that for a long time, though. Maybe I wasn't willing to believe it." I straightened my shoulders, adjusting in my seat. "I know it now."

Roman and Dorian scrunched their eyebrows, hesitant that this was going their way. Which was to say, it was not as planned.

I frowned, mentally pushing to Ezra. *They don't believe me.*

Can you blame them?

I wanted to argue it, but I knew deep down he was

right. I wasn't sure I would have believed me either if I were sitting in their seats. I sighed. *Not really*, I admitted. *I don't know what I can do here. They expected me to disagree and to pushback, but I'm not going to. Now that I haven't, they're unsure about what that means.*

It's not a level of distrust here. Don't take it that way. They desperately want this to be real for you. It's up to you to show them that. I can't.

I grunted under my breath, grabbing the attention of the room. It was real for me. As real as it could get. I refused to let Azrael scare me. I refused to allow his hold over me to carry on into my daily life. Into my psyche. Into my relationships. No more. It was done.

Rava walked into the room, rubbing her arms as though she had a chill. Her eyes were slightly red, but puffiness hadn't set in yet. "Pria's asleep. Caitlin fell asleep next to her."

I swallowed thickly. "Is she okay?"

She lifted a shoulder slightly. "As okay as she can be for now."

A thought came to me, and I knew I was risking something big if I attempted it and was turned down. But I had to try.

"Rava, can I ask you something?" I said, choosing my words carefully.

She raised her eyebrows in surprise, but she didn't have judgment on her face. She wasn't going to tell me to go back to Hell for what had happened. "Sure, I guess . . ."

I nodded, going with my gut. "I'm done with drinking. Like, done-done. I'd like to start—uh, well, I think I should start therapy of some sort," I said.

"And not like the 'therapy' you did with Vlad the Impaler," Hades interjected. When I shot him a look, he fluffed his feathers. "What? I'm being serious. Counting to ten before stabbing someone isn't an actual healthy coping technique. Rava will back me up. You know I'm right."

"That wasn't what I did. It was 'count to ten so I wouldn't stab'," I angry-whispered at him.

He gave me a deadpanned look. "And if you got to ten and you were still ragey?"

I glared at him. Through gritted teeth, I said, "Then I stabbed."

"I rest my case," Hades huffed. "Anger management, my ass. You always said you wanted to reform the guild, Fury. Start there."

I rolled my eyes, tempted to count to ten and stab him now that I knew he would just reappear. I shook it off, focusing on Rava and the hesitation she was exhibiting. Her mouth had fallen open slightly, taken aback. "Fury, I don't know . . ."

"Hear me out," I said, holding my hands up. I didn't want her making a decision without listening to me first. "This isn't about making amends for tonight. I know I screwed up. I can't change that. I don't want you to be my therapist so I can earn your forgiveness or anything like that. You're a hybrid, you're part of the pack I'm in, and I trust you. You're my family. I know you'll be real with me and hold me accountable. I need this. I need to work through my past, and I know it won't be easy. I know that. I need someone strong enough to walk me through it." Realizing I might have guilted her into it, I added, "If you say no, I respect that. I won't ask again. I'd only ask for you to make some referrals to someone. I can sift. They can be anywhere. The bird is an asshole, but he's . . . not wrong. I need it to be real this time."

Silence weighed heavily in the room. Dorian and

Roman's expressions had changed from dubious to mildly shocked.

I met Ezra's gaze. *I didn't do it for them to believe me. I need this.*

I know. They know it too.

Even Dorian? I asked, wondering if he could read him now.

I can't read him, no. Just a hunch.

Rava closed her eyes, taking in a deep breath. "Our pack," she said.

"Huh?" I said, making the confused sound before thinking better of it.

"You said I'm part of the pack you're in. It's your pack. Our pack. You belong somewhere now, even if you never felt like you did before." She looked at Roman, dipping her head respectfully. "If this is what you want, I have provisions. We won't discuss what happened here tonight. I'm not the person for that, but we will hit hard on your past. You'll learn actual coping skills," she said, nodding in agreement with Hades, "but we can do it together."

I released a breath I'd been holding since she started to speak. "I've got to save the world first, but then we get started, okay?"

She barked a laugh, but there was still a seriousness to her expression. She met eyes with Roman, shifting to Dorian, and then Ezra.

"You're going to face Azrael again," Roman said, rubbing his hands together. "We all are. Are you ready for that?"

"I don't have a choice but to be ready. This is happening whether we like it or not. There's no time to dwell on it. I'm not letting him hurt the ones I love anymore. He's not in my head. I can deal with the past after I find a way to stop him," I said, steeling my posture. "And if destroying that motherfucker and extinguishing his soul brings me trouble up here"—I tapped my head—"then I'll deal with that in therapy too."

"There's the Fury I know," Hades murmured, tilting his head with a glint of fire in his eyes.

I looked around the room, seeing the expression on my mates' faces and they finally matched. Dorian and Roman could read and feel my sincerity. Ezra knew my heart, and there was no keeping the truth from him.

I stood up, walking to them as Roman wrapped his arms around me. Dorian stroked my hair softly, and Ezra placed his hand on the small of my back.

This was it. I was done. I'd lived a traumatic life and left this Earth when I died a tragic death. We'd escaped a potential tragedy tonight. It was a wake-up call, one that could have ended so differently. Azrael didn't own any part of me anymore. Not my heart, not my mind, not my body, and not my past.

That was all mine. It belonged to me. I owned it, I lived it, and I was over shoving it down and chasing it with a bottle.

It was the start of a new day. Or it would be, after I got some much-needed sleep.

Hades cleared his throat, sort of squawking as he did. "I hate to ruin this moment, but I wanted to get a word in here before we all started singing kumbaya."

"What now, feathers?" I asked, stifling a yawn.

"Nothing overly important. Just the small matter of the Dukes trying to rain fire on Earth here in a few hours."

Right. Just them.

I just wanted to stop the prophecy. Save the world, and everything in it. Prevent everything and everyone in existence from being wiped away. Was it too much to ask that the universe throw me a bone and help me out?

Apparently it was.

"I suppose we have to do this now, don't we?"

"Take a seat. Better to know the enemy now," Hades said as he nodded, seeing that each of my mates had agreed as well. I motioned for him to start. "Have you ever watched squirrels play in the road, dodging cars?"

I stared at him, gaping. This wasn't the best way to start, and I really hoped we weren't the squirrels in this scenario.

CHAPTER 24
EZRA

The talk had gone better than any of us could have expected. It didn't take long for Fury to show me the sincerity in her choices. I saw the decision she had come to, and I could easily see why she did.

No one could read Dorian, but I listened to Roman's internal struggle. He had wanted to believe her, but when she's fought us on so many things before, it was hard to accept her being so agreeable. She was right when she knew he had the desire to fix her too. I'd seen enough people suffer from their own tragedies to know they could only fix themselves. She had our support, but she had to want that change.

I'd have to process with my own ordeal. I had no desire to, but moments of the torture and memories of the pain came in short bursts, flashing in my mind. That wasn't going to go away any time soon. I didn't want her to know how much it was simmering under the surface. It was new and raw, the same as my regenerating skin.

"Ezra?"

I heard my name, snapping my attention up to the

room. I hummed in question before speaking. "Sorry. What was that?"

The crow fluffed up. "I'm sorry, was I boring you?"

"Yes, now that you mention it," I said, wiping my eyebrow and smoothing it out. "What were you saying?"

He glared at me in return.

"He was babbling on about analogies with squirrels that have no plans, taking risks that end up with them being flattened by a much more powerful machine," Fury answered, her tone dripping with annoyance. I reached out to her mentally, feeling her exhaustion.

"Well," Hades said, throwing out his wings. "Tell me I'm wrong."

Dorian sighed loudly before she got into a fight with him. "You're not wrong, but it's not helpful yet." He motioned for Hades to continue.

"Tell us what we need to know about the Dukes," I said. "All of us. Dorian and I know what we heard in Jake's office, but there's more to this. You said we need to know our enemy. They're your brothers. Start with that."

Roxanne looked confused. "Brothers?"

Fury snorted. "Wait for it."

"First off, there's three of them. They are not the Four Horsemen , no matter what they call themselves," he started. "Anubis, Typhon, and Orcus."

"Which one are you?" Fury asked. "What's your real name?"

He narrowed his eyes at her. "Hades."

I am going to find out who you really are, you bag of feathers. I have questions, dammit.

I chuckled under my breath when I heard her. She shot me a look, and I shook my head.

"Who I am is not important right now. They are," he said, trying to push the conversation forward.

"I thought—" Roxanne started, but Hades didn't give her the opportunity to finish.

"Look, everything you think you know, throw it out. Mythology, religion, history books, all of it. That's all manmade; nothing but stories passed down over generations. Not only was it lost in translation, but it was also embellished," he said.

"And in some cases, made up entirely as a rumor," Dorian added.

"In some cases," the crow mumbled. "Anyway, the point is, what I am telling you is real. Not what you think you know. Are we in agreement?"

The room nodded collectively, but Fury spoke instead. She had so many thoughts running through her mind, it was hard to hear them all. "I scanned through pages of a book that Jake had," she said, looking at Roman and Roxanne. "The destruction they caused was massive. Death everywhere. They enjoyed it. The events we know about in history are a warmup compared to the genocide they led."

"What happened?" Rox whispered. "I don't want gory details. Just—what happened to make them that way? Why did they do it?"

Hades shrugged. "Jake thinks they couldn't handle time and what it does to us. I think they were always a little unsure of their place. So close to control of everything, to leading the Afterlife, but it would never be in their grasp. Maybe time urged the crazy forward, and the combination is what caused them to explode. Who knows."

"And they did what exactly?" Roman asked.

"They almost wiped humanity from the face of the Earth," Fury answered quietly. I closed my eyes, seeing the pages in the book she'd flipped through when we were in Jake's office, looking at the details through her memory. The carnage. The lives lost. There wasn't a word bigger than genocide to give it the meaning it deserved. I didn't know how humankind had even survived it. So many parts of history were never written, and in this case, it was a good thing. "What man passed down as the story of the great flood? It was real, but it was them, and there was no arc to save anyone. Ancient plagues and wars that we know nothing about or that we only know as a myth—it happened. The Dukes came close to wiping out civilization. Then Jake imprisoned them in Lethe."

"Fantastic," Roxanne said sarcastically. "I'm going to take a wild guess here and assume that's Azrael's realm?"

"Bingo." Fury pursed her lips, pointing at Rox.

"And Azrael has the power to release them," I said. The silence in the room would have been deafening if I couldn't hear so much internal chatter.

"Which he plans on doing," Hades added.

"Tell me what their powers are," I said, running my hands through my hair, preparing myself for the worst of it. We needed to know what we were looking at. "And are their powers specific to them?"

"Of course they are. What kind of story would this be if they weren't?" Hades asked. He took a deep breath, no doubt troubled by what he was about to share. "Typhon has an elemental control that surpasses all, and he has no problem using them all at once. Anubis is much like a fae in his ability to control and persuade. He can turn throngs of people against each other on a whim, so keep him out of your head. Orcus is just a toxic octopus. He's going to wrap his poisonous smoke around you. Each of them is a master in their abilities, as you would expect."

"That's not great, but it's not too bad," Dorian said. "It sounds like they're supernaturals. You said they could end the world. What about them can—"

"It's the combination. That's what gives them the ultimate power," Hades said, knowing exactly where Dorian was going with his train of thought.

Like fucking He-Man, Fury thought.

I almost snorted. *Like what?*

She looked at me, somewhat surprised. *That cartoon? He was all like 'I have the power' because he was the master of the universe or something? That's what these dudes sound like. Totally full of themselves.*

I looked down at the floor to hide my smile while I shook my head.

I wonder if we can use that? she pondered, looking for my opinion.

I mentally shrugged. *Perhaps. You should ask.*

Fury relayed her thoughts to Hades, but he didn't seem on board.

"So, no hopes of convincing them to join our side?" Fury said playfully. "They sound like they want to be the winners, so . . ."

Hades huffed a laugh. "They are the winners, every time."

"Except when Jake extinguished them," I said.

"Yes, except then." Hades looked in my direction. "That is a luxury we don't have this time around. They know better than to go to the Afterlife, and Azrael has finally lost his last marble so he's just giving them a key to walk out the door."

"But they are vain," Fury said quietly, the wheels in her mind turning. "They know they're invincible."

"I'm not seeing how that helps us," Roxanne interjected. The sound of worry in her voice ran deep. "It sounds like this is a losing battle." I reached out, hearing her concern for the pack. The children in it. Stretching that fear out to every innocent life that would be lost. Her empathy was overpowering, threatening to suffocate me. I pulled away quickly before it began to melt into me.

"It's not a losing battle," Fury murmured, as she tried to piece together a plan. "They want to end the world, and they don't see a way they could lose."

"Do you see a way we can win?" Roman asked.

She didn't answer, and neither did Hades.

He said their combined abilities was what gave them the unbridled power. I suppose the same could be said about you three, Fury said to me.

I shot her a look, wondering if that meant more than she intended.

What do you think that means? I asked.

She shook her head ever so slightly. *I don't know yet. I'm working on it.*

"We're not going to win without a plan," Dorian said, walking over to a window and looking out. "First light is in a few hours. Lyra is safe now. That plan worked. Now we have to come up with what to do for Azrael and the Dukes."

Roman blew out a long breath, and Roxanne leaned forward, placing her head in her hands.

Exhaustion was taking over everyone.

While it did, I listened to my mate.

She sat in the room silently, but her thoughts were racing. As I tried to see them all, hear everything she was saying in her mind, parts of it started shifting and becoming cloudy in my vision, like it was damaged and skipping.

A mild panic shot through me, feeling an odd disconnect between us.

What's happening? I asked her.

Do you remember when you were shocked that I'd kept Lyra's existence from you?

I mentally acknowledged my recollection. It hadn't made any sense.

Well, it wasn't intentional. But after it happened, I realized I had kept something a secret because it was important to someone else. I connected the dots and figured out it was part of my fae abilities. She met my gaze, her voice becoming gentler in her response. *I've been practicing how to shield my thoughts from you.* Before I could respond, she jumped to finish. *It's not because of privacy. I have all these powers. That has to mean something, so I'm trying to use it when needed. There are things I need to keep to myself, for your benefit and mine. I mean, how else am I going to buy you a birthday present if I can't keep secrets from you?* She smiled at me. *For this, I need to keep things close to the chest.*

I nodded, understanding and respecting her choice, even if I didn't want her keeping things from me.

I trust you, I said.

And I trust you.

She rubbed her hands on her thighs, leaving them to rest on her knees. "We're not going to do our best work when we're dragging. We need to think on it and get some sleep." When everyone nodded in agreement, she stood up, gesturing to Hades. "You," she said. "Come with me."

He tilted his head, but he went along with her request. He flew, landing on her shoulder. "I go where you go," he said.

"Wait—" Roman and Dorian said in unison.

"I'll be back in a little bit," she said, not bothering to explain herself.

Then she sifted from the room and disappeared.

They looked at me instantly, concerned and confused. "Where is she going?" Roman asked, frustration leaking in his voice.

"I don't know," I answered honestly. "But she's going to find a way to win this."

Dorian looked furious that she sifted and he didn't know where. Both he and Roman hated not having control of a situation. They hated feeling vulnerable, knowing that they couldn't follow her and protect her.

That made three of us, but I wasn't saying so.

CHAPTER 25

Tick.

Tock.

Tick.

Tock.

My fingernails drummed against the table, counting down the seconds till the end. Hades used to say the phrase goad me . Somehow, I'd adopted the saying as well, almost like a mantra of sorts. Now I sat, feet propped up on the chair across from me, staring into the early morning dawn through the wide dining room window.

Lyra and I had destroyed several rooms, including the main kitchen. But the formal dining room was on the other side of the mansion, accompanied by an industrial chef's kitchen. The smell of coffee drifted through the doorway, followed by the scent of cinnamon.

Ezra took a seat beside me, sans shirt, wearing only a pair of low-riding sweats that belonged to Dorian. "Eat," he said, pushing a plate and mug toward me.

My eyes flicked down, taking in the displayed cinnamon rolls.

I lifted an eyebrow. He shrugged. "Seems that Dorian's butler has quite the sweet tooth. It was this or candy."

I briefly thought about James, the fae assistant that had been by his side for over a century. I wondered where he was now. What he was doing. If he knew the end was upon us.

Ezra lifted a cinnamon roll to my lips and repeated in a harsher tone, "Eat."

I took a bite, then winced. Cinnamon dough covered in icing was a little sweet for my early morning tastes. I usually preferred a more bitter breakfast of gin and tonic.

But seeing as my drinking days were over, I chewed the sweet sticky bun and swallowed it down.

Ezra smiled faintly at me. "That so hard?"

"Yes," I responded stubbornly. Not that I meant it. I didn't give a damn what I ate for breakfast with everything else going on, but these little moments of happiness— bantering about something so inconsequential as a means to escape the crushing sensation in my chest—they meant everything to me.

Ezra leaned forward, his tongue flicking out to lick my top lip. "Mmm," he hummed, nipping softly at my bottom lip when they parted. "You know what else is har—"

"Now I know damn well you can hear our thoughts," Roxanne griped from the kitchen. "I feel like it's just a common courtesy to save that for when there's not an audience all of fifteen feet away."

My lips curled up at the devilish smirk in Ezra's eyes.

"If we're going to talk about my ability to listen in, Rox, then I feel obliged to say that you're quite the fan of watching—"

Another cup clapped down on the table on my other side. I glanced up at Roman, who was glaring at Ezra. "I don't want or need to know what my sister likes," he said, only just keeping the growl out of his tone.

Ezra dipped his head, acknowledging him. I lifted the mug to my lips, hiding my smile behind it as I took a tentative drink.

Probably not the best time to mention she'd totally be up for watching us in a group thing if not for this one over here, Ezra added mentally.

I choked, spluttering coffee from my nose.

"Ezra," I admonished. He ripped off a paper towel from the center of the table and passed it to me. I blotted at my face, semi embarrassed as Roxanne and Caitlin both took seats across from me.

"Yes, kitten?" he asked innocently, green eyes smoldering with heat and mirth in equal measure. I glared at him, pursing my lips.

"Don't 'kitten' me—"

The doorbell rang.

I paused, casting the rest of the table a wary glance. Next to me, Ezra stiffened.

Hades appeared out of thin air, landing on the table. At the same time, Dorian came striding into the room. If not for the briskness of his approach, I might not have stopped to take a second look. He wore jeans and a T-shirt of all things. His long hair was wild and unkempt. Golden eyes glowed with a ravenous sort of rage.

"We had a visitor," Hades said slowly, not taking his eyes off Dorian. "I think Fury should be the one to check it—"

Dorian was already moving. Despite the uncertainty of the moment, it struck me as off that something had worked him up. He never fell apart. Not in the same way I did. This was more than last night . . .

I sifted as I stood up, appearing on the front porch.

For a moment, time stood still.

I had to work to process what I was seeing.

A hand. A foot. An arm.

Pieces. A body that had been torn to pieces.

I tilted my head, trying to focus on the face. It was half hidden in the pile.

Biting my lip, I bent at the waist to grasp the hair—

Snarling rang through the air.

I didn't look up. I already knew it was Dorian behind me.

It took me a second to recognize the face. I'd seen many bloody crimes. Torture sessions that went beyond. Things that would turn most people's stomachs, but that's not what caused the delay. When someone died, their face took on an almost fake quality. Like plastic. There was a stiffness that wasn't there before. A blankness that occupied the shell where there was once a person.

Without his personality, it was hard to recognize, but when I did, I understood.

James.

It was James.

"Fury," Hades said, trying to get my attention. I glanced up to see light illuminating from beneath Dorian's skin.

It flashed like lightning, making his veins appear like dark streaks in contrast.

"Dorian," I said his name. Once. Twice. On the third attempt I grabbed his chin, forcing him to look at me. His golden gaze was nearly unhinged.

"Take a deep breath." When he didn't listen, I grabbed one of his hands and pressed it to my chest. "Do it with me."

In. Out. In. Out.

It took a few tries for him to finally listen and follow me. When I could tell I had at least part of his attention, I changed gears.

"What color is my hair?" I asked.

His eyebrows twitched. "Red."

"Like fire truck red?" I prompted. "Sunset red? Describe it."

He scowled. The flashes slowed. "It's dark, like liquid fire. At night it looks black until the moon catches it just right..."

Almost as if he realized what he was doing, he paused, looking from me to the pile at our feet.

"My eyes," I said, pushing forward. "Describe them."

It took him a second. Indecision warred in his features before he finally said, "They glow, similar to the wolf's, but it's not your raven. It's like the center of the flame. They're not gold like mine... they're light. Like the sun."

If not for the labored way he stopped and started, forcing himself to make words, it might have sounded flowery. As it was, I paid little attention to the compliments themselves and instead focused on the crackling beneath his skin and the way it receded to mere flickers.

"You'll need to learn to do that," I said. "When the power becomes too much and threatens to carry you away, focus on things you see. Describe them. Make the words. It will ground you long enough to take back control."

Dorian shifted, staring at the pile that was his butler, assistant, and closest thing to a friend.

"I'm sorry," I said quietly. We hadn't said who was at fault, but it's not like it was a question. This was Azrael's work through and through.

"He didn't deserve this," Dorian said after a moment.

"No," I agreed. "He didn't."

A gasp from behind Dorian drew our attention. At the door, Roman, Roxanne, Caitlin, and Ezra stood. My vampire was the fastest to react and grab Caitlin's hair when she bent at the waist and hurled.

"This is what I was talking about," Hades said, shaking his head.

"In what way?" I asked quietly. "I don't recall you mentioning *this* would happen."

"No, I mean Azrael being unhinged. After not finding you in the Afterlife or Lethe, he turned to tracking down anyone close to you, and he settled on someone close to your mate."

Whether Lyra was sent, or she'd gone rogue, she hadn't returned to him. I knew my ex, perhaps better than anyone. He'd lost his control over her, and this was the result.

It was that thought that made me take a closer look at the pile of limbs.

I squatted down, pushing my feelings aside. This wasn't James. It was a body. A shell. An empty vessel that was sent here for a reason.

So I looked for it.

My heart constricted when I found it. There, in one of the hands. A letter smudged in blood.

I reached for it without thought.

The parchment was rough against the pads of my fingers, and I pulled it from the severed body part.

Numbly, I opened it.

The first words drained me of whatever emotion I had left.

My Dearest Wife,
I miss you and the games we play. I long to taste your tears once more. Lyra's were never nearly as sweet.

I'll forgive your transgressions if you come home and submit to me. Refuse, and the Dukes will destroy everything you hold dear. If you bring one of those animals you've let touch you, I'll be sure to give them a warm welcome in Lethe.

I'll be waiting.

Yours,
Azrael

I don't know how many times I read it. Only that at some point, someone took the letter away. Arms wrapped around me, walking me back indoors. Sometime later, I put a name on the growing feeling inside me.

It was more than fear. More than dread. More than hate.

It was absolution.

Around us, words were flying. Everyone wanted to go after Azrael, and yet none of them could because the simple fact of the matter was he couldn't die.

He couldn't be extinguished.

Each one of us had tried to push away the tension. We had been taking time to appreciate the morning together. Be with each other. We knew what the night would bring. We knew Azrael was coming. We knew he was releasing the Dukes. Without saying so, we all wanted a moment to share where everything was normal.

That was long gone.

The few hours of peace we were trying to create were shattered.

War meant casualties. Always. And James' dismemberment was the startling reminder that more death was to come.

We all knew damn well I wasn't giving myself to Azrael.

The talking around me continued. The sounds of their voices were muffled, like they were speaking with their hands over their mouths, drowned out by my own thoughts.

I didn't say anything. I let them talk. Let them plot.

It would make them feel better and save me from having to tell them the truth.

That I would have to return to him alone to finish this—and neither life nor death would stop me from going through with it.

I scanned the room, focusing on each one of them.

Dorian, my refined brooding fae. In control, well-kempt, regal in so many ways. His heart hurt for his daughter, and his loyalty to the ones he loved was unending. He would do anything for me; remind me that I could have all that I had earned in right and name in my afterlife. Ensure that it was okay to want those things, and to enjoy them. That it was okay to be myself.

Roman, my nature-bound shifter. The protector. He was passionate in every way, and the love he had for his pack ran bone-deep. The responsibility he felt to every one of them was heavy, but he would always carry that burden—and he would never complain about it. He gave me a place to feel a connection. To be respected and seen as an equal. To let my raven be a part of something powerful and never-ending.

Ezra, my soulful vampire. My confidant in so many ways. My support. When it was hard to explain how I felt, hard to share what I was going through, he knew. It was effortless. There was so much he didn't take seriously, and he was just the balance I needed between the three of them.

I could laugh with all of them, but he was different. He gave me a place to work and feel fulfilled. To continue the path I had set, so I wouldn't toss aside the purpose I had found. He gave me the gift of protecting my identity. More than anything, he always trusted me. I would need that now more than ever.

Roxanne, my first friend. My best friend. I loved her more than I could say. More than I realized I could love someone in a platonic way. I knew full well that friendships could come and go—I was a demon by trade, after all. I knew an awful lot of dead people, and I knew their stories. But I also knew there were times that people would meet someone, and it was kismet. That's what we were. Fights, disagreements, different viewpoints: none of that would separate us.

Rava, Caitlin, Pria . . . I could be an auntie too, just like Rox. I think I'd like it.

This was my family. It took death and an afterlife to find it.

I wasn't going to lose something so precious. Azrael would never take this away from me.

You aren't going to lose us, kitten. Ezra's gentle voice brushed my mind.

I smiled sadly. *Some hard decisions are going to be made today. I need you to be by my side. Trust me. I know what I'm doing.*

I'll always be by your side.

I lifted my chin, holding his gaze, shielding my thoughts once more.

I cleared my throat, rapping my fist on the table so they could hear me through the chatter. When the room silenced, and eyes looked my way, I spoke. "I want

Roxanne, Caitlin, Rava, and Pria taken to an undisclosed location. I want them in hiding. This isn't their fight."

Dorian and Roman instantly agreed, taking no time to process it. They weren't willing to risk the lives of those mentioned. Roxanne opened her mouth to protest, but she snapped it shut, seeing the look in my eyes. I wasn't yielding. She appeared to reconsider her words when she took a couple of breaths but said nothing, and I gave her a moment to gather her response. "I agree that Caitlin, Rava, and Pria need to go, but this is my fight. This is my family."

I pressed my lips together and shook my head. "That's exactly why I want you in hiding too. You're my family. Azrael will come for all of you to hurt me in any way he can. I know you're powerful, and I won't dispute that for even a second. Your wolf is a force to be reckoned with, but you can still die. You all can. And if you're there, that is exactly what is going to happen. You can't beat them. All they need is that stupid deathstick and you're gone with a single touch."

Understanding reached her, and she sniffed, her eyes becoming glassy as they filled with tears. She nodded. "I know a place we can go. No one knows about it."

Roman's eyebrows raised in surprise, and she returned his gaze with a look of guilt. She'd kept something from him, but in this case, it turned out to be a good thing. She walked over to Roman and hugged him tight, whispering 'I love you' in his ear.

"Go. Take them now. There's no reason to wait," he said to her quietly.

"How will . . . how will I know?" she asked, unsure how to finish her sentence. Scared to say the words I knew she was thinking. How would she know if we survived? How would she know if we succeeded?

"You'll know because the world will continue spinning," I answered honestly. It was the cruel reality of what we were about to face. "Keep a mirror nearby."

She blew out an unsteady breath and whispered, "Okay." She approached me, wrapping me into her embrace, taking her time before letting me go. "I don't know what your plan is," she said in a shaky voice, "but I expect you to destroy them."

I huffed a small laugh. "I'll try not to fuck it up."

She released me, giving a nod to Dorian and Ezra as she wiped a small tear from under her right eye. "I'll go get them now."

"No goodbyes with them. Just have Rava sift you there. I don't want to put Pria through this. Tell them I love them too. Keep them safe."

She inclined her head in acceptance, then left the room to get our extended family and put them in hiding.

When the room was empty, I turned my attention to my mates. Hades was perched on the back of the chair, remaining quiet through the exchange. He waited patiently, knowing every bit that was coming.

"I'm sensing you already have a plan," Dorian said.

"I've been working on one, yes. But I can't share it in its entirety."

"Wait," Roman said, stepping forward. "Why not?"

Ezra urged me on silently, grazing a psychic hand over mine in reassurance.

"In case Azrael gets one of you," I said, not sugarcoating it. Glossing over the truth wasn't going to be helpful. We needed the facts, cut and dry, as harsh as they might have been. "I've figured out how to shield my thoughts from Ezra. Not fully blocked off like Dorian, but that part of fae that runs through my veins has given me access to it."

"Even I don't know all of what's going through her head. Parts of it are clouded, like there's a piece of opaque film over it," he admitted, confirming my ability.

Dorian crossed his arms. "He took Ezra with ease. He can take any one of us. I don't want to agree with you, but it's the smartest move."

Roman pulled out a hair tie, reaching back and securing his dreadlocks out of his face. "All of us except Jules and Hades."

"Exactly," I said, pointing to him. "They are the only ones that can't be compromised." I called out for Jules, and she appeared in a framed mirror above a credenza.

I had intended on greeting her but was taken aback for a moment. Her hands were on her hips, and she proudly wore a metal Viking-styled helmet embellished with horns. "I . . . what is on your head?" I stuttered.

"A Veksø. I'm ready for battle," she answered like it was obvious.

Dorian's mouth popped open. "That's not a Veksø . . ."

She creased her brows. "It's close enough."

I pressed my lips together, trying not to laugh. "It suits you." She knew full well she couldn't physically help. If that's what motivated her for the small part she'd play, I was for it.

She dipped her chin in my direction with a smug look on her face.

I rubbed my hands over my thighs, feeling the friction of the material against my palms. It gave me something to focus on, readying myself to say the things I knew wouldn't go over well.

Say it, Ezra encouraged.

Dreading the pushback.

You might be surprised.

I sighed, taking in a deep breath through my nose, exhaling loudly through barely parted lips. "We aren't going to be together in this fight," I started, waiting for the immediate grumbled responses from the two mates who couldn't know what I was about to say. When none came, I sat in surprise for a moment, then continued. "Azrael wants me, and if he can find a way to go after you, it'll end up distracting all of us. You'll want to protect me; I'll want to protect you. We're going to lose quickly if our attention isn't where it needs to be."

Roman blew out a breath, and Dorian silently stewed. It was times like this I wished I could read them the way Ezra could read me.

"What do you suggest?" Roman asked after a suspended time.

"Azrael isn't the only one that needs to be dealt with. Even if we can take him out, there's still the Dukes. I need you three dealing with them so I can focus on Azrael ," I said.

"Wait, his brothers are in this?" Jules asked, raising her brows and looking at Hades.

I shot her a look, just as surprised. "You know about them?" Realization struck me. "Wait, you know Hades is a duke?"

She huffed in annoyance. "Oh trust me, I know. Imagine my surprise the first day you summoned me and standing beside you in crow form is the Great Duke of the Afterlife."

I gave Hades a curious look. "Yes. Imagine that."

He covered his face with his wing, no doubt wishing he could escape this. One day, bird. One day we would talk. My raven reminded me she'd shit on him if he didn't answer. I smiled at her internally, appreciating the support.

"The Dukes," Dorian said, bringing us back around. "So

the three of us fight them. The question is how." I gestured to Hades, and he shuffled his body forward.

"They're more destructive than any group of supernaturals could ever be. Together, they're unstoppable," he said.

"Comforting," Roman said sarcastically. "So how do we stop the unstoppable?"

"Hades is going with you. He can slip between the veils and realms somehow. It's his power—"

Jules snorted, and Hades shot her a dirty look, narrowing his eyes.

"Apparently it's one of his powers," I amended. "We can't give these cards away too soon. Not yet. He's going to give each of you the piece you need when we know you are who you are."

Roman pursed his lips together, figuring it out. "And you'll know that because you'll be somewhere else with Azrael."

"I will," I said quietly. "And you have to let me. You can't protect me from him."

I waited for the arguing. I waited for the alphas to tell me how it would be, and that they wouldn't accept this plan. That they wouldn't leave my side. All of the things that would get us nowhere and would lead straight to death.

Instead, I was met with what could best be described as a reluctant accord as both Roman and Dorian paused before inclining their heads with a single nod.

I told you, Ezra said.

Did you already tell Roman? Did you tell him what I was going to say or tell him not to fight it?

I would never speak for you like that. Especially not in something as important as this.

A rush of warmth coursed through me. Appreciation

and love for the mate who gave me exactly what I needed. For the mates that trusted me, just as I trusted them.

"What if you need us? He's death incarnate, is he not?" Dorian asked.

"I know where he wants me to be," I said. "I'll go to him, but not to surrender. I'm going to end him. I'm the only one that can."

Ezra smiled, but it didn't reach his eyes. "And you won't share the how."

I shook my head solemnly. The truth was, I wasn't entirely sure. I shielded all of that from him. I couldn't tell them I was flying by the seat of my pants. Hanging by a thread of hope that what I thought I could do would actually work. There was a tiny tendril of anxiety that whispered, 'this won't work'. And if it didn't, I would try again and again and again, exhausting every single idea I had considered.

I'd made a trip to the Afterlife post-intervention, spending the pre-breakfast morning hours having a conversation with Jake and Hades. I replayed it in my head. He'd answered my questions, helping me build the course of action I planned to take. He fueled the hope that I could finish this. Was it all a fool's hope? Maybe. I didn't care. It was all we had.

"Where does Jules fit in? The fight is here," Roman asked, he looked at her apologetically. "No offense."

"None taken," she said, shrugging a shoulder. "I know what I am."

"I'm going to fill her in on my plan, but she's the contingency in case"—I halted, hating the possibility of what I had to say. I sighed. "She's the messenger in case we don't fully succeed. She goes to Roxanne. She knows how to find her. If the Dukes are defeated, but in the end it still winds up being one crazy suicide mission, it's Azrael that's left. She'll keep them safe and protect them."

Understanding washed over their faces. Roman closed his eyes, struggling with that concept. I only knew a fraction of that pain. When he opened them, he looked to our favorite poltergeist, and simply said, "Thank you."

A small smile graced her lips. "I'll take care of them. It's all I can do."

The room went silent for a moment as everyone processed the information I'd given.

"Hey Jules," I said, "do you mind giving us a minute alone?"

She waved, the mirror warbling and going fuzzy as she disappeared. In a split second, it was back to a flattened glass, showing the reflection of the room.

I looked out the window, watching the sky change color, and I knew we didn't have much time before the waning crescent moon would be glowing high above us.

Before Azrael showed his angelically beautiful face. A face I hated with every fiber of my being. I wanted to feel better inside. I wanted to heal from the damage and from the trauma. I wanted to breathe freely for the first time.

I wanted to let go of the hate.

But if that hate would drive me, I was going to hold on tight and let it fuel every strategic move I had.

"A penny for your thoughts," Ezra said, choosing to share his comment with my other mates.

"Not sure there are enough pennies," I said, my voice flat.

"Try us," Dorian added.

I did have to force myself to smile as I looked at my three mates. They brought me genuine happiness. I didn't want to say goodbye. That felt too real. Goodbyes were permanent. They meant it was the end. This wouldn't be the end. We'd finish this, and it would be a new beginning.

"I love you," I said, settling on what I wanted to say. "I love all three of you, and I don't regret one second of our time together since I took that mission and ended up in this weirdness. I'd rather have it than anything else in the world."

I walked up to each of them, grabbing their face and pulling it to mine as I drank in their scent and lost myself in a kiss.

It wasn't goodbye. And I told them each that.

"I'd follow you to the ends of the earth," Roman whispered as he pressed his forehead to mine. "If you make me come to Lethe, I'm going to destroy it."

I chuckled, gently brushing his lips one last time.

I gazed at Hades. "Draw the Dukes out. Control this situation."

He flapped his wings, taking flight and hovering in place before landing on Dorian's shoulder. "I don't have anyone else I love-hate as much as you, so I'd appreciate it if you didn't die."

I snorted and my raven reluctantly hummed. "Wow. I'm touched." I placed my hand over my heart. "I think you should put that on a greeting card. It would sell amazing."

"I'll cross-stitch it for you." He let out an obnoxious squawk, then he winked. He whispered into Dorian's ear, then turned to my mates as he said, "We're staying here."

"Where will you go?" Dorian asked.

"Where he asked me to meet him." I mouthed 'I love you' once more, then sifted out.

I appeared in Ezra's empty penthouse and walked to the bathroom in silence. I placed my hands on the counter, looking down at my feet.

I looked up, seeing my reflection. I stared at my eyes, seeing the glimmer of the girl I had once been. I saw the woman I had become. I saw love and rage, unwavering stubbornness, and perseverance. I grinned at myself devilishly. I knew who I was. Azrael didn't have a clue what I was capable of.

I wasn't afraid of him.

I just wanted—well, I wanted Death to die.

I straightened my posture, then whispered Jules' name. The glass waved, and she appeared, a questioning look on her face. "I need one last favor," I said.

She cocked her head, intrigued. "I'm listening."

I patted my pocket. "How do you feel about traveling?"

I wanted the impossible. I was going to make it happen.

Angel. Demon. Shifter. Fae. Vampire. Woman.

Fuck the Angel of Death.

I was as close to a god as one could get.

CHAPTER 26

EZRA

She'd sifted away from us, refusing to share her location. None of us liked it. It went against every instinct we could have as a mate.

Honor. Worship. Guard. Protect.

There was one that was always left out. Trust. It was something that should have been there when you had a mate, or any type of relationship. For alphas, it was never at the forefront. It wasn't our nature. It wasn't a matter of loyalty or monogamy. The very nature of the mate bond was devotion, but if we broke things down, there wasn't the ability to trust they could do it without us.

Our first mates died. Trust wouldn't have prevented any of their deaths. That path, it would seem, was already set. With Fury, there was a great chance that not having trust in her would lead to everyone's demise. She wasn't cut from the same cloth. She was more than capable in so many aspects of her existence, yet she was vulnerable at times. She needed us, only in a different way.

Not to save her. Not to protect her.

To fight with her. To believe in her abilities.

She needed us to *see* her for who she really was, and not just see her as our mate.

We did. We listened, and we accepted . . . even if our baser instincts fought against it.

Although Dorian was shielded from me, I knew he understood. I could tell that he wasn't that different from the rest of us. He could wear the flat affect all he wanted, but I could see through it. Roman's voice was loud if I chose to listen, but he wasn't struggling to keep control. Something about Fury had changed him. Something had settled the fiery wolf within. He raged inside, just as I did, but she kept us grounded somehow.

It was trust.

The moments ticked on, and we sat in silence as the sun set further, the hazy disc slipping below the horizon.

The Houston pollution created a bright sunset, shooting streaks of color out in rays, illuminating the clouds in pinks and oranges.

It was our clock. The sand in the hourglass draining to the bottom. The moon was now visible, and it would soon be the only celestial orb in our sky.

Hades lifted a foot to scratch his neck, tilting his head to the side and closing his eyes as it clearly felt good.

"You'd think for as old as I am, waiting for this wouldn't feel like my soul was being sucked from my eyeballs," Dorian said, pressing his palms to his eyes and rubbing.

I snorted. "For as much as you stand by windows and stare out of them for what seems like hours on end, I find that surprising."

"Right?" Roman chuckled, leaning forward with his elbows on his knees. "In all seriousness, what do you think about when you do that?"

The fae smiled faintly and exhaled a light huff from his

nostrils. "Everything. I'm a planner. In control of every-thing. Even with something that's out of my control, I'm making a plan for how to reverse that." The smile faded, and he looked down to the ground, almost as if speaking to his feet. "For a millennium I was searching for answers to fix my daughter. It was always at the forefront of my mind. Always pouring through the scrolls and ancient texts, then replaying it in my head. I was sure I'd overlooked some-thing. I would try to consider what pieces of the puzzle I was missing." When he looked up, his eyes were slightly glazed over, but it faded quickly. "Now Lyra's safe."

I could see how that would take up a lot of mental energy. "So what makes waiting so hard right now?"

"I have no way to plan for the pure unknown," he said with a laugh. "I'm out of my element, and apparently that isn't something my mind is able to comprehend just yet."

I stood up, rubbing my hands on my jeans. "Well, I'm used to waiting, and this is still a nightmare."

Fury wasn't here, and I wouldn't pour a drink in front of her until she was ready. If that never happened, then so be it. I would respect that forever. Right now, it was me and her two other mates. Right now, we sat and waited for Jake's rogue offspring to make their world-ending appearance.

I walked to a bar cart, pulling the stopper out of a bottle of fae wine. I poured it into three small glasses and wrapped my hands around them to bring them to the coffee table. I set them down carefully, then handed one to Dorian and Roman. They accepted theirs, looking at each other cautiously.

I remained standing, raising my glass in each of their directions.

"A toast before we fight Hades' boyband of younger

brothers." They each laughed, then stood up, and I contin-ued. "There was a time when I didn't like either of you. We've done little to help one another, mostly tolerating each other over the years. Now we've passed toleration and we might possibly even *like* each other. The jury is still out on that one. What I do know for sure is that we share something else, aside from our mate. Respect for each other. Fury brought us together in ways we never saw coming. She brings out the best in us. Even you," I said to the crow and he snort-squawked. "With her, we look forward to the future, even if we see our futures differ-ently. I never expected to have a mate again, much less have to share one. I never thought I'd be here, waiting to take on harbingers of death from the Afterlife. But here we are, and I'm honestly glad it's you two fuckers I'm standing with."

Dorian smiled, then dipped his head graciously before raising his glass. Roman laughed, pursing his lips, and nodding his head, then he shrugged. Glass poised in the air, we said 'cheers' and drank.

"Dear god, now you three are like a boyband," Hades said.

I barked a laugh, turning to his perch on the back of a chair, but I never got a response out.

A rumbling reverberated through the walls, shaking the floors, and making every item in the room rattle.

"Guess they're here," Hades said, sighing. He took a deep breath. "You should sift now. They're going to blow things up first." He shook his head, muttering, "So unoriginal."

"Then why aren't we outside?" I shouted. That damn bird . . .

He slipped into his realm, not answering.

Dorian grabbed us, sifting us away just as a blast forced its way through the outside wall.

A burst of hot wind blew over my skin just as the ground felt like it was pulled from beneath me, and then I landed hard, trying to secure my footing on impact.

Dorian grunted, letting us go. "Sorry about the rough ride."

We stood shoulder to shoulder, three immortal alphas, staring down the burning flames on the west wing of Dorian's estate. Smoke billowed from the fire, the debris of his destroyed home littering the ground.

Three beings emerged from the fumes, walking side by side, slowly approaching us. They each had shoulder-length black hair to match their black eyes, a stark contrast to the pallor of their skin. One had enormous wings, and if he didn't look like he was the walking dead, I'd almost describe his feathers as angelic. An unnatural wind blew around us, picking up the haze and swirling it around their bodies.

Hades appeared, landing on my shoulder. "Look at them walk like they're in a shampoo commercial," he huffed. "Tools."

I pressed my lips together in an attempt to hide my smile, focusing on the seriousness of what was about to happen. Hades didn't seem to have a worry. I had to believe he knew what to do.

Fury trusted him.

He trusted Fury.

Trust.

That's what would get us through this.

The winds grew, their speeds increasing, sending leaves fluttering across the ground as it quaked. Lightning split across the sky, sending a thunderous crack in its wake. *Typhon.*

A tendril of darkness appeared, snaking around a duke's arm, a pungent odor beginning to permeate the air. *Orcus.*

Psychic pressure made its presence known, pushing inward and demanding entry to my thoughts. *Anubis.*

"Hello, brother. It's been a long time," Typhon said. His voice had an eerie snake-like quality to it, dragging out the 's' in a hiss. "Yet, you come to us in your crow form. Father must have punished you as well, though not nearly to the same extent it would seem."

Hades sighed deeply. "Are we really doing this? You're gearing up to give your evil soliloquy before you attack? C'mon. You can't die," he said, holding his wing out in our direction. "They're immortal. It's pointless. You could just go back to Lethe and call it a day. Save me the trouble."

Orcus huffed a humorless laugh. "You should have joined us."

"Yes, clearly I missed out on the losing side," he retorted. "Have you changed your name to the Three Horsemen yet? It doesn't quite have the same ring to it."

Roman shook his head to the side, a loud sniffing sound coming from him as he did so.

Roman, are you still with us? I asked him, mentally reaching out while listening to the exchange between Hades and his brothers.

I am. The pressure from Anubis is getting stronger.

Fight it. We can't lose our control to him.

Anubis raised an eyebrow, holding his hands out and gesturing around us, extending his wings to show off. "*Losing?* We are here, are we not?"

Dorian chuckled, drawing their attention. Anubis' eyes widened as the fae mocked him, clapping slowly. "Your goal was to get *here*? In Houston?" he asked, looking amused at the mere thought. "Why? That's a hell of a long game if this was your intention. Poor planning. I'm guessing you're not the brains of the operation." He turned to Hades. "I really don't see the family resemblance."

Hades snorted. "In my father's defense, everyone makes mistakes."

I quietly laughed as his words rubbed them the wrong way. Fissures ripped through the ground, shooting columns of earth upward toward the sky. Pressure eased off my mind as Anubis' gaze was laser-focused on Dorian.

Flashes of unbridled anger reached me, and I realized Hades and Dorian had cleverly played to their emotions. As their rage increased, it became their focal point. Now they weren't even bothering to protect their minds. All their energy was moving toward fighting us, and Anubis had foolishly set his sights on the only supernatural present whose mental shield he couldn't break.

I mentally shouted to Hades and Roman, telling them I could read the dukes' minds. *It's jumbled, and disorganized, but it's there. Some of it's random. I can't see what their purpose is yet, but it's getting clearer.*

Purpose, Hades repeated in a jaded tone. *They have very little purpose, and they're sensitive as all get out. They react to any stimulus, good or bad. They're like walking testicles. That's what we're fighting.*

I nearly busted out laughing. *Well, I do like to fight dirty.*

Reading pieces of their disjointed thoughts, I saw it happening in their heads. Poorly planned, as Dorian said, but it was happening.

They had every belief they could kill us. They had some clever ideas. I'd died in many ways. Roman had been ripped apart as a young wolf. We always regenerated. The Dukes had every intention of incinerating us to ashes and taking us to the four corners of the world. So that was new. Even if we could regenerate from that, it wouldn't be fast, leaving more than enough time for them to wipe out every being on the planet. And they were angry enough to do it. They had stewed in that hatred for millennia. They wanted revenge.

I passed it on, letting them know what I could see in their thoughts. Roman nodded tersely in response. I wished I could tell Dorian, but he would catch on.

Hades' urgency reached me. *What we talked about, Ezra. Follow Dorian's lead. Make it happen. Without it, I can't do my part.*

The crow and I had shared pieces of the plan. Dorian had his portion, as did Roman. None of us knew it all. We couldn't. If Anubis was able to persuade and take control of us, if he could fully penetrate our minds, the entire thing could go to shit. The fae had the most solid barrier. Whatever was happening—whatever our plan was—would be safely hidden in there.

My job was to keep one of them busy. Distract. Make him aim for me. If the Backstreet Boys of the underworld focused their powers together, Dorian couldn't do his part.

I've got it, Hades. Go. Roman, Orcus seems like he's going for you. Typhon for me.

. . . NOW.

Hades let out a loud caw, flapping his wings and taking flight. He banked hard, gliding directly into his realm, disappearing before our eyes.

The Dukes' reactions were delayed, confused as to why their brother left the fight before it had even started. It gave us a brief upper hand.

In an instant, all hell broke loose. Roman exploded in a full shift, his wolf landing on all fours, cracking the ground beneath him with the impact of his weight. At full speed, his paws pounded against the earth in a steady beat. He aimed straight for Orcus, lunging, and flying into the air.

Tendrils of death and decay wrapped around Roman's body, slowly killing pieces of his flesh, but it hadn't slowed him down. In his wolf form, he was more powerful. He could regenerate faster. His paws landed on Orcus' chest, and he reached around with his gaping jaws, gripping hold of an arm right at the shoulder, ripping it right out of the socket. Tossing it to the side, Roman continued to nip at him as the poisonous rot attacked his body. Each of them would recover, but it would slow them down. Whatever his plan was, I had to trust he could handle it.

Dorian sifted, appearing across the massive lawn. Anubis' attention faltered for a brief moment. Lightning crackled beneath Dorian's skin, and the ground trembled beneath him. He was enticing him, and it worked. A harsh grin curled up Anubis' lips. He wanted more than anything to take control of the fae and use the powers he saw. He turned his full attention Dorian's way, walking toward him at a leisurely pace. He was too cocky. Maybe they both were. I had to fight my fight and watch Dorian simultaneously. *Follow Dorian's lead.* Those were my instructions.

Trust.

Typhon and I stared each other down. His hands rested at his sides, palms turned out while his fingers twitched. I was poised to run, using my speed to my advantage.

I reached out mentally, peeking into his thoughts. I saw his next moves. I smirked, then playfully winked.

He shot his hand up, throwing wind in an attempt to lift me from the ground so he could toss me into the fire. Hard pass. I'd had more than enough raw skin growing back in recent days. I just needed to keep him occupied. I wasn't going to let him mutilate me.

I dashed past him, his elemental grasp missing me entirely. He took chunks of broken earth, raising them high and using the air to catapult them toward me. I dodged them easily, watching his thoughts and predicting where each piece would land. He couldn't keep up as I darted away, never knowing where I was going.

He was infuriated with each miss, which was a delight for me, honestly. I laughed as his anger increased. His mind raged with thoughts of me on fire.

The problem was that level of wrath brought along an erratic desperation. He wasn't thinking anymore. He was just *doing*.

Shit.

A fire tornado burst to life, the gale force winds pulling the flames from Dorian's house, twirling them in a cyclone as it picked me up.

I spun within it, losing my sense of direction. My skin burned, melting away in patches, exposing muscle and nerves. Pain exploded through me, taunting parts of my psyche that had endured torture at the hands of Azrael. The fire and wind held me, sending me spiraling in its circle while smoke filled my lungs.

Burning flesh reached my nostrils and the olfactory memory pulled me into the house in the Afterlife. The moments before I took my eyes. Azrael wearing Fury's beautiful face, working to break me as he flayed my tattoos slowly. When the skin grew back, he did it again. My blood flowed freely, draining my power over and over and over as I tried to regenerate.

My mate flashed in my mind, and an anger grew within me. I knew what Azrael wanted to do to her. He'd told me repeatedly, and he relished in the idea he'd have her for an eternity. He knew how strong she was. He knew how long it would take her to break. He loved it. He wanted nothing more than to lick the tears from her face as he fractured her soul. His words echoed in my ears, replaying the sound of his voice while he stood over me, taunting me while every piece of me tried to grow back.

Michael hid her. He got to keep one of his line. I kept no one. Destroying them was my punishment. Do you know what that's like, Ezra? Killing the very beings you created? It took a part of me that never returned. And it was all Michael's fault.

He thought he could keep one. A final heir. Hiding the last descendent generation after generation after generation. But I found her, and she was just too perfect to destroy. Her pain was delicious. She was so much like Michael. I refuse to let her go.

The fire continued to lick at the regenerating skin, burning it off all over again in a sick loop. But ire coursed through my veins, and I felt a wave of light travel through my muscles, crackling over the pieces of skin that remained.

Fury's power . . .

I pushed it out with minimal force, not really knowing where I was anymore or how to control it. Just testing the water, so to speak. I may as well have set off a bomb. I was in the middle of it.

An explosion shot outward from my center, knocking Typhon down and blowing him back a hundred yards. The fire tornado dissipated, and I came crashing back down to the ground, landing on my back with a hard thud that almost knocked the air out of me. I turned my head to see I'd blown a hole in the side of Dorian's mansion. The entire side of the building was exposed, its walls crumbled all around it. A gaping hole showcased the damage, and I spotted the industrial kitchen fully demolished. A medium-sized metal object was on fire. It was the trash bin.

A literal dumpster fire.

Seemed fitting.

I groaned, sitting up and looking down at the skin that was regrowing at a record pace. Electricity ran over my body like I was a live wire. I surveyed the damage again, realizing I'd barely tried when I used that power. I just wanted the fire to stop.

That could be a problem.

I couldn't see Dorian. Off in the distance, Roman continued to shred at Orcus as his body took hit after hit of decay. It looked like acid wrapping itself around him, burning off fur and flesh, leaving a bubbling ooze before it went to find another piece of living skin to attack. I didn't know how much longer he could do that before he lost the ability to quickly recover.

He was apparently feeling that too.

Orcus reached a tendril out like a smoky black hand, closing its fingers around Roman's throat and I saw Roman's icy blue eyes flash yellow, the same shade as Fury's.

A sudden understanding hit me.

The prophecy had once said we three combined could end the world.

And here we were, carrying Fury's power.

If the Dukes didn't end the world . . . we would.

I reached out to Roman, panic filling my voice. *Don't use her power! You can't control it. We'll destroy everything before—*

I can control it. I've been in control of my own for longer than you know. A small smile crept up his wolfish jaw.

I didn't push back, but the uncertainty filled me quickly.

I flicked my eyes between Typhon as he got up, and to Roman as fur melted off his body where Orcus held him.

Trust me, he said.

That damn word was going to be the end of us.

Then I watched as his wolf grew. Muscle regenerated and expanded, layering itself on top over and over. Bones popped as they enlarged to hold his everchanging frame. His fangs elongated, his jaw opening as drool dripped from his jowls.

Orcus lost his focus, removing his death smoke from gripping Roman's neck, but it wasn't simply the sight of Roman's monstrous wolf. When he growled, the very earth shattered beneath our feet. What looked like molten lava poured from his eyes.

What in the actual . . .

My mind went blank in pure shock. Motion in my periphery pulled my attention to the English-styled garden and hedge maze Dorian kept.

He and Anubis were fighting, disappearing, and reappearing in new places as they fought. They blinked in and out, sifting through Dorian's power and exchanging blows.

A small ripple appeared, just a tiny wave in the fabric of space.

Hades came flying through it, dropping an object into Dorian's outstretched hand, then vanishing through another split into his realm.

Anubis figured out what it was just as I did.

It was that deathstick Lyra had brought.

They couldn't be extinguished, but if that was part of the plan, he needed to use it.

Dorian sifted, but Anubis was prepared, moving himself quickly and planning his next move. I could see his thoughts. He'd taken note of Roman's hellwolf, and he had every intention of using that to his advantage.

He reached into Roman's unguarded mind, grabbing onto his psyche with determined persuasion, pulling him away from Orcus. He'd been stalking toward the Duke when he suddenly stopped and shook his head. Turning toward us, he ran in our direction. His paws shook the ground, breaking it apart like an earthquake chasing a fault line. He let out a roar as red magma poured onto the ground.

Fucking hell.

Typhon threw his arms deep into the dirt, pulling at it and creating an earthquake that sent splits shooting across the estate. Giant chasms appeared, creating a minefield to run through.

Dorian sifted, then disappeared, then sifted again, working to make his way to Anubis as he avoided him.

Mind reading and vampire speed. That's what I had to my advantage. I used it.

As I crossed the quaking terrain, I hopped over each crevice as it appeared, the separating increasing as Typhon shoved his elemental control into it.

I had no way to reach Dorian, but I saw my opening. Hoping he caught the reference, I shouted, "Dorian, catch!"

Fury's power crackled over my skin, building up. I only needed a little. Just a little.

As I came up on Anubis with lightning speed, I threw out what I hoped was just a small pulse of her power. The ground behind Anubis exploded, sending him flying forward . . . right to where Dorian sifted, landing in a crouch. He shoved the deathstick up and outward, his eyes filled with the same electric quality I had under my skin.

Anubis crashed into it, releasing his mental hold on

Roman, who came to a sudden stop. The giant monster shook his head back and forth, regaining control of his mind and body.

Anubis fell to his knees. His form flickered in and out, as though it were trying to extinguish, but it couldn't. He coughed as he laughed, knowing his power would return momentarily.

"Your arrogance will be your end," Anubis said.

"Funny you should say that, brother." Hades' voice sounded as he stepped through his veil.

My jaw dropped when a man walked out. His jet-black hair was long on top, slicked back and away from his face. His dark olive-toned skin was covered in tattoos, hints of ink peeking out from his collar. The long sleeves of his crisp black shirt were rolled up, exposing extensive designs on his arms. I met his black eyes, but they carried a slight warmth I recognized.

Without a doubt, I was staring at Hades.

"Arrogance was always your downfall," he said, a cruel smile curved on his lips as he approached Anubis. His brother flickered quickly, trying to fully recover his power so they could be on equal footing, but Hades tsked, grabbing him and pulling him through the veil.

They vanished.

"Heads up," Dorian shouted, and it snapped me out of my trance. He tossed the deathstick at me, and I caught it. Following his gaze back to Roman, I saw he'd turned his hellwolf back around, aiming for Orcus.

I didn't have a clue where Hades had taken Anubis, but his brothers knew what was coming now.

"One down, two to go."

CHAPTER 27

HADES

I'd watched the fight unfold from the split between worlds. A place of veiled darkness, filled with silence that hummed in my ears. A place only I could go.

My realm.

It was uniquely mine, the way another realm had once been. I'd chosen to share that one. I gave it away to keep her safe.

I interfered.

I still didn't regret it.

Even if I lived the remainder of eternity in my crow form, she was safe.

She was worth it.

I closed my eyes, breathing in deeply as I readjusted to my human form. I felt my limbs, having long forgotten what it was like to use parts of my body. I extended my fingers, opening and closing them repeatedly, strengthening the joints and tendons. Tilting my head to the side, I cracked my neck, the popping sound and the relief filling my senses.

Exhaling, I readied myself to enter the battle once

again. This time my brothers knew I was coming. The element of surprise was gone, but it needed to be this way.

Fury, Jake, and I knew what we needed to do. I carried more power than my idiot brothers. The 'Four' Horsemen , indeed. What a joke. But we couldn't cancel each other out. We were designed that way. Created from the same source, unable to destroy each other.

I didn't need to destroy them. I just needed them temporarily weak. I couldn't pull them through my realm at peak strength.

"One down, two to go."

My lips curled into a cruel smile.

Roman's hellwolf exploded in a run, aiming toward Orcus. I wouldn't lie. That was a bit of a surprise. We knew he was enormous in his power, but the tales of what he could become hadn't been shared. Perhaps his people were too scared. If you didn't speak of it, it wasn't real. The monster wouldn't return if you didn't give it a name.

Yet, he was real, and I watched him in awe. A true hellwolf, filled with so much anger and power it rippled across his body in waves. The icy blue eyes of his standard wolf were long gone, replaced by glowing yellow orbs dripping lava to the ground.

He pounded against the earth, my brother's poisonous tendrils of decay clashing with him in mid-air, throwing him to the side while his fur and flesh melted. Dorian sifted, trying to appear in front of Orcus, but he anticipated this, constantly changing his position. He threw out a black branch of smoke, wrapping it around the fae's arm, burning the skin off like acid. It shriveled, and Dorian's recoiled, catching the deathstick he'd been holding with his other hand before sifting out of the way.

Ezra was managing Typhon's erratic temper tantrum as

best he could. God, what a twat. He always had been. He had the emotional range of a reptile.

I wanted to level the playing field.

And maybe have a little fun.

I shifted into my crow form, slipping through a rift high in the sky, flying fast and aiming toward Typhon.

My brother was shooting balls of fire, harnessing wind, and throwing chunks of whatever he could find. He never really was a man with a plan.

I twisted, curving in the air, keeping my body pressed together tightly as I dove down. My speed picked up, and I threw my wings out to break against the current, extending my feet out to grab. I cawed loudly, giving my position away on purpose. I wanted him to see me coming.

Typhon looked up just as I wanted him to. Legs fully outstretched, I hit my target, digging my claws into the squishy orb, curling my talons around the soft flesh, and ripping it out with a sickening, wet pop. I grinned internally as I flapped my wings hard, taking flight away from him, carrying my new prize with me.

He screamed in rage, glaring up at me with his one good eye. A deep pit in his face poured a black ichor from it.

I flew toward Roman, cawing again, tossing the eye out in the open like I was playing with a toy.

A feral grin curled up his wolf lips, and he jumped into the air, catching it in his mouth, chomping once for good measure, and then swallowing. He landed back on the ground, the impact shaking the ground and sending a plume of dust around him.

Did Roman just eat *your brother's eye?* Ezra yelled in my mind.

I laughed, mentally making sure he could hear my response. *He sure did. You know, I always liked that shifter.*

I'm not eating body parts for your approval. Making that clear right now.

I chuckled again, turning around in flight to return to the fight. *Awfully judgy for a bloodsucking vampire.*

Different and you know it, he said as he sped away from Typhon's fire.

Is it though? I hadn't pegged you for someone with a weak stomach, I taunted. I found a good current and hovered, taking in the carnage below me.

At least I didn't throw up when Fury sifted us, he retorted.

I shuddered. That was a rough ride, and I'd spent over four hundred years as a bird.

I floated, contemplating how to get Orcus out of the way. I just needed an opening. He was so good at keeping anyone away from him. Easy enough to do when you reeked of death.

I knew Fury would succeed on her part. She always would. She didn't know how to fail. That's why she was chosen. A piece of Michael was in her veins, yes, but that wasn't what made her unstoppable. It was her humanity. She was uniquely balanced in the gray area, accepting her faults and the darkness, always striving to increase the light. If we didn't complete our part, Azrael would win.

Equally as important, my asshole brothers would win.

I couldn't live with that.

I turned my attention to Roman, watching as he roared and prepared for his next move. He charged Orcus again, his great body protecting him from inflicting too much long-term damage from the tendrils of decay.

From my vantage point, I saw Dorian in the hedge maze, watching carefully as the shifter fought. Roman snapped at limbs, his razor-sharp teeth shredding at pieces of Orcus' body while my brother retaliated with poisonous fumes. Roman took a hit and rolled, getting back on all fours, and shaking his body.

Do me a quick favor and piss Typhon off, I said to Ezra.

He glanced up to where I was in the sky, half smirking, a fang peeking through and hanging over his lip.

Any requests? he asked.

Make me laugh while you do it. Yeah, we were fighting to save the world, but I was at least going to enjoy my brothers' misery. And yes, their misery made me laugh.

Ezra cackled, taking off at a breakneck speed. While Typhon was throwing all sorts of elements at the vampire, I needed one thing from him to pull off my next move. I was counting on his predictability.

In a sudden twist my brother didn't see coming, Ezra zoomed toward him, stopping for a fraction of a second, then poked him in his one good eye—speeding away before Typhon could retaliate.

He'd grabbed his face, screaming and cursing.

Immortal, supernatural, god-like creature, demon spawn: it didn't matter what you were. That hurt like a bitch.

I almost fell out of the sky as I squawked with unrestrained laughter. The sounds of my wheezing snorts caught my brother's attention.

I sent my thanks to Ezra, who gave me a salute and a wink.

Roman ate an eyeball, but you might be my new favorite, I told him.

Typhon's chest heaved up and down as clouds built above us, rolling like waves as they gathered and became larger. Lightning cracked and split across the night sky; thunder rumbled deeply, sending heavy vibrations to the ground below.

Perfect. Predictable. Just like the dumbass I always knew.

Tell Roman I need a decoy, I shouted to Ezra, knowing he would pass it on to the shifter. I had my own way of communicating with Dorian.

I cawed loudly in three short bursts, and the fae nodded, seizing the moment to sift in front of Orcus with the deathstick extending outward, aiming for his chest. He thrusted forward, but it fell short as Orcus pulled back, grabbing Dorian around the middle with his phantom smoky arms. He lost his grip on the weapon, and it bounced with a thud as it hit the ground. The decay burned around his waist, no doubt causing unbearable pain.

Fury's mates couldn't die, but I knew they could still feel everything.

Roman didn't hesitate and lunged haphazardly toward Orcus, right on cue.

Typhon threw one hand above him, pulling the elements from the sky, harnessing the lightning, gathering it like a ball of power in his hand.

Internally, I grinned.

I banked hard, flying into a rift, appearing in my realm.

I shook, feathers disappearing as I took my human form.

This is going to hurt, I said, preparing myself. Fucking my brother up was worth it.

I reached through the veil, my arm appearing right in front of Typhon as I snatched the orb of crackling electricity. It pulsed through my body, sending waves of burning pain in every direction. Shoving my hand through the fabric of space, a rift opened in front of Orcus, and I took another form. One that allowed me to pass directly through matter.

I might have been a little out of practice, but it was like riding a bicycle.

I was the OG poltergeist, after all.

Orcus' mouth fell open in surprise when I shoved the ball of lightning into his chest. I yanked my hand back before the bolts shot from their confinement, splintering apart inside his sternum.

He looked down at his body, then gazed up at me in shock. I winked at him while I took my steps back.

He dropped his hold on Dorian and Roman, and they fell to the ground. Dorian rolled onto his back wheezing. "Fucking hell, you took long enough," he coughed as the skin on his abdomen bubbled and regenerated.

"Sorry about that. Great job, though. Give yourself a pat on the back," I said, reaching down to give him a hand.

He caught my extended offer, pulling himself up. "I don't want a pat on the back," he grumbled. "I want to not burn anymore."

Roman stood on all fours and vomited black poison on the grass. He shook like a dog, sending growing fur and pieces of rotting flesh flying off. I scrunched my nose and made a face.

"Well, that's new. I've never seen anyone ingest his power before."

Roman snapped his jaws once, then licked his lips, running his long tongue over his nose to the other side of his snout.

Dorian gave him a look of disgust while he rubbed his mid-section.

Crackles and pops sounded as my brother looked at his chest while he flickered in and out. His black toxic smoke wafted from his eyes, curling around his neck and his mouth.

I opened my mouth to speak, but snapped it shut when Typhon's scream of rage pierced the air.

Always interrupting. Nothing ever changed with them.

I turned around to see him throw his hands into the earth, reaching deep. Pebbles shook over the surface, and the earth quaked and began to get warmer. A stream of red and orange liquid rope came out of the ground, coiling like a snake under the control of its charmer.

I sighed.

Magma.

So predictable.

He stood up tall with his legs spread apart, manipulating his newest weapon.

"I'm coming for you," he called out to me.

I stared at him blankly. "Okay," I said mockingly. "To do what exactly? You can't kill me."

"I'm going to make you suffer." He narrowed his eyes on Dorian and Roman. "All of you."

For fuck's sake, his talking is enough to suffer through, Ezra said in my mind.

I shifted my gaze, realizing he wasn't in my sights.

Roman barked, grabbing my attention. A wind gusted past us, and I saw it then. Ezra. A blur in my vision, falling to the ground, sliding across the terrain like he was stealing home base. He dug his feet into the dirt, keeping them close together, sending up a cloud of dust as he came to a stop in front of Typhon, his legs sliding between my brother's.

Typhon looked down as Ezra smiled, thrusting the deathstick up into my brother's chest. His mouth formed an 'o' as his eyes rolled into the back of his head and he fell to his knees, convulsing. He flickered in and out, his indestructible soul trying to die. We had a few moments before they'd regain power. It was all I needed.

Ezra got up, swinging the deathstick at Typhon's head, landing it across his temple in a sickening smack. My brother tipped over to his side, pieces of electricity buzzing over his head. "You really are predictable."

He tossed it in the air, and I caught it. I extended my arm, shaking the vampire's hand. "Nice touch. Probably a bit overkill, but nice all the same."

He shrugged. "I haven't run like that in years. I'm pissed off."

I chuckled. He sounded so much like Fury, and he didn't even know it.

I held the deathstick up and looked at it. Lyra had no idea how helpful she'd be when she brought that. Make no mistake, she intended on using it. It just turned out to be useful for us. Azrael was a shitbag, and he never should've had something this powerful just lying around. It was going back to Jake's office to be hidden away safely. I tucked the weapon under my arm and reached for Typhon. I grabbed a handful of his hair and dragged him over to Orcus, dumping him unceremoniously.

"Well, this went better than I expected," I said to Fury's mates.

"Are we just going to skip over the fact that you're a person now?" Ezra said. "What the fuck is that about?"

"Of course I'm not just a crow. The three stooges here are my brothers and you don't see them covered in feathers. It's complicated." I shrugged. "I'm on a tight schedule. Only have a small window of time to get these assholes off this realm."

Dorian reached his hand out, patting me on the shoulder. "Where are you taking them, anyway?"

I placed a hand on Typhon and Orcus' shoulders. Their powers were still unsteady, but flashes and sparks were beginning to surface. Their strength was returning. It didn't matter. Where we were going, their power was useless.

"Back to our dad's place," I said, an evil smirk on my face.

I slipped into darkness, laughing while dragging my brothers back to Hell.

Contentment hummed through my veins. It was validating knowing my three siblings were about to get what was coming to them, but the real war wasn't over. The reality of that fact settled in my mind. Roman, Dorian, Ezra, and I succeeded, but winning here only got us to the halfway point.

Fury still had Azrael to contend with, and he was a much bigger problem.

CHAPTER 28

I sifted mid-step.

One moment I was walking out of Ezra's penthouse.

The next, I stood on the driveway of what was once my greatest nightmare.

Bright lights illuminated the dining room. The flowered wallpaper we had was long gone, replaced by a bright yellow paint. Inside two parents moved around a giggling baby with ginormous cheeks and a full head of dark hair. The kid flung food off its highchair toward the waiting Pitbull. The dog wagged its tail, happily chowing down whatever pureed mash it was given while the baby squealed in delight. They were definitely in cahoots. The mom shook her head in amusement while the dad scrambled to stop the baby from doing it again.

They seemed so happy. Picture perfect in the same house that haunted my dreams for decades. Sure, it looked different now. The exterior had been repaired over the years of natural wear and tear. It had a garage now. The ugly bushes that sat in front of the windows were long gone, replaced by a flower bed filled with color. The surface was new, but the bones of the place—the foundation it was built on—there was no changing that.

I walked around the front, toward the yard. A white picket fence surrounded it on three sides. I reached up, hooking my hand around the rough wood edge before jumping. My feet landed quietly on the other side. A soft breeze drifted up from the lake, lifting my hair, blowing strands over my shoulders. I started down the hill for the small dock at the edge.

A hundred years ago this lake was the place I went to when the walls closed in and the air felt stifling. John would come and go, but as a housewife, my duty was here.

Cooking. Cleaning. Dressing up like a living doll and going through the motions.

But when my makeup couldn't quite cover the bruises and the tears wouldn't stop coming, this was where I would retreat.

Azrael told me to come home.

I knew what he meant.

I half-expected him to have the house redone; reverted to the picture of our old life so that he could torture me just a little bit more with it. To make me play the doll—walking, talking, breathing in fear.

Perhaps he simply hadn't gotten to it yet. Maybe I was early. All I knew was that we had one last game to play, but this time the tables had turned.

He thought he held all the cards. That the rules were set and there was no escape.

He was mistaken.

"Sunny."

His voice was low and husky. Silky smooth. He always did know how to charm. After all, he was the greatest liar in history.

"Azrael," I answered, not nearly so pleasant. I glanced over my shoulder, taking in his pale blond hair, bone white skin, and icy blue eyes. He wore John's face. A tactic meant to throw me. Intimidate me.

But there was nothing intimidating about a coward who hid behind a mask.

"After all this time I would've expected you to show me your true face." Turning around, I looked at him. My reaction surprised him, and he tilted his head as he considered my words. "You're threatening to end the world just to have me. Seems a little strange you want me to spend the rest of eternity with you and I don't even know who my captor is."

His eyes narrowed on the word captor. To call it anything else would've been a kindness he didn't deserve. We both knew why I was here. He wanted to hurt me. Torture me.

This wasn't some long lost love.

It was obsession.

Madness.

"You have a very high opinion of yourself," he mused, stepping forward. Only four or so feet remained between. I brushed my damp hands against my jeans, then stuffed them in my jacket pockets. "It's not the most becoming quality in a lady, though I will enjoy slowly stripping it away."

I stayed silent, lifting an eyebrow.

"Because you followed my command and came alone, I will tell you a truth," he continued, taking another step. I might have broken past the fear, but I couldn't stop the way my heart rate picked up. Good. I needed him to believe he still had that effect on me. As if he heard it, Azrael smiled. It was lifeless and cruel. "They are all my faces. Whichever one I was made with, I forgot long ago."

I let out a soft exhale.

"I suppose it follows that you forgot who you were along with it. Was that before or after Michael saw to it that you slaughtered your children?"

He closed the distance between us, standing before me. His head ducked down, hovering only inches from mine.

In my first life, I'd sometimes thought I'd seen a glimpse of something in his gaze. Something inhuman. Something monstrous.

As I watched him, I saw it now in the way shadows drifted through the blue of his eyes, darkening it.

"You speak of things you know nothing about," he said, voice deadly.

"I know that's why you became obsessed with hunting angels' children," I replied. "And why you were after me." His hand came up as if to cup my jaw. Instead, it curled around my face, squeezing hard. I had to fight the sliver of panic that hit me, threatening to ruin everything.

"If you're looking for a reason why I am the way I am, you won't find one. If you're thinking there's something redeemable in my soul, that you can somehow coax it out —you won't. I've been the Angel of Death a long time, Sunny, and I'm bored. The descendants of angels are no more. I ensured that when I beat the whelp out of you." His callous way of describing our child, *my child*, made me clench my hands. I was thankful they were in my jacket pockets, or he might have seen beyond the façade. He might have suspected that my heart wasn't beating simply because I had the desire to run, but instead, a desire to fight. To kill.

"I would have died anyway. You beating me just prolonged my torture."

"As I said, I'm bored. You were the first thing to interest

me since I killed Michael. Needless to say, it's been a long time. Most of the angel hybrids were so far removed from the source. Their blood was diluted and they barely held any power, but you . . . you had his hair. I was struck by the unnatural shade of red that only he and his true offspring carried. Somehow your line wasn't weakened. I saw in you the same anger that filled him. This disgusting sense of what was just. You couldn't just lie down and take what life gave you, even when I used you. Broke you . . ." I flinched when his lips caressed mine, just the slightest of touches.

"Then I went too far. Hit too hard. I do regret that. Killing you so soon, especially when you weren't extinguished as you should have been. I was expecting you in Lethe, but you escaped me. I was saddened I didn't get to play with you. It was truly unexpected. I bided my time, watching you from afar. But there were times I missed you too much. I couldn't help myself. I took stranger's faces and met you at bars, sex clubs—enjoying my fill of you when you had no idea." My face drained of color. He smiled, pressing his body closer to mine, and I could feel his erection against me.

"You remember the night at Hail Mary's?"

I couldn't forget.

It was the night I'd hooked up with a demon I'd never seen before and went back to his place. We'd fucked like savages, but at some point, I'd passed out. Something that never happened. I awoke to my arms and legs bound while the same demon was using me . . .

I blew him up. It was one of two times I'd lost control of my power and extinguished someone.

That was the last time I'd fucked anyone outside of a group setting in the Afterlife.

"That was you," I said, fighting the acid crawling its way up my throat.

"I had to be more careful after that incident since my angel had finally grown into her powers. Still, you never knew. Not until I took the vampire's place."

"You're a sick fuck," I spat.

His grip on my jaw tightened, digging deep into the flesh, desperate to leave the bruises he'd so enjoyed. Making his mark.

"I've paid my dues. I ran this world and the Afterlife for thousands of years while Satan—I'm sorry, 'Jake'—fucked off. Forever is too long but I can't die, and I'm beyond caring about what is right or wrong or *just*. I want you, and I'm going to take you. You'll be my angel in a cage long after this world is gone. Existing for my enjoyment alone."

Hades said Azrael had lost his last marble. I didn't doubt it before. I wasn't searching for some hidden moral compass or compassion that would allow him to come back. It was just an incredible understatement.

I laughed once, cold as death himself.

Azrael tensed against me, not liking the sound.

I pulled my hand out of my pocket and flipped open the makeup compact.

A hand appeared, reaching through the glass. It fisted in his shirt, twisting the material.

Azrael saw it coming and he released my face, shoving me to the side without care. I twisted to avoid landing in the lake, and instead slammed my head into the side of the dock.

I blinked, clearing the stars in my vision. Azrael grabbed the wrist holding him. As the compact fell to the ground, more and more of Jules' body emerged. She couldn't escape.

Azrael looked down at me, ignoring the dangling poltergeist he held captive.

"This was your grand plan?" he asked me, incredulous. "I knew you wouldn't come easily. But really, this? You thought I'd fall for the same thing you did to Lyra?"

He laughed, then tossed Jules aside.

His foot came down on the compact, shattering it into tiny pieces that he kicked into the lake.

"I have to say, though, I do love that you give me excuses to punish you."

He knelt beside me, grabbed my ankle, then twisted— the entire time he watched my face, waiting for the reaction that would give him satisfaction.

Snap.

My lips fell open in a silent scream.

Oh that piece of shit was going to pay.

Gritting my teeth, I leaned up, using my elbows to brace me. Light danced on my hands and face. Any part of my body that had visible skin lit up like a star on the brink of going supernova.

Now he'd done it.

"Jesus Christ, you just love to hear yourself talk, don't you?"

Azrael narrowed his eyes. "And you just don't give up."

He reached higher, for my knee. I jerked forward, slamming my forehead into his.

He shot back, falling ass first on the dock.

"You're over here talking shit, saying you know me so well. If that were the case, you'd know I wasn't looking for anything redeemable in you. I know there isn't, and even if there was, who the fuck cares?" I rocked forward, sweeping my leg behind me so I could lean up on my knee. That ankle was broken; there were no doubts about it. It would heal, but I wasn't quite sure how long that would take. I was strong, but I didn't heal like Ezra who could regrow eyes in a flash.

I glanced up, taking in the crescent moon that was now high in the sky.

It reflected off the lake in front of us like an open portal into the universe.

"Maybe you weren't always a monster. I don't know. But you're a sadistic, evil shitbag now. If I'd been given your casefile, I'd tell them to extinguish you. But you can't die. That's the kicker, right?" He stared at me with unveiled hatred. I wondered if he saw his obsession and loathed himself for it. It controlled him. It drove him. He'd never be able to let it go. It owned him. Therefore *I* owned him. So no. He wouldn't blame himself for it. He'd save all that hate for me.

"You're going to regret that."

"No," I said firmly, fangs descending. "I don't think I am."

He launched across the deck at me.

I was ready for it.

I downright wanted it.

I'd positioned myself on the very edge of the dock. Coming at me from his angle, we'd topple clean over the side.

He expected me to block. To fight him.

He didn't expect my embrace. My arms closed around his shoulders, one going up to grab a fistful of his hair. Not to pull him away, but to bring him closer.

In the blink of an eye, between him slamming into me and us falling off the dock—I set my sights on the carotid artery in his neck.

Then I bit him.

Latching on, I pressed my fangs deep into his flesh, holding tight while I reverse fed.

It wasn't time yet. I didn't need to give blood, but I knew I could. Dorian was right when he said I needed to just get ahead of the urge.

The only urge I had now was to end Azrael. When he sent that shifter after me, I'd learned something of vital importance. The bite of a supernatural was lethal in Afterlife blood.

Unless you were mates.

Jake said mine saved me.

In return, I'd unknowingly claimed them.

But Azrael?

He was nothing to me.

My blood and power rushed into him as we went airborne. But where the water should have broken our fall, it didn't.

For one that had lived so long, he was horribly arrogant.

I'd banked on it.

The makeup compact was just plan A. One that both Jules and I knew would likely fail. It was too easy. He was too cunning. We'd hoped that it would work, but we knew better than to come without a backup plan. In demanding I come home, he'd positioned us next to a far larger mirror.

One he couldn't break.

One he'd never considered.

Lit by moonlight and reflecting our images on its calm and quiet surface, the lake provided just what we needed.

Jules was ready and waiting to open the door to her realm. When we should have hit water and sank into its depths, we crossed dimensions, falling through the entrance and landing on the other side.

Our bodies crashed into wooden planks, and the dock

cracked under the weight of our combined ascent. Or descent, depending on how you wanted to look at it.

Fire licked along my back, or at least it felt like it as we skidded before sliding over the edge, landing in the shallows.

Azrael grasped either side of my head, wrenching me away from where I kept my teeth buried in his skin.

I took a chunk of his neck with me; blood dripped from my lips, down my chin. I spat his flesh out, baring my fangs. Water soaked my jeans, my shirt, my jacket. Every part of me was either dripping or submerged as a bitter cold settled over us.

I embraced it, maneuvering my stiff fingers to my jacket pocket. It was still there. It hadn't fallen out during the scuffle.

"There's no ending where you don't end up mine in Lethe. I should —" He paused, eyes narrowing as he cast a downward look at himself.

The light wasn't simply dancing beneath my skin.

It was under his.

Like a venomous bite, the mark on his neck turned black. It didn't heal as it should, instead gaping open and bleeding as his veins darkened—trying and failing to process my blood.

A harsh breath escaped his lips. His grip on me loosened. Chest panting hard as his heart began to slow.

"Clever," he spat. His blue eyes turned dark as obsidian.

"You don't know the half of it," I said. Using my free hand, I shoved him back. He tilted, giving me the space to crawl away, getting halfway up shore. I sagged against the grassy bank of the lake and looked up at the sky. "Over the next few minutes you'll lose the ability to move. Loss of speech comes next—although that seems to be setting in even faster than it did for me."

"This won't kill me," he said, straining to get the words out. He tried to turn and face me. To follow me. But he just ended up face-planting into the water.

"Jules," I said softly. I pointed to my unhealed broken ankle. "Help a friend out, will you?"

She appeared next to him and grabbed onto one black wing, using it to haul him up hill, toward me.

She managed to get the upper half of his body out of the water, taking more than a dozen feathers out while she was at it. Her face was set in a grim mask as she unceremoniously dropped him at my feet and then handed me a knife.

"This next step has to be yours." She gave me a knowing smile.

"Every bit of it." My hand closed over the blade's handle, and I nodded to her, giving her my thanks. "This part is my closure."

"Make him pay," she said before disappearing once more.

I maneuvered to the side, wincing as pain shot through my leg. I shuffled over , sitting just above his head so I could see every facet in his reaction. Every contortion of his face. Every flinch of his body as my power spread further in his veins. Deeper into his being. Embedding itself in him.

Part of me wanted to drag this out. Enjoy it. Make him feel the way so many others had when they suffered by his hand.

The rest of me was tired of it all.

I was ready for the games to end.

I was playing for keeps.

No more moves. No more strategy. Winner takes all.

"Still think you won't die?" I asked. His gaze flickered

toward me. His eyes pitch-colored like pure evil. "I see the fight hasn't properly left you yet, even though you find yourself powerless—probably for the first time ever. In case you haven't put it together, I'm going to spell it out for you. You will die. Here and now. Killed by the supernatural powers I was imbued with when you tried to have that shifter extinguish me. My mates changed me in order to save me. Without that, I never would've evolved. I'd still just be an angel-demon hybrid, and nothing more. The part that I needed to defeat you? It was theirs, and neither of us knew it." My voice was cold and hard and unyielding. I didn't possess an ounce of power in this moment, but that didn't matter. Because neither did he.

"Supernatural magic doesn't mix with the Afterlife, Azrael. No exceptions. Except one. Me and the handful of others that found our mates. Our bodies accept that change. I'm not your mate, though. I'm not your wife. I'm nothing except your executioner. You will die from that bite, make no mistake." His arms began to shake. His hands curling to fists, but he couldn't lift them. He couldn't speak. He was well and truly immobile.

"But as you've continued to point out, you're the Angel of Death, so I've covered my bases."

I pulled the starlight orb out of my pocket.

"Without this, you'll die here in the mirror realm, but you'll still come back. You'd be trapped here forever, sure. And I could do that. Forever alone is a good punishment, but it's better than you deserve."

With my other hand I lifted the knife. It was a short blade. Sharp. Serrated. It would do the trick.

I tilted my head as I used it to cut his shirt away.

Beneath his skin the light was growing.

My time was almost up, but it would be enough. I'd

carved up enough bodies in my time to know the fastest way to a man's heart. Between the fourth and fifth ribs, I stabbed at the flesh, hacking away at the organ desperately trying to beat in his chest. Blood coated my hands, making my grip slick, but I was determined.

Demon strength would have made it easier, but I'd create a five-inch pocket all the same. I set the knife down beside me and slipped my fingers into either side of the incision, then pulled.

His body jerked.

It was nearly time. I shoved the orb into the hole I'd created in his chest. Then used all my weight to burrow it as deep as I possibly could.

When I felt the surge of my power along his skin, I fell back, scrambling to get away. The broken ankle made it hard to move quickly, but Jules was right there. She grabbed my hand and blinked us away.

We sat on the mirror realm version of the Willis tower. Miles and miles away from the little Indiana town outside Chicago where my old life was. Where my ex lay on the shore of a lake.

Together in the darkness, we both waited and then watched as Azrael self-destructed. Gold and orange and red wove together, exploding outward.

It was the best fireworks show I'd ever seen.

"You're sure he won't be able to use his powers anymore?" Jules asked.

"I'm sure."

The starlight orb was made of Afterlife magic, or maybe our magic was made from the orb. I didn't know. What I did know was that it could trap it. Hades said so. It's what prevented me from healing in Jules' realm. The orb didn't strip us of magic. Nothing could do that. But it could confine, and that's what I did with Azrael's powers.

I rendered him all but human.

"Take me home," I said as the light faded, and the darkness closed in once more.

"You don't want to get in one final hoorah?" she asked, legs dangling off the edge of the skyscraper. "I do love a good gloat."

I smiled. "Nah. His punishment begins now. He won't be seeing me ever again."

As she took me across the country, back to the mansion I hoped was still standing—I could have sworn I heard a cry of anguish on the wind. Almost like . . . death.

And I knew that Azrael—the Angel of Death, wearer of a thousand faces—was gone.

He may not have been able to die, but for the rest of eternity he'd wear the same face as John. He'd live his life as John might have.

Powerless.

There was no greater punishment for a twisted sadist like him.

And no greater peace for me.

CHAPTER 29

We stepped through a mirror in the hallway of Dorian's estate in Houston. Jules turned around, staring at it in silence for a moment. I wanted to give her time to say goodbye. She was technically leaving the only home she'd had for centuries. I could understand the longing she felt.

"Do you think you'll miss it?" I asked, knowing it was a type of grief she was likely going to experience.

She shrugged. "Maybe? Probably." She pulled her braid over one shoulder, picking at the ends of it absentmindedly. "Yeah, probably. But it'll be nice to socialize differently. See people again in a new way. Watch TV shows that I want to watch when I want to watch them. Even go to the beach," she said, smiling. "That'll be fun. Maybe we could go together."

I creased my brows, looking at her from the side. "The mirror realm has lakes but not beaches? You said it's an exact replica of this world."

"Oh, it is. But the beaches are empty. Lonely." She rubbed her arms as though she were cold. "I was safe, but that didn't mean I was comfortable. This'll be good. I'm excited to see what the future holds. You know, now that I have one."

I chuckled. "C'mon. I don't hear explosions and yelling, so that's a good sign." I turned, looking at the broken side of the house. Smoldering piles of rubble and ash littered the ground. I frowned. "Well, 'good' might be a bit of a stretch."

She followed me as I headed down to the library. I had no idea where the guys would be, so I walked the halls, calling out their names.

"Where are yo—"

Dorian sifted in front of me, and I walked headfirst into his massive chest, letting out a loud umph sound on impact. Before I could react, he wrapped his arms around me tightly, resting his cheek on my head.

Returning the embrace, I breathed in his scent as he no doubt breathed in mine.

A warmth bloomed in my chest, content and happy to have my mate with me.

Ezra's familiar voice filtered in my mind, stroking my jawline with his psychic touch. I felt the barest hint of a phantom kiss on my lips. *Welcome back.*

Hey, I said lamely. In all the years I had been rehabilitating troubled souls, no one ever treated me this way after a hard day at work. No, my job hadn't involved trapping the Angel of Death and preventing what boiled down to an apocalypse, but all the same. The greeting threw me off guard and I wasn't sure what to say. What I knew was I liked the contact with them. I liked seeing their faces and hearing their voices. *I see you blew the place up. Looks like Dorian is going to have to rebuild here.*

We'll help him.

I raised my brows in surprise. *Is that . . . comradery? If I didn't know for a fact it was you, I'd question whether or not you'd been kidnapped. What did I miss?*

He chuckled. *Let's just say we have a newfound respect for each other. There's trust there.*

I smiled against Dorian's chest. I never expected them to have a guy's night, but there was something nice about the possibility they might do more than tolerate each other for my benefit. They might actually get along.

I hoped they would. Eternity was a long time.

Roman's voice bellowed, echoing off the walls. "You plan on bringing her back here, or do I have to come to you?"

Dorian grumbled, then realized Jules was in the room with us. "I didn't expect to see you here," he said, dipping his head to her in a sign of appreciation. "We have a lot to discuss, it would seem." He held out a hand for her and she accepted, sifting us from the hallway to another room, one that hadn't been destroyed by fire or whatever bomb had gone off here.

He let me go, and Roman lifted me off the ground, pressing his lips to mine in a forceful kiss. He wrapped his fingers through my tangled hair, inhaled deeply, drinking me in. I hummed in response, kissing him in return.

Jules cleared her throat after an unknown amount of time. It didn't seem that long to me, but it was apparently enough for her.

Roman released me, looking at her and pointing in surprise. He gave me a questioning look about her presence while I wiped the edges of my mouth off, smirking and not at all ashamed.

I smoothed out the wrinkles on my shirt, moving my hair away from my face. Looking around, I said, "I see you tried to level the place."

Ezra walked over to me, giving me a soft peck on the lips. *I'll take more of that later. When no one can interrupt us.*

My cheeks heated and I pressed my knees together slightly. I had no arguments there. His greedy smile told me he already knew that.

"You and Hades set us up for success, really. We followed his lead, doing what you two planned, and we pulled it off," Ezra said, shrugging. He crossed his arms, tilting his head to the side in Roman's direction. "That one turns into a hellwolf too, so that didn't hurt."

I stared blankly for a moment, turning to my mate in question. "I'm sorry, what? A . . . hellwolf?"

"Oh yeah. Dripping lava and everything," Hades said. "You should've seen it."

I turned at the sound of his voice, finding myself looking for a crow, but staring instead at the tall, dangerously handsome son of Jake in human form.

"Hades," I said in greeting.

A smile curled up one side. "In the flesh."

"Have to admit, I was looking for feathers. I didn't realize you'd show up as a person."

"A person you and your raven can't easily shit on," he said with a grin.

"I'm not sure that's a challenge you should just throw out there. Never know what I'll do to prove a point." He twisted his lips and hummed in response. "You know, I think I liked you better as a crow," I said. My inner raven agreed. A smaller bird was something she could dominate. This new Hades was something else entirely. After being confined by mirror realm magic in my fight with Azrael, she was ready to pick a fight.

His hands were in his pockets while he leaned up against a doorframe. He lifted a shoulder in response. "I'm actually quite attached to both shapes. They serve their purposes." He turned his gaze to Jules who stood behind a chair, her posture rigid. He dipped his head to her. "Happy to see you're out of your realm safe."

A crease formed between my brows when I heard him change his tone while speaking to her. I looked back and forth, from Hades to Jules, then back again, piecing together something I hadn't caught before.

She knew him in *this* form.

His human form.

The way she looked at him spoke volumes.

My jaw fell.

"It's *you*," she whispered, her eyes traveling the length of his body. She looked surprised to see him, just not in the way I'd expected.

I held my hand up. "Wait just a damn minute," I started, walking toward them. "You know him when he's not a crow? Like, you *know* each other waaaay more than you let on. When did—"

"I'm sorry to interrupt you—" Hades said.

"No, you're not." I narrowed my eyes and pursed my lips.

"No, I'm not." He smiled at me. "That aside, it's time we head back. There's the final matter of my brothers' punishment that needs to be dealt with, amongst a few other things."

My mates shared a look of discomfort, and I had a feeling I knew what it might be.

"It's okay. Jake and I have an arrangement. I'm not staying in the Afterlife." I could hear the collective relief they felt. "C'mon. We're all going for a visit. There's a lot to catch up on."

Hades held his arm out. "After you."

I walked over to Ezra and Roman, placing an arm on each of them. "Dorian, will you bring Jules?" He cocked his head in question.

"I can't—"

I pressed my lips together and smiled. "You can. Trust me. You have my powers, and I have yours. Jake and I figured this out. If I can sift there, you can too." He looked slightly unsure, but he agreed. I focused my energy on sifting us to the Afterlife.

We appeared in the waiting room, and Francine looked up. "Do you have an appointment?"

"I . . ." I sighed. "Not technically, no."

She picked up her phone, ready to dial Jake's intercom extension. "Name?"

I grit my teeth together. "Are you . . . are you fucking joking?"

She looked me dead in the eye with a flat expression, and not even the twitch of a smile. "I never joke."

I stormed forward, opening my mouth to give her a piece of my mind when the door flung open.

"Give it a rest, Francine," Jake said, gesturing for us to come inside. "You need to find someone new to pick on. Fury's off limits now."

I glared at her, motioning to my eyes and back to her. Twat. Then I led the way into his office, Jules and my mates following quietly behind me.

Hades was already in there waiting for us.

"Take a seat," Jake said, snapping his fingers. Four more chairs appeared, giving each of us a place to sit.

I plopped down in my familiar chair while everyone else sat. Dorian looked stoic, as usual, but he'd been in this room before. Ezra was taking it in, recognizing the scent of it, but considering he didn't have eyes the last time he was in the Afterlife, he was seeing it for the first time. Roman looked curious, but oddly comfortable. Jules looked downright concerned, assuming she was going to be extinguished or imprisoned at any moment.

I cleared my throat once everyone was settled. "So, where are they?"

Jake took a heavy ball out of his pocket, setting it on the desk. To the average person, it looked like a paperweight. A crystal ball, of sorts.

I pointed at it. "They're in there?"

"For now," he said. "It's a very, very temporary situation. This won't hold them, and it would be stupid of me to keep them confined where someone could let them out."

I cocked an eyebrow. "Yeah, in your defense, you wouldn't want to make that mistake again."

He narrowed his eyes playfully, letting me have my jabs. Good. I'd earned them.

"I figured Jules would like to do the honor," he said, turning to the woman in question.

She looked at him with wide eyes. "Why? Hades knows how."

He shrugged. "You gave up your realm. You were an essential piece in stopping all this. If you want me to, I'll give it to Hades."

"Wait," Dorian said, shifting his body forward. "What do you mean? You're putting them in the mirror realm?" He turned to Jules. "You're not going back? What about Lyra?"

"Don't worry." Jules rested her hand on Dorian's arm, reassuring him. "We found another place for her. She's safe."

My mate's worried eyes met mine, and I gave him a small smile. "She's here, Dorian. It's okay." I nodded my head over to Jake. "We worked a few things out."

Jake locked his fingers together, resting them on his desk. "Fury drove some hard bargains—"

I scoffed. "No, I didn't."

"You did, actually. I don't give away favors."

"Whatever, Jake. I told you what I wanted to do to save the world. It was sort of a team effort here. I needed certain leniencies to get it done. It wasn't an ultimatum."

He considered me for a moment. "Weren't they? If I had said no to your demands, what would you have done?"

I sat for moment, letting the silence tick on. "I still would've saved the world, and I would have done what I wanted behind your back. And if that didn't work, I'd have fought you until my dying breath, but the world wasn't going to end. That wasn't an option."

Jake smirked, nodding his head slowly. He turned to Hades. "This is why. I always saw this in her."

Hades tilted his head side to side. "She's all right. She grows on you. Like algae."

I scrunched my nose. "How is that a compliment?"

He shrugged. "It grows on sloths, and they're cute. It's not a bad thing."

I squinted at him. "You're the 'cute' sloth in this scenario. I'm a plant."

He grinned a Cheshire smile, saying nothing more.

Asshole.

My mates kept quiet, pressing their lips together as they looked down at the floor, but Ezra was laughing in my mind, getting a kick out of my bantering with Hades.

"At any rate," Jake said, starting up again, "I made some concessions. One of which was Lyra. We're going to keep her here in the Afterlife. She's not dead, nor will she be extinguished. Her case is specifically under Fury . . . and me."

I reached over, resting my hand on Dorian's knee. "I'm going to work here on special cases, mainly Lyra for now. I can sift into the Afterlife to work with her and sift back home for dinner. I can be the one to help rehabilitate her properly. She needs a level of compassion and empathy others don't have." I took a deep breath. "I dealt with Azrael's abuse. I know it, intimately. So does she. She needs me, and she'll be safe here."

Dorian placed his hand on mine, squeezing gently. He looked up to Jake, clearing a scratchy spot in his throat. "Thank you," he said softly.

Jake inclined his head. "Duke is back, and he's already set up a comfortable place for Lyra. She's getting settled in. You can see her when we're done here if you'd like." Dorian nodded once. "In the meantime, Jules gave up her realm entirely to imprison Azrael. Fury and I decided his fate."

"What about Lethe?" Roman asked, resting his palms on his thighs. "What happens to it? That's where the extinguished souls go, right?"

Hades groaned. "I'm looking after it."

Jake turned to him with a sour expression. "Don't try so hard to hide your displeasure."

"Does that mean you're staying in Lethe like Azrael did?" Ezra asked. I tilted my head, listening closely to Ezra's thoughts. There was an admiration there. Whatever my mates and Hades had gone through fighting together, I think it bonded them in a way.

That and he found him far too entertaining.

"Hard pass." Hades shook his head. "I belong in the Afterlife, and on Earth." His gaze briefly flickered to another in the room, and I didn't miss it. "I'll manage it. The extinguished souls aren't all bad. As we've all learned over the courses of our lives, nothing is black and white."

Roman sat forward, his long dreads spilling over his thick shoulders. "What does sending the terrible triplets into the mirror realm accomplish?" Hades snorted at Roman's nickname for his rogue brothers.

"Well for one, they can't get out," I answered.

"And second," Hades said, "they'll be locked in there with Azrael, who is now powerless."

Dorian's eyes rose in surprise. "How so?"

I smirked, sharing a knowing look with Jake and Hades. "He'll live forever because *someone* here made him the Angel of Death—yeah yeah, I know, 'hindsight'," I said to Jake before he started to explain himself again. Turning back to Dorian, I added, "But he has no power anymore. The orb trapped it."

"She sliced him open and shoved it inside him," Ezra said, reading my thoughts.

I shot him a quick look. *I love you, but I still need you to at least pretend like you don't hear my thoughts. I don't want to shield you like Dorian does.*

Noted, he said to me, and the sincerity in his voice was strong.

My mates gave me an approving nod at Ezra's comment, and I couldn't help but preen under the quiet praise.

"Look, my brothers have no love for Azrael. He was their warden for a very long time." Hades crossed his arms, leaning against Jake's desk. "You saw them. They have temper tantrums and short fuses. Now they get to spend eternity in the mirror realm, tormenting Azrael."

Roman barked a laugh. I could tell that thought pleased him greatly. Dorian looked relieved. Not only was Lyra going to be taken care of, but her abuser was going to spend a literal eternity paying for his crimes. Ezra was just happy to be with me now that it was all over.

Jules sniffed quietly, picking at invisible lint on her jeans. "And *our* bargain, Jake?"

He swiveled in his chair. "I'm a man of my word."

She kept her head down, but lifted her eyes up, glaring at him. "You aren't a man."

"Fine. I never go back on my word," he amended. "Better?"

She pressed her lips together and gave him a single nod.

"Jules, you gave up your realm. What do you get out of it?" Dorian asked her, taking in the tension between them.

"Freedom," she whispered, a small smile playing on her lips. "No one is coming after me this time. I have no reason to hide."

Jake held out the crystal ball, waiting for her to accept it. "Toss them in, then come back."

She took it in her hand, then stood up from her chair. Hades moved out of the way, showing her a mirror that had been set on a bookshelf just for this occasion. Taking a deep breath, Jules pushed her arm through, quickly disappearing into the realm. Moments later, she pulled herself out, as though she'd just walked through a portal.

She wiped her hands off. "It's done."

Jake dipped his chin, then turned to my mates. "Dorian, I'll have Duke come take you to see Lyra. Roman, I imagine you'd like to see your sister and let her know everything is okay. Hades is going to take you and Ezra back to Earth while Fury and I settle a few other minor details."

"Jules?" Hades asked, offering his hand to her. "Are you coming?"

She looked to me in question. "You're family. You're coming home with us," I said, standing up to give her a hug.

She squeezed me in return. "Roxanne will get you all set up. She lives for this kind of stuff."

"Think she'll make me a Bloody Mary?" she asked, a spark of hope in her eyes.

I chuckled. "She won't be making anything for me, but I bet she'll be happy to make a drink or two for you."

My mates stood up, walking over to me, grabbing the back of my elbow gently while they kissed my lips.

One by one, they left the room.

The extra chairs disappeared.

Now it was just me and Jake.

It felt like old times somehow, even though so much had changed.

I tucked one leg under the other, balling myself up in the chair, enjoying the silence.

Jake leaned back in his chair, putting his hands behind his head, interlocking his fingers. He exhaled loudly. "Man, tough day."

I snorted. "You barely did anything."

"I made decisions," he countered. "That's very, very hard work. I'm very busy and important."

I huffed a small laugh. It did feel like old times. Jake, my Afterlife Resources caseworker. He just happened to be running basically everything. Nothing serious. Death. The Afterlife. Existence.

I'd seen him countless times in my one hundred- and three-year stint, but none stuck out as much as the first day. The day he comforted me. The day he took a scared and broken girl and gave her another chance.

"The day you brought me in here to offer me the assignment, did you mean what you said?" I asked, picking at a nail. "You said if I succeeded, I earned my retirement."

He cocked an eyebrow. "Why does it matter? You

succeeded and our agreement was you get to stay on Earth with your mates."

I gave him a doubtful look. "You didn't know I was going to have mates, much less three of them. By your own admission, it took everyone by surprise." He waited for me to finish, but he still didn't speak. Realization dawned on me. "You weren't going to let me retire, were you?"

A burst of anger shot through me.

"I don't know," he admitted. "I never go back on my word, and I did offer it to you. Retirement isn't what people think it is, and you weren't ready. I wanted to offer you something better."

I scoffed. "Like what? A seat next to you?"

He shrugged. "I'd considered it."

I paused, taking in his response. "I was just being an asshole."

"I know, but I wasn't."

"You really considered that? Why? What for?"

He gave me a disappointed look. "C'mon, Fury. You're Michael's descendant. I knew what you were the first day you landed in my office. You were something special. You still are. After you succeeded, and the alphas were reformed, I didn't want to see you quit. You have a lot to offer. There's a lot you can change." He leaned forward in his chair, placing his arms on the desk. "The trouble with the angels over the millennia was that they lost touch with humanity. You embody everything they'd lost. You hold on tight to it. It's what got you through every rough night you've had."

"I'm young, though, in comparison to them," I said, gesturing around me. "This place is *old*. Am I eventually going to be like the other angels? Descending into madness? I mean, if that's what runs in the family, I need to know now."

"Why?" he asked. "It's not like your mates can take you in the backyard like a rabid dog and end it like Old Yeller."

My mouth fell open. "No, but—"

"They never had what you had. You didn't live your first life as an angel. You were human. You have your own unique human spirit. Couple that with your angel heritage, and it made something special. I wasn't sure I wanted to let you give it up. Not when I knew you had potential."

I frowned. "That wasn't for you to decide."

"It's not," he agreed. "Which is why I said I don't know. I hadn't come to a decision, but I didn't like my options."

"I'm not sure you liked the options you had today either, but here we are."

"I made the trades I did because it was worth it. You weigh your choices the same as me. And look, we both got what we wanted. The alphas didn't end the world and Azrael and my other three sons are imprisoned, and Hades is going to manage Lethe. I can't complain about the outcome here."

Hades ruling Lethe seemed so strange to me. He clearly didn't want it. Though he'd mentioned that was exactly why Azrael had been a bad choice for all his roles. Maybe this would make him good at it.

Hades, crow and protector of extinguished souls. I needed to get him business cards made. Maybe that would be a good present.

A thought occurred to me, and I perked up. "Jake?" He hummed in question. "Do you think I can get one more favor?"

"You can ask," he said. That was fair.

"Now that Hades can control Lethe, is it possible that

he can un-extinguish a soul?" I looked down at my feet, not wanting to meet his eyes. But he didn't speak. He waited for me to look up. When I finally did, his voice was calm. It was the same voice he used the day I first arrived in his office. That's when I knew the answer.

"I'm sorry, Fury. Truly. But no. Only Azrael carried that power." He met my gaze, holding it with gentle eyes. He knew what I wanted. The real John. It was my fault. My anger. And it was never him that'd hurt me. "We have to live with the choices we make, good or bad. You aren't in control of what happens to you. You're only in control of how you react. That's what life is. What you do with it is entirely up to you."

I pressed my lips together, taking a deep breath in. "It was worth a shot."

"I would give that to you if I could."

I saw the sincerity on his face. The one thing Jake wasn't was a liar. He may have kept his real identity hidden, but that was different. In all the years I had known him, he'd always been honest with me, even when I didn't want to hear it. "I appreciate that." I meant it.

I'd just have to add it to my list of things to work on in therapy.

"For what it's worth, that rule applies to everyone. Even me," he said.

I looked at him in question. "Which one?"

"We have to live with the choices we make," he repeated. "So do I. I don't get to turn back time and change it. Sometimes I wish I could."

"What would you change? One thing?" I asked him quickly, hoping my fast speech would make him answer immediately and honestly.

"I'd bring back my daughter," he said.

"Shut the front door—what?" I was moments away from picking my jaw up from the floor.

He nodded slowly. "I told you, angels can't bear children." He looked at me, straight in the eye. "I was arrogant. I didn't protect her. I believed she was of my bloodline, and she would be indestructible, just as I was. All their mothers died. But my daughter would live. That's what I foolishly believed."

"But . . . you made them. Didn't you make all of this?" I asked in confusion.

He wobbled his hand from side to side. "It's more complicated than that. Everyone wants to point to some divine source, but they always overlook nature. Even me, it would seem."

"She died in childbirth too?"

He nodded. "It apparently doesn't matter what line you carry. A woman bearing a child of Afterlife magic can't survive it. The power is too great."

"I'm sorry," I said. It was lame. It felt so weak and insincere, but it really wasn't. I just didn't know the best way to respond. Then I realized, honesty was probably the best way to go. "I don't know what to say."

"Sometimes there's nothing you can say." He gave a half-smile. "She birthed a son, then she died."

"Did her son survive?"

He met my gaze. "He did. It was Michael."

My stomach tightened in a knot. "I . . . we . . . I'm from Michael, and he's from your daughter, and she's from *you*," I stuttered, feeling like the wind was knocked out of me. "Why are you telling me this now?"

I'd come to terms with not having a child. I'd accepted it when I died and appeared in the Afterlife, but my newfound status as uber demon-angel-supernatural had given me the slightest inkling of hope. Just a little. When he told me in front of Dorian and Ezra what would have happened in my mortal life, I knew what that truly meant. This just solidified it. But more so, I was still technically dead. The demon part of me was there. The living human girl that would age and grow was long gone. If I wanted children, I'd have them. They just wouldn't be from my body. I was okay with that.

But *this*.

"You deserve to know. This is your lineage. It wasn't some cruel joke that prevented you from bearing children. It was never intended to be a punishment. It just *is*. I didn't want to take that away from you or from anyone. I'm sorry for the way that turned out," he said.

"I . . . does this mean we have to invite you over for holidays?" I asked with a smirk, breaking the tension.

"Can't come," he said, snapping his fingers. "But I wouldn't say no to pie. I love pie. And cocoa bombs."

I blinked a few times. "You're the weirdest concept of a devil anyone could've ever imagined."

He shrugged. "You can guess how much I care what people think."

"Guess that runs in the family." I snickered, but saying those words made me think of something he'd mentioned. "When I was here the other day, you said you knew who I was the day I landed in your office. You let me live because I was Michael's descendent . . . but it's because I'm yours too."

"No," he said, a sad tone taking over his voice. "The angels did have to destroy their lines. When they arrived, they were extinguished. It was cruel and unusual punishment for humans to be damned the way they were, passing down a bloodline that was guaranteed to end every woman born. I lost my daughter. I wouldn't wish that on anyone. I wasn't going to allow it to continue for thousands and thousands of years. It's inflicting pain unnecessarily. I chose to keep you because I saw who you really were. You made the best parts of Michael thrive within. Not the other way around."

"It was cruel and unusual punishment to make them kill their line. What about those people? They were innocent too," I pointed out.

He sighed, but he didn't disagree with me. "You sound a lot like Hades."

"You just made me realize we're related. I don't know how I feel about that." I twisted my face, letting my head fall back with a groan. I was never going to hear the end of that. I snapped my head up. "Wait. You gave Hades his body back so we could fight his brothers. Are you going to let him keep that form now that we're done, or is he still being punished?"

"He's back to his charming self. Saving the world gets him a pass." He tapped the desk a few times. "Besides, it's been long enough."

"What did he do?" I asked.

Jake shook his finger at me. "No, no. That's not my story to tell. You're welcome to ask him."

I pursed my lips, knowing he was entirely too secretive. He wasn't going to tell me shit. "Fine," I said. "I'll ask Jules."

I watched him carefully, but he said nothing. A spark twinkled in Jake's eyes, and he gave a half-smirk, and that was my answer.

I smiled, letting my legs drop to the floor.

"Get home, Fury," he said, moving to stand himself up. "You know where to find me if you need me."

I stood, reaching my arms above me to stretch. I was

ready for a nap. I'd earned it. I could finally rest, not worried about impending doom or failing the entirety of the world.

I'd earned my retirement. It just looked a little different than what I'd imagined it would be. I was perfectly okay with that.

"I'll stop by tomorrow after I work with Lyra," I told him as I walked to the door. Turning over my shoulder, I added, "I'll bring pie." I saw him grin as the door closed behind me.

Francine sat behind her desk, smug as ever. "I like pie."

I glared at her. I'd read a book where a scorned woman baked shit into a chocolate pie. "I'm feeling generous. I'll bring you one too," I said, and she beamed in response.

I sifted out, laughing to myself. She was in for it.

I appeared in Roman's living room at the compound. It was just a guess, but it was the right one. Jules sat on a chair on the front porch watching the shifter cubs play while Pria used her pink swirling magic to chase them. I could hear Roxanne making sandwiches in the kitchen while talking with Rava and Caitlin.

Roman, Dorian, and Ezra were sitting on the deck, over-looking the lake. They weren't even talking, but they were together. Seeing their faces filled me with an overwhelming feeling of fulfillment. Something I had never really experienced before.

I had so much to tell them.

I supposed this is what people had meant when they talked about coming home to someone you wanted to share your day with.

I had that now . . . times three.

I had no complaints.

CHAPTER 30

Three years later...

"All right, everyone. Gather 'round," I called.

A dozen kids were on me in seconds as I placed a few discreet plastic bags on the table. A few other adults took notice, but for the most part no one seemed to be paying much attention. I glanced across the yard at my friends and family. Roman was grilling hotdogs, hamburgers, and brats on the grill, chatting with Caitlin and Rava. Dorian, Roxanne, and Ezra were deep in conversation about the enforcer program I'd created. It was a bit of a pet project of mine that I'd been playing around with for a while and finally launched about six months ago.

We'd come a long way since the end of the world. Physically and figuratively.

After our violent battle ended with the Dukes and Azrael, no one really wanted to stay in Houston. They'd only ever agreed on it as a central location for meeting. When they said they wanted to relocate, I certainly didn't complain.

Roman took his pack north to the Rocky Mountains and set up an amazing ranch there. Ranch was a bit of an understatement. It was closer to a town of all shifters, but there were the occasional fae and vampire that decided to join us. We welcomed it. Kelly said she couldn't let us have all the fun. She came along and worked with Rava to set up a school for hybrid kids like Pria.

I would soon be marking three years since I'd started therapy with Rava. It was hard in the beginning. After the initial drive to get sober had settled, I'd be lying if I said I didn't have weak moments. Days that I struggled to deny myself a drink. But I'd kept my promise and not picked up the bottle ever since that night. My life with them was too important to lose to alcohol.

Dorian restored Avalon to its former glory, pre-Lyra ransacking. It was still cold as ever, but the castle wasn't so frigid. Fae lived on the island again, working happily. He spent very little time there these days—preferring to visit me or play an active role in rebuilding communities his daughter had hurt deeply. Especially the shifters. It touched me that he took that responsibility so seriously. He wasn't simply funding the rebuilding, but also helping people relocate, finding homes for orphans, and keeping up with them to try to ease the tensions that a lot of the survivors had developed surrounding fae.

Ezra and I had a different journey to follow. Not in regard to our bond. We tattooed each other, just as he said we would. I loved every minute of it. But we were also connected in another way the others couldn't understand. Both of us had suffered horribly at the hands of Azrael, and that lasting damage wasn't going anywhere. Beyond therapy, I needed an outlet for myself. A purpose. For a while that meant becoming an enforcer for Ezra, but it didn't take long for me to see that changes needed to be made there—and in the Afterlife, for that matter. Too many people ended up in positions of power, lording it over others and too often it turned into abuse. Because of the trauma we'd been through, Ezra helped me come up with a plan to truly reform the way we handled punishments and infractions. I didn't just want to stop with the vampires, though. I wanted to make changes across the entire supernatural world.

But I'm just one person.

Badass mini-god though I may be.

So Roxanne stepped in and became my recruiter, of sorts. We went around the world finding supernaturals that were like us; those wanting to make a difference for the right reasons. Capable of reforming others without falling into their own darkness.

Don't get me wrong, there were still some broken kneecaps along the way. Reforming wasn't all sunshine and flowers, but there was a lot more to it than simply punishing.

That's how the Enforcer's Guild came about.

In the Afterlife, everyone belonged to one, but the supernatural world divided themselves by species. I wanted people from all walks of life to be a part of it, and while it was still new—I had this feeling that my work here was only just beginning.

My eyes dropped to Pria. Standing beside me with a toothy smile, she looked at me with admiration. She'd been saying for months that she wanted to be an enforcer when she grew up. Whether or not she would—only time would tell, but it didn't hurt the feeling inside that assured me I was *finally* where I was meant to be. Doing what I do best. Fixing people. Making a difference. Fury style.

"Now," I said, looking around the group of kids. "Everyone is going to take one." I opened the bag directly in front of me to reveal several colored glass bottles. I suppose I should have predicted the problems that would ensue when there were only so many pink and purple ones. "Color doesn't matter," I reminded them. "You're going to be blowing them up, anyway."

Rava's keen ears perked up, taking notice of my demonstration.

I pretended not to notice as she slowly turned her head, that inscrutable parent-eye falling on me. Pria giggled, completely aware of what was going on.

I pulled out two unmarked containers. They were filled with 100% alcohol.

Not the kind that would even come close to tempting me. Mix this stuff with acetone and you had nail polish remover.

"Set your bottles down so I can pour some of this in —*no*, you cannot drink it," I added, seeing the curious look on one twelve-year-old boy's face. I knew this one in particular because Pria had a crush on him. His name was Junior and apparently his wolf had 'the cutest little white paws'. I shook my head, a smile curling around my mouth as I filled the bottles—and then had to remind them a second time not to drink it.

One kid took a sniff and gagged, solidifying what I told them from the beginning.

"Fury . . ." Rava said, slowly trailing over.

Welp. They were going to find out soon enough.

I opened the last bag. It was full of rags in different colors. I picked up one of the spare bottles, and said, "You're going to stuff half of this in the bottle, but don't take it out or tip it over. Okay?" They nodded along, but I knew at least one of them wouldn't follow instructions. There was always *that one*. I stepped back, letting their little grabby hands go for the bag as Rava approached.

"What are you doing?" she asked, eyeing the table in question.

"Um, well," I started, shoving my hands in the back pockets of my pants. "In my defense, Pria asked for this—"

Out of nowhere, a deep, rumbling laugh drifted over the yard.

"Did you really just use that excuse?" Hades said, striding forward. "Because I remember your exact response when Jake tried to—"

I whacked him on the shoulder as he approached, pursing my lips. "This is completely different. I was put in charge of organizing a child's birthday party. Jake handed over the means to end the world to that shitbag—" I stopped; mouth snapping shut.

I was pretty sure 'shitbag' wasn't something I was allowed to say at an eleven-year-old's party. Even if said eleven-year-old was my niece.

Hades chuckled, throwing an arm around me. "It's good to see you too, Fury."

"We're ready!" Pria called, running up to me to present what she'd made. "Look Mama, it's a Molotov cocktail."

Rava gave me a not-amused look, though in a certain light her lip might have been curving up. At least I hoped so.

"I see that," Rava said, lifting her eyebrows as she looked between me and her child. Beside us, Hades started choking from laughing so hard. I elbowed him in the ribs, which didn't help. My raven asked to take control, wanting to tell him off, but I gently reminded her to wait until he was a crow. Then she could have a go at him. She bristled but was content to wait. Rava pinned me with her glare, adding, "I'm *so* curious on how Aunt Fury plans for you guys to set these off."

"We're throwing them into the mirror realm," Pria said happily.

On cue, Roman's garage door opened. Out stepped Jules wearing a light blue summer dress she'd picked up on our last trip to Hawaii. Her brown hair was bound in a long braid that went to her waist, decorated with flowers, courtesy of the birthday girl who'd asked for all this.

Beside me, Hades stopped laughing. His attention shifted, hyper-focusing on the poltergeist as she rolled out a large circular mirror on wheels. I glanced between them, noticing the change . Jules hadn't seen him yet, but Hades had definitely noticed her.

Rava's perceptive stare caught my eye, she was totally thinking what I was.

"All right, kiddos, line up in front of the mirror—" I didn't even have to finish the sentence before they took off like a herd of puppies that just heard a treat wrapper open. Pria dashed across the grass, her light-up sneakers blinking away as she approached the mirror first.

I gave Rava an apologetic smile and said, "It's better to ask for forgiveness than permission?"

To my relief, she snorted. "Under normal circumstances, I'd say you're a hundred and twenty-nine years old and you can do whatever you want. Next time, just a little heads up with what you're planning would be nice where it concerns my kid, though, okay?"

I nodded along, agreeing with her, while internally hoping Pria didn't ask for another unorthodox birthday activity. Last year was bad enough when I had to say no to base jumping off the Eiffel Tower without parachutes. 'Just sift us, Auntie Fury!' That girl. If Rava thought this was bad, she was in store for a hell of a time as her daughter got older. Pria was a total adrenaline junkie and Caitlin gave into it even more than I did.

As if she heard me thinking her name, Caitlin peeled away from Roman and pulled a lighter out of her back pocket. "Who's ready to make some bombs?"

Rava's mouth dropped open.

"Am I the *only* one that didn't know?"

"Yeah," Hades said.

"Kinda," I mumbled.

"Yep," my mates chimed in.

Rava lowered her head in her hand and sighed. "Apologies then, Fury. It seems my wife is the one I should be talking to."

As she spoke, Caitlin flicked the end of the lighter. The rag on Pria's bottle caught fire before she threw it as hard as she could at the mirror. Jules used her magic, and it went flying straight through. Pink glass exploded on the other side, causing an eruption of 'ooooos' and 'ahhhhs' from the kids standing in line.

"If it makes you feel better, I still have to remind Ezra to put the toilet seat down," I said, resulting in Dorian and Roman laughing a little too hard. "Roman is a blanket hog and I wake up freezing. And Dorian has gotten my cat into the worst habit by bribing him to leave the bedroom with wet cat food. Now he stands outside the door screaming at me for food at six am." I grimaced at Dorian, who smirked and shrugged. Pretty sure he and the damn cat were in cahoots because that furball magically never did that when Dorian was over. The cat got his food, and Dorian still got to make me wake up early even if he wasn't there. It was a win-win for them.

"Rava brushes her teeth in the most obnoxious way, getting toothpaste all over the mirror," Caitlin said. "It drives me crazy."

"At least I clean the mirror," Rava huffed, blowing a strand of pale purple hair out of her face.

"You have it easy," Ezra chimed in. "Fury is incapable of picking up her clothes and shoes. Try waking up at five in the morning to take a piss and stabbing your foot on a belt buckle after you trip over a boot."

Roman and Dorian nodded in agreement. I pressed my lips together in an awkward smile. It's not like I could say much since I'd started the bantering session.

The truth was that I wouldn't change a single second of my life.

For over a hundred years I worked toward retirement, but I'd come to learn that the concept of retirement was highly overrated. I'd rather have our crazy family and friends—unconventional as it all was—over a life of complacency, just passing the time. The days didn't just pass by unappreciated. I treasured them. Birthday parties, lifted toilet seats, and all the in between.

EPILOGUE
DORIAN

I sifted onto her front step. The house was small, but attractive. She'd painted it yellow two decades ago when she decided to live on her own. There was a white picket fence out front and a little vegetable garden along the side. She enjoyed that, these days. She'd said that working in the dirt made her feel at peace in a way few things did.

I didn't care what she did to get to that point. I was just happy she was happy.

I lifted my hand to knock on the door, but the knob turned before I could, followed by the wooden panel swinging open.

Lyra smiled. It wasn't broken or chaotic as it had once been. It was soft. Sincere. There was a hint of an apology in it; the same apology I saw in her eyes. Fifty years had passed since she'd come to the Afterlife. It was here she was finally able to get the help she needed. Here that she found another family with Duke and his wife and girls. Here that Fury saw her multiple times a week to work with her—never missing a session and never giving up, even on the hardest of days.

I was almost sixteen hundred years old and I never for a second thought the day would come that I'd be having Sunday dinners with my daughter.

Because of my mate, I was able to.

I loved her for many reasons, but this—*this* went beyond my love for her. Fury gave me something irreplaceable when she committed to helping Lyra.

To say that my daughter was as good as new would be a disservice.

She'd been through immense trauma. The damage done to her psyche wasn't something she could simply heal from. She'd never be the same as before.

There was no going back.

No forgetting.

The only way she could go was forward, and with Fury and Duke's help, she did.

Years after years of therapy and working through her problems made it so that we could eventually connect again and build a new relationship.

One that involved us traveling back and forth between our worlds. While being mated to Fury and gaining her power somehow gave me access to sift into the Afterlife and use my magic here, Lyra could not. She was supernatural at her core—but she didn't care.

On Earth, she was essentially a god. Powerful in a way that only few of us were.

But here she had peace.

If you asked her, she'd tell you that was worth more than all the power in her veins.

Lyra opened the door wider and two excitable corgis rushed around her to greet me. She'd adopted them from the rainbow bridge. Strays that didn't have families waiting for them, much like Fury's cat that she'd taken from here back to Earth.

She and Lyra made weekly visits across the bridge, spending time loving on animals and getting something out of it themselves. After all the death and destruction, they both needed that extra support. Even beyond family, there was a certain kind of love that pets provided that helped heal beyond measure.

Fury found that in her cat, Mr. Waffles.

Lyra found that in her dogs, Sterling and Stitch.

While I wasn't one that ever needed the companionship of animals, I had to admit that watching them both with theirs softened me to the prospect of having one of my own. Fury often thought I'd benefit from the company of a dog but she didn't want to push the subject. I'd yet to tell her that I was getting an Old English Sheepdog I'd met on our recent day trip across the rainbow bridge. Something about the way he bounced up to me and looked at me with deep brown eyes that said 'you belong to me' had tugged a heartstring or two.

"I think they missed you," my daughter said, bending at the waist to pick up Sterling. He was a rotten dog, but perfect for her. The little monster made gremlin noises about being picked up that caused her to laugh.

I loved the sound.

Perhaps it wasn't as pure as when she was a young girl, but it was real. Genuine.

Which is why she could have all the dogs she wanted as far as I was concerned.

"I think they were hoping Fury was with me. She's the one that always brings them treats." It wasn't as if the Afterlife didn't have them, but she enjoyed the simplicity in going to the pet store. While we led interesting lives traversing the continents, her work with the Enforcer's Guild, and my own with rebuilding communities and improving fae relations around the world—it was the simple things she loved most.

Curling up with her cat on the lanai, overlooking the black sand beaches in Hawaii. Shopping for pet treats. Flying as a raven and teasing Hades to no end.

I shook my head, smiling to myself.

"There's probably some truth to that," Lyra said, chuckling as she closed the door behind me. She leaned over to let Sterling down and the corgi took off, doing laps around the kitchen table, Stitch following after him.

I looked at the pair of feet that I saw standing next to the pups.

We weren't alone.

"Jake," I said politely, but confusion edged my voice. While we still saw him from time to time, Fury more often than me—the last place I expected to see him was my daughter's house.

"Dorian." He inclined his chin in my direction while setting down a large dish on the small dining table. It smelled like Lyra's chicken tortilla casserole. Something she'd learned to make in her time here. Cooking was another hobby she picked up; one I certainly didn't mind benefiting from. My mate always appreciated any leftovers I brought home as well. She knew where her strength and weaknesses were. Fury may have been approaching two hundred now, but she still found a way to burn water.

"To what do I owe the pleasure?" I said, stepping toward the table. Lyra stalled between us, twisting her hands in her pleated skirt.

"Athair," she said, falling back to her Gaelic, something

she did when she was trying to soften me up. I had an inkling of what it was this time, and I didn't like it. "Jake and I have been . . . seeing each other."

My mind blanked for a moment.

This was another first in my sixteen hundred years of existence.

"You're seeing one another?" I said slowly, resting my hands on the back of a chair. "As friends? Extended acquaintances?"

"I'm dating your daughter," Jake said bluntly. Lyra shot him a look of annoyance and the fucker just shrugged. "What? He knows damn well what seeing someone means."

"How long?" I asked, my hand slowly curling and uncurling around the wooden frame.

"Oh, just a little while—" Lyra started.

"Fifteen years," Jake said.

Fifteen years.

Fifteen. Fucking. Years.

Time wise, it was a blip. That was nothing to me. To Lyra. Especially to Jake.

But it was more than a little while. This wasn't some casual fling.

"Please tell me she knows who you really are," I said, torn between sitting in the chair and breaking it over his head. It wouldn't do anything, but it'd sure make me feel better.

Jake nodded. "She's aware."

I turned to her, forcing the aggression away. I had no problem beating the shit out of him, but I wouldn't come at her like that. "You know that he's essentially Satan, and yet you're still willing to pursue something?"

"Hold up now," Jake started. Lyra lifted her hand to call him off and he went quiet.

"One, that's rude. You know it's more complicated than that, and he doesn't go by that name," she said, sounding so much like Fury it made my heart ache. "Two, it doesn't matter who he is. He makes me happy. He supports my choices. He doesn't disrespect me or my boundaries. And he doesn't care what I've done." Her final admission made me flinch. It was a topic we rarely brought up. Fury had told me a long time ago to let Lyra choose when to talk about it and not a moment sooner. I'd always done just that. "Isn't that what you would want for me?"

Her pointed stare made me shift.

"I—yes," I sighed. "I am happy you have found someone that makes you happy. I just wish it hadn't been this fucker—"

"Athair," she chided.

"Really, Dorian?" Jake t'sked. "You don't have much room to talk. I know you and Fury fucked on my desk when I refused to build a statue in her honor—"

"So you date my daughter?" I snapped.

"Only because she hasn't agreed to the Aeternum ceremony."

That stopped me cold in my tracks.

"Aeternum?" I repeated, lowering my voice. I couldn't believe what I was hearing. "That ritual solidifies a union. Forever. It's the equivalent to a *mate* ceremony."

"I'm aware of that," he said coolly.

I didn't know what to say so I looked at Lyra instead.

"Jake, we talked about this . . ."

"I know we did," he said, walking up to me. "But he needs to know I'm serious and not fucking around with you.

I can understand the concern, but I don't want the disrespect." She sighed. This conversation not new to her apparently. "Before you start blowing things up, this isn't me asking your permission. I've already asked her. Repeatedly. Lyra wants to take things slower, though. That included me meeting you as her partner and not just the deity you enjoy fucking with on occasion just because you can."

I sighed, rubbing my temples. "You're serious about him?"

Lyra nodded, pulling a seat out for her to sit. "I am."

I took a deep breath and sighed. Then slowly, I pulled the chair out and sat down at the table.

"You get her pregnant, I'll find a way to kill you."

Jake nodded once, understanding that I was being completely serious. One might find it funny, but I knew what happened to his son's mothers. Fury had a long talk with us about why she could never biologically have children, even if we wanted it someday.

"Oh that won't happen. We're safe. Fury helped me get a magical contraception from Kelly."

The fork I'd picked up bent in my hand.

"I don't think that helps, love," Jake commented.

"Lyra, sweetheart, I want you to be able to tell me anything—except that. Also, how long has Fury known about this?" I eyed them both.

Jake started scooping casserole while Lyra turned a bit red, staring at her cuticles.

"Fifteen years," she whispered, and my eyebrows shot up. "Fury was the one that convinced me we should tell you. I wasn't sure how you'd take it."

My mate had neglected to tell me something this big for fifteen years. I was going to have a long talk with her about what all she knew about Jake and Lyra's relationship. I could hear her now. 'It wasn't my secret to tell.' It'd be hard to argue with that, but I'd find a way.

"I am sorry if I've made you feel like you can't tell me things—"

"It doesn't help when you light up like a disco ball at the mention of it," Jake remarked. Lyra kicked him from under the table.

"It's not exactly that," she said. "I know that you worry about me, and I don't want you to. I know I've made a lot of mistakes, but this isn't one. I wanted to be sure before I told you *because* you mean so much to me—and also because I was a bit worried you might try to blow Jake up if you found out some other way."

She gave me a lopsided smile.

There was still an apology in it, one that didn't have its place there, but I smiled back.

He took her hand from across the table, squeezing her fingers lightly. Lyra visibly relaxed, her features smoothing as anxiety drained away.

It was then that I realized perhaps there was more to their relationship than I'd initially wanted to acknowledge or admit.

And that maybe, it was quite possible, that I was being overprotective.

Maybe.

She was my daughter, after all, and this was the devil. God. Jake.

Whatever the fuck he wanted to be called.

The End.

AND I'M THRILLED to offer a sneak peek of my bestselling why choose demon romance, Lucifer's Daughter. **Perfect for fans of Jaymin Eve, Tate James, and Ivy Asher.**

Sneak Peek of Lucifer's Daughter

HELL MUST HAVE FROZEN OVER.

That's it. The only possible excuse for why Kendall Clackson, our resident Bible fanatic, was strutting through my favorite diner on a Saturday morning. She usually saved her shenanigans for earlier in the week, on days I didn't have off. Coincidence? Not likely.

I froze in my spot and considered bailing, but that thought only lasted about half a second before her smug face made me stomp across the diner and settle into my usual booth.

Fuck it. I've done the same thing every day for the last ten years. I'm not changing now.

Swinging my legs into the booth, I didn't even pick up the menu as Little Miss Georgia Peach approached me with all her southern charm.

"Ruby! What a pleasure seein' you here, hun."

I turned fractionally and nodded once, hoping she would get the hint. If there was anything that Kendall didn't understand, it was how insufferable I found her exaggerated southern accent to be. We lived in Portland for devil's sake.

"I hope you weren't comin' here lookin' for Josh. He's playin' golf with some of the other men in our church. Bless him. Found his way to the Lord through me."

I could barely contain rolling my eyes. *Oh, yes. I'm sure he did. Just as soon as you gave him what I wouldn't.* I snorted to myself, but didn't say anything. Kendall made it her job to remind me, and everyone else, that he had left me for her and God.

"What's so funny? You know, Ruby, you should find a church. It might help with your"— she dropped her voice low—"*issues.*" Several regulars threw us curious, and somewhat scathing glances. It was an unspoken rule with us Saturday folks that you kept to yourself and didn't start trouble. Like Kendall was currently doing.

"Issues?" I asked, pretending to be mildly surprised by her comment. I knew damn well what she meant. I had a bit of a temper, but in my defense, there's only so much you can do when you're half-demon.

I waved down Martha on the other side of the diner, and she took one look at Blondie before rolling her eyes. Yeah, this wasn't the first time this had happened, but clearly, *I'm* the one with issues.

"You know, your anger—"

"What can I get for you this morning, Ruby?" Martha asked, appearing beside Kendall and seeming not to notice her at all.

"Black coffee and four orders of bacon, please," I said, not bothering to look at the menu.

Martha chuckled under her breath. "I'm not even sure why I ask anymore," she muttered as she walked away.

Kendall resumed her preaching, knowing full well her

advice was unwanted. "You know, Ruby, you really should lay off the fat if you ever want to find a nice Christian man."

Something like heat prickled inside me, but I clamped down on it hard. Kendall could pick at me all she wanted. I knew it wasn't actually me she was angry with. It was my cheating ex-boyfriend that wouldn't leave *me* alone, despite my repeated attempts to send him away. It wasn't unreasonable that she was pissed with him. It was unreasonable that she stalked *me* for it, and made *my* life hell. Particularly, when she was the one he had cheated on me with in the first place. Yet, somehow, she didn't see the irony in all of this.

"Hmmmm…let me think about that. Bacon or church? Bacon or church? Well, it's really a no brainer, Kendall. I'm atheist, so I think I better go with the bacon," I said, smirking at the way her mouth popped open. I did enjoy riling her up. What could I say? I have a penchant for trouble.

"Is that Satan talkin,' or just your jealousy, Ruby? You should've known that Josh would find his way to our Lord, with or without you."

This was too much. I couldn't hold back my laughter and I failed miserably when I tried to disguise it as a cough. "Kendall, I hate to be the bearer of bad news, but we split up because he fucked you in a broom closet, and unless 'God' is what you call your vagina nowadays, I think you're fooling yourself." I gave her my most mocking of smiles and made a shooing motion with my hand. Even beneath the orange of her spray tan, I could see her face reddening. She thought she could come here, in my sacred space, and offend me. Slander me and throw my break up out there for everyone to see. She thought it would embarrass me. What she failed to see was that I didn't care. Josh was someone to pass time with, and his dick got the better of him. As a half-succubus, it wasn't my nature to believe in love. Not when the "heart" could be swayed by a pretty face and a three minute fuck.

Kendall's anger seemed to intensify. She put on a saccharine smile as Martha came around the corner carrying my bacon and coffee, but I didn't miss the look in her eyes.

"Bless your heart," she sneered, turning on her heel. I breathed a sigh of relief, but it was a second too early. Her foot came out and caught Martha's black sneaker before I could say anything. Next thing I knew, heat flamed my chest as the coffee splashed across my maroon sweater. It wouldn't burn me, but she didn't know that.

Martha caught herself, but the damage was already done. My bacon lay on the table, soaking in a puddle of coffee that was dripping into my lap.

Her white apron and yellow shirt smeared with grease and coffee, Martha spluttered, "I'm so sorry about that, Ruby! Can I—"

"It's okay, Martha," I said, glaring at Kendall. The bitch had returned to her seat where three other Stepfords sat, each blonde and almost impossible to tell apart. They wore the same impossibly pleasant smiles with their impossibly perfect makeup. Kendall had strength in numbers and gave me a little wave for show as she took her seat.

I. Saw. Red.

Standing from my seat, I hastily helped Martha clean up the mess. She kept repeating to me: "She's not worth it, Ruby." Not that it mattered. Someone needed to teach Ms. Upstanding Citizen a lesson. This was the third time she'd tried to corner me this week, and while it was funny playing with her, what she just did was unacceptable. Not that I deserved any of this, but Martha certainly did not. She wasn't even involved. Kendall could fuck with me all she wanted, but dragging Martha into this and nearly hurting her crossed the line of bullshit I was willing to take. It was time for her to reap the consequences for being a shitty human being.

I placed a ten on the table and left the diner without another word. The door jingled as it swung shut behind me, and I turned my eyes on Kendall's baby blue Mustang.

A fit of glee came over me as my inner demon smiled. I went to my car and grabbed the baseball bat and a lighter I kept in the driver's side door.

Josh should have warned you what happens when you play with fire.

START LUCIFER'S DAUGHTER NOW

Author's Note

While Fury is fictional, the abuse and trauma she experienced is a reality for countless people. She'll have an eternity to work on healing, but unfortunately, our time is finite. It's never too late to ask for help.

If you or someone you love needs help, please reach out to a friend, a family member, a counselor, or one of the resources below.

Alcoholics Anonymous
  https://www.aa.org

The Substance Abuse and Mental Health Services Administration
  https://www.samhsa.gov/find-help/atod

The National Domestic Violence Hotline
  https://www.thehotline.org
  800-799-SAFE (7233)

United Nations Domestic Abuse
     https://www.un.org/en/coronavirus/what-is-domestic-abuse

ACKNOWLEDGMENTS

Ending this series together presented some challenges. Not with each other, but just the time constraints and hurdles in life. Without our support team, we couldn't have pulled it off.

From Kel:

Amanda, Heather, and Emigh. You've been incredibly supportive friends during such a difficult time in my life. You've been some of my biggest supporters over the past several months, and not just as authors, but in just life itself. This year has been difficult beyond measure, but you've made it a little bit easier.

Friends and Family. For visiting, calling, and helping me hold myself together, even when the days got dark and dreary. You were the bright spots that kept me going. You know who you are.

Aurelia. For not just holding my hand in life, but quite literally dragging me across the finish line. We did it. We wrote a whole fricken series. The first of many, and I am so excited for our future projects together. Through ups and downs, you've stuck with me, and there's no going back now. I'm like glitter, and once it's on you, it doesn't come off.

Matt. For 2am CVS runs so I could sleep, for holding me up when I can't hold it together myself, and for forever forgetting to put the toilet seat down. You make me believe in soulmates and all that other flowery shit. I love you.

From Aurelia:

Ian. You have no idea what your support means to me. You're my favorite brother, and I love you. The good, the bad, and everything in-between, we share it all and I'm happy you're in my life.

Kel. Thanks for badgering me for a year to write with you. I'm glad you were persistent. I'm glad I gave in, and I'm so incredibly lucky to do this with my best friend. I can't wait to show the world what else we can do together.

Mr. Jane. You're TMFS. The best man I know. I love you until the world blows up. Your beard is pretty spectacular too.

My kiddos. I'm done. Let's go decorate cookies.

From the dynamic duo:

Maegan, a million points to Hufflepuff. You know we can't survive without you by our side. You make all the bits and pieces work behind the scenes. Hades came to life because of you, even if he took on a personality we didn't expect. He's forever yours.

Dom, I hope you know how awesome you are. We can't thank you enough for all the hard work and time you have invested into this series. Can't wait to share new stories with you!

And finally, our readers. Without you, none of it is possible. We hope you join us for more adventures. If you keep reading them, we'll keep writing them. We have a lot up our sleeves.

Until next time . . .